Fallen Star

The Helyan Series – Part Two

S.M.Tidball

Copyright © 2020 S.M.Tidball

First Edition

The right of S.M.Tidball to be identified as author of this work has been asserted by her in accordance with section 77 and 78 of the Copyright, Designs and Patents Act 1988.

All rights reserved. No part of this publication may be reproduced, stored in a retrieval system, or transmitted in any form or by any means, electronic, mechanical, photocopying, recording, or otherwise, without the prior permission of the publishers.

The characters and events portrayed in this book are fictitious. Any similarity to real persons, living or dead, is coincidental and not intended by the author.

Cover design by: daniellefine.com

ISBN: 979-8-6368-6331-1

DEDICATION

For my family and friends – thanks for continuing
to believe in me.

1

The waters of the Rosado Sea turned red with blood. My blood.

As the dark shadow of the Mantra shark circled, panic rose in my throat, and despite the warm water, ice chills shivered over my skin. My heart kicked hard under my ribcage and my chest tightened until my lungs protested.

I stared through the water, watching the predator disappear into the dark, eyes so wide they began to ache. The aqua-lenses stung, and I forced myself to blink, my vision part obscured by the tiny air bubbles expelled from the small tube regulator as I hyperventilated. Even though I was metres below the surface, I had a violent urge to rip the device from between my teeth, but instead I forced myself to concentrate – slow breath in… slow breath out…

In the distance the dark shape glided gracefully into view again and my stomach flipped over, the controlled breathing forgotten in a plume of bubbles.

The pain in my leg had dulled to a throbbing ache and I looked briefly down at my thigh. Moments earlier, the razor-sharp pectoral fin of the waking Mantra had sliced easily through skin and muscle, but the wound was healing quickly. The silver-blue light radiating from my leg glowed bright in the water, illuminating the delicate fins of the tiny sea-wisps floating around me.

The cut didn't worry me because I knew I'd heal, just like I did from every other bullet hole, plasma burn, knife cut, and broken bone. But a Mantra attack was in a whole new league, and there'd be no coming back from that; dead is dead. What worried me more was that the nocturnal creature was awake when it should've been dormant. It should've been hovering in a kind of trance just below the surface, basking in the heat of the day. Like all the others, it wasn't supposed to wake until dusk.

The indistinct purple-grey shape moved sluggishly in the distance and I knew I had to get to the safety of the reef. During the attack, I'd lost my bearings, and I knew I only had one option; I kicked my legs and propelled myself to the surface. Removing the regulator, I took a deep breath, but a wave caught me by surprise ripping the tube from my fingers. I tried to grab for it as it sank in a spiral of bubbles.

A shadow passed below me, the regulator disappearing into a gaping mouth. I gasped, swallowing sea-spray, and choked – coughing until I could get air back in my lungs. I pulled my legs up tight to my chest, using the smallest movements to keep myself afloat.

The sky darkened, and the sun sank low on the horizon, the last rays glinting crimson in the distance. It was later than I'd thought, and cold fear rippled through my chest. I wasn't facing one, anomalous shark; I was out in open water with hundreds of monsters about to wake and feed. Bile rose, burning the back of my throat.

I had to swim for the safety of the reef, it was my only chance, but I also knew the odds weren't in my favour. I put my face into the water to see what was happening below, but the sun was setting quickly, and visibility was poor. It was impossible to know what monsters hunted below and panic fluttered in my tummy.

Looking back towards the reef, I mentally gauged the distance, but just as I kicked my legs, the three fins of a Mantra broke the surface directly in my path. It seemed lethargic, still waking, but I was so focussed on it, I wasn't prepared for the one that brushed past me from behind. It was so close, the rough, scaled armour on the creature's flank tore the skin off my shoulder and I felt the usual tickling sensation as I began to heal. The wake from the muscular twin-finned tail pulled me down and tumbled me through the churning sea, and when I made it to the surface, I choked and gasped for air. More of my blood was in the water and within seconds at least four distinct sets of fins appeared.

One of the predators turned with a splash of the tail and I froze as it sliced through the water towards me. As it drew closer, something else grabbed me, crushing my arms. At first, I thought it was another shark, but then I was lifted from the water, the metal of the skiff freezing against my skin. I pulled my legs clear, swinging them over the edge of the boat, just as the creature hit the side with its flat snout – jaws wide, with an impressive set of knife-sharp, black teeth on display.

The skiff rocked violently, throwing me backwards, and I realised I was lying on top of Brother Asher. He had a tight grip on my arms and they began to hurt, but I was too afraid to move – and I wouldn't have dared complain. Eventually he released me and I rolled over, falling on to ice-cold metal. The shock forced the air out of my lungs and it took me a moment before I could take another shaky breath.

Brother Francis sat in the stern of the boat, and even in the fading light, the anxious lines mapping his tired face were obvious. I knew he'd be mad at me and I waited for him to say something, but he simply shook his head and looked away. I stared at him, confused and hurt.

"What the hell do you think you were doing, Shae?" Ash

suddenly barked, making me jump.

"I... I..." I stuttered, completely shocked. Not because he'd shouted, I deserved that, but because of the rage that bulldozed its way through the mental Link between us. Ash was the nearest thing I had to a brother, and I loved him more than anyone in the entire Universe, so his anger hit me like a punch in the guts.

"Is this how you're dealing with Finnian's death?" he continued, his eyes fierce. "By getting yourself killed as well?"

"No! Of course I wasn't trying..." I broke off, gulping back sobs.

"Francis, take us in," Ash grunted as the skiff rocked from the charge of another Mantra.

The journey back was short but uncomfortable as Ash fell into a furious silence. He glared at me from the opposite side of the skiff and I wanted to say something, but every time I opened my mouth, I realised there was no excuse I could give that would make things better. In the end I took my lead from him and kept quiet.

When we got to shore, Francis manoeuvred the boat parallel to the short stone slip, where it jolted in the water as it butted up to the docking clamp. He cut the engine and there was an awkward moment before anyone moved, then Ash and I stood at the same time causing the skiff to rock – water lapping musically against the hull. I lost my balance, but he caught me, like he always did. His hands were warm on my frozen, goose-bumped skin, but as soon as I was steady, he released me and stepped away. Even the sweet smell of the roseberries drifting down from the kitchen garden couldn't make me feel better.

I shivered as I waited on the slip. It was practically dark, but a well-lit pathway led up to the rock plateau where the Brotherhood of the Virtuous Sun had built Sector Three's primary monastery.

"Ash, Francis, you have to believe me. I wasn't trying

to… I just… I lost track of time, that's all."

"I can't talk to you right now, Shae. I'm too angry, and I'm afraid I'll say something both of us will regret." Ash's voice was as cold as I felt, and his grey eyes flashed dangerously, but then his shoulders relaxed a little and his voice softened. "Why don't you take a shower and warm up? I'll get someone to bring you some soup and we'll talk in the morning."

I was twenty-nine years old, but somehow I felt like a child again. Maybe I deserved it. Perhaps there was no maybe about it. I hung my head and mumbled my agreement.

"We'll talk tomorrow," Ash repeated. "After that, you'll have to see Investigator Manus. You can't hide from him forever."

"Great. Can't wait," I replied sarcastically, and if it was possible, I felt even more miserable.

Back in the warmth and safety of my room, the magnitude of what'd happened finally hit me, stirred up by Ash's own maelstrom of emotions through the Link. Not the Mantra attack, but the loss of Finnian – the closest thing I had to a father. I rested my head in my hands and cried for the first time since we brought his body home. By the time I'd wiped away the last tear, I knew two things: one – I would never forget what he meant to me, and two – he would never have wanted me to fall to pieces the way I had. He would've expected me to be strong. Brave.

I took a lengthy shower, using my most expensive soaps and gels as if it would help to wash the hurt away. By the time I'd finished, my skin felt soft, my shoulder-length, dark brown hair bounced into soft curls, and I smelled like roseberries after spring rain. But I was paler than usual, and my eyes were bloodshot and sore.

I'd just drawn the heavy drapes across the glass window that covered almost one entire wall of my room, when there was a knock at the door. The last person I expected to see was Francis, but he came in and put a tray of food on my desk before turning to leave without saying a word.

"Wait…" I begged. He stopped, but didn't turn, so I got between him and the door. "Sit with me a moment," I added, trying to get eye contact. Eventually he raised his head and nodded wordlessly before slumping on the side of the bed. I settled myself next to him, feeling tiny beside his bulk, but he still didn't say anything.

"Please talk to me, Francis," I pleaded.

He turned his head and looked at me with sad, brown eyes that glistened with the first hint of tears. "It'll be a week tomorrow since Finnian died," he said finally, his deep voice wavering. "It's tough enough making sense of his death… then today we almost lost you too. Don't you know what that would've done to the rest of us? To Ash? To me?" He sighed deeply and rubbed his eyes. "You're my sister and I love you. I know you weren't trying to kill yourself, and whatever Ash says, he knows that too, but since we got back you've been so distant. Everyone's worried about you."

"I'm sorry," I said weakly. "I shouldn't have…" I didn't know what else to say, so instead I put my arm around his broad shoulders.

We talked for ages and by the time Francis left we'd come to an agreement – he would share his feelings with me, and in return I would try to be less reckless. We were both happy with that.

The dinner tray sat untouched.

The following morning was the first time since Finnian's death that I woke without a hollow feeling in the pit of my tummy. I brushed the grogginess of sleep away, noticing the blinking green light on my desk plexi-screen. I'd avoided looking at my coms-log since I'd been back, but I knew I couldn't put it off any longer. I sighed and reluctantly got out of bed, feeling the thick-pile rug between my toes.

The screen flickered on the moment I touched it. "Display messages," I said through a stifled yawn, and the listing told me there were twenty: three from Investigator Manus, probably demanding to know why I was avoiding him, three from Jake, and five from Jared. The rest was standard monastery information. I didn't want to know what Manus had to say, and as for Jake and Jared... it was all too complicated. My lips twitched as I contemplated giving the delete-all command, but in the end, I simply turned off the screen and walked away.

As I entered the refectory, the smell of baking bread and freshly ground coffee reminded me how hungry I was and my tummy grumbled loudly. Ash and Francis sat at a table by themselves, and when I joined them, Ash put his arm around me and I naturally sank into his side.

"Promise me you won't ever, ever," he reiterated, "do that again. Ever."

"I promise," I said into his chest.

"Good. Then we'll say no more about it." He let go of me.

Over breakfast we talked, and laughed, and mocked each other, and by the time we'd finished, we were back to normal – family.

"Have you spoken to Jared?" Ash asked casually.

"No. Should I have?" I replied.

"He's left you messages. You did get them, didn't you?"

"I got them, but I haven't looked at them yet," I mumbled, blowing on my second mug of hot coffee. I thought for a moment and then my forehead creased. "How do you know he's sent me messages?"

"Because he sent me one too, asking me why you haven't responded to the ones he sent you."

"The guy's nothing if not persistent," added Francis.

"You think?" Ash replied, but he gave me just a hint of his trademark lopsided grin. I punched him playfully on the arm.

"Stop it, both of you. I don't want to talk to him. Or Jake," I continued hastily before one of them asked.

Ash held up his arms in a gesture of surrender. "Fine. You don't want to talk about either of them at the moment, I get that, but you can't avoid them forever." I raised my eyebrows to indicate that I could try, but Ash just frowned in response.

"Uh oh. Here comes trouble," Francis whispered.

I turned to see what he was looking at then ducked behind Ash.

"I told you yesterday, Shae, you can't avoid him forever," Ash said, moving to the side.

"I don't see why I have to talk to him at all. Surely the two of you have covered everything that happened," I replied. Truth was, I just didn't want to talk about Finnian's death anymore; it was too hard. I looked over my shoulder and swore under my breath as the pristinely suited Investigator Manus caught my eye, detouring in our direction. He was tall and lanky, with a gangly walk that was almost comical as he navigated the refectory tables.

"He just wants to get the facts from everyone involved," said Francis.

"I don't care. I don't want to talk to him," I grumbled.

"I don't think you have the choice," Ash whispered before standing to shake the investigators hand. "Investigator Manus, good to see you this morning. I trust you slept well?"

"Thank you, I did," Manus replied stiffly, then wasting no time, he turned to me and added, "I understand you don't have duties this morning, Shae, so I'll expect to see you in the Primus's office in one hour to go over your account of the recent events." I began to protest but he smiled and repeated, "One hour," before walking away without a goodbye. I was left open mouthed.

Exactly sixty minutes later, Ash frog-marched me to the Primus's Outer Chamber where he practically sat on me until Brother David ushered me into the office which had once belonged to Finnian. Goose bumps skittered across my skin as I realised I hadn't been in there since we'd returned from our mission. The stone-walled room was plain, but it had some homely touches which Finnian and I had added when he'd first become Primus. Memories flooded back and I had to work hard to stop them overwhelming me.

The centrepiece of the room was a huge, ornately carved wooden desk that was usually covered in a mountain of paper and data-pads, and it was always home to a cup of Brother Thomas' Goldflower tea. Finnian's favourite.

Now, Investigator Manus sat behind a clear tabletop.

I reluctantly made my way to sit opposite him but he got up and indicated to the lounge chairs by the bay window.

"I don't understand why we have to do this," I said, already combative. "You've got my After-Action report; it details everything that happened. I don't see what can be achieved by going through it all again."

"I'm not your enemy, Shae," Manus said. I must've looked sceptical because he tucked a few stands of thinning black hair behind his ear and added, "I'm here to get the facts of the events that led up to Primus Finnian's death. That's all. I'm not here to catch you out, and I'm certainly not here to lay blame. I already have Brother Asher and Brother Francis's accounts. Once you give me yours, I'll be able to complete my report and present it to the Supreme Primus." He paused, and for a moment a wave of sadness crossed his pallid face. "Finnian was my friend also." He didn't elaborate further, but I thought perhaps I'd judged him unfairly.

"Fine," I said, taking the chair by the window. "What do you want to know?"

The Investigator sat opposite and placed a data-recorder on the coffee table between us. "There are no trick questions," he said. "I just want you to talk me through your version of events. I'll ask questions to clarify as we go along." I nodded silently. "Let's start with your arrival on Angel Ridge. Tell me everything you can remember."

I let my mind wander back to that day. It seemed like forever ago, but in reality, only twelve days had passed. I began my brief, meticulously detailing what I could remember – starting with the fact that we were there to find out about a possible assassination attempt.

"So Nyan had only given you half the information when Captain... err..." Manus consulted his notes. "Captain Marcos arrived with his Troopers?"

"Yes. He was there investigating stolen Fleet weapons."

"It had nothing to do with your investigation?"

"No. But I'm guessing the local ARRO sympathisers weren't too happy to see them."

"Ah yes, the Anti-Royalist Rebel Opposition. Quite the thorn in the Crowns' side, so I hear."

"You think?" I said incredulously, standing up. "ARRO was directly responsible for Finnian's death, and I don't appreciate your glib comment."

"I apologise," Manus replied quickly as I turned to leave. "That didn't come out how I meant it. Please..." He indicated towards my chair, but I hesitated. "Please?" he repeated.

"Fine." I sat grudgingly – not because I wanted to, but because I knew Ash would give me hell if I walked out.

"Good, good. Let's continue, shall we?" Manus continued, oblivious to the fact that he was now at the top of my 'People I'd most like to punch' list. "What happened after the Captain arrived?"

I continued to describe the events that unfolded: the riot, the fighting, and much to my regret, Nyan's death.

"Then what?" the Investigator pushed.

"Then we returned to Lilania and met with Primus Finnian. Even though Nyan hadn't been able to tell us who the intended target was, or even when it was supposed to happen, Finnian believed there was a credible threat and authorised Ash and me to continue with our investigation. He had other plans for Francis. Ash and I travelled to GalaxyBase4 to track down a possible lead, which is where we bumped into Jared… umm, Captain Marcos, again. It's also where we accidentally screwed up an undercover mission led by Marine Colonel Jake Mitchell. We were running out of time, so Ash decided to bring them in on our mission – so we could utilize their resources."

"I see," Manus said, but I wondered if he really did. "Do you agree with Brother Asher's decision to share details of a Brotherhood investigation with the Royal Earth Force?"

"Absolutely. We couldn't have completed the mission without them," I replied, a little too vehemently.

"It was just a question, Shae," the Investigator said carefully. "Please, continue."

I painstakingly detailed all the events that led to the night Finnian died. When I got to the moments before his death, I felt my heart constrict in my chest and my voice broke. "Francis is the only one who can tell you exactly what happened. He was there; I wasn't. But I do know there was absolutely nothing he could've done to save the Primus," I said defensively, eyeing Manus carefully.

"This isn't a witch-hunt, Shae." He seemed momentarily offended. "I'm simply getting to the bottom of what happened."

"What happened, happened quickly. Finnian was shot twice in the chest trying to apprehend a terrorist." I took a deep breath and then completed my account of the mission. "And that's everything," I concluded.

I looked at the com-pad on my wrist and realised I'd been talking for four hours.

"Thank you, Shae. I think that's everything I need about the mission," Manus said. I started to rise from my seat. "Just a couple more questions before you go, though."

I sank back down with a frustrated sigh. "You just said

you had everything you need."

"About the mission, yes, but I'd like to clarify a few other things. From what you've said, both Captain Marcos and Colonel Mitchell are aware of your… ability shall we call it?"

"Yes, that's correct."

"I see." He paused, as if trying to collect his thoughts. "The Brotherhood has worked extremely hard to keep your ability a secret. What I'm trying to ascertain is whether you trust these strangers to keep that secret as well."

"They're hardly strangers," I replied, thinking about how much we'd all gone through in such a short amount of time. "Of course I trust them, but I also need to be realistic. They're military men. If given a direct order, they may have no option but to share what they know. Besides, you know what gossip's like. Every member of Jared's crew has probably heard what happened to me on the Planet of Souls, so I'd say it's likely that at some point High Command will find out what I can do. What they'll do with that information is anyone's guess."

"I see," Manus said again, and I worried that if he said it one more time, I was going to do him a serious injury. "So you wouldn't be surprised if this information got out?"

"I think I just said that. Disappointed – not surprised. But it was either reveal what I can do, or let people die. What was I supposed to do?"

"I appreciate your honesty," the Investigator replied, but I noticed he hadn't answered my question. He leant forward and turned off the recorder.

"Was there anything else?" I asked overly politely.

"Well…" He shifted in his seat and looked more awkward than usual. "I do have another question, but it's more of a personal nature."

I scrunched up my nose, thought for a second, then indicated he could continue.

Manus cleared his throat. "You're something of an

enigma within the Brotherhood," he said eventually, but I was so surprised I snorted a laugh. "Really," he added. "It's an honour to finally meet you after everything I've heard."

"Thank you... I think." I wasn't sure if he was being sincere or sarcastic, it was difficult to tell.

"You're the subject of much discussion and debate. Practically every monastery I've ever visited talks about you like you're some kind of miracle."

"A miracle? Really?" I said, trying not to laugh. "I'm just a normal person, like everyone else."

"But you're not like everyone else, are you? You were brought here as an orphaned baby and accepted by the Brotherhood for reasons unknown. Since then, you've been trained by the Warrior Caste as one of their own, even though you're female. But…"

"But what? I may not be a monk, but I wear this tattoo with honour and pride." I lifted the sleeve of my shirt to show the black-ink Sun and Rune tattoo with the words Protect the Unprotected in delicate, ancient script underneath. The ink, mixed with sacred black rock from the Brotherhood's first and most revered monastery, sparkled lightly in the afternoon sun.

"My case in point," Manus continued, looking slightly in awe. "You were awarded one of those tattoos – the only female or non-monk to ever have one. Plus, you have remarkable, unexplained abilities – something we're expressly forbidden to talk about outside the Brotherhood, by the way. You can understand why monks from the other monasteries would be fascinated by you."

"Perhaps you're right," I conceded. "I've never really thought about it before. So, what's your question?"

"My question is: why?"

"Why?"

"Why did Primus Bernard allow you to stay when Finnian brought you here as a baby? I mean, they didn't know about your abilities at that point; you were just a baby girl. It's just so... mysterious. Don't you think?"

It wasn't the first time somebody had posed that question, and I'd asked Finnian the same thing many times. His answer was always identical.

"Because a promise was made to a dying woman, and the Brotherhood honoured it," I said.

"Really?" Manus' tone was a mixture of surprise and disillusionment.

"Really."

"But they could've placed you in a safe, loving home; somewhere you could've been normal. The Brotherhood could've checked in on you to make sure you were okay. Why keep you here?

"I can't answer your question any other way than I already have, Investigator. Just before my mother died on the *Nakomo*, she made Finnian promise that the Brotherhood would look after me. I guess both the Primus and Supreme Primus decided that a promise was a promise."

"And that's it?"

"That's it."

"So why are you still here? You could've left a long time ago."

"And leave all this?" I indicated to life outside the window. "Besides, where else would I go? The Brotherhood is my family, my life. They took me in when I needed a home, when I needed love. Over the years they've looked after me, trained me to be a Warrior, and in turn I help protect the unprotected. Plus, as you've already pointed out, I'm not exactly 'normal'."

"It's lucky the *Nakomo* was in the vicinity when they were needed. Any idea what they were doing that far from home?"

"Not sure. Something to do with a humanitarian mission, I think. Can't tell you more than that, I'm afraid."

"Well, I guess that's it then." Manus stood, looking

dissatisfied. "I'll have my report ready for the Supreme Primus when he arrives the day after tomorrow." When he shook my hand, his grip was weak and clammy.

I was heading back to my quarters when I bumped into Ash on the patio overlooking the bay. "How did it go?" he asked as I sat beside him.

"It was horrible, but it's done now," I replied pragmatically before lapsing into silence.

When the wind blew in our direction, I got the faint scent of washed cotton from the traditional funeral drapes. They'd been brought out of storage, cleaned, and were now out drying in the warm, breezy, afternoon sun.

The investigator's comment about the Supreme Primus arriving had started me thinking about who he would announce as Finnian's replacement. The obvious choice would be Ash – brave, honourable, smart and caring – but I knew that if he was named, he wouldn't be able to come on our off-world missions anymore. I hated myself for it, but part of me hoped it wouldn't be him.

"Hey, I was thinking," I said, trying to sound casual. "I know it should be you… but on the off-chance it's not, who do you think Isaiah will name Primus?"

Ash sat back in his chair and raised his face to the sun. "Brother Artimus maybe," he replied.

"Seriously?" I said, choking back a laugh. He turned his face towards me, opening one eye.

"Sure. Why not?" he said sincerely.

"Umm, let me think… probably because Brother Artimus is a stuffy Doctrinal Caste academic, not to mention loquacious and bombastic; the complete antithesis of the Warrior Caste," I said, copying the same flamboyant language Artimus used. "But I suppose he's not that bad – if you can manage to stay awake." I caught the mischievous twinkle in Ash's eye. "You're having me on! I can't believe I fell for it!" I thumped him on the arm and his face broke into a beautiful, lopsided grin.

"Yes, but only partly. As a Ninth Degree, he is eligible. What about Brother Andre?"

"Still Doctrinal… but a better choice," I concluded. "As Finnian was Warrior Caste do you think Isaiah will purposely go Doctrinal?"

"It's possible." Ash thought for a moment. "No. I believe he'll go with the best candidate, regardless of Caste."

"Then it should be you. You're the best candidate." I tried to sound cheerful and happy for him, but he always knew when I was faking – damn Link.

"I know you think that, but you're biased."

"I'm not the only one that thinks it."

"I appreciate the faith you, and others, have in me, but I'm way too young and inexperienced. There are more qualified candidates, like Benjamin or Noah. Both would be good choices."

Francis sauntered up and sat his stocky, muscular body in the chair opposite me. It groaned in protest, but he ignored it and raised an inquisitive eyebrow. "Good choices for what?"

"Primus," Ash replied. "We're speculating over who might be Finnian's successor. We think Artimus—" The rest of his sentence was drowned out by Francis's guffaws.

We took it in turns to throw weirder and more ridiculous names into the pot until I couldn't breathe and my sides hurt from laughing. Eventually the suggestions stopped long enough for me to get my breath back.

"We really should be doing something to prepare for the Supreme Primus's arrival," I commented half-heartedly, though I figured there were enough monks flapping around cleaning and polishing, scrubbing and mopping.

The laundry had gone into overdrive to make sure the monk's floor-length ceremonial robes were all cleaned and pressed, and the normally vibrant pink of the north lawn had been replaced by a sea of blue. The Warrior dark blue and the Doctrinal light blue shimmered in the distance like waves in the mid-day sun.

Normally, a visit from the Supreme Primus was a joyous and auspicious event – a cause of real celebration. The entire monastery would hum with the excitement of his arrival, but that afternoon the mood was sombre, and the monks worked in virtual silence.

"I think the chores have been adequately allocated," Ash said. "I don't think there's anything we need to be doing right now, so I suggest we just enjoy a few minute's peace together." I smiled at him gratefully.

The rest of the afternoon passed quickly as the three of us talked about Finnian's life instead of his death. Occasionally monks joined us on the patio, sharing fond memories of the Primus, before carrying on with their chores. It was late, and the sun had long set, when we went our separate ways.

After the unpleasant task of talking to Manus, it had been an enjoyable afternoon, and remembering the good things about the man I considered my father had eased the painful knot in my chest. By the time I retired to my room, I was able to smile when I thought of him, and I was asleep as soon as I shut my eyes.

2

"Shae, wake up!" My head was foggy and the voice sounded distant and muffled. "Shae, you have to wake up." The tone more urgent.

I knew who it was, but I ignored him. I was warm and comfortable, and quite happy clinging on to sleep – until Ash shook me so hard, I had no other option. I opened my eyes and they seared from the bright overhead light, so I shut them tight, then blinked continuously until I'd acclimatised.

"I'm awake. Stop shaking me. I'm awake," I grumbled, trying to fend him off. I was angry at the way Ash had woken me, but it quickly morphed into panic. "What's going on? What's happened?"

"It's Captain Marcos," Ash replied, looking me directly in the eyes to make sure I was awake enough to understand.

"What about him?"

"I've just spoken to Commander Tel'an," Ash continued, but he seemed reluctant to say more. I felt a wave of anxiety flow through the mental Link between us and fear froze the pit of my stomach.

"What is it Ash?" I pleaded. "Just tell me."

"Jared's missing," he said bluntly, obviously taking me at my word. My breath caught in my throat as I digested the words: Jared was missing. Another wave of unease flooded through the Link from Ash, and for a moment I was overwhelmed.

"What happened?" I asked slowly.

"Tel'an didn't have long to talk, and she couldn't say much, but she told me the *Defender* had been sent to the Western Agricultural Region near Chartreuse."

"Why would they send one of the most prestigious ships in the Royal Earth Force to a peaceful strip of farming planets at the outer border of the Sector?" I asked, confused.

"Seems it's not so peaceful at the moment," Ash replied. "Over the last few months, the region's been prey to a gang of thieves. Hit and run jobs mainly – credits, jewellery, small equipment, that sort of thing, and mostly during the day when everyone's at work. But recently the attacks have been escalating, getting progressively more violent and brutal. The latest raid left an entire community razed to the ground, the crops burnt, and five farmers dead. I guess the REF wanted to put a stop to it once and for all. Send a message, so to speak. The *Defender* was closest."

"Okay, so what went wrong? A few gun-thugs should've been a cake-walk for Jared's troopers."

"When the *Defender* got to the region, there was already a raid in progress. Jared took a squad of troopers—"

"Of course he did," I interrupted without thinking. "Why does he always have to be in charge of everything? He's the godsdamn captain! When's he going to learn to delegate? He shouldn't be putting himself in unnecessary danger like that."

"Yes, well, that's as maybe, but you know what he's like."

"Stubborn and pig-headed?"

"I was going to go with hands-on and leading from the

front, but I think you're probably right as well. Anyway, he took a Warrior and followed the target ship into No Man's Land between our Sector and D'Antaran space. The Warrior took out their engines and forced the thieves to land on the nearest planet, but once they were down, they ran. It should've been a straightforward cat-and-mouse round up, but something happened... the Captain disappeared."

"What do you mean, disappeared? What happened to his locator beacon?"

"I don't know, Shae. By all accounts... maybe it would be better to let Tel'an tell you the rest."

"Ash, if you know more, you'd better tell me," I demanded, feeling heat rise in my cheeks.

"Okay, but this is all I know." Ash sighed. "Jared and the troopers followed the gun-thugs into the forest and managed to pin them down. It was dark and there was a firefight, but the last reports indicated the troopers had the upper hand. Then they were attacked—"

"Attacked?" I didn't mean to interrupt again, it kind of blurted out. "By who?"

"Not by whom, by what. The trooper who called it in said they'd been attacked by some kind of creatures. When back-up got there, they found the mutilated bodies of two troopers and three hostiles. Once they'd rounded up the survivors, they discovered Jared and one of the thugs were missing. Shae, they found Jared's Sentinel and it had blood on it. Doc Anderson confirmed it's his."

I felt sick.

Even though I'd only known him a few weeks, the thought of losing Jared terrified me. "And that's all you know?"

"That's all I know for now. Tel'an will give us an update when we get there."

I dressed quickly, pulling on my combat trousers with such haste I almost fell. I grabbed my worn, military-style boots and sat on my bed to put them on, my hands shaking so badly I could barely tie the laces.

"Not that I'm complaining, but why did Commander Tel'an contact us?" I asked, picking up my utility belt and buckling it around my hips.

"Probably because Francis is one of the best trackers in the Sector," Ash replied. Francis, who'd been lurking silently by the door, gave an exaggerated cough. "Sorry, Francis. The best tracker in the Sector."

"Thank you," Francis said smiling.

"You're welcome."

The banter was good, lifting the mood, but I couldn't help thinking Tel'an had an alternative reason, and I knew Ash sensed what was going through my head.

"Maybe she contacted us because she thought that you… that we would want to help. And maybe it would be prudent to have you close by. Just in case."

I slotted my Sentinel and Cal'ret into their respective holsters as Brothers Artimus and Noah arrived at my room. Noah knocked, even though the door was wide open, and I appreciated the gesture.

"What's going on?" spluttered Artimus, looking at each of us in turn. "Surely you're not thinking of leaving?"

"We're needed," Francis replied. Short, but to the point.

Artimus looked bewildered. "But the Supreme Primus is due tomorrow, Ash. You have to be here." He turned to look at me. "And what about the funeral? You can't possibly think about going off-world."

"I can't possibly think about not going," I replied bluntly, but I was hurt that he'd think anything would keep me away from Finnian's funeral.

"Artimus," Ash said carefully. "Supreme Primus Isaiah won't be arriving until lunchtime tomorrow. Chartreuse is a three or four-hour flight tops; we can be there and back by the time he arrives. Besides, if we don't find Captain Marcos by then, I don't think the chances are…" he trailed off.

"But with so much going on?" Artimus continued unabated. "And with the Supreme Primus choosing a new Primus for Sector Three. Surely that and Finnian's funeral should take priority?"

I saw red. And I'm sure Ash felt the blast wave coming through the Link because as I opened my mouth, he cut me off. "Brother Artimus, we both knew Finnian extremely well. Do you really think that he, of all people, would want us to put pomp and ceremony ahead of a man's life?"

Artimus squirmed for a moment. "Yours is a fair point made well, Brother Asher," he conceded, the colour in his cheeks exposing his embarrassment.

Noah smirked silently behind him from the doorframe, but after an uncomfortable pause he stepped forward into the room. His presence was immediately felt.

"Brother Asher's right, you have to help find Captain Marcos. Besides, the rest of us are more than capable of holding the fort. Don't worry about a thing – I'm sure Artimus can handle the ceremonial preparations, and I can greet our visiting monks and make sure they have everything they need. We're already well prepared, I'm sure we can spare the three of you for a short while. Isn't that so Artimus?" Noah's question was heavily loaded and left Artimus little room but to agree.

I patted myself down to check that I had all my weapons and tactical gear, leant past Artimus to grab my jacket, and then gave Noah a quick kiss on the cheek. "Thank you," I said quietly.

Running up the stone steps to the *Nakomo's* landing pad, I was surprised to see Brother Andre standing at the bottom of the boarding ramp holding a data-pad. The *Nakomo's* engines were already warming up, and although Jared's engineers had given her an overhaul during our last mission, there was something comforting about the unexplained rattle that still came from the port engine.

"I heard what happened," Andre said. "Thought you might be needing the old tub."

"Hey! Less of the old," I replied. "But you thought right," I added with a grateful smile.

Andre handed Francis the data-pad. "She's fuelled and ready to go. I've done the external checks and she's warmed up nicely. You just have to do the internals and you're good to go."

Our home was a beautiful little planet surrounded by a cloaking shield, hidden behind a large and deadly asteroid field. When we got to the shield, a small window appeared, just big enough to fit the *Nakomo*. It closed quickly behind us and Lilania disappeared, leaving what looked like a great big empty area of nothingness.

It took Francis a little over half an hour, and a lot of concentration, to pilot the safe path through the asteroids. After checking there were no ships on the other side of the field, he took us out into Deadspace – an area of Sector Three that was virtual wasteland. The *Nakomo's* FTL engines kicked in and we started our journey to rendezvous with the *Defender*.

As we came into visual range of the Cruiser, I was momentarily reminded by how magnificent she was. Leaving dry-dock just over six months ago, the ship was a brand spanking new Vanguard Class Cruiser. Fast, highly manoeuvrable for her size, and armed to the eyeballs.

The *Defender* was imposing, even I could tell that, and although I'd never say it to Jared, she was pretty. She had state-of-the-art FTL engines, plasma cannons on the top and sides, and at least four Starflower Railguns; a beautiful name for such a deadly and destructive weapon.

The *Nakomo* was dwarfed by the Cruiser as we pulled up alongside, just a speck against her hull. I expected to receive docking codes from one of the flight controllers, but instead we were hailed by the Officer on Watch.

"Commander Tel'an is awaiting your arrival at the

temporary Command Centre on 758-C2," he informed us. "I'm sending you the coordinates now."

758-C2 was a mid-size, Category Two planet. It was still early, but the sun was rising quickly, and the pale-rock landing site was bathed in a white, blinding glow that gave the planet an eerie, ghostly feel to it.

As soon as we had boots on the ground, we were approached by a familiar face. "Brothers, Shae," Lieutenant Grainger said, shaking our hands in turn. "I'm sorry we have to meet again under these circumstances, but I'm glad you're here. You need to put these on." She handed us protective glasses. "Something to do with the sunlight and polarisation, Doc says. This way."

Grainger was the Fleet Officer I'd saved while I should've been looking after Nyan. I didn't regret saving her life for a second. It'd been the right thing to do, even if the result had been Nyan's death. I'd made peace with that.

I followed as she led us towards a huge Command Tent that was pitched in the middle of a clearing. The whole area was a hive of activity, but Grainger took us straight inside, where data-screens and workstations had been hastily erected. Commander Tel'an was leaning over a holo-table displaying a topographical map of the area.

"Thank you for coming so quickly," she said with just a hint of a soft Santian accent. "I have it on good authority that you're the best tracker in the Sector, Brother Francis. We could certainly use your help."

"Of course," he replied. "I'll do everything I can."

Tel'an was one of the most beautiful women I'd met in my life. Most of the time she was immaculate, even managing to make her plain Fleet uniform look good, but I was struck by how anxious she looked. Her half-Santian genes normally gave her skin a pale coffee and cream marbled effect, but it was noticeably several shades deeper. On the flight, I'd tried to convince myself that everything would be okay, that Fleet was overreacting, and Jared would simply be lost in the forest, but Tel'an's physical reaction to the threat scared the hell out of me. I tried to quell the feeling by telling myself her colour-change was just a trick of the light in the tent, but then she turned her almond-shaped eyes on me and the usual bright amber was almost obscured by the blackness of the slit irises. She blinked a third eyelid which closed from side to side, and said, "Let's get to work then."

Despite the change in her appearance, Tel'an seemed in perfect control of the operation. She moved gracefully around the tent, pointing to various plexi-screens as she filled us in on what'd happened. Just as she was concluding her brief, Doc walked in.

"Any news?" he asked.

"Nothing yet," Tel'an replied. She turned to Francis. "So that's everything. The *Defender* has scanned the area and found no sign of the Captain, or his locator signal – though our equipment is being severely hampered by the particle polarization in the atmosphere. It's been…" she looked at one of the data-screens, "nearly ten hours since Captain Marcos was first reported missing."

"Okay." Francis gathered his thoughts. "Speed is essential at this point, but so is thoroughness. I need to see where the Captain was taken, then I want your tracker to walk me through what she's done so far. No offence, but I want to check nothing's been missed."

"Of course. Follow me," Tel'an said, leaving the tent. "Tristada, with us," she ordered to a female trooper, who immediately fell in with our group. The Commander led us into the forest until we came to another clearing, where plasma burns and bullet holes peppered the surrounding trees and rocks.

"Watch your step," Francis said as I almost trod on one of the large animal paw prints covering the soft ground.

Maroon tarpaulin sheets covered five mounds. Doc stepped forward and pointed to a rough cluster of three tarps on the far side of the clearing. "Those three are the remains of the bad guys. That one and that one," he pointed to the remaining two in turn, "are what's left of the Fleet troopers. We've left everything in place so you can get a feel for what happened." I started towards the nearest tarp. "You might want to prepare yourself," he suggested.

Ash and I stood next to the body as Francis pulled back the stiff material and my stomach lurched as I surveyed the carnage inflicted on the poor man. He'd been torn open by claws or teeth, or both – it was impossible to tell because of the extent of the damage. A pool of blood stained the ground around the body and I turned away when I'd seen too much, swallowing repeatedly to stop myself being sick.

There was so much blood.

I steadied my breathing and got myself under control as Ash dropped to his knees, his eyes closed, and his lips moving silently in prayer.

"Where's the Captain's Sentinel?" asked Francis as he carefully replaced the sheet.

"Over here," said Trooper Tristada, pointing to the left of us. We followed her over. "It's definitely the Captain's."

The Sentinel, one of two Jared wore on missions, lay on the dark, red-soaked mud, covered in congealing blood. "Is all this Jared's?" I asked, my own blood turning cold.

"Yes," said Doc. "It must've been quite an injury to—"

"Brother Francis," Tel'an interrupted, quickly changing the subject. "Trooper Tristada's our best tracker – she's at your disposal."

"Excellent," Francis replied, before turning to the young woman. "I need you walk me through your process."

"Sure. The first part's simple; you can see from the tracks here and here, and the marks over here, that the team was attacked by two large quadrupeds. This was also confirmed in the surviving troopers' After-Action reports." She walked carefully around the clearing, pointing out large footprints in the mud and slash marks on the tree bark.

"I've no idea what kind of predator they are; we have little information on the indigenous animals in this part of No Man's Land. What I do know is they came in from that direction but left that way."

The trees around the clearing were unusually tall, with narrow, deadly-straight trunks. My fingers traced over three deep parallel grooves carved into the ash-white bark, and my eyes followed the gouges up the trunk towards a shock of purple and magenta leaves in the branches high above.

I'd seen the damage the creatures had done to trees and flesh, and couldn't help imagining what those same claws had done to Jared. Tristada was still talking and I tried to concentrate on her words, pushing visions of a bloodied, mutilated Jared to the deepest recesses of my brain.

"I would estimate one of the creatures to be about six hundred kilos, the second a little less, maybe five-fifty. It's difficult to tell, because of the extreme damage to the bodies, but I'd say they have three razor-sharp hunting claws on their front paws and six shorter, blunter claws on the back paws. From the bite marks, they have exceptionally strong jaws with a set of six canine-type teeth – four on the upper jaw, two on the lower." Tristada paused and shook her head.

"What is it?" Francis asked.

"I've been thinking." She turned to Tel'an. "Commander, I know I didn't say this earlier, but I now believe the creatures have some resilience to our weapons – at least to our TK70's."

"On what evidence do you base that opinion?" Tel'an replied.

"We know from the directionality of gun fire that our squad targeted the creatures, and with the number of rounds expended, some of them had to hit the targets, but the blood... Doc's tested it, and he says it's all human. There's only one small trace of unidentified animal blood where drag marks lead off to the left. The evidence suggests these creatures have a type of thick, armoured skin – one that even protected them against our rifles."

"I see. Give me a moment," said Tel'an before removing herself from the group to talk quietly into her communicator.

Francis double-checked Tristada's observations, while I found myself standing alone in the centre of the carnage, watching Ash as he moved between each tarp-covered mound. Images of Jared I'd tried to bury bubbled to the surface, and just when I thought I might collapse into a heap of uselessness, Ash put his hand on my shoulder and I was able to pull myself together.

"I'm sure he's fine," Ash said confidently, but the hit I got from him through the Link couldn't have been more conflicting. I was about to answer when three Troopers arrived, each carrying two cases which they laid on the ground before flipping the clasps to reveal weapons I didn't recognise.

"TK80 Handheld Assault Cannons," Tel'an explained, handing me one. "Prototypes. The *Defender* was chosen to test them – I guess now's as good a time as any."

The gun felt heavy in my hands, but I was used to my Sentinel which was a much lighter handgun. Subconsciously my hand dropped to my side to confirm it was still holstered.

"Okay, now what?" I asked.

"Now we follow the trail," said Francis.

Tel'an checked her com-pad. "I'm afraid this is where I must leave you," she said. "As much as I want to help, I have to update Central Command. Doctor Anderson, you're with me; Doctor Carter will go with the rescue team."

"But—"

"That's an order, Doctor. I can't risk our Chief Medical Officer disappearing as well."

"Okay, listen up" Francis said loudly to get everyone's

attention. "The search team will consist of me, Tristada, Shae, Ash, Doc Carter and Trooper Team Three. Stay behind me and watch where you step. I'll give further instructions along the way. Clear?"

We followed him and Tristada silently into the forest.

I flicked my eyes left and right for any sign of Jared, but there was nothing except a blanket of dense foliage – the washed-out whites and creams occasionally tangled together with bright heliotrope flowers. The contrast was both beautiful and unnatural at the same time.

We walked along the trail for about a mile, the two trackers exchanging information the whole way. Dead leaves littered the forest floor, so dark they were almost black, so dry and brittle they crunched noisily under foot.

The track led towards a rocky area with large bone-white boulders, eventually running parallel to an almost sheer rock face. The ground beyond began to rise steeply towards a small mountain range in the distance.

"This is far as I got," Tristada said. "It looks like there was a rockslide and the trail just disappears. I tried to pick it up over there and over there," she pointed left and right, "but nothing."

"Okay, then. We're going to have to do this old school," Francis replied before giving us specific search instructions and individual map co-ordinates to concentrate on. Just before we headed out, I noticed he hadn't allocated himself a search area.

"Where are you heading?" I asked.

"Up there," he replied, pointing to the rock face behind him.

"Seriously?" I craned my neck up.

"Yeah. I've got a hunch."

We synchronised com-pads and set off, meticulously studying the ground, leaves, brush, trees... hell, everything, for signs of a trail. After about two hours of searching, my eyes ached and I had a splitting headache.

Coms had been quiet for so long, I jumped when I heard Francis's voice in my earpiece.

"I've got the trail, sending you co-ordinates now. I suggest everyone converges on my position asap; there's a pathway up through the rocks just to the west. Be careful though, the ground's unstable."

We found him waiting for us about quarter of a mile from the top of the cliff. "I guess your hunch paid off," said Ash, looking at the new pool of blood. "How did you know they went up the rock face?"

"I didn't. But Tristada's a good tracker and she said she hadn't seen any signs of a trail below. I'm thinking the creatures climbed the cliff and it was their combined weight that caused the landslide. It was an educated guess, nothing more."

Francis suggested we take a short break to re-focus and have something to drink before following the new trail. I managed to sit for a minute and ate some crackers from my MRE, trying not to look at the drying blood on the ground. When I was done, I got up and started to pace, drifting off from the rest of the group. The sun had risen high in the sky and it had become uncomfortably hot. When I took off my glasses to rub my eyes, I realised how blindingly white the light was, and put them back on quickly.

I turned to return to the group but a sharp, deafening crack, like the snap of a whip, split the air and I felt the ground move. I froze. Birds took flight from the branches high above, dislodging leaves which fell gracefully to the ashen grass around me.

The air became still and silent again, the ground motionless.

I caught Ash's eye and he raised his arm, gesturing for me to re-join them. I'd taken two, maybe three steps when the earth shook again, and the air filled with a deep, ominous rumble.

3

My head hurt like hell and it took a moment for my brain to focus. Blazing white sunlight had been replaced by total blackness and I blinked a couple of times to make sure my eyes were really open. Wherever I was, I couldn't move, and as my breath quickened, my lungs filled with cool air that smelled damp and musty like the lakebeds on Larrutra.

Through the aching in my head I heard Ash and Francis talking, though I only caught the odd word. My immediate thought was that they were trapped like me, but as they became clearer, I realised the jumbled, urgent voices were coming through my earpiece.

"Ash," I croaked, my throat stinging. "Ash…"

"Shae!" I fixed on his voice and that helped to clear my head a little. "Thank the Gods. I thought…" His fear vibrated through the Link. "Are you okay? Are you hurt? Shae? Answer me?"

"Whoa, Ash, if you quit yakking for one second, I might get a word in," I grumbled.

He laughed briefly. "My apologies. You have our full attention," he mocked.

"What the hell happened?" I asked.

"Best guess... an earthquake opened up a sinkhole and you—"

"Fell in it?"

"Exactly. We've been trying to get to you for twenty minutes, but the ground's too unstable. We had to back off before more earth collapsed."

On cue, a light shower of soil covered my shoulders.

"Let's start with the basics." Francis took over. "Are you injured?"

"My head hurts, but it's getting better; score one for instant healing."

"Now's hardly the time for jokes," he cautioned.

"Okay, okay," I replied. "No need to get all serious." He huffed loudly in my ear. "I seem to be vertically wedged in some kind of shaft or fissure, but it's so dark down here, it's difficult to know for sure. My right arm's pinned between my hip and the rock side, and my left arm... what the... hang on..."

"And you're left arm..." Francis pushed. "Shae? What's wrong?"

"Oh, wait, it's ok. I was a little freaked out for a moment. Wasn't exactly sure where my left arm was, but it's wedged above my head, completely numb. Hold on, I'm going to try something."

With effort, I bent my elbow and managed to knock the glasses off my face with an uncooperative hand. Unhindered by the polarized lenses, the crack in the earth seemed marginally lighter. As my eyes acclimatised, I looked up to see a small shaft of light seeping through a moon-shaped hole in the rock canopy.

"I can see daylight above, but it's impossible to say how far down I am."

"Okay, we'll worry about that in a bit; I'm more concerned with you. So, apart from your head hurting, what about the rest of you? Legs? Ribs? Internal injuries? Does anything feel out of place?" Francis pressed.

"No, everything seems fine. My legs feel weird, but I think that's because..." I bent my head forward to get a better view of the shaft below me, crying out in pain as I smacked my head on the barely visible jagged rocks in front of me.

"What happened? You okay?"

"It's nothing," I grumbled, too embarrassed to say anything more. My skin had already started to tickle and the crevice filled with a pale silvery-blue glow that dissipated quickly.

"What were you saying about your legs?" Francis asked.

"Well, they're kind of hanging. I've swung them around a bit but can't feel the side of the crevice."

The ground shook and I was covered in another shower of rock debris. I hacked to clear my throat and my eyes stung from the grit that had invaded before I'd had the sense to shut them tightly. The ground rumbled again and I dropped a fraction, bracing myself against the rock walls.

When the earth stopped shaking, I was able to move my left arm and carefully rotated my shoulder, allowing me to drop it to my side. I felt the blood flow to my fingertips and there was a moment of calm before my entire arm exploded with pins-and-needles. I gritted my teeth and waited for the pain to disappear.

"Shae, we can't get to you at the moment." It was Tel'an's voice in my earpiece. "The ground up here is too unstable; every time we try to get close, more earth collapses. I have an engineering team on their way down from the *Defender* and we'll get you out as soon as they arrive."

With difficulty, I retrieved a chemstick from one of my pockets, the green glow lighting up rocks that were too close and rough. With a bit of careful twisting, I saw that below my hips, my legs dangled in open space. I dropped the chemstick and it fell about seven or eight metres before landing, illuminating a small cave. Another shower of rocks fell, only they were larger and heavier, and my arm was no longer above my head to protect me. The ground rumbled threateningly.

"Tel'an, I'm not sure nature's going to wait for your engineers to arrive. There's a cave below me, I think—" I was cut off by more falling debris, but that time it started to pile up around my shoulders. "I don't think I can stay where I am," I spluttered, spitting soil out of my mouth. "I'm going to get buried any second."

"Can you drop down into the cave?" asked Ash.

"My Cal'ret is wedged into the rock face, but if I undo my belt, I should be able to." I looked at the cave below, glowing bright green, and realised there was no way I could fall that far and not do myself some kind of injury. Unease fluttered in my chest. Sure, I'd heal, but that didn't stop a broken leg, or worse, from hurting like a sonofabitch. I wasn't overly enamoured about the prospect, but then the decision was made for me.

Falling soil built up around me, covering my mouth and nose. I held my breath and desperately fumbled with the clips and buckles of my utility belt, feeling the lurch in my stomach as I dropped. The moment I landed, a bolt of pain shot up my leg, then ribs crushed in my chest and I heard a snap from my wrist. I ignored it all, rolling out of the way of the earth and stone falling through the crevice with me, the small window to the outside world disappearing.

The luminous green from the chemstick mixed with the sparkling silver-blue flush from my body. My eyes watered and I gritted my teeth as bone reset beneath bruised skin.

I lay on my back and closed my eyes, panting from the pain as it gradually morphed into a dull ache. Eventually I sat up, assessing any lingering damage. "Ash?" I croaked.

"You have got to stop scaring me like this." Ash tried to sound casual, but the Link always gave him away.

"This time it wasn't my fault," I replied, cautiously standing and putting weight on each leg in turn to test them.

"Hmm, maybe," he conceded. "The engineering team has arrived and are assessing the situation, but we've had to move further away from the site after the last collapse. It's going to take some time to get to you so just sit tight, okay?"

"It's not like I've exactly got a choice. Ash, I've lost my belt and weapons, and I've no idea where the TK80 is. They're either stuck in the fissure still or buried under rock somewhere. Do you think Jared will be pissed I've lost one of his shiny new toys already?"

"I think that's the last thing he'd be worried about," replied Tel'an kindly.

I picked up the chemstick and walked around the cave, finding a small opening on the far wall, just big enough to crawl through. The skin on my arms goose-bumped from the cool, soft breeze blowing through it, and the sound of running water was so faint I wondered whether I'd imagined it.

I wriggled through the opening until I was four or five metres in, listening harder. In the tunnel, the sound of running water was unmistakable, the wafts of air damp on my cheeks. "Ash, I've found a passageway I think leads to water," I advised. No response. "Ash?" Lowering my mental roadblocks, I searched the Link for him. Still nothing. I reversed my way back out of the tunnel. "Ash! Ash!" I called, panicked.

"What? What's happened?" he said. I was overwhelmed by a sudden hit through the Link, and quickly put my roadblocks back in place before explaining. "Stay in the cave, Shae. This is not the time to go wandering off," he chastised.

"Thing is, this cave doesn't look overly secure," I replied, watching the ceiling gradually crumble. "The tunnel definitely leads to water, and the breeze must be coming from somewhere. What if it's a way out?"

"And what if it isn't? What if it takes you further into the mountain and away from us?"

"Okay, you make a fair point, but—"

"Shae, this is Tel'an. Our subterranean scans are dealing with a great deal of interference, but it looks like there's a network of underground springs covering this entire area. Some look like they lead to the outside, but others criss-cross each other and lead nowhere. We're working to enhance the imaging, but it's going to take time."

"I don't think I've got time, Commander," I said, side stepping a cascade of falling rocks.

"Whatever's distorting our scanners and affecting communications, is also preventing us from picking up your locator beacon," Ash explained before sighing heavily. "We won't know where you are, or if anything has happened to you. It's not safe."

"I understand," I replied. "But it's hardly safe where I am." I heard him sigh again as the ground rumbled. "Look, how long do you reckon before the engineers will be able to get to me?"

"They've advised it will be about an hour before they can stabilise the ground enough to start digging," Ash said.

"Then give me the hour to investigate," I reasoned.

"Fine. One hour – but if you haven't made it out by then, I want you back in the cave. One hour. Not a second longer. Do you hear me, Shae?"

"I hear you. See you soon," I replied before slipping back into the tunnel.

About ten metres from the cave, the passageway narrowed and I had to drag myself along the ground. The jagged rock sides were close, and in the dim light I noticed the walls continued to taper. After a while, drops of sweat ran into my eyes, stinging them, and I allowed my head to drop until my forehead rested on my arm. The green glow faded as I took a minute to get my breath back.

By the time I'd gone another few metres, the tunnel

sides where almost touching my shoulders and I felt confined and claustrophobic. I began to regret my decision to investigate the tunnel, but the thought of Jared, alone and injured, spurred me on. In front, the tunnel bottlenecked, looking like a gaping black mouth in the ghost-green light of the dying chemstick.

I squeezed and pushed myself forward until I couldn't go any further. My shoulders were wedged, and the rough, sharp stone of the tunnel walls cut through my skin again. I rocked backwards and forwards, only managing to progress a little. Fear escalated and I had to stop, taking deep breaths to calm myself before trying again. Just as I thought the panic was going to take over, my left foot found leverage against the wall and I pushed for all my worth. Skin ripped at the top of my arm and I cried out in pain, but then my shoulders were free and I was able to pull myself through the rest of the way.

A pale, silvery shimmer momentarily filled the passageway. As it subsided, so did the last light from the chemstick. I cracked my last one, clipped it to my vest, and pressed on. After another few minutes of wriggling, the tunnel opened out into a small cave that was big enough for me to stand up in.

I stretched my body out, rubbed my arms and legs to get the circulation going, and tried to contact Ash – on the off-chance. The response was nothing more than taunting static.

I slid and slipped my way across slime-covered rocks and through a small opening on the far side, coming to a large rock conduit only a few minutes later. The narrow waterway that ran gently through it was crystal clear and I dropped a stone in, watching it sink into the deceptively deep channel.

I checked the time, surprised I'd been gone a fraction over half an hour. The sensible part of my brain told me it was time to return, but the thought of venturing back through that rock bottleneck didn't fill me with joy. Plus, I didn't want to be beaten by the godsforsaken place, so I decided to track the tunnel downstream for other five minutes.

The river continued to run steady, showing no sign of any change, and I finally had to admit defeat, leaving me with no option but to return. As I turned to retrace my steps, my foot slipped and I put my hand out to stop myself falling. My palm touched the wall of the tunnel and I only had a fraction of a second to register that something about the surface felt odd before the rock face gave way. I tumbled through the hole, falling into the river that ran through a new, parallel passageway.

The ice-cold water took my breath away and I was swept up by the strong, fast-moving current. I tried to stop myself, but it was impossible; the sides were smooth and there was nothing for me to grab on to. The water tasted clear and fresh, from what I'd inadvertently swallowed, and for a moment I allowed myself to believe the river might carry me to the surface.

I didn't even see the waterfall until it was too late.

I battled the churning foam and broke the surface, coughing and spluttering. That's when it hit me.

The stench flowed over me like a tidal wave. I couldn't get my breath, my eyes burned, and my stomach lurched violently. Something bumped me from behind and I splashed around, ready to defend myself. The rotting carcass of a large animal knocked gently against me in the frothing water, lit up in all its gory detail by the aluminous green light from the chemstick. I gagged and pushed the horror away, but as I tried to swim towards the edge of the small pool, I was engulfed in death. A half-decayed head suddenly bobbed up right in front of me, and I just managed to haul myself out of the sickening soup of body parts before almost passing out. The putrid smell of death seeped into my brain and it refused to focus.

I've been in some hideously smelling places in my time – Angel Ridge, the Lava Pits of Santorra, the slums of Genesis, to name a few – but that cave was worse than all of them put together. Before I knew it, I was on my knees emptying the contents of my stomach on to the cavern floor. Gradually the violent spasms subsided and I wiped my lips with the back of a shaking hand, one thing going through my head over and over: breathe through your mouth.

My chest ached from the strain of retching and my throat burned, but gradually the physical reactions to the reek began to subside. In all that time, I hadn't looked around, too scared to take in any more than I was already trying to process.

I checked my com-pad – ten minutes until my hour was up. The river had swept me a long way, but I had no idea in which direction. I could've been almost to the edge of the mountain, or I could've travelled deep into its heart, it was impossible to know. I made a half-hearted attempt to call the surface but wasn't surprised when there was no reply. I was on my own.

The cave was almost pitch-black, but the chemstick lit it up enough for me to see the source of the smell. The floor was littered with dead animals, all at various stages of decomposition. Stripped, gnawed bones lay in grisly heaps and my stomach heaved again.

Jagged, dark-grey stalactites hung from a high ceiling, and I could just make out that the small lake, with its ingredients of body parts, took up about half of the floor space. On one side of the cave, the waterfall – which marked my point of ingress – frothed and gurgled, on the other, a small stream flowed out through a tunnel.

My pulse quickened at the thought of a possible way out of the nightmare I was in, but in my enthusiasm, I forgot to breathe through my mouth and ended up dry-heaving on the floor again.

The shortest way to the tunnel would be to get back into the pool and swim to the other side, but the thought of what else was in the water made me queasy. It wasn't just the rotting heads and putrefying flesh – though that in itself was bad enough – it was the juices and fluids that were mixed in. I tried not to dwell on the fact I'd swallowed some of that water.

My only other option was to walk around the edge of the pool, over the carpet of decomposing carcasses. I made myself look at the closest remains, my eyes lingering on the distinct parallel slashes carved deep into the creature's flank.

I couldn't believe it. By complete fluke, I'd ended up in the nest of the very creatures we'd been tracking. For a second, I felt elation. If this was the beasts' nest, perhaps they'd brought Jared here… but then again, everything I'd come across so far was mutilated and maimed, and most definitely dead. My blood turned cold and my spirits sank.

Should I call out his name? Hope that he answered? I hadn't been attacked, so logic suggested the creatures weren't home, but the way my luck was going… I decided to risk it, but the only answer I received was my own voice echoing back at me.

Standing up, I quickly got my bearings, reminding myself it was just dead animals, nothing more. I climbed across the remains of a variety of beasts, some big, some small – all part eaten. I guess the creatures liked their food very, very dead.

I detoured to my right to avoid a particularly ripe and gloopy cow-like creature, catching something out of the corner of my eye.

My heart stopped.

Focusing the fading light, I made out the bottom half of a human leg sticking out from behind an animal's torso, on the end, a black, military boot. A vicious thump in my chest told me my heart had started again, and as I forced myself nearer, it pounded hard under my ribcage. The mutilated body of the man lay face down on the cave floor. Even from a distance, I could tell he was ripped and torn beyond my help, his wounds so extensive I couldn't even tell for definite if it was Jared or not.

I knelt next to the man's back, what was left of it, and with a shaking hand took his shoulder and turned him over towards me. I saw the cropped, military haircut, strong features, square jaw and soft mouth, and a strange, guttural cry escaped my lips, echoing around the cave.

The dead, unfocussed eyes of a man I didn't recognise stared at me through the darkness, and relief flooded every part of my body. I started to cry big, wet, uncontrollable tears, and it took me a moment of looking at the poor man before I could pull myself together enough to get off my knees and push on through the cave.

The body hadn't belonged to Jared, but my hope of finding him alive waned by the second. I barely noticed the horror in the cave anymore.

I wasn't far from the tunnel entrance when I practically stood on him. He was partially covered by dead animals, looking so horrific that I froze to the spot. His injuries were severe, and I struggled to process all the damage. The T-shirt and skin on the right side of his chest was torn back, rib bones cracked and bloody. Bite marks covered his legs and shoulders, and one of his arms lay at an unnatural angle.

"Jared…" His name escaped my lips, but it was barely a whisper.

Sinking to the ground next to him, I turned his face gently towards me, opening the raw, jagged gash that ran from his temple, down his face, and across his neck. I put two fingers against the undamaged side of his neck.

In the seconds it'd been since I'd found him and seen the damage, I'd convinced myself he was dead, so when I felt the faintest of heartbeats against my fingertips, I cried out with relief.

I pulled dead animals off him and dumped them to the side, not caring that my fingers tore into rotting flesh.

I ripped open what was left of his shirt and retched, swallowing down bile as I got a better look at the gaping wound. I wasted no time, placing my hands over his chest.

Closing my eyes tightly, I took a few steadying breaths, imagining him whole and unbroken: the mid-brown, military-cut hair, damp from a shower; the mischievous, boyish grin I loved so much spread across his strong face; his beautiful, unusual, blue eyes sparkling gently; his uniform clean and pristine…

In my mind, he was perfect.

A deep tingling sensation started in the pit of my stomach, gradually radiating out to my limbs. Warmth flowed down my arms and stopped at my wrists for the shortest time before arcing to Jared's chest. I opened my eyes and the whole cave glowed with the silver-blue light shining from the two of us. Dancing strands of energy flickered between my hands and Jared's skin, and excitement shivered in my chest as I watched the gaping hole above his ribs begin to close. It was slow, and I had to concentrate so hard to keep the connection strong, but I didn't care. It was working.

I took a second to glance around the cave, clearly illuminated by the glow of healing, and wished I hadn't, but Jared's deep, throaty groan brought my attention back to him. His eyelids fluttered, his fingers twitched, and I allowed myself to smile. It was difficult to tell in the bluish light, but I was sure his cheeks pinked as the wide gash down his face healed to a thin red line.

But then a deafening wail reverberated around the cave, echoing off the walls, and I flinched. Distracted, the connection between us instantly broke, and the silver-blue shimmer dissipated quickly.

Even with the light from my chemstick, it was impossible to tell exactly what had entered the cave, just that something huge and black had. I listened as the creature crossed the pool, but it wasn't until it hoisted itself out of the water about five metres to the left of us, that I got a good look. The animal shook itself vigorously, spraying me with fine droplets of water. I didn't dare move, trying to keep my breath as shallow and noiseless as possible.

The monster's thunderous howl echoed again, and I flinched. Jared stirred, his eyes fluttered, and he groaned.

The creature's head whipped around in our direction before it put its nose in the air, sniffing loudly. It raised its head higher and sniffed some more before letting out another thunderous screech.

I felt Jared move and I glanced down to see him coming around. Before he could make a sound, I put my hand over his mouth and watched confusion fill his eyes. I pressed my finger to my mouth to indicate silence then pointed slowly to my left. His eyes followed and then widened as he took in the terrifying vision of the creature, still sniffing the air, padding backwards and forwards. He slowly nodded his comprehension and I removed my hand from his mouth.

The creature started towards us, smelling rotting corpses as it came nearer. I slunk down next to Jared before rolling on top of him. He groaned, and I felt bad for causing him pain, but I had my reasons.

"They eat rotten meat," I whispered, trying to explain. "And you smell... well, rotten. I'm not quite so bad." I think he understood; I think I even saw a hint of a smile.

The snuffling noise got louder until I felt the damp heat of the creature's breath on the nape of my neck. It smelt worse than Jared, which was saying something, and my stomach turned. A rough tongue ran over the side of my face and I had to work hard not to move or scream, or vomit. A large glob of saliva dripped onto my cheek and both Jared and I held our breath.

4

The creature sniffed me again before picking up the scent of an already half-eaten animal to the side of us. It snuffled the meat, smelled me a few more times, then picked up the carcass in its mouth and padded back to the other side of the cave. A moment later, the squelch of tearing flesh and crunch of bones echoed through the cave. I filled my lungs and wiped the putrid spit off my face.

Jared let out a low, painful moan as I rolled off him and I glanced quickly towards the creature, waiting to see if it would respond. I turned back to whisper something to him, but he was already unconscious again.

I don't know how long I sat beside him watching his chest rise and fall with each breath, the pale pink, ragged scar a reminder of the wound that'd once been there. I couldn't risk healing him more, the light would draw attention from the beast, but the longer we stayed, the more danger we were in.

After a while, the crunching slowed and then stopped, replaced by a deep, rumbling snore. It was time to move.

"Jared," I whispered. "Jared, can you hear me?" I stroked the side of his face and he stirred, opening his eyes slowly. I think, for a second, he'd forgotten where we were and a smile flickered across his lips, but then his eyes darkened and his face hardened. "Can you move?"

"I think so," he whispered, his voice weak.

"The creature came back while I was healing you. I'm not sure what's still broken."

"I'll manage. Thank you," he added quietly, taking my hand.

"You don't need to thank me, Jared. You just need to help me get you out of here, okay?"

"Okay," he replied, squeezing my hand.

I helped him sit up. He swayed silently, and his eyes glazed over. Fearing he was about to pass out again, I put my hand to his cheek and rubbed it gently until his eyes refocused.

I contemplated finishing his healing, but I didn't dare risk waking the snoring beast. Instead, I concentrated on finding the easiest route out of the cave.

The last thing I wanted to do was go back into the pond, but I knew the water would support Jared better than I could on my own, and it would be easier on his injuries. When he was ready, we shuffled towards the edge. It was slow, tough going, and he was clearly in a lot of pain, but he pushed through it without complaining. I lowered myself into the pond first, pushing away the largest bits of flesh, and then gently guided him in as best I could. A loud splash, followed by the gentle rippling of water against the rock edges, resonated off the cavern walls. We stayed still for a moment, waiting, listening. A few large grumbles broke through the darkness, followed by steady, rhythmic snoring.

Jared seemed more comfortable in the water, but when I put my arm around his chest to tow him the short distance to the mouth of the tunnel, he winced in pain. I was grateful the stream remained deep enough that I could wade, allowing me to continue pulling him through the water, but after about fifty metres, it became shallow, and the rocks were too sharp and jagged for us to continue like that.

I indicated to Jared that we were going to have to go the rest of the way on foot and he nodded uneasily. He stood on shaking legs and I could tell he was trying not to put too much of his weight on me as we struggled along the tunnel wall. My heart ached every time he grimaced or groaned, and when it was impossible for him to take another step, he slumped against the side and I couldn't bear it anymore.

"Enough," I whispered. "I need to finish healing you."

"No." He was defiant. "It's too dangerous. You should leave me here and go on alone. Bring back help."

"Are you kidding me?" I cried, before covering my mouth. My voice echoed loudly down the tunnel. "I didn't come all this way to leave your sorry arse here now." I scowled at him, annoyed that he was smiling.

"Not that I'm complaining, but what are you doing here?"

"I thought that would be obvious," I huffed. "I came here to help save your miserable, ungrateful backside."

"Trust me, I'm extremely grateful." He gave me a brief, boyish grin. "But, how did you find me?"

"Well, let's just say I found you more by accident than design… you're welcome, by the way," I added sarcastically before pulling him back to his feet. "Now move, Captain. I don't intend on letting either of us die in this shitty, stinky, hell-hole."

We shuffled along the tunnel in silence and gradually it began to get lighter until I could make out the bright white light of an opening.

"Shae? Shae, do you read me?" I was so surprised to hear Ash's voice in my earpiece, I almost dropped Jared. He shot me a worried glance and I mouthed the word 'Ash' while pointing at my ear. "Are you okay?" Ash continued urgently.

"I'm fine," I replied.

"Thank the Gods." I heard the relief in his voice, but I couldn't feel him through the Link, so he couldn't have been close. "You scared me. Again."

"Yeah, I know. I'm sorry, I got… never mind. I'm near the surface now, which must be why I'm picking up coms. Hey, guess what? I found Jared."

There was a pause. "Is he…"

"Alive? Yeah." I smiled. "We also found the creatures' nest, so stay alert. I've got no idea where we are, but we're moving along a tunnel and should hit daylight soon."

"I've got your locator signal and we're heading your way now. We'll meet you at the tunnel entrance."

"Good. I don't suppose Doc Anderson's with you, is he?"

"Actually, he is." His tone was cautious. "He re-joined us after you disappeared."

"Great. You may want to suggest he breaks out the Hazmat gear."

"Why? What's happened? Have you been exposed to something?"

"Relax, Ash. I'm sure we're fine. We're just a little…" I tried to think of the right word. "Ripe," I concluded. "You'll understand when we get to you."

We were about twenty-five metres from daylight when Jared surprised me by asking, "Why didn't you return my coms?" I was about to tell him it wasn't the time to have that particular discussion, when a thundering growl stopped us in our tracks and an enormous shadow passed in front of the tunnel mouth. We immediately braced ourselves against the wall and I shot Jared a terrified glance.

The second creature splashed along the stream. At first it didn't seem to notice us, but as it drew parallel, it must've picked up our scent because its head whipped around. Its snout was no more than a few centimetres from my face and its breath stung my eyes. It snuffled my cheek before it moved sideways and sniffed at Jared's chest. The water had washed some of the stench off him and I hoped it would be enough to discourage the animal, but the creature opened its mouth, baring fearsome teeth. It let out a horrific screech before turning away and continuing up the tunnel.

Jared puffed out a slow, deep breath, sweat dripping from his forehead, and I realised it'd taken all his effort not to keel over in front of the creature. Before I could prop him up, his legs gave way, and as he slumped, his foot knocking a rock which splashed noisily into the stream.

There was a second's silence and then the tunnel filled with a throaty roar and the sound of huge feet charging through the water back towards us.

"Run!" I gasped, pulling Jared to his feet.

We stumbled out of the tunnel, immediately blinded by the blistering white sunlight, but I could just make out the shapes of four or five people.

"Get down!" Ash shouted, and I wasn't going to argue. I flung both of us to the dirt as the thundering beast reared up behind us.

I put my hands over my ears to block the sound of weapons fire and the creature's shrieks. The ground shook as the animal swayed, planting its massive, heavy feet too close to where we were huddled on the grass. Jared pulled his body over mine as protection and I appreciated the gesture, knowing it wouldn't have made a difference if we were trampled.

The barrage of weapon's fire continued until the beast let out one last ear-piercing scream before crashing to the floor.

I felt Jared's weight lift from me and I flipped on to my back, covering my eyes with my forearm to block out the sun.

"Hey," said Francis to get my attention. I turned my head to see him approaching but he stopped dead, a look of disgust on his face. His nose wrinkled. "I'm glad you're okay and everything, but… good Gods! You stink!"

"Thanks for stating the obvious, Francis," I replied. "Does that mean you're not going to come over here and help us up?"

"Umm… no. I'm good here, thanks. I'll let the medics get you. I've got something that will cheer you up, though."

"Is it Chocomel ice cream?"

"If it's Shatokian coffee, I'll take some," said Jared.

"Sorry, neither," Francis replied, holding up my belt with the Sentinel and Cal'ret still holstered. "The engineers found it while they were digging for you." He took a couple of steps away from us, almost gagging. "Seriously, do you know how bad you smell?"

"Actually, I—"

The massive black-armoured body of the first creature lunged out of the cave. It picked up one of the Fleet troopers in its jaws and tossed him to one side as if he were made of nothing more than cotton wool. Without hesitating, it attacked again, sending a med-tech flying – three large gashes opening up the bright orange Hazmat suit she wore.

A volley of TK80 fire brought down the animal before it could do any further damage. It lay whimpering on the ground as Tel'an walked right up beside it, putting a shot directly between its bloodshot eyes.

"Are there anymore?" she asked, her face flushed but not a hair out of place.

"I only saw two," Jared answered weakly.

"Me too," I confirmed, to a collective sigh of relief.

"Harper, get your team to set up a twenty-metre perimeter. I don't want to be surprised by any more of these things," said Tel'an. The Lieutenant nodded and began to round up troopers, giving quick, precise orders.

"Hey, Captain," Francis yelled. Jared turned his head towards him. "It's ridiculous the lengths some people will go to just to see us again. You could've just invited us for lunch, you know. It would've been a lot easier!"

Jared opened his mouth to reply but didn't get the chance.

"Listen up," shouted Doc Anderson. "We don't know what contagions or pathogens the Captain and Shae have been exposed to, so I'm treating this as a Level Two Hazmat situation. That means no-one approaches either of them without a suit. Anyone not wearing protection needs to move to a ten-metre perimeter. Now! Also, everyone, and I mean everyone, must go through decon protocols before leaving the planet. Understood?" There was a murmur of agreement. "Understood?" Doc repeated louder. That time he seemed content with the response.

I rubbed my eyes and sat up as one of the med-techs in an orange suit and plastic helmet handed me a pair of polarized glasses. They made it easier to see the damage the creature had done. Jared, still lying on the ground next to me, tried to swat away the med-tech without much success, but as he wasn't in immediate danger, he could wait. There were others to take care of first.

Doc knelt over an unconscious female, pressing a field-dressing on her wounds to staunch the blood.

"What you got for me, Doc?" I asked.

"Are you alright to do this?" he asked, flicking concerned eyes over me. I nodded. "Okay, if you're sure. The three large claw marks across the back have caused extensive damage to both tissue and muscle, and there's severe internal damage. I think the spinal cord is at least partially severed here, and here," he pointed to the worst areas, "but I can't be sure without a full scan back on the *Defender*."

"No problem. Easy peasy." I smiled reassuringly, and although he looked sceptical, he moved out of the way to let me get closer. A couple of minutes later, the med-tech was sitting up and talking with not a mark to be seen. I stood, swayed, and Doc's gloved hand rested on my arm to steady me.

"That was... well, that was simply amazing," he said, shaking his head as if he was still trying to process what I could do – even though he'd seen it first-hand several times. Doc was an older gentleman, kindly and gracious, with distinguished greying hair and gentle eyes. As he studied my face with a combined look of concern and pride, he reminded me a bit of Finnian. "Although amazing doesn't seem to cover what you just did," he continued. "Are you sure you're all right? You look exhausted."

"I'm fine," I lied. "Honestly." I walked over to the other trooper who'd been attacked and was glad he didn't look too badly injured. It was no more than a light workout to get him fixed up and back to full health.

By the time my attention had returned to Jared, he'd been strapped to a gurney and was about to be taken to the Warrior. He and Doc were having a difference of opinion about something, which, if I had to guess, was probably Jared saying he was fine, and Doc disagreeing. Standard stuff for the pair of them.

Ash and Francis were with Tel'an at the Hazmat 'safe' perimeter. I smiled and waved at them.

"We have to go decontaminate," Ash shouted. "Then we're going to take the *Nakomo* back to the *Defender* for a debrief. Doc wants you to go with them so he can check you over. You okay with that?"

No, I wasn't okay with that. I didn't want to go with Doc, and I certainly didn't want to go back to the *Defender*. I wanted to heal Jared and get the hell out of there before he started asking more questions about why I hadn't returned his coms.

"Don't you think we should be getting home?" I suggested. "We should be there to greet the other Primuses, no?"

Even from a distance, I could tell by the look on Ash's face that he was suspicious, but the hit I got through the

Link confirmed it.

"They can wait a bit longer," he replied, narrowing his eyes.

All the healing had made me tired and hungry, and more than a little grumpy, and on top of that, I was still trying to reconcile my feelings for Jared. Being in such close proximity to him had made everything more confusing, and all I wanted to do was to return to Lilania and bury my head in the sand again. Unfortunately, I knew damn-well I wasn't going to be able to change Ash's mind.

"Fine," I grumbled, before shuffling over to the gurney where Jared lay wincing every time Doc poked him. Even with my glasses on, he looked worse than I'd feared. "Right, let's get this over with," I said, trying to sound strong and in control, but Jared swung his arm out and tried to push me away. He was so weak he couldn't put up much of a fight when I tucked it back by his side.

"You need to rest. You've done too much already and I'm fine," he protested.

"Yeah, right." I prodded his side and he groaned. "Don't be such a martyr."

"I'm not being a martyr."

"You are."

"Am not."

"What are you? Six?"

"Fine! I'm not fine." He was angry and that took me by surprise. "But neither are you."

"I'm okay."

"No, you're not. Now who's being the martyr? You look like crap," he added bluntly.

"Thanks very much," I replied, sulking.

"And you know what else? You smell bad!" His lips twisted up at the side and I couldn't help but return his smile.

"Nice try, Marcos, but you're not going to put me off. You might as well just lay back and think of Earth."

"The Captain's right, Shae. You don't look so good," added Doc, a worried frown crossing his forehead. "Maybe you should rest."

"After." My tone was blunt, and my message was received because Doc moved out of the way. Jared continued to protest, but it was easy to ignore him as the usual tingling sensation grew in my tummy, spreading through my veins until we both glowed silver-blue.

Just as I was sure he was completely fixed, a wave of fatigue flooded through me and my knees buckled. I vaguely remember someone putting their arms around me, lifting me off the floor, but I couldn't stop myself from drifting away.

I could smell Roseberries and... vanilla maybe? Yes, definitely vanilla. I was warm and comfortable, and my skin felt like it was covered by liquid silk. I knew exactly where I was and felt myself smiling as I forced the last moments of sleep from my head. The lights were low, but I recognised the ornate furniture and luxury fabrics filling the beautiful VIP quarters that had been my home during my last stay on the *Defender*. I stretched and listened to the low voices coming from the lounge.

A quick glance at my com-pad told me it was just before 21:00 hours. I could've easily turned over and gone back to sleep, but suddenly had a dire need to pee. Typical then, that Ash chose that exact moment to check in.

"Feeling better, I see?" he called after me as I dashed into the bathroom.

When I emerged, wearing a warm, fluffy dressing gown I'd picked up from the heated shelf by the basin, Ash had returned to the lounge. I strolled in expecting to see him and Francis, but I hadn't counted on Jared being there.

"Hey, Sleeping Beauty," he said. Before I could take defensive action, he'd crossed the floor in a few steps and pulled me off my feet into a tight hug. When he let me go, I noticed his eyes were clear, intense, and back to bright blue – almost sapphire around the edge of the iris and ice-silver blue in the middle. He smiled, and he looked beautiful.

For a second, the urge to kiss him bubbled up inside of me, and I had to take a step back before I did anything stupid. His smile faltered momentarily, and his eyes narrowed.

I turned to say something to Ash but got completely side-swiped by a wave of emotion that wasn't mine. And it wasn't Ash's either; after years of practice, I'm able to recognise and differentiate his feelings. My eyes widened and my stomach flipped as I realised it was Jared I was reading.

I stared at him, open mouthed, unable to form any words.

I'd healed Jared back from the edge of death; I should've realised there'd be a residual Link between us. Why was I so surprised? No. I wasn't surprised – I was petrified. If I could feel his emotions, he could feel mine, and I couldn't let that happen. I retreated quickly to the other side of the room, knowing full-well that we were still too close for it to make the slightest bit of difference.

Another wave from Jared crashed through my head, but it was jumbled and impossible to read. I tried to ignore it, focussing instead on building a mental brain-block, desperate to keep my own emotions from seeping through the Link back to him. The only way to solve the problem would be to put more distance between the two of us. I had to get off the *Defender*.

"Give me a few minutes to throw on some clothes and we can head home," I said, turning towards the bedroom.

"Whoa, slow down," replied Ash. "I've spoken to Brother Noah and we've agreed that the three of us will spend the night here and return to the monastery in the morning. You need more rest… and we'll still be back with plenty of time to spare before the Supreme Primus arrives."

"But... what if we get held up tomorrow? What if the Supreme Primus arrives early? You should be there, and I'm really okay. Perhaps we should head off tonight. Just in case," I rambled.

Ash frowned. "Relax, Shae. Tomorrow morning will be soon enough." He'd made up his mind and I gave up complaining.

"Well, if we're staying, I'm going to need something to eat," I said, trying to make the most out of a bad situation.

"Dinner's on its way," Jared said. "I ordered it as soon as we knew you were awake." He sat on the sofa and relaxed into the cushions. To his credit, he didn't mention his coms, or my blatant disregard of them, but instead filled us in on what he and the *Defender* had been up to. I listened as he spoke, but as I watched him my mind wandered. I remembered how damaged and broken he'd looked in the cave and recalled the feeling of absolute heartache and anguish when I thought he was dead.

What would I have done if he had died?

Jared had been an arrogant arse when we'd first met, but the more I'd got to know him, the more I'd wanted to know him. We were friends, sure, but it was more than that. Why did I keep turning to him when I needed support? Why did I trust him so unconditionally? If it'd just been the two of us, maybe things would've been clearer – but it wasn't just the two of us. There was Jake.

The next hour or so was filled with eating and talking. After Jared had finished telling us what the REF was doing to round up old ARRO cells, Ash and Francis filled him in on the preparations for Finnian's funeral and the forthcoming announcement about the new Primus. Fortunately, neither of them found it necessary to inform Jared about the shark incident, or about how I'd had a complete meltdown over the last week. I tried to listen, but random thoughts about Jared kept meandering through my brain. As I picked through yet another memory of him at death's door, it hit me like a punch in the guts.

The room was suddenly silent, and I looked up to see all three men staring at me. Jared looked perplexed, his forehead puckered into a deep frown, Francis looked mildly irritated, like he did when he thought he was being left out of something, and Ash looked… relieved. A half-smile lingered on his lips.

I knew immediately what'd happened.

Without meaning to, I'd broadcasted my true feelings for Jared through the Link. It was obvious Ash would've picked up on it, I just couldn't comprehend his response. Unfortunately, he wasn't the only person in the room I was Linked to. I knew from his expression, Jared had also got a hit from me, I just hoped he hadn't understood it.

Ash must've sensed my ensuing panic because his smile dropped and he switched to protection mode. "It's been a long, eventful day," he said standing and stretching. "We could all do with some rest."

He and Francis headed for the door, but Jared remained by the couch looking preoccupied. "Shae?" he said hesitantly. "Can we talk… privately?"

"It's late, and Shae's exhausted. Can it wait until morning?" Ash asked bluntly as I tried to calm the butterflies fluttering nervously under my ribcage.

"Please," Jared pushed.

"It's okay," I said to Ash.

"Are you sure?"

"Yes, I'll be fine."

"All right. I love you."

"I love you too. See you in the morning."

I watched Ash and Francis disappear down the corridor before stepping back into my suite, the door whooshing quietly shut behind me. Jared stood by the desk with his broad, strong back to me and his hands on his hips. He turned slowly.

"I…" He paused and took a few steps towards me, but I

retreated to the other side of the couch, unexpectedly nervous about being alone with him. He looked at me strangely. "What's going on, Shae?"

"What do you mean?"

"I thought we were friends. I thought…" He let the sentence hang, but he sounded hurt.

"We are friends," I said, shocked he would think otherwise.

"Then why are you avoiding me?"

"I'm not," I lied unconvincingly.

He shook his head slowly. "The night before you returned to the monastery with Finnian's body – the night all of us spent in the bar, here on the *Defender* – you were avoiding me even then." He was right of course, but I didn't think I'd been that obvious.

When our last mission was over, we'd all returned to the *Defender* to drink to our loss, and our victory, and there'd been way too much Fire Whisky consumed. I knew Jared had wanted to speak to me privately that night, but I didn't trust myself to be alone with him. I'd stuck to Ash's side for protection the entire time.

Ash had been great as always. He'd been a gatekeeper – fielding off the attentions of both Jared and Jake without making things more awkward. At least so I'd thought.

"You've ignored my coms, not even looked at them. And now," Jared paused, pain clear in his eyes, "now you can barely stand to be in the same room with me. I don't understand. Did I do something wrong?"

"No," I cried, taking a step forward before realising what I was doing. "Jared, you've done nothing wrong. Nothing."

"Then what's going on?" he asked again.

I wanted to rush over and throw my arms around him, tell him everything was okay, but I couldn't. And besides, everything wasn't okay. "It's complicated." I sighed and looked intently at my feet.

"Then un-complicate it." The harshness of his voice made me look up and I noticed he'd moved closer. He looked uncomfortable for a second and then said, "I've never met anyone like you before."

"Well, you know, the whole healing thing is pretty unique," I quipped, trying to make light of the situation, but I knew as soon as the words were out of my mouth that it'd been a mistake.

"That's not what I meant."

"I know," I replied quietly.

"I can't stop thinking about you. In truth, you're everything I think about." Tears filled my eyes and warmth radiated through my chest. "I think... I think I'm falling in love with you," he added. The tears spilled over, splashing down my cheeks, and I smiled, but I still took a step away from him when he approached. He stopped dead. "I've tried not to. Fall in love with you, that is. You're an infuriating, emotional, pain in my backside most of the time, but there it is. And..." he looked directly into my eyes, "I think you feel something for me as well."

My legs buckled and I slumped heavily into a chair. Jared was on his knees in front of me before I could blink away a fresh set of tears.

"Jared, I—"

The rest of my sentence was silenced by his lips pressing gently on mine, and they were just as soft and warm as I'd imagined them to be. Before my brain could fire off a warning shot, I kissed him back.

Excitement simmered in my chest, hampering my ability to think clearly, so it took a few seconds for the alarm bells to start clanging. "I can't do this," I cried, using every ounce of strength I had in me to pull away from his arms. The baffled pain in his eyes was like a knife to my heart. "I can't. I'm sorry." I stood up and made to run away but Jared grabbed my wrist. He caught my gaze, and I couldn't look away, tears falling uncontrollably.

"Is it because of Jake?" he asked, hurt dripping in his voice. I didn't reply. "Answer me one question: do you love him? You owe me that much, Shae. Do you love Jake?"

"Yes," I said after a moment. A sad shadow crossed his face and he let go of my wrist. "Yes, I love him. But I'm not in love with him."

"What the hell does that mean?"

"It's complicated."

"Isn't everything?" He was sarcastic, and I couldn't blame him.

"You know everything that's happened between Jake and me. There's never been secrets." I was frustrated and confused, and I compensated by becoming confrontational. "Yes, I'm physically attracted to Jake. Yes, I think he's a good man, an honourable man, and a damn good Marine. And yes, we slept together. You know all of that." I tried to figure out the best way to explain. "But no, I'm not in love with him in a relationship kind of way. I love him like a really good friend. A best friend."

"A best friend you just happen to sleep with?"

"Grow up, Jared!"

"But you did sleep with him!"

"Yes. Once." I was angry, and shouting. How dare he judge me? "We were both single, consenting adults." My emotions were getting the better of me. "But I didn't know then that I…" I stopped myself in time.

"That you what?"

"It doesn't matter," I said fiercely. My heart beat too fast and my skin was hot and flushed.

"What?" Jared demanded. "You didn't know what?"

"It doesn't matter," I repeated.

"It does. What aren't you telling me?"

"Nothing."

"What didn't you know back then?"

"Nothing."

"Tell me."

"I can't!"

"Tell me," he shouted.

"That I loved you!" I was shocked I'd actually said it, but it was out there now. "I didn't know back then that I was in love with you. Are you happy now?"

A huge grin exploded across Jared's face.

I sat on the sofa and put my head in my hands. My confession had only made things a hundred times worse.

I felt his fingers caressing the back of my neck and I looked up to see his strong, handsome face and sparking blue eyes. Tears flowed again and he stroked my cheek, wiping away the tracks with his fingertips. He smiled, but I knew he wouldn't be for long. I reached up and gently removed his fingers from my skin.

"You need to leave, Jared."

"What?"

"Please," I said carefully, rallying myself for what I needed to say. "I love you. It's taken me a while to realise it, but I do love you."

"Why do I feel like I'm not going to like what you say next?"

"Because you're not." He tried to interrupt so I continued. "It doesn't matter."

"What doesn't matter?"

"That I love you." His forehead puckered. "People I love die, Jared. My parents, Finnian… even you nearly died today. Losing Finnian ripped me apart more than you know. I can't afford to let myself get that emotionally attached to anyone again. If you and I were… if we were… I don't think I'd survive if anything happened to you."

"I'm not going to die," he said.

"And you know that how? I'm sure that's what you thought when you went to apprehend some gun-thugs and ended up almost getting yourself eaten by rampaging creatures. If I hadn't found you today, you would be dead. You know that, don't you?" A chill ran through me. "I'm sorry, but I can't let myself get any closer to you. I can't afford to get my heart ripped open again."

"Shae, this is ridiculous." He sighed heavily. "You can't cut me off because of something that may never happen. I love you, and you love me. You can't ignore that."

"I'm sorry," I turned my face away from him, "but I have to. You need to leave now."

"But—"

"Please." My voice was hollow and broken. "Ash was right; I'm exhausted. I need to sleep now."

"Okay," he conceded after a brief pause. "But this conversation isn't over. We will continue it in the morning."

"No, we won't."

He leant forward and briefly brushed my hot, damp cheek with his lips before he stood and walked to the door. As he left, he repeated, "This conversation is not over."

"Yes, it is," I replied, but I knew he hadn't heard me.

5

It was dark in the putrid-smelling creature-cave.

I could see the way out, but as I scrambled over rotting carcasses, the stinking bodies of long-dead animals fell on me, blocking my path. Nausea and panic roiled over me in waves as I tore at decomposing flesh, pulling the animals off me one by one. Finally, I was free and able to move forward, but that's when I saw the stranger's leg and boot, just like I'd done in the real cave, and I went to him, kneeling beside his shredded body. I reached out, turning him to towards me, but it wasn't the stranger; it was Jared. His dead eyes, striking but hollow, stared unfocussed at the ceiling of the cave.

I was still screaming when I woke.

At first, I wasn't sure where I was. It was pitch-black – was I still in the cave? Had escaping with Jared been the dream and the reality was that I was still trapped?

"Lights!" I gasped.

The VIP bedroom was suddenly reassuring and calming, and I pulled the soft sheets up to my neck as if to protect myself from my own thoughts. I vaguely heard a buzzer, but ignored it, still trying to remove the vision of Jared, dead and decomposing, from my head. More buzzing, then banging – loud, heavy thumps. For a split-second I thought it might be Jared and flew out of bed, careering off the doorframe as I hurtled into the lounge.

Ash barely waited for the door to release before he forced his way in. Without a word, he wrapped me up in his arms and didn't free me until I'd stopped shaking. After he let go, I curled up on the sofa with a blanket wrapped around me, feeling better purely because he was there.

"I felt your fear through the Link," he said as he handed me a glass of water. "It woke me up. I knew it must've been bad; you've never done that before."

"I'm sorry. I didn't mean to."

"You were screaming, Shae. I'm worried about you." He looked strained and pale.

"You're cold," I said, noticing the goose bumps on his bare skin, and trying to change the subject.

"Didn't exactly have time to stop and dress," he explained. "Just grabbed enough to keep me decent." He picked at his trousers – the only thing he wore. We sat in silence for a bit before he said, "Talk to me, Shae. Let me help."

He held my hand as I explained how I'd realised I was in love with Jared. I thought he'd be surprised or disappointed, after all, I'd known Jared such a short amount of time, but he simply nodded and smiled. Just like he had when I broadcasted the emotion to him earlier.

"Why are you grinning like a cantooa?" I asked.

His lopsided grin widened. "I'm glad you finally worked it out. You took your time."

"What? You knew?" I stared at him, open mouthed.

"Umm... of course." He cheeks pinked.

"What do you mean of course?"

"Well, it was kind of obvious. We all knew."

"It wasn't to me," I grumbled. "Why didn't you tell me?"

"Would you have believed me? I wanted too. I hated seeing you go through all that, but you had to work it out for yourself."

"Maybe," I conceded. "Who's all?"

Ash fidgeted. "Me and Francis knew. Oh don't look like that. I felt it through the Link, and Francis knows you better than you know yourself."

"And…"

"And?"

"Don't play games with me, Ash. You said, we all knew. So who's the all in that sentence? And don't tell me you meant just you and Francis, because then you'd have said, we both knew. I know you as well, remember."

He got up to refill his water glass and I knew he was buying time. When he returned, he said, "Me, Francis and Jared, of course." I looked at him suspiciously. "You said yourself Jared told you he thought you had feelings for him. So, he knew, right?" He looked pleased with his argument.

"Hmm." His answer was plausible, but I had a feeling he hadn't told me the whole truth.

"So, the nightmare?" Ash asked, changing the subject. "It's just a dream, Shae. Your unconscious mind playing tricks on you."

"I know." I sighed. "But I haven't told you what happened with Jared after you went to bed." Sadness shivered through me as I explained the last part of my story to Ash, but I knew he'd get it. I knew he'd tell me I'd done the right thing.

When I finished, he looked at me with sad, grey eyes. "Shae." It was more like a sigh. "I understand. I do." I knew he would. "But you can't turn away someone you love just because you're afraid of losing them."

"You sound like Jared."

"Maybe because we're both right. Please," he begged, "think about what you're doing. You owe it to yourself to be happy, and I want you to be happy."

"I can't lose anyone else I love."

"What does that even mean? Are you going to cut me and Francis out of your life as well?"

"Don't be an idiot," I replied, a little annoyed.

"But that's what you're saying. That you can't afford to love people in case they die? Well, what about me? What about Francis? Are you going to pull away from us too?" I was horrified at the idea. "Don't you see? It's the same thing."

"It's not the same thing at all. You're family. Our lives have always been together."

"I don't see the difference," Ash said before trying to argue his case again, but my mind had been made.

"Look, you're stuck with me whether you like it or not," I said finally, trying to draw the conversation to a close. "But if you up and die on me, I will kill you."

Ash laughed softly. "Fair enough. But—"

Thankfully his sentence was cut off by a knock at the door and he got up to answer it.

"Umm, aren't you a bit underdressed for breakfast?" Francis asked. "We did agree to meet the others at zero-seven-thirty, didn't we?" He checked his com-pad.

I hadn't realised the time, and the thought of seeing Jared over the breakfast table made my stomach flip.

"Change of plan. We're leaving now," I said, getting off the sofa.

"We are?" Francis said, frowning. "Right now? Before food?"

"Long story," Ash said. "We'll fill you in on the *Nakomo*."

"Okay," he replied slowly, confusion replaced by intrigue. "I'll contact Commander Tel'an and let her know we won't be joining them."

"No!" I said, too loudly. "If you tell Tel'an we're leaving, she'll tell Jared, and he'll try and stop us."

"Huh?" Francis went from intrigued to perplexed. "Why

would Captain Marcos want to stop us leaving the... never mind. Tell me on the *Nakomo*."

I located my faded ready bag on the chair next to the bed and dressed swiftly. Ash appeared at the door as I was hunting for my lucky boots.

"They're gone," he said with mock reverence. "Finally deceased."

I sat heavily on the bed. I knew it was irrational to have a pair of combat boots as lucky charms, but those boots had seen me through my worst times. Under normal circumstances, I would've been devastated at the news, but given everything else that had happened, it seemed a little ridiculous to get upset over footwear.

"Oh well, nothing lasts forever," I said pragmatically, causing Ash to raise a surprised eyebrow. I pulled my spare pair of boots out of the bag and put them on. When Francis and Ash were also ready, we headed quickly to the *Nakomo*.

"We can't just take off and leave without anyone realising. There are protocols," Francis explained in the lift. "I have to do the pre-flight checks and get authorisation from flight control. As soon as I request departure for the *Nakomo*, Captain Marcos will find out."

"That's okay. Jared can go anywhere on the *Defender* he chooses," Ash explained, "but he can't come on the *Nakomo* without express permission. You won't have to speak to him, or even see him, if you don't want to," he added to me.

"What if he doesn't authorise our departure?" Francis asked.

"He has no valid reason to prevent us. He knows we must get back to meet with the Supreme Primus, and besides, he's not going to risk a diplomatic incident. His love-life isn't exactly a legitimate reason to hold us."

"Love life?" Francis said, grinning. "This story's going to be good, I can tell."

When Francis had asked for our departure authority,

he'd been told to hold for a response by Flight Control, but I was relieved to be safely onboard the *Nakomo*. While we waited, I busied myself by completing the internal pre-flight checklist, while Ash did the external checks. He was about to raise the ramp when Jared's voice rose up through the hatch.

"I need to speak to her, Ash."

"Now's not the time."

"You're wrong. Now is exactly the time. You can't leave… she can't leave like this. Not after last night." There was a pause. "I take it you know what happened?"

"I do."

"Then you know it can't be left like this. I can't believe you agree with her."

"I'm sorry, Captain, but whether I agree or not, Shae doesn't want to speak to you."

"But—"

"It's not going to happen," Ash said finally.

We arrived back at the monastery mid-morning and were greeted off the shuttle by a harassed-looking Artimus, who made it quite clear he still thought we shouldn't have left Lilania. I didn't have the energy to argue with him, to tell him that Jared would've died if we hadn't gone.

Noah casually sauntered up as Artimus began reeling off a list of things that apparently needed Ash's immediate attention. He dramatically raised his steel-grey eyes to the sky and shook his head, but Artimus was deep in flow and didn't seem to notice.

I liked and respected Noah. Even though he was in his early fifties, he was still incredibly fit, and he'd taught me a lot during our combat training sessions. He was a good, strong leader – dedicated and disciplined, and behind Ash, an excellent choice for Primus. He'd once had jet-black hair, but now it was flecked with grey. A fraction shorter than Ash, and not as powerfully built, he was clearly tough.

When Artimus finally stopped for breath, Noah stepped forward. "I hear your trip was a success. I trust Captain Marcos is well?"

"The Captain's safe and mended, thanks to Shae," confirmed Ash. He left it at that.

"Good," said Noah, genuinely pleased by the news. Artimus muttered in the background. "As I was explaining to Artimus before he dashed off to greet you, Thomas has already spoken to Primus Augustus about his dietary requirements. David has solved the seating arrangements for the Ceremony of the Setting Sun. Supreme Primus Isaiah's chambers are ready for his arrival, and I've personally dealt with all the other small issues as they have arisen. We really are as ready as we are going to be. Ash, please don't take this the wrong way, but there's really nothing that needs your attention."

Ash's lopsided grin spread across his face. "Best news I've heard all day."

After Artimus finally accepted there was nothing for us to do, he shuffled off muttering something about catering and seating plans. Ash left to say hello to the visiting Primuses, and Francis and I ambled back to our quarters to get changed for the big arrival. It took a while to get to my room because everyone we passed stopped to talk. Our own monastery monks welcomed us back with congratulations on a successful mission, and the visiting monks stopped to introduce themselves and pass on their condolences. As it turned out, I had just enough time for a shower before heading to the courtyard.

The flagstone yard was full, with every monk turned out impeccably for the formal welcome. Thankfully, we didn't have to wait long in the blazing sun before Supreme Primus Isaiah arrived. Ash helped the elderly man to the raised platform, and I noticed he looked much older and frailer than I remembered. Isaiah had risen through the Doctrinal Caste before becoming Primus to Sector Four, then

Supreme Primus to the Brotherhood. Next to Ash, he looked waif-like, and his angular features, thin lips and small eyes made him look severe. His limp and slow, deliberate movements betrayed his years.

"Brothers… and of course, Shae…" Isaiah began. Francis nudged me with his elbow and I was touched that the Supreme Primus had been thoughtful enough to include me. "This is a sad time for us all, and I wish I was standing before you under different circumstances. That said, I am honoured to be here. Primus Finnian was a good, honourable man, who presided over this monastery with fairness and wisdom. His death is a great loss to us all." There was a moment's silence before Isaiah continued. "As is custom, I will be officiating at the Ceremony of the Setting Sun on the beach at dusk today. After which, Primus Finnian will be laid in state in the Great Hall until the funeral tomorrow afternoon."

Tears welled, and I tried really hard not to cry.

After a few more words, the Supreme Primus excused himself, and I wasn't surprised to see Investigator Manus trailing behind him towards the Primus's Office. The courtyard had thinned considerably by the time Ash appeared at my side.

"Isaiah's meeting with Manus now, but he wants to see all of us at fifteen-hundred," Ash said.

At our given time, we were chatting to Brother David, Aide to the Primus. "Investigator Manus is still in there," David explained quietly, giving an exaggerated raise of his eyebrows, which made me smile. "Shouldn't be too much longer," he added.

Almost an hour later, the door to the office creaked open and the Investigator strode out.

"You can go in now," Manus said amiably. I tried to read his expression, but Ash was already nudging me past him into Finnian's office.

"Please, sit," the Supreme Primus said, waving his hand

towards the lounge chairs by the patio doors. "Let me start by saying I know how close you all were to Finnian. I'm deeply shocked and saddened by his death, and I can only imagine what you're all going through. My thoughts and prayers are will you all – especially you, my dear."

"Thank you," I said. His touch was gentle as he patted my arm.

"Before we go any further," he continued, "let me clear up the matter of Investigator Manus' enquiry. He tells me you were all extremely cooperative, and I thank you for your patience; I'm sure it couldn't have been easy reliving those painful events. Manus has concluded that Finnian's death was an unavoidable tragedy, and that he was an unfortunate casualty of the mission. I'm pleased to say the enquiry is now formally closed."

I was glad Manus hadn't blamed anyone for Finnian's death, but I was upset that Isaiah had made it sound so black and white, so unemotional.

"And you, my dear," he continued suddenly, making me start. "I'm especially aware you had a particularly close bond with Finnian. I want you to know that I'm here for you if you need someone to talk to."

My eyes started to well up again and I choked back tears. I wasn't going to cry. I was not going to cry. A lone tear defied me and ran down my cheek soaking into my top. "Thank you," I croaked.

"I don't wish to detract from the loss you've all suffered, but I do want to express my personal thanks for your outstanding work during the mission. Without you, the Four Sectors would be in chaos. Something that's not lost on the Tetrarchy of Souls – who have personally asked me to pass on their own gratitude."

The Tetrarchy was made up of the ruling monarchs from each Sector. The four of them were responsible for every Human across the galaxy, and they presided over the administration of all Sectors including politics, business, commerce and the military. Isaiah was correct – our mission had been a success. There was no denying that things would be exceptionally different had we failed.

"I was here, at the monastery, the day Finnian brought you back as a baby. Did you know that?" Isaiah said. I shook my head; no-one had mentioned that before. "I was Ninth Degree back then, and here doing some research. I have to say, for such a tiny little thing, you caused quite a big commotion." He smiled as he reminisced. I was enthralled to hear a new take on the stories I'd been told since I was old enough to understand. But when he drew them to a close, I felt there was more he wasn't telling.

"By the Gods, where does the time go?" he said, looking at the clock on the wall. "I must prepare for the Ceremony of the Setting Sun, but before you go, I have a few more things to cover. Firstly, I hear you had quite the adventure yesterday. It seems more congratulations are in order for successfully locating and saving Captain Marcos."

"Wow, news really does travel fast," I said.

"Not a lot goes on that I don't know about, child," he said kindly. "However, this brings me on to my next piece of business. Investigator Manus is concerned that your… gift is becoming common knowledge, Shae. I understand Captain Marcos and Colonel Mitchell, along with their respective crews, are aware of your abilities. I have to say this concerns me greatly, and while I know the situation couldn't be helped, I worry. The Brotherhood has worked extremely hard to keep you a secret. I want you to let me know immediately if you receive any unusual attention from the military… or anyone else, for that matter."

"There's been no indication the REF knows," said Ash. "Both Captain Marcos and Colonel Mitchell agreed not to include that particular information in their After-Action reports."

"So I understand," replied the Supreme Primus. "But we cannot assume they won't find out. All I'm saying is this: be extra careful, and extra vigilant. I want to be kept informed of any developments in this area. Personally. Am I making myself clear?"

"Of course," Ash replied, and I felt a hit of intrigue from him through the Link.

"Good. Now, one final piece of news to end on a happier note, I hope. I've been contacted by the House of Palavaria. King Sebastian apologises for the lack of ceremony afforded when he granted Ash and Shae the Order of Royal Battle. Although, given the circumstances, I don't think anyone can blame him for that. Anyway, he wishes to make up for the oversight."

"To be honest, I feel like a fraud," said Ash, and I had to agree with him. "We were given the honour because it was the only way to get us access to Tetrad Summit. And we needed to be at the Summit to protect the King. It feels wrong to hold such status when we did nothing to earn it."

"It seems King Sebastian had a feeling you might say that." The Supreme Primus smiled knowingly. "I've been asked to remind you that during the course of the investigation, your actions did indeed meet and exceed the criteria under which the Order is given. The King has made it extremely clear that his decision was based on merit and stands absolutely."

"I guess that does make it clear," Ash said.

"Quite so," agreed Isaiah. "It's well known that the King hosts quite the party every four years after the close of the Tetrad Summit. This year he has decided that the two of you, Captain Marcos, and Colonel Mitchell will be guests of honour. Sebastian would like to keep the presentation of your Orders a surprise for his guests, so keep it to yourselves."

Francis huffed loudly.

"The party is one week from today," the Supreme Primus continued. "The Wolfpack has also been invited to thank them for their part in the investigation." Another loud huff and Isaiah smiled. "As have you, Brother Francis."

Francis grinned broadly.

"This is high honour indeed," Isaiah continued. "And diplomatic relations aside, you're all exceptional ambassadors for the Brotherhood and I'm sure you'll have a wonderful time. Good," he said exuberantly, clapping his hands as a cue for us to leave, but as we headed for the door, he asked Ash to remain behind.

"What do you think that's about?" asked Francis as we crossed the courtyard.

"No idea," I replied.

Just before sundown, Francis, Ash and I joined the monks on the beach for the Ceremony of the Setting Sun. Flaming torches flickered in the light evening breeze, the sand sparkling in the reflected glow.

Isaiah's words were kind and heartfelt, and I thought Finnian would've liked it. After the sun had set, the torches were extinguished, and his coffin was carried to the Great Hall where he would remain until the funeral, allowing the monks time to pay their individual respects.

I'd thought the day of Finnian's funeral would be impossible to get through, but when I woke the next day, I felt at peace.

I spent the morning meeting the other Primuses and visiting monks, listening to their stories of Finnian – many of which were from before my time – and I enjoyed hearing about what he was like as a young monk. Ash was kept busy on various errands, and when I did finally get a few minutes with him, I purposely didn't ask about his conversation with Isaiah. He didn't mention it either.

Like the Ceremony of the Setting Sun, the funeral went as well as could be expected. I sat at the front, flanked by Ash and Francis, and when Ash got up to read the eulogy, I couldn't stop the tears running down my cheek. After the service, several of the monks made it their business to come and express their sympathies to me personally, and I was touched by their kindness and consideration.

Brother Thomas and his team excelled themselves in catering for the wake, and before long the mood lifted and there was the general drone of happier voices filing the monastery. When Brother David took to the raised platform to inform us that Supreme Primus Isaiah would be starting the Naming Ceremony shortly, my pulse quickened and nerves crept through my chest.

Francis and I waited patiently while Isaiah went through the formal preamble, but just before he got to the big announcement, Ash appeared silently at my side. I looked up at him, confused, but he smiled and indicated I should focus my attention on Isaiah. I was completely floored when the Supreme Primus named Brother Noah as Sector Three's new Primus.

I turned to Ash, expecting to see... disappointment maybe? But he was clapping and smiling like everyone else. And it wasn't the begrudging best wishes from the losing candidate, but true, honest congratulations. He was genuinely thrilled for Noah. It took me a moment to digest, then I joined in the celebration. Noah was, after all, an excellent choice.

After a couple more hours of chatting, way too much food, and a few glasses of Brother Thomas' super-lethal moonshine, I excused myself and headed to the beach. I took off my shoes and let my toes dig into the sand, which was still warm even at that time of night. I smiled happily as Francis sat and put his arm around me, and I let my head rest on his shoulder. We didn't talk, we just sat in silence, listening to the gentle lapping of water against the beach and the laughter coming from the monastery. Thomas' moonshine was clearly still flowing freely.

I guess I fell asleep because I woke briefly as Francis laid me on my bed, covering me in my blanket. "Go back to sleep," he whispered before kissing me on the forehead. I didn't argue.

The following morning, I searched high and low for Ash before I found him and Noah at the boathouse. It was the first time I'd had a proper chance to tell Noah how pleased I was that he was our new Primus, and we chatted for a while before he excused himself to attend a meeting with the Supreme Primus.

"So?" I asked, somewhat cryptically as Noah disappeared up the path.

"So... what?" Ash replied, but I knew from the sparkling eyes and the lopsided grin that he knew exactly what I was talking about.

"I was sure it was going to be you," I said. He actually guffawed, but I frowned until he got himself under control. He looked around us.

"Just between us," he paused and gave me his or else look, "the Supreme Primus offered me the position. Kind of."

"I don't understand. What do you mean kind of? And if he offered you the position, why didn't you take it?"

Ash smiled again. "Isaiah said the position was mine, if I wanted it, but there were other things to consider."

"Like what?"

"Like... I'd have to stop going on off-world missions for starters. And I'd have to withdraw from the Guardians. But also, there's you."

"Me?"

He laughed again. "Yes, you. Who would stop you from getting into trouble if I was stuck on Lilania? And there's something else—"

"Wait, please don't tell me you turned down Primus because of me?" I interrupted.

"Relax, Shae. You were a part of the decision, but I'm not ready to hang up my Cal'ret just yet. There's still so much work to be done out there." He waved his hand towards the sky. "And being a Guardian does sound pretty exciting, right? Besides, Noah's a far better choice for Primus right now."

"Does he know about you?" I asked.

"Yes, he's fully aware of the situation. But no one else is – except you, and I know you'll keep it confidential." He rubbed my shoulder. "Don't look so sad. Isaiah said I'm still young enough that it's possible I'll have another chance."

"That does make me feel a little better," I replied.

"Besides, I could hardly walk away from the Guardians before we've even had our first mission. Look, the Tetrarchy and the Brotherhood believe that putting together elite, covert teams, made up of Marines, Fleet and our own Brotherhood, will be the key to dealing with threats to the Crowns. But until we get called on a mission, we'll just carry on with our own business."

"But if they activate our team, you and I will have to work with Jake and Jared again," I grumbled.

"Oh well, there's a downside to everything," Ash joked, putting his arm around my shoulders. "We'll cross that bridge when we get to it."

"Guardian of the Crowns does sound pretty impressive though, doesn't it?"

"Yes, it does," he replied. "Even if we do have to keep it Alpha-Secure. I hate not being able to talk to Francis about it."

"Me too." I watched him carefully. "What was the other thing?"

"Hmm?"

"I cut you off, but you were about to say there was another reason for not accepting Primus."

"Oh, it's nothing." He shrugged his broad shoulders and looked out across the bay.

"Are you sure?"

"Shae, it's nothing. I can't even remember what I was

going to say."
   I got the feeling that wasn't exactly true.

6

The following days flew by. The Supreme Primus returned to Sector One the day after the funeral, and the other Primuses and their entourages left gradually until only our own contingent remained. Routines returned, and things eventually got back to normal. We were halfway through the week when Brother David came to my room. The door was wedged open to let the warm sea air flow through, so he knocked on the doorframe.

"Delivery for you," he said.

"For me?" I asked, frowning at the large package he carried in both hands.

"Got your name on it. And the Palavarian Royal Seal. It came in via one of our outposts." He put it on the bed and I looked at it sceptically, pursing my lips. "I don't think it's going to bite," he added.

"Hmm, we'll see," I mumbled as I peeled off the attached envelope, cracking the official wax seal as I opened it. The precise handwriting, with exotic curlicues and flourishes, was unmistakably Josephina's, King Sebastian's only daughter, and probably the closest thing I had to a female friend.

'My Darling Shae,' the note read. 'If I know you even half as well as I think I do, you haven't even thought about what you're going to wear to your party this weekend.' She'd double underlined the word 'your'. 'So I hope you'll forgive my interference and accept this small gift. I'm very much looking forward to seeing you all again – you disappeared so quickly after the Summit, I didn't have the chance to say goodbye. Until this weekend. Forever your friend, Phina.' She finished the letter with four kisses.

My serrated hunting knife easily sliced through the ribbon holding the box sealed. The top lifted off with an impolite slurp, and I peeled back layers of delicate purple tissue paper to reveal a beautiful gown. Lifting it out of the box by the shoulders, the dress unfolded to floor length.

"Wow," said David.

"Wow, indeed," added Ash from the doorway – I had no idea how long he'd been there.

I hung the dress up on the outside of my wardrobe door and dug around in the rest of the tissue, discovering a pair of very high-heeled shoes and matching jewellery. Phina had certainly gone all out to make sure I would look the part, but Ash must've caught a hint of something through the Link.

"What's the matter?" he asked, already knowing the answer.

"It's a gorgeous dress, sure, but totally unnecessary. I'm not going to the party."

Ash looked at me with well-practiced exasperation. "Shae…" He said it slowly, like it was more of a warning.

"Don't Shae me, Ash. I don't want to go."

"But—"

"Isn't it my decision?"

"Well, not exact—"

"Would you look at the time," David interrupted awkwardly. "Things to do, people to see," he added, ducking around Ash to make a quick exit.

"I thought you might try and pull a trick like this," Ash said, sitting in the armchair next to the patio doors.

"I guess I'm just too damn predictable then."

"Guess so." He sighed.

"I have my reasons. I—"

"I know exactly why you don't want to go, so you can save your breath. Jared's going to be there, and so is Jake, but you're going to have to face them eventually. We're all Guardians, you know we could be pulled together at any time to go on a mission."

"That's different."

"How so?"

"Because that's business. We would all need to keep things professional. Jared and Jake included. The King's party... that's social. It's different... and I'm not going," I repeated, letting down my mental roadblocks long enough to send a hit of obstinate annoyance through the Link.

"If it makes it easier, think of it as a mission," Ash suggested, undeterred. I scowled at him. "I'm serious. Yes, it's a party, but as Isaiah said, it's also building diplomatic relations. Imagine it's just another run-of-the-mill assignment. All you have to do is turn up, receive the Order, be a good Brotherhood Ambassador, have a couple of drinks, then leave. Mission accomplished." He made it sound so easy and reasonable that for a moment he almost had me believing him. For a moment.

"I'm not changing my mind, so there's nothing else to say. End of," I announced, bringing the conversation to an abrupt close.

"We'll see," he said, getting up and giving me a kiss on the forehead before leaving.

The day before the party, I was summands to the Primus's office, and it surprised how much it bothered me that Finnian's personal possessions had been removed.

"Shae, I'm not sure there's any other way to say this

other than to just say it, so... you're going to the Palace of Palavaria to receive your Order from King Sebastian," Noah said.

"But—"

"I haven't finished," he continued firmly. "It's none of my business why you don't want to go, unless you wish to tell me, but the Supreme Primus has the expectation that you, Asher and Francis are attending. He's responded to the Palace as such. He feels, and I agree, that this is an excellent opportunity to cement the groundwork for future collaborations, giving us a strategic advantage in Sector Three."

"But—"

Noah silenced me again by holding up a hand. "I'm appealing to your sense of honour and duty, Shae." Damn him for hitting me with the one thing I couldn't argue with. I closed my mouth and sat in silence. "I could order you to attend the party tomorrow, but I really don't want that to be the first directive I have to give as Primus. It's up to you."

So, there were my choices: agree to go willingly, or get ordered to attend. Either way, it looked like I was going.

"You don't have to make the order," I said begrudgingly. "I'll go, and I'll be the perfect Ambassador for the Brotherhood."

"Thank you." Noah sighed with relief. "You have no idea how much I appreciate that."

We left for Decerra, the home planet of the House of Palavaria, after breakfast the following day. I still wasn't happy about going, and after a few half-hearted words with Ash and Francis, I took myself off to the corner of the main cabin to read. I'd hoped to take my mind off things, but after reading the same page four times, I realised that all I could really think about was Jared – and the conversation we'd had back on the *Defender*.

I went over it again and again, reliving every hurt word,

every confused look in his beautiful blue eyes, every pained expression on his face. And each time I did, the pit in my stomach deepened. For a moment my resolve waivered, but then I dredged up the image of Jared in the creature-cave, and I was sure I'd done the right thing. So what if he didn't understand my decision – he'd have to accept it.

I knew it was for the best, but I was startled by how detached I'd become from the situation. Like something had hardened inside of me, or something had broken. But if I was broken, it wasn't anything my gift could heal.

Colonel Jake Mitchell, however, was an entirely different animal. The instant attraction and the unexpected heat between us was impossible to ignore. I tried to, but the desire was mutual, and it wasn't long before the inevitable happened. He was charming and attentive… and a little bit dangerous.

I hadn't lied to Jared when I'd told him I wasn't in love with Jake romantically, but I couldn't dismiss the fact that I cared for him deeply, that I loved him as a friend. I just didn't know how Jake would feel about that particular piece of information. Like Jared, I'd avoided him on our last night on the *Defender* and had purposely ignored his coms. We hadn't exactly talked much about what'd happened between us, and I had no idea how he felt about me, or how he'd react when he saw me again. To say I was nervous about seeing them both again would be a colossal understatement.

I'd just attempted to read my page for the fifth time when I lurched sideways, banging my head hard against the cabin wall. Shaking off the pain, I ran to the flight area, but the concerned frown on Ash's brow didn't ease my own fear.

"What the hell happened," I asked, rubbing my temple. "Why did we drop out of FTL?"

"Two very good questions," Ash replied, raising an enquiring eyebrow in Francis's direction.

"Give me a minute," he replied, leaning over one of the flight consoles briefly before disappearing out through the main cabin. A few minutes later he returned looking hot and irritable, wiping dirty hands on a rag. "The port Farnam coupling has sheered, damaging the nacelle that separates the FTL engine from the main fuel conduit." I stared at him blankly. "We're dead in the water," he clarified. "Or space... you know what I mean."

"Can you fix it?" I asked. A glimmer of hope grew as I wondered if we'd miss the party after all.

"Maybe. I told Brother Michael months ago that the coupling looked fatigued. If he's put a new one in the parts locker, and if I can mend the damage to the nacelle, I might be able to get us to Decerra in one piece." Hope waned as Francis disappeared to check the locker for the new coupling.

"Perhaps we should contact the palace and tell them we're not going to make it due to technical difficulties," I suggested to Ash, who narrowed his eyes in response.

"Or... perhaps we should contact the *Defender* and ask them to send a Warrior to come and pick us up. What do you think?" He was teasing, I knew, but I still took the bait.

"I think—"

Fortunately, I was interrupted by Francis, who arrived with a chunk of metal in his hand and a triumphant grin on his face.

"The good news is, we have a new Farnam coupling and the right tools to fix the nacelle. The bad news is, I estimate it's going to take me a good couple of hours to strip out the old part and fix in the new one."

"That's going to put us about thirty minutes late for our grand entrance at the party," I said, doing the maths. "No point in going really," I added optimistically.

"I'm sure they'll understand our predicament," said Ash before accessing the com-system to let Decerra know the situation.

In the end, Francis's estimation turned out to be pretty accurate. After a lot of puffing and grunting, he got the new part in and working, and in just over two hours, we continued our journey. Much to my disappointment. When we were half an hour out, I went to get changed.

The dress was simply stunning – there was no denying the fact – and the simple, black crystal jewellery was the perfect compliment. I removed my own necklace, careful not to let the two small objects slip off the chain. Both held sentimental value, but for different reasons. The small, beautifully elaborate version of the Ninth Degree medallion was given to me by Finnian in recognition of my achievements within the Brotherhood. It symbolised honour and loyalty, two things I held dear.

The second object was equally unusual. Roughly the same size, it was brushed bronze in colour, with a light blue stone in the centre and raised nodules that ran around the edge at random intervals. I rubbed my thumb over in the engraved symbols, not found anywhere else in the Sectors according to the Brotherhood scholars.

Before my mother died, she gave Finnian two things, making him promise that I'd get them when I was old enough. The pendent was one, the other was a small piece of ripped, bloodied paper with three words written on it: Family, Honour, Courage. I don't know whether they have specific meaning, maybe they were a family motto or something, but they're words I've chosen to live by.

I stowed the chain and pendants in my locker and added my com-pad and earpiece.

The black crystal choker glinted under the harsh lights as I applied a small amount of make-up. I couldn't deny that Phina had good taste, but I wasn't keen on the shoes. I'd spent most of my life in boots, wearing any kind of heel was a disaster waiting to happen.

Ash and Frances were deep in conversation when I returned to the cabin, and no matter how many times I saw them in their ceremonial robes, I was always surprised by how impressive and grand they looked.

"Wow," said Ash, turning around. "You look beautiful."

"I agree," Francis added. "Everyone's going to be blown away."

I blushed outrageously and punched him on the arm.

It was dark as we came in to land, but the illuminated Palace stood proud against the countryside, guiding our way. As soon as the ramp lowered, we were accosted by Martha O'Donnell, Princess Josephina's Personal Aide, and quite possibly the most officious person I've ever had the misfortune to meet.

"Whilst I fully appreciate you being here is a total surprise to our guests, you're late! And you've thrown my entire schedule off," she snapped irritably, while tapping fake, talon nails on her data-pad. I had a violent urge to break them all off.

"Good to see you again too, Martha," I replied sarcastically, which won me a dig in the ribs from Ash.

"Good evening, Ms O'Donnell," he said diplomatically. "I'm afraid our tardiness couldn't be helped."

"Well… I suppose you're here now." The scowl temporarily faded, but after checking her itinerary, it returned with a vengeance and she announced irritably that we should've been receiving our Orders in the Great Hall right at that very moment. She huffed indignantly, and then at a speed not conducive to me wearing high heels, she hurried us across the landing pad, through security, and towards the Great Hall.

The Palace, which was usually packed with staff and King's Guard, was extraordinarily quiet.

"They're all at the party," Martha explained. "The King gave orders to invite everyone but essential staff and key Palace Security. It's quite the social gathering the King's hosting for you." For a moment she looked vaguely impressed, but then she reverted to type and made it quite clear we'd caused her a great deal of hardship by having to rearrange the sequence of events. "The King, Prince and Princess are already in attendance at the party, but Captain Marcos and Colonel Mitchell are waiting for you ahead of being announced," she explained.

I hardly had time to register the swell of panic before Martha ushered us through a plain door into a luxurious antechamber.

The Wolfpack, Jake's Special Operations team, were laughing and drinking in a group, but Jake and Jared stood to the side, chatting together amiably – which was weird given they usually went to great effort not to like each other.

Jared saw us first and managed a half-smile, but his eyes were tinged with something I couldn't place. Disappointment? Confusion? Pain? He shifted his weight, making no attempt to approach.

Jake followed his glance, a grin breaking across his strong, square face. "Babe, you look… stunning," he said. Before I could protest, he'd gathered me up into his arms, kissing me hungrily on the lips. "You have no idea how much I've missed you. God you smell good," he added, practically drooling. As he placed me back on the floor, I noticed he was clean shaven, a contrast to the two or three days' worth of stubble he normally wore. He raked his fingers through shaggy, dark-brown hair, which always seemed to look messy, no matter what he did with it.

A light tingling in my tummy reminded me why I hadn't been able to resist the Colonel's charms in the first place, but one look at Jared quickly extinguished the smouldering embers. I felt guilty and was close to running from the room when Martha's loud tutting distracted me.

"Brother Francis, you need to come with me," she said, waving an impatient hand towards a set of old, wooden doors that I guessed led to the Great Hall. "And you… Wolfpack," she added, as if it was a dirty word, "you too."

In the centre of one door was an ornate wrought-iron knocker, which Martha banged three times. Latches clicked and both doors swung slowly open with a protesting groan. A King's Guard stood each side of the opening, looking splendid, if over the top, in their Court livery. Martha fussed with their finery as she walked past, tutting again.

None of the men had followed, so she turned and aimed a withering stare towards the Wolfpack. "Don't dawdle," she griped with clear disdain.

Kaiser, Jake's second in command, chewed on his tongue to keep control of it. He tugged at the collar of his Dress Uniform, which looked tight across his broad chest, and scowled. "I miss my leather jacket," he grumbled.

"Come on, big guy," said Connor, the team's weapons and explosives expert. "Might as well get this shit over and done with. Sooner we get this show on the road, sooner we can get the fuck outta here."

I guess the Wolfpack wanted to be there about as much as I did, but they shuffled into the Great Hall and the doors closed heavily behind them. In the wake of their departure, the four of us stood in awkward silence.

"So... are congratulations in order, Ash?" Jared asked eventually.

"No, not this time."

"Really?" Jared's eyebrows raised. "The way Shae was talking, it sounded like a done deal."

"What can I say? She's my biggest fan," Ash said laughing. He put his arm around my shoulder and pulled me into a hug.

"Am I missing something?" Jake asked, his hazel eyes narrowing.

Ash told him about Finnian's funeral and the naming of our new Primus. "Like I said, it's not my time. I still have a lot of good I can do in the field... and with the Guardians."

Jake's eyes narrowed further, and deep frown lines cut across his forehead. "Are you telling me you've all been in contact since that last night on the *Defender*?" he asked as he made the connection, but as we explained the whole creature incident to him, he laughed so hard I thought Jared was going to punch him.

"Looks like we've got quite a bit of catching up to do, Babe," Jake said when he'd composed himself. "Which reminds me... didn't you get my coms?" He slipped his arm around my waist as he spoke, but I got flustered and flicked a confused look towards Jared, who still stood a few steps away.

Jake turned to follow my glance, a shadow passing across his face. "What the fuck have you done now?" he said, glowering at Jared. I guess he must've thought the distance between us was because we were fighting again. Jared shifted his weight but remained silent. "Surely you can't still be pissed she chose me?" Jake taunted.

Of all the things he could've said, that was probably the worst, and I sighed, knowing that Jared had the killer of all comebacks. I prepared myself for the fallout, but Jared didn't say a word. He simply looked at me with sad eyes that seemed to ask, what do you want me to say?

With a loud creak, the ancient doors swung open just long enough for Martha to sweep back into the room, totally oblivious to the atmosphere. I don't know whether I was relieved or annoyed.

"In five minutes, these doors will open again, and the Master of Ceremonies will announce each of you," she said. "Walk forward to the balustrade, smile, and then take the steps to your left before making your way to join King Sebastian on the stage. Do not deviate from these instructions." For a moment she was actually quite scary, reminding me of the creatures Jared and I had encountered in the cave. "At least try to do this one thing right," she added harshly.

I was halfway through telling her exactly what I thought of her when the unmistakable sound of gunfire and screaming stopped me in my tracks. My hand automatically dropped to my thigh to retrieve my Sentinel, but it wasn't there, it was stowed in my locker on the *Nakomo*, along with my com-pad and earpiece.

The gunfire continued, followed by the heavy thud of a body being thrown against the wooden door. Martha's face drained white and her eyes widened. Her mouth fell open and I watched her chest rise as she took in a lungful of air. I pounced on her, covering her mouth with my hand to muffle her scream, pressing hard because she struggled against me. I felt her teeth against my skin and a bright red line of blood trickled through my fingers. I forced her to the ground, pushing my knee into her chest to stop her escaping. Her eyes flickered, wild and unfocussed like a trapped animal, as she twitched and bucked beneath me.

"Shut up," I ordered, but when I removed my hand she twisted sideways and sucked in another deep breath.

In the heat of the moment there seemed only one swift and viable solution, and after I'd knocked her out cold, I looked up guiltily. Ash cocked his head and gave me a brief look of disapproval, which was half-hearted at best, then he turned his attention to Jared, who was trying to quietly open one of the heavy wooden doors.

Jake crouched next to me, grinning. "I've wanted to do that since the moment we met her," he whispered. "I'm so jealous… and I have to admit, a little turned on right now."

"Jake!"

A metallic click signalled the release of the latch, followed by a low creak as Jared opened the door just wide enough for him to peek through. The majority of gunfire had ceased, and shrieks had been replaced by sobbing. We froze as a shadow passed the door, then Jared closed it carefully.

"Well?" whispered Jake.

"Well, there are people with guns—"

"Really, genius? Tell us something we don't know."

"Okay. There are lots of people with guns, Jake. Big guns," Jared replied impatiently. It wasn't the best time for the uneasy truce between them to disintegrate.

Ash sighed impatiently. "Stand down gentlemen. Let's try and focus, shall we?"

"Of course. My bad," said Jake, making a continue motion with his hand towards Jared, which Jared purposely ignored.

"I counted at least eleven men, all armed with Seekers, all wearing tactical gear and masks," Jared continued.

"Seekers? You sure?" Jake asked.

"Yes, I'm sure. Would I have said it otherwise?"

"Jared, what are Seekers?" Ash asked, breaking the tension.

"They're new REF rifles designed for close quarters combat. They're not even in general circulation yet."

"You're saying those people are Royal Earth Force?"

"No. They may have our weapons, but they're not us. Their tac-gear's wrong and they've not deployed like us. They're scrappier, less disciplined, but they're just as deadly, and they've no qualms about killing. The two guards and the Master of Ceremonies are dead." Jared pointed to the wall just to the right of the doorframe. "And there are several others as well who—" Jared silenced as voices filtered through the door. We waited for whoever it was to pass.

"Did you see King Sebastian? The Wolfpack? Francis?" asked Jake.

Jared shook his head. "We need reinforcements," he added, pressing a button on his com-pad. "*Defender*, this is Captain Marcos... *Defender*, respond... Nothing. It's dead; not even static. They must be blocking off-world communications."

"Kaiser, can you hear me? Connor? Ty?" Jake shook his head. "Ours are down too; they must be blocking all communications. You need some pretty high-end shit to knock out our military encoded signals. Very specialised, very expensive. Who the fuck are these fuckers?"

"That's what we need to find out, and fast, before anyone else gets killed," Ash said. I felt his unease through the Link. "We have to get eyes on the situation."

"Agreed," Jake said. He took a deep breath and grinned. "Why is it that every time the four of us get together, bad shit happens?"

"Just lucky, I guess," Jared suggested with a shrug of his broad shoulders. "Looks like the Guardians have their first mission, even if it's not officially sanctioned. So where do we start?"

"What about the Queen's Balcony?" Ash suggested.

"What about it?" Jake asked.

"It's high up on the west wall of the Great Hall, facing the throne platform," Ash explained. "It would make the perfect vantage point, and the door to the stairway's not far from here. There's a small antechamber where we'll be hidden, problem is, we'll be out in the open until we get there."

"Best make sure we're not seen then," Jared said.

"Okay, sounds like we have the start of a plan," I said before pausing. "Just one problem…"

"What?" asked Ash.

"What are we going to do with her?" I pointed to Martha, who was still out cold on the floor. "We can't just leave her like that."

"Shove her behind the couch," said Jake. "At least she'll be out of sight. She should be okay… and if she's not, is that such a bad thing?"

"Seriously?" I scolded, but he just gave me a mischievous grin. "What if she wakes up? I don't like the woman, but that doesn't mean I want any harm to come to her." I massaged my hand and corrected myself. "I don't want any further harm to come to her." I looked around for inspiration and noticed some notepaper on the bureau.

Grabbing a sheet, I wrote, Palace under siege. Stay hidden. DON'T MAKE A SOUND. It was short, but I think I made my point. Jake grabbed Martha's wrists and pulled her behind the couch, and I placed my hastily written note into her right hand.

Ash rolled up the sleeves of his robes and Jared and Jake both removed their jackets, stuffing them behind the couch with Martha. After a quick glance up and down the corridor, we headed out.

As soon as I stepped off the carpet into the hallway, my high heels clicked loudly against the flagstones. I mouthed sorry as I slipped them off, hiding them behind an ornate plant pot, but a few steps later I tripped over the hem of my dress and had to grab Jake's arm to stop myself falling. Gathering up the material in both hands, I followed the others, staying close to the wall.

Ash led us slowly down a deserted hallway, pausing at corners to check for bad guys. A couple of minutes later, we stopped at the dead end of a short corridor, where a ceiling to floor tapestry hung on the wall.

"Hold this," I said, pulling the side of the tapestry away from the wall to reveal a small alcove with an old, plain door. With Jake keeping the drapery out of the way, I dipped into the alcove to open the door, but a moment later I returned to the hallway. "It's locked. I need…" My sentence hung as I looked around for something I could use as a pick. "That." I pointed at the Brotherhood medallion on Ash's belt. "I promise I'll be careful," I said as he anxiously handed it over. On the back was a short metal pin – exactly what I needed to get the door open.

The lock was stiff, and it took me longer to get the door open than I'd anticipated. I was still working on it when Jake hissed, "Keep working. Don't come out," before letting the tapestry drop.

Every part of me wanted to find out what was happening, but I disciplined myself to do what Jake had asked. It was dark in the alcove once the artwork was back in place, and I automatically went to my wrist to activate the light on my absent com-pad.

I blindly fiddled with the lock, using my fingertips to feel the vibrations in the metal, listening hard for the tell-tale sounds that would indicate a tumbler had fallen into place. From the other side of the tapestry I heard muffled cries followed by grunts and scrapping, but I remained focussed on my task. A final click indicated the lock had opened and I turned the handle. The door remained stubborn, and at first I thought there must've been a secondary catch, but after I'd put my full weight against it, it swung open.

Ash appeared around the side of the wall-hanging. "Good, you're in. Never doubted you," he said as Jake pulled the tapestry back further to allow him to drag a body through. I held the door open my side as he hauled the man into the round antechamber, no larger than three metres in diameter. Jared appeared, dragging the body of a second bad guy.

As soon as Ash released the tapestry, the room fell into total darkness.

"Where's the god-damn light switch?" Jake grunted impatiently.

7

I heard Jake fumbling in the darkness. "Don't touch the switch," I said quickly. "All the lights, including the ones in the balcony, are on the same circuit."

"You sure?" he asked.

"Yes, I'm sure," I snapped back. "I have been here before, remember? Anyway, forget the damn lights, what just happened out there?"

"Minor incident, Babe. Nothing to worry about," Jake said, his voice cocky in the darkness.

"I don't consider two dead gun-thugs nothing to worry about, or a minor incident. In fact—" I had plenty more to say on the subject, but lost my train of thought when I was blinded by a beam of light.

"Sorry," Jared apologised, aiming the torch away from me and towards the body of the hostile next to him. He pulled a second torch from the man's utility belt and tossed it to Ash before going through the rest of his things.

"Well, if you're not going to tell me what happened, at least tell me you're all okay?" I conceded.

It was Jared who answered while he pointed to the bodies. "These two were on perimeter patrol and they come straight at us. In case you hadn't realised, there wasn't exactly anywhere to hide." I was stung by the coldness of his words, and perhaps he realised because when he continued, his tone was gentler. "We had to take them out before they radioed in our position. There was no option. We're all fine."

"That's all I wanted to know," I said, still bothered by his attitude.

"Still, at least we have guns now," Jake chipped in cheerily, holding up two Seekers. He looked at Jared briefly, then passed one to Ash with a dry smile.

"And this," Jared said, pulling a knife out of one of the bad guy's boots. He leant over and checked the other man's leg, removing a second blade which he gave to me. I felt happier knowing we all had weapons, although in the grand scheme of things, I would've preferred a Seeker.

I stood up, immediately tripping over my hem again, and in a fit of pure frustration, I plunged the knife through the material in the skirt and started to cut a jagged line.

"That's a bit drastic isn't it, Babe?" Jake said. I glanced up from cutting to see them all watching me.

"The dress is too long, and I keep tripping over it," I said, thinking that would've been obvious. "Call it a pre-emptive strike if you like. It's either a drastic re-styling, or I take the whole damn thing off." I caught the hungry look on Jake's face and knew what he was thinking. "Stop it," I aimed directly at him.

"Stop what?" he replied innocently, but when Jared coughed loudly, guilt rippled through my chest and I returned my attention to the dress. By the time I'd finished, my beautiful floor-length gown finished in a ragged line at my knees. At least I could move without the fear of falling flat on my face.

"At the top of the stairs is a second door," Ash explained. "It shouldn't be locked, but the way our luck is going... anyway, we can't all go up there. The more of us there are, the greater the chance of being seen."

"Agreed," said Jared. "Shae, you're the smallest. Tactically, you're the best choice."

"On it," I said, heading for the steps, but I stopped when I felt someone at my shoulder.

"Wait up," Jake said quietly. "Captain Charisma might be happy to put you in harm's way on your own," he looked pointedly at Jared, "but I'm not. Besides, my men are in that Hall, I need to see what's going on."

The stone stairs were cold under my bare feet and goose bumps sprung up on my skin. The air smelled old and musty, and for a change it was the sound of Jake's military boots that echoed softly through the narrow passageway. When we reached the door, I held my breath and said a silent prayer before slowly turning the handle. The catch turned, and the door opened under the slightest pressure, just wide enough for me to squeeze through.

I dropped to the ground and shimmied across the floor to the wooden-slatted banisters. Jake appeared silently at my side, and I wondered whether it was entirely necessary for him to have positioned himself quite so closely. I pushed the thought aside and peered through one of the thin gaps in the railings.

I counted hostiles into the double-figures, all dressed in black tactical gear, all wearing balaclavas. They were also heavily armed, which told me whoever was in charge of the operation had to be both extremely connected and well-funded. Commanding a private, well-trained army, willing to take on the Palace of Palavaria using stolen REF weapons, would take money, loyalty, and above all, balls.

The terrified party guests had been herded into a group at the far end of the Hall, forced to their knees with their hands on their heads. I located Francis, King Sebastian, and Princess Josephina together towards the left of the group and was relieved to see they all looked physically fine.

Kaiser knelt a few metres behind them with Prince

Frederick, looking equally unhurt, but as I located Ty and Connor on the other side of the group, I saw that Connor was holding a bloody cloth to his head. He was conscious and looked alert, so I hoped it wasn't too serious.

A woman appeared from somewhere beneath the balcony. She was about my height and build, but it was her wavy, flame-red hair that first caught my attention. Although she wore the same tactical gear, the black masquerade mask made her stand out from the other balaclava-wearing gun-thugs.

She called over a few of the hostiles and gave them an order I couldn't hear, then they moved into the huddle of guests and began pulling people out at random. No, not at random – they were singling out members of the King's Guard. One tried to resist and was shot mercilessly at point-blank, the sound echoing off stone walls, followed by a cacophony of screaming and shouting.

"Silence," the woman ordered, her thin lips hard and resolute. "I said silence… unless someone else wants to get shot." Guests cowered as she waved her gun around arbitrarily.

After that, the rest of the King's Guard were weeded out quickly. As they were escorted to a room off to the side of the Hall, I noticed one of the bad guys showing the red-headed woman something on a data-pad.

"Well, well, well," she said loudly in an accent I didn't recognise. "It appears we have some interesting guests here this evening. Would the Spec Ops team, otherwise known as the Wolfpack, mind showing themselves?" Jake stiffened beside me and I glanced at him, noticing the strained muscle flexing in his jaw. A murmur went through the hostages, but none of the Wolfpack identified themselves. "Come now. Don't be shy," she taunted. "We'll be able to find you by your uniforms, but believe me, if I have to come looking, there will be consequences."

A hostile seized an elderly gentleman from the front of

the group, dragging him towards the woman. She put the muzzle of her gun to his temple and I put my hand on Jake's arm to calm him.

"We can't help them from here," I whispered into his ear, but Kaiser's voice turned my attention back to the far end of the Hall.

"Stop," he said loudly as he stood up, holding his arms out to the side. "You don't need to hurt anyone else."

Ty and Connor also stood, though I noticed Connor didn't look too steady.

"Good," said the woman. "It seems like we understand each other after all. Although next time, I will not repeat myself." She pulled the trigger, the flagstones turning instant red.

"No!" Kaiser yelled, starting forwards, but the bad guy next to him brought the butt of his Seeker down hard on the back of his head knocking him unconscious. I felt sick. Not just because Kaiser had been injured, but because that old man had been killed... for what? To make a point? The woman was cold and calculating, which was a dangerous combination in itself, but the fact that she looked like she was enjoying herself added an extra level of evil.

"Put them in with the others," she ordered. The bad guy grabbed Kaiser's wrist, dragging him towards the side room. Connor and Ty followed under protest. "Now isn't that better? Deakes?" A tall, stocky man started towards her. "I want the rest of the guests split into two groups. Half this side, half that."

Deakes and his team immediately set about separating the guests, and chaos erupted until the woman fired a warning shot into the air.

"Hey, look what we have here," Deakes yelled, pulling Francis to his feet. "Brotherhood – Warrior Caste. And a pretty high ranking one at that."

"Really?" The red-headed woman glanced over, looking momentarily interested, but it faded quickly. "Whatever.

Stick him out of the way with the others."

It looked like Francis was going to resist for a second. I held my breath, knowing what had happened to the last person who'd defied her, but then he reluctantly moved towards the side room.

I felt a tap on my left hand and looked to where Jake pointed. A group of five men had entered through a door on the far side of the Hall. I watched as two of them greeted the woman with familiarity, and if I was reading it right, affection. Like her, they wore black masquerade masks, but unlike her fatigues, they wore business suits, tailored and expensive by the looks of it. Something about them seemed familiar, but I couldn't put my finger on it.

"Any problems?" asked the taller, slimmer of the two men, whose beaked mask and black outfit made him look like an evil raven. His accent was similar to the woman's, but I still couldn't place it and that bugged me.

"A few minor issues," she replied, and for a second it reminded me of what Jake had said earlier. "I took care of it."

"So I see." The tall man, who I took to be in charge, surveyed the dead bodies that littered the Great Hall. "Were they all completely necessary?"

"Of course they were." She smiled maliciously. "We had some interesting additional guests though – an REF Special Ops team."

"Really?" The second, shorter man sounded surprised. "Where are they?" he asked, his shaggy hair and stocky frame reminding me of a black bear.

"In the side room with the King's Guards. One's unconscious, and I think another one has a concussion; they're not going to be a problem. The only way out is through that door." She pointed. "And as you can see, I have it well guarded."

"Excellent," said the tall man. He raised a hand and touched her cheek gently. A girlfriend perhaps? Lover?

Wife? "You've done well." She started to respond, but he cut her off with a dismissive wave of his hand before turning his attention to the guests. "Ladies and Gentlemen," he said loudly as he mounted the throne platform. "May I have your undivided attention? King Sebastian... please, come forward." No one moved.

"I believe you know what happens if we have to ask again, Your Highness," the woman added, gun raised.

"I'm here." The voice came from the left-hand side of the room. The King stood and made his way through the group to the centre of the floor. "There's no need for further bloodshed." The woman marshalled him to the floor in front of the stage and pushed him to his knees with the muzzle of her gun. "Whoever you are, you're making a huge mistake," he continued furiously.

"Ah, Sebastian, you say that like we care what you think." The tall man sneered.

"We're not scared of you," the shorter one added, spitting on the ground.

"Are you ARRO?" the King asked.

"ARRO?" the tall one spluttered with such discussed he practically choked. "Hell no. ARRO are weak-minded terrorists who hide behind anonymity and mindless violence. We are true criminals. Artists if you will. What we do requires skill and brains, not plasma bombs and scare tactics."

"Then what do you want?" Sebastian asked, his voice strong and angry.

"What do we want?" The man in charge considered the question carefully, tapping his finger against his temple. "What is it that we want?" he asked the shorter, suited man, who was meandering through the group to the right.

"Let's see... oh yes, we want... this," he said, yanking a jewelled choker from around a woman's neck. "And... this." He helped himself to the bracelet from another lady's wrist.

"You're thieves?" The King was disgusted, like he'd expected more.

The tall man laughed – an unattractive, airy, nasal snort. "That's as good a word as any I suppose." I thought it odd that he seemed amused by the accusation as he turned to address the room. "This is how it's going to work. In a moment my colleagues are going to come amongst you and gather your fine collection of valuables. That includes rings, brooches, bracelets, medals, cufflinks… I could go on, but I'm sure you get the point. You will hand over everything or… my dear, please tell our lovely guests what will happen."

The flame-haired woman stepped forward looking manic and spiteful. "You'll do exactly what we tell you to do, or one person from the other group will get dead." A low mutter erupted amongst both parties. "If one person resists – one person dies. If you don't give us all your jewels – someone dies. If you piss me off – someone dies. I assume you're seeing the trend here?" She was enjoying every second.

"You won't get away with this," said Sebastian.

"Who's going to stop us?" asked the tall man, who'd jumped down from the stage and was crouching in front of Sebastian. "Your Guards? I wouldn't count on them if I were you. We've sealed off most areas of the Palace, and right now I have men rounding up what's left of your pitiful Security Team. And don't even bother hoping that they managed to get a distress signal off-world. We have a super little gizmo thingy that turns all of your sophisticated communications equipment into nothing more than useless chunks of metal and wire." The King's head lowered slightly. "There's no help coming."

A hostile approached the shorter, stockier man, whispered something, then retreated quickly. The man instantly bristled at the news, and he beckoned the woman away from the guests until they were practically below the balcony.

"We've lost contact with one of our perimeter patrols," he said quietly. "Could one of the King's Guards have gotten away before you locked down the Hall?"

The woman looked disgusted. "No way, Blain." So that was his name. Why did it sound familiar? "The plan worked flawlessly; I was spectacular as always. There's no way anyone got past our guys."

"What about the Wolfpack, Vita?"

"I told you, they're locked up with the Guards."

"All of them?"

"Yes."

"All four of them?" Blain pushed.

"Four?" Vita said loudly, drawing attention from some of the closer hostages. She lowered her voice again. "No, there were only three names on the list."

"There are four members to a Wolfpack, you idiot. Shit! There's one missing. You have to tell Vanze."

"Can't you tell him?" For the first time, she looked unnerved.

"No way, Sis. This is all on you. You screwed it up, you deal with it."

"Thanks for the support, Blain," she hissed as she turned and stalked back up the Hall.

Vanze wasn't happy with the news, backhanding the woman across the stage before calling Deakes over to give him orders. Deakes rounded up six other bad guys and left the Great Hall through the main doors. It wasn't a stretch to guess Vanze had sent them after the fourth member of the Wolfpack.

Vanze stalked towards Sebastian before dropping down to crouch in front of him. "Where's the safe?" he grunted.

"What safe?"

"Let's not play this game." Vanze sighed noisily. "The safe. The vault. The secure storage facility. The strong-room. Whatever you want to call it. I want to know where it is. Now."

"I don't know what you're talking about."

"I know you have a vault for all the Palavarian family treasures, and if you don't… oh never mind." He sighed again before standing up. "Perhaps you need a little encouragement to jog your memory. Bring me Princess Josephina."

"No!" shouted the King, trying to rise, but Vanze elbowed him across the temple forcing him back to his knees. "I'll show you. I'll take you there myself," continued the King desperately. "If it's just the treasures and artefacts you want, you can have them. Just don't hurt anyone else."

Vanze smiled victoriously and pulled the King to his feet. "Lead the way," he said with greasy politeness, holding an arm out towards the door. "Bring the Princess as well," he added to the hostile restraining Josephina. "A little leverage might come in handy. And my dear?" He turned to Vita. "Can I trust you to keep an eye on things here?"

"Of course," she replied, rubbing the side of her face gingerly.

Vanze and Blain left the great Hall with the King, Phina and three hostiles, leaving their sister in an even more dangerous mood.

Jake touched my hand again to get my attention, indicating it was time to leave. I shimmied to the door and headed back down the cold, musty stairs.

"We were about to send out a search party," Ash said.

"Sorry," I apologised. "There was quite a lot going on."

Jake condensed what we'd seen into the key facts. "The King's Guards, Wolfpack and Francis were removed from the group and marshalled into a small side chamber. From what I could tell, there are only civilians left in the Great Hall," he concluded.

"They know one of the Wolfpack is missing, but they don't know who it is," I added.

"What about us?" asked Ash.

"Ty, Connor and Kaiser must've been added to the guest list, not sure about Francis, but we were supposed to be a surprise. They don't seem to know about us at all," I replied.

"That swings things in our favour," said Jared. "It would also explain what I've been picking up on their coms." He held out an earpiece that he'd obviously taken from one of the dead bad guys. "There's chatter about a search grid. I thought they were looking to round up stray Guards, but after what you've said, it sounds like they're looking for Jake."

"Aren't I the honoured one?" Jake scoffed. "Anyway, you haven't heard the best bit. We're dealing with the Khan Brothers."

"The Khan Brothers?" repeated Jared, his voice dripping with distain.

"And their not-so-little psychopathic sister," I added.

"We've been after those bastards for years, but they're too well connected," Jared said. "We always got there just too late. I can't believe they have the audacity... or stupidity, to take the Palace. They must be insane. Surely they know what the repercussions will be? Did you get what they're here for?"

"Jewels," I said, but I couldn't shift a nagging feeling that something wasn't right. "Vita's men are picking the guests clean as we speak, but the brothers have taken the King and Phina to some kind of storage facility to collect the rest of the Palavarian antiquities." I noticed Jake studying my face in the pale torchlight.

"I know that look. What's up, Shae?" he asked.

"I don't know exactly, but this seems all wrong."

"What do you mean?"

"Something's bugging me. Actually, there are two things bugging me. Firstly, I have to agree with Jared... nobody in their right mind would attempt an all-out assault on the Palace, especially for something as meaningless as theft. If its jewellery and trinkets they want, there are far softer targets that would reap the same benefits, if not more. Granted the artworks and antiquities are worth millions of credits, but they're unique. The Khans may be able to shift a few items on the black market, but even low-life fencers aren't going to touch the bulk of the stuff. Plus, there's no way the Tetrarchy would let anyone get away with something like this. You can guarantee they'll commit every resource across the Four Sectors to bringing the Khans to justice."

"It does seem illogical," Ash agreed.

"I think we're all with you on that one, Babe. So what was the other thing?" Jake asked.

"Huh?"

"You said there were two things bugging you."

"Yeah, sorry, I was still thinking about the repercussions from the Tetrarchy. The other thing is the Khans themselves. The Brotherhood has been after them for years, and we've had just as much trouble pinning them down as you guys. They've obviously got a vast network of connections that help them evade us, but fundamentally they're just meathead thugs – ruthless and cold-blooded certainly, but thugs none the less. They run guns and drugs, and they've cornered the market on loan-sharking and prostitution, but they've never done anything as organised or blatant as this. It just doesn't seem like them. Call it a hunch if you want to, but this just doesn't feel like a run-of-the-mill robbery."

"Something's definitely off. We need to find out what else is going on," said Ash. "But we can't blunder around blindly, especially with hostiles out searching for Jake."

"What about Security Operations?" Jared offered. "I know it would've been the first place the Khans took when they arrived, but we can take it back. From there we can see everything that's happening in the Palace and grounds."

"Hey, that's a great idea," said Jake. "If we ask really

nicely, they're bound to open the door and welcome us in. They might even make us tea and everything."

"Have you got a better idea?"

Jake's silence was his answer.

"For what it's worth, I say we go," I said to end the awkwardness. "We have weapons, and we have the element of surprise. I say we do it."

By my calculations, we made it almost half way before we encountered our first patrol. Two hostiles were so quiet that when they swept around a corner, they were practically on top of us. One of them was right in my face before either of us realised what was happening, and I instinctively raised the knife that Jared had given me. I felt a jolt as Jake pushed me roughly to the side of the hallway and I stumbled, my shoulder colliding painfully with the wall.

I watched Jake punch the hostile hard in the throat before he ducked under the man's flailing arm and got behind him, plunging his knife into the man's back and forcing it up and under his ribs. He died instantly.

Ash and Jared dealt with the second man. Having disarmed him, Jared had his arms pinned to the side of his body while Ash snapped his neck using a relatively easy Tok-ma manoeuvre called cal'tar. Tok-ma was the unarmed fighting style used by the Brotherhood, mixing ancient combat techniques with a modern brawl twist. I'm skilled to a high level, which was why I was particularly pissed that Jake had felt it necessary to barge me out of the way.

Jared slung the strap of a Seeker over his shoulder before passing me the second. I readied the weapon before cautiously opening the nearest door, and after confirming the all-clear, grabbed the foot of the nearest body and tugged it into the room. I hadn't realised Jared was so close behind me, so when I turned, I almost walked straight into him.

"Oops, sorry," I said, stopping myself just in time.

"No problem. Listen, Shae—" Jared started, but I was

already in the hall and didn't catch it if he said anything else.

We managed to avoid the next patrol because they were making so much noise, we could hear them coming from a mile away. So far, we'd been lucky, and none of the hostiles had managed to get a warning out to the Khans before their demise, but we knew our luck wouldn't hold out forever. Our team sat that round out in an office until the black shadows had passed.

We got to Security Operations without further trouble, but after a check of the approaching corridor, it was obvious that our luck had, indeed, run out. The office was about ten meters down on the left side of the hallway. Two heavily armed hostiles flanked the door, and there was no way to sneak up on them without being seen. We retreated to a small lounge area with an oversized couch and a couple of armchairs.

"We're not going to take those two by surprise," Jared whispered. "They'll get a warning out to the Khans before we get four metres."

"There's one way to stop them before they can make the call," Jake replied, tapping his gun.

"No way," Jared hissed though his teeth. "The noise will draw in every hostile in the area."

"Exactly." Jake grinned. "They're looking for a member of the Wolfpack, right? So, let's give 'um one. I'll take out the two scroats by Security, drawing in as many of the other bastards as I can. You wait here until I've led them away, then you can hit the office."

"No," I gasped. "That's suicide. There has to be another way."

"Given the circumstances, I don't think there is," Ash replied. I gave him a withering glare in response.

"You guys hide behind here until the coast is clear and I'll catch up with you when I can." Jake indicated to the giant couch. He started to leave but I caught his arm.

"Don't do this," I begged.

"I'll be fine, Babe. I do this for a living you know," he joked. His lips broke into a wide smile before he kissed me briefly and turned away. I tried to follow but Ash yanked my arm and I had no choice but to sink behind the couch with him. I watched around the side as Jake stopped briefly before throwing himself into the next hallway, the sound of the Seeker on automatic fire splitting the air. A moment later, pounding boots passed in front of the sofa, and when we were sure no one else was coming, we headed to Security.

The open door was flanked by two dead bodies, and the bullet-riddled walls dripped blood like tears. Most of the bad guys had headed off after Jake, leaving only one to man the office. Jared dispatched him quickly with his knife and dumped his body on the floor beside the corpses of the King's security team. Ash locked the door behind us.

I studied a wall of plexi-screens, each showing a different part of the Palace. "There," I said, pointing at a cluster of four images. "That's the Great Hall. And there," I tapped the screen, "is Vita." Her long, flame-red hair made her easy to identify amongst the other hostiles.

"Does anyone see the King, or Princess Josephina?" Ash asked. I shook my head. "Jared?"

"No, but Jake's made it outside and he's leading the hostiles away from us. He looks okay so far, and he's taken out two hostiles while I've been watching. I'm impressed – just don't tell him I said that."

"It looks like all the landing pads are being patrolled," I said. "And there's a ship on the West pad which is almost certainly the Khans. The rest of the screens show roving squads rounding up the last of the Guards, and it looks like they're taking them all to the King's dojo. There are only two ways in and out, so it would be easy for them to control the environment. Unfortunately, it also makes it practically impossible to get to without being seen – or without a small army."

"Which we don't have," Jared reminded us, as if that was necessary. "There are too many hostiles. If we had Francis and the Wolfpack—"

"That's not such a bad idea," Ash interrupted. I gave him my, I don't have a clue what you're talking about, frown. "We have to take back control of the Palace and find the King, right? Which by default means finding the Khan Brothers as well. And as you quite rightly said, Shae, we can't do any of that with just the four of us. Look here." He indicated towards the plexi-screens. "The only hostages left in the Great Hall are dignitaries and diplomats. They're terrified but subdued, and they've been conditioned not to do anything stupid or someone will die. They're not going to cause any trouble at this point. Now count how many hostiles are controlling them."

I skimmed the four monitors, counting. "Four including Vita," I concluded. "That can't be all, surely?"

"From what you and Jake heard earlier, Vita's role was to take the Hall, manage the hostages, relieve them of their belongings, and keep things under control while the brothers located the rest of the antiquities. She's cocky and arrogant, which we can use to our favour. She probably thinks her job's done and I bet she dispatched the rest of her men to help round up Jake."

"If we take back the Great Hall, releasing the Guards and the Wolfpack, we'll have enough people to clear up the rest of the hostiles and do a proper search for the King," Jared said.

"Precisely," Ash replied.

"The three of us should be able to take on the four of them no problem," I said confidently.

"The two of you," Ash corrected, picking up a com-pad and earpiece kit. "This plan stands a much better chance of success if I stay here and watch the monitors. I can guide you around patrols, help you to avoid any nasty surprises, and let you know exactly where the hostiles are in the Hall before you breach."

"I agree," said Jared, "but our coms are down, remember?"

"Our coms are, yes, but give me minute and I should be able to adjust these earpieces to piggyback off the Khans' own signal."

"Won't they know that?" I asked.

"I can adjust the frequency slightly so they won't have a clue," Ash explained.

"Outstanding." Jared looked impressed. "Wait, something's happening in the Great Hall."

I watched as Prince Frederick was hauled out from the hostages. There was no sound, but it was clear Vita was laughing as she pistol-whipped him across the temple.

"We need to get in there now," Jared said. "How are you doing, Ash?"

"Done," he replied as he handed us an earpiece and com-pad each.

"Okay," continued Jared. "This needs to be a surgical strike, quick and accurate. Agreed?" Ash and I nodded. "Shae, you happy you can take two targets out?"

"Do Carmichaels make the best ice-cream ever?"

"A simple yes would have sufficed," he replied, smiling.

With guidance from Ash, Jared and I made it to the Great Hall with only one slight delay as we ducked into a storeroom to allow a group of hostiles to sprint past. It was cramped and dark, and I had to stand closer to Jared than I was comfortable with.

We separated just before we got to the Hall. Jared headed towards the main entrance, while I detoured around to the side. I reached the door that marked my breach point and checked my weapon to make sure it was in full working order.

"Shae, wait for Jared. He's not quite in place yet," Ash instructed.

I located the nearest camera and looked directly into the

lens, giving the thumbs-up. "Understood. Tell me when," I whispered.

"Shae, target one has moved about four metres left of his original position. Target two is still in exactly the same place. Jared?"

"Go ahead."

"Target three is pacing by the hostages, but he's not moving too far. Target four, Vita, is towards the front of the Hall, just off-centre right."

"What about the hostages?" Jared asked.

"They remain against the walls in their two groups, except Prince Frederick who's still where Vita hit him. He's conscious but looks groggy. Breach on my mark. Ready?"

"Confirmed," Jared said.

"Confirmed," I repeated.

"Okay. On my mark then," Ash said as I gripped the door handle. "Three... Two... One... Mark."

8

I yanked the handle and burst through the door, immediately locating my first target. Out of the corner of my eye, I saw Jared appear through the main Hall doors and our first shots rang out so closely they sounded like an echo. My hostile crumpled, dead, and without pausing I swung around and fired off a shot in the direction of my second target. The force of the bullet to his forehead flung his whole body backwards and he crashed against a wooden door with a hollow thud.

Jared's second shot was followed by a high-pitched scream from Vita, but as I turned, another shot rang out. From the direction of the sound, I knew it hadn't come from Jared's gun, and a split second later I was aiming my own weapon at the flame-haired woman, blood oozing from a wound to her left shoulder. She held Prince Frederick as a shield, but she wasn't looking at him, or me.

The muzzle of Vita's gun was raised to the Prince's temple, but I followed her gaze towards Jared, watching a red stain spread across his grey t-shirt. Trickles of blood seeped through his fingers as he pressed his hand to the bullet hole in his left flank.

"Give it up, Vita," I ordered, trying to remain calm and in control of myself, but she merely laughed. I pressed on regardless. "Your men are dead, and you're out numbered. Put your weapon down and give yourself up."

"I don't think so," she scoffed, laughing louder. "Last time I checked, I have the advantage here." She tapped the gun against the Prince's skull and he recoiled, wincing. "I think you should put your weapons down. Oh, and I guess I don't need this anymore seen as you obviously know who I am," she added, removing her mask. Her eyes were feral. I'd heard many stories about Vita Khan, none of which were complimentary, and most of them described her as a violent psychopath. I'd thought they'd been exaggerated, but with her wild stare and maniacal laughter, I wasn't so sure. She'd certainly proved that she could kill mercilessly and without cause. "Nice dress by the way," she mocked, her eyes twinkling maliciously.

Vita watched Jared sway and fail to stifle a low groan. She laughed again and I wanted to kill her with my bare hands. An image of my fingers around her throat, squeezing the life out of her, temporarily filled my thoughts.

"You don't look so good," she taunted as Jared collapsed on to one knee, then on to the ground, the Seeker clattering noisily against the flagstones. My finger tightened on the trigger. "Well, hun." She turned her attention back to me. "Looks like it's just you and me. Oh, and of course, the Prince here." She kissed him roughly on the cheek before shaking her long red hair and laughing gutturally. The woman was certifiable – and I was left wondering how I was going to negotiate with crazy. "Put your gun down," she continued. "Don't make me ask you again or I will shoot him. And trust me, hun, you do not want to test my resolve."

I was a good shot, but it was impossible to know whether I could get off a kill-shot before Vita put a bullet in Frederick. Worse still, I could hit him myself. But if I gave up, there was always the chance she would kill me just for the fun of it, or kill the Prince anyway to punish us for the death of her men. Or just because? Did a psychopath need a reason to do anything?

Ash was ominously silent in my ear.

"Do I need to ask you again?" Vita sneered.

"Okay," I said reluctantly, putting my hands in the air, the barrel of the gun pointing towards the ceiling.

"Just shoot her," shouted Frederick, but it was too late. Vita smiled unpleasantly, and I wanted to wipe it off her face – with my fist.

"Put the gun on the floor," she ordered. "Carefully... that's it... now kick it away. Good. On your knees."

I did as I was told, knowing the mistake I'd made.

"Seriously?" she goaded. "How stupid are you?"

She pushed the Prince out of the way and aimed her gun directly at my head. I closed my eyes and heard the gun fire, but after a second it occurred to me that I was neither dead, dying, nor writhing in agony.

I opened my eyes and saw Vita lying on the Hall floor, her face bent towards me, her eyes open but empty. A small drop of blood ran from a hole in her temple, and a thick, dark puddle of red seeped out from beneath her skull, running along the joins in the flagstones like tiny red ribbons. Jake stood in the Queen's Balcony, his weapon still pointing at Vita's body.

"You okay?" he yelled.

"I'm fine. Jared's been shot."

"I'll be right down."

I pulled Jared's t-shirt up to reveal the ragged bullet hole in his side. His eyes flickered open and he moaned as I pressed my hands firmly over the wound to stop the bleeding.

"Tell me again how nothing's going to happen to you," I said, suddenly angry with him. He answered with a groan before resting his head back on the floor. I felt a hand on my shoulder and I raised my gun instinctively.

"Whoa, it's me," Jake said quickly, pushing the muzzle of the weapon gently to the side. I took my finger off the trigger. "How is he?"

"Not good, but he'll live," I replied coldly. It was irrational, but I was annoyed with Jared for getting himself shot, and I must've sounded harsh because Jake gave me an odd look. I ignored his enquiring eyes and looked around the Hall. The two groups of hostages had come together into one big, chaotic and frightened mass at the far end of the room. "I need to fix him, but I can't do it here in front of all these people."

"I know," Jake replied. "Hold on, I'll get the others."

He unlocked the heavy wrought iron bolts and released the captives. Sergeant Mollere was the first out and Jake had to duck a punch before Mollere realised who he was. The Sergeant issued orders to his Guards, who quickly gathered up the discarded Seekers before deploying to the Hall entrances to stand sentry. I handed my Seeker to a passing Guard because it was more important that he used it to hold our position.

"You still with me?" I asked Jared. It was unfair of me to be so callous, even belligerent towards him in his condition, but I couldn't help it – it was my way of protecting myself against the anguish of seeing him hurt. He groaned as I moved my hand to get a better seal over the seeping hole in his side. "Hold on," I told him, my tone softening as my defences collapsed.

Footsteps made me turn to see Jake approaching with the others. I was glad Ty and Francis looked uninjured, and even Connor seemed more alert, but Kaiser looked pale and bilious.

"Ty, Con," Jake said. "Take Captain Marcos and Kaiser to the antechamber, the one we were in when this shitstorm kicked off. Sergeant—"

"Ash!" I interrupted, hearing his voice back on the

coms. "What happened? Where did you go? Are you okay?"

"Sorry I had to leave you. I had a few... umm... issues of my own to deal with in Security. A number of unwanted guests, you could say."

"Are you all right though? Are you hurt?" My interrogation continued, but I relaxed when he laughed.

"I'm alive," he joked, but I reprimanded his levity. "Really, it's nothing serious. Nothing a massage and a soak in a hot bath won't cure."

The Prince pulled up a chair and sat heavily, looking slightly confused and unfocused from the concussion. Aids fussed around him, more of a hindrance than a help.

"Be careful with him," I begged as Ty and Connor pick up Jared. I wiped my bloodied hands on the front of my dress, noticing Mollere's interest. "It's just a scratch," I said, trying to sound nonchalant.

"Really?" One eyebrow practically disappeared into his hairline.

"Really. It totally looks worse than it is. He'll be fine in no time. If you'll excuse me though, I'll go check on him."

The Wolfpack had laid Jared on one of the couches. Unwanted dark images of the death-cave swirled in my head and it was impossible at that point to say whether they were real memories or echoes of my nightmare. I closed my eyes and forced them into the mental box marked never to be thought of again, which sat in the deepest part of my brain.

I took a breath and turned my attention to Jared. Clearing my thoughts, I began to feel the usual tickling sensation begin in the pit of my stomach. A warm, comfortable heat started to radiate through my chest and my breathing calmed, my heartbeat synchronising with the rhythmic pulses of energy flowing through my veins. The force continued to build inside me, and I knew that any second it would pulse down my arms, through my hands, and arc to Jared's chest. I opened my eyes and the room shimmered from the pale silver-blue glow radiating from my skin. In that moment I felt so calm, so at peace, it was like everything around me had gone quiet and still. The Wolfpack, the chaos, and the Khan Brothers simply ceased to be. All that was left was one simple, basic, primal thought—

A high-pitched scream shattered my concentration, breaking the energy flow and returning the room to the warm orange glow from the table lamps. My brain was foggy and confused, like I'd been woken abruptly from a really deep sleep.

It took a second before I saw Martha standing behind the couch. She looked directly at me, silent just long enough to draw a sufficient amount of breath to let out another ear-piercing shriek.

"Shut her up," Connor ordered quickly.

Kaiser was nearest, and even though he didn't look too steady, he ducked around the side of the couch and grabbed her from behind. He wrapped one thick arm around her shoulders, pinning her arms to her side, and used his other to put his hand over her mouth. Her eyes opened wider, and then she bit him. He yanked his hand away, swearing, and it looked like she was going to scream again until Connor punched her hard in the face.

Her body fell limp in Kaiser's arms, but instead of laying her down gently, he just let go and she dropped to the floor with a thud.

"Shae," Ty said, but I wasn't paying much attention. He snapped his fingers in front of my face. "Shae, you have to focus." I looked at him vaguely. "Oh, man. Please don't tell Jake I did this."

"Hey, what the?" I snapped, my cheek stinging from his slap.

"Shae, concentrate. Captain Marcos is hurt and you have to heal him. Forget all the other shit that's happening, we'll make sure you don't get interrupted again." He took my jaw in his hand and gently twisted my head until I faced Jared.

As soon as I saw the raw, oozing bullet hole, the fog cleared and I knew exactly what to do. As the sparkling silver-blue strands of energy flickered between us, the red-raw skin around Jared's wound began to knit closed and the uneven edges smoothed to a pale pink scar before fading to shinny white and then disappearing altogether. His ashen skin coloured into a rosy glow, and when he opened his eyes, they were their usual piercing blue. He sat up and inspected his side.

"Thanks... again," he said, looking sheepish.

I was so glad he was okay, I forgot all about being angry with him and flung myself tightly around his neck. I didn't even worry when he closed his arms around me, pulling me so closely to his body that I felt the strong heartbeat in his chest. For a moment I was warm and safe and happy, but it quickly came crashing down when my head reminded me I was supposed to be distancing myself from him.

I pulled away from his arms and turned my attention to Kaiser, who'd just thrown up into a bin.

"Sit," I ordered the big guy, looking into his glassy eyes. He seemed dazed and did what I asked without protest. I placed one hand on his clammy forehead, the other on the back of his neck. "Hold still, this'll only take a moment."

Although he said he didn't need my help, I fixed up Connor's head laceration as well, just for good measure. "What we going to do about her?" he asked once I'd finished, disgust wrinkling his nose.

"Hasn't she woken up yet?" Jared asked. I was confused until I remembered he'd been unconscious when Connor had knocked her out for a second time. When I'd finished explaining, Jared said, "Just leave her here, we've got more important things to deal with."

"She saw what Shae can do," Ty explained.

Jared thought for a moment. "Nobody will believe her if none of us back her up. They'll just put it down to concussion. Where are the others?"

"Ash's still at Security Operation, and Jake's in the Great Hall briefing Francis and Sergeant Mollere," I said. "This thing isn't over. We still have the King and Phina to locate, plus a whole heap of hostiles to round up."

"What are we waiting for then?"

We left Martha where she'd fallen and returned to the others, who'd been joined by a couple of the Sergeant's men. As we walked through the Hall, I noticed Jared looking at Vita's dead body with contempt.

"You do that?" he asked me.

I shook my head. "Jake."

"One down, two to go then," he said flatly. "Sergeant, good to see you again," he continued, extending his hand.

"Captain Marcos," Mollere replied, taking it firmly, his eyes dropping to Jared's bloody t-shirt.

"Just a scratch," Jared said lightly before turning to Jake. "Where do we stand?"

"Okay, this is the situation…" Jake paused, tapping his earpiece. "Ash? You still there?"

"Got you loud and clear," he replied.

"How did you get coms?" I asked, pointing to Jake's ear.

"I gave the hostiles the slip over by the North hangar then doubled back to security. Ash gave it to me before sending me here to help you two out," he explained. "Sergeant Mollere's men have the Hall locked down, and Ash say's there's no activity in the vicinity so we're safe for the moment. There's been no chatter on coms to suggest the Khans know what's happened, but that's going to change as soon as Vita fails to check-in. A squad of King's Guards has been dispatched to the armoury; half will return here with weapons to protect the guests, the other half will go to the dojo, spring the rest of the Guards, and start rounding up hostiles. Ash's coordinating everything from security."

"Yeah, about that… I could do with a little help," Ash

added.

"As soon as the guests are secure, Mollere will join you in Ops to help coordinate the round-up of remaining hostiles," replied Jake. "That leaves us to locate the Khan Brothers."

It wasn't long before the Guards returned, carrying large canvas holdalls which they lined up in the middle of the dance floor. They swiftly unpacked a small arsenal, laying out handguns, rifles, concussion grenades, knives and wrist cuffs.

Without waiting to be invited, I grabbed a handgun and automatically went to tuck it into the back of my trousers. I sighed at the inconvenience of my dress, or what was left of it, and passed the pistol on to Jared, picking up a rifle with a shoulder sling instead. I watched enviously as the guys tucked grenades into pockets and guns into belts.

"So where do we start looking for the Khans?" I asked.

"Ash?" Jake said. "You got any sign of them on the monitors?"

"Negative. It's like they've disappeared."

"You think they've left?"

"No ships have departed since we re-took security, so I think it's safe to say they're still here... somewhere. Somewhere where there aren't any cameras," Ash suggested.

"Sergeant, is there anywhere in the Castle that isn't monitored?" asked Jared.

"Quite a bit, to be honest. None of the personal living quarters have cameras," offered Mollere. "And neither do the offices of the Royal Family and Senior Staff. Pretty much everywhere else is covered one way or another though."

"What about the vault or safe Vanze was asking the King about?" Jake asked.

"There's a safe in the King's office that contains legal and historical papers, and possibly some ceremonial jewels, but most of the Palavarian legacies are kept..." Colour drained from the Sergeant's face.

"What?" Jake asked.

"The Third Seal," Mollere replied grimly. "The Third Seal is in the safe. King Sebastian had it brought up especially for the ceremony, and there are no cameras in his office."

"Could this get any worse?" Jared sighed, pinching the bridge of his nose. "So one of the Sector's most powerful objects is relatively unsecured?"

"I'm afraid so," confirmed Mollere.

"I'm lost," I said. "Surely it's just a chunk of metal. Can't be that powerful, right?"

Mollere's mouth opened and closed a couple of times and his cheeks pinked. "Just a chunk of metal?" he repeated in astonishment. "The Seal is the tangible embodiment of King Sebastian's right to the Throne, and therefore his ruling power over the Sector. To lose it would have devastating consequences for the King. It's our duty to make sure it doesn't fall into the Khans' hands."

"Okay, so I get its importance, but devastating consequences? Isn't that overreacting a little?" I asked.

Mollere huffed with frustration and suddenly I felt stupid for asking the question. "It would be argued that a Ruling Monarch who can't protect their Seal is incapable of protecting an entire sector," he explained. "A vote of No Confidence from the Sector Senate would see Sebastian removed from office and the entire Palavarian family forced to abdicate. The repercussions would ripple throughout the Four Sectors."

"Maybe that's the real reason for the Khans being here," Jared suggested.

"Maybe," said Jake.

"Is it a coincidence that this happens directly after we foil a plan by ARRO to destabilise the Four Sectors?" Jared continued. "Do you think they had this as a back-up to weaken the authority of the Royals should the first offensive fail? Or is this something altogether separate?"

"The Khans are scroats, but they've never been affiliated with any anti-royalist terror organisations like ARRO," said Jake. "I know we can't rule it out, but I'd bet this is something different."

"Your argument is logical," Jared agreed, "but if not that, then what?" His eyes narrowed as he thought. "Sergeant, you said the King had the Seal brought up for the ceremony?"

"Yes, normally it's kept in..." He paused, looking conflicted. "As you know, the entire South Wing of the Palace is a museum, displaying historical and cultural antiquities from Sector Three as well as Earth itself. Below—"

"Ash, do you have eyes on the South Wing?" interrupted Jake.

"There are several cameras in the museum," Ash replied. "I'm watching a group of men boxing up artefacts as we speak. The good news is they're taking exceptional care with them, the bad news is there's no sign of the King or Princess." Jake relayed this new information to Mollere.

"Okay, but if you'd let me finish, you'd know that the museum is actually of no importance. It's common knowledge that below the museum are the Restoration Rooms and the storage facilities for the rest of the Palavarian Collection," he explained. "But what's under that, is classified Alpha-Secure. I can't tell you any more than I just have."

"Technically you haven't told us anything, but you can," clarified Jared. "We all have Alpha-Secure clearance, given to us directly by the King himself."

"You do?" Mollere was surprised, and doubtful, and for a moment he looked conflicted again. "Well, it's not like I can check right now, so I'll just have to take your word for it and deal with the fallout after. Under the Restoration

Rooms are the Catacombs; a series of vaults used to store artefacts rescued from Earth during the War of Unification. A long time ago, to minimise the risk of losing our remaining heritage, the collection was secretly distributed between the four Royal Families for protection and safekeeping."

"And the Seal is normally kept there?" Jared asked.

"Correct. But it was secretly brought to the King's office in preparation for your surprise ceremony. If the Khans know about the Catacombs, like they seem to know everything else around the palace, they may still believe it's down there."

"I take it there are no security cameras in the Catacombs?" I surmised.

"No. As far as most people are concerned, the Restoration Rooms are the lowest level in the palace. The vaults don't even appear on building blueprints."

"Okay, at least we have information to work with," Jake said. "There are two potential targets: the safe in the King's office, which actually contains the Seal, and the Catacombs, where the Khans might believe the Seal is being stored. We need to cover both. Ty, join Ash in security and get internal coms up and running. Con, go with him; I want you to co-ordinate the King's Guard's counter-offensive. Francis, if it's okay with Ash, I'd like you to stay here and protect the Prince. I trust you to keep him safe."

"Of course," Francis replied.

"I'll check out the King's office with Shae," Jake continued, winking at me.

"I think I'd be more use taking the museum," I suggested. "I know the way and the layout of the rooms." Plus, I didn't think it would be appropriate to be alone with Jake.

"Agreed. I'll come with you," Jared added, but I wasn't sure whether that option was any better.

Jake narrowed his eyes and glared at Jared. "Kaiser,

you're with me," he grunted eventually.

I'd been standing still for so long, my bare feet had warmed the stone flooring, so when I moved it was like stepping on to ice and goose bumps sprang up across my skin. Remembering Vita was about my size, I wandered over and measured my foot against one of her boots.

I was double-knotting the laces around my ankle when Prince Frederick approached Jake. "I'm coming with you," he said unsteadily.

"With all due respect, no way, Your Highness. You need to stay here with Brother Francis. Your safety is priority," Jake replied. "Besides, you don't look so good."

"I'm fine, and it wasn't a suggestion. My father and sister are still in danger, and if you think I'm…" I heard the anguish in his voice and he took a second to control himself. "If they're not there, you'll need me to gain access to the safe. Next to the King, the protection of the Third Seal is the priority, not me."

I thought Jake was going to protest again, but instead he primed a rifle and passed it to the Prince. "I take it you know how to use one of these," he said. Frederick nodded. "You do what I say, when I say it," Jake warned.

"Fair enough," the Prince agreed.

"Let's move then."

Jared and I were almost to the South Wing when we heard from Ash again. "We're picking up chatter on the Khans' com-channel," he said. "Looks like they know what's happened, and they're not exactly happy, but weirdly, there's nothing from the Khans themselves. It's like they've dropped off the face of the planet."

"That is weird," Jared said. "Now the cantooa's out of the bag, we should move with purpose."

"Agreed. You've got a clear path all the way to the museum entrance."

The main double-door entrance to the South Wing was wide open. As Jared swept right, I headed left, walking quietly between rows of tempered glass display cases. A shiver rolled over my skin – there was something about the cool air and ominous silence of a library that always gave me the creeps.

I crouched by the open archway leading to the Literary Section, listening to Ash's instructions. "Two armed sentries are at your ten and two. Three unarmed men are loading crates at your twelve, about fifteen metres in."

Jared used hand signals to indicate which sentry he wanted me to take, then on his three-count we launched from our positions, entering the room simultaneously. Jared fired, hitting his target, but mine proved more elusive. He took a bullet to his arm but was able to dive behind one of the large, wooden storage crates.

An exchange of bullets shattered a climate-controlled case into thousands of miniature toughened-glass nuggets. The floor in front of me sparkled like the ice lakes on Larrutra, and tiny shards crunched under my feet as I moved forwards. Once I was past the broken glass, I dived to the floor, rolled to the left, and aimed at the hostile's ankles, just visible below the packing box. The man hit the floor screaming, giving Jared the opportunity to swing around the side of the crate to take the kill-shot.

Without their armed protectors, the remaining men gave themselves up peacefully. Jared used flexi-cuffs to fasten the three of them around a large stone pillar by their wrists.

"If any of you tries to escape, or even make a sound, I will come back and shoot you all in the head. Do you understand?" he said. The men nodded frantically. "We'll be watching," he added, pointing to the nearest camera.

As he walked away from them, he had a broad, cocky grin on his face, reminding me of the Captain I'd first met back at Finnegan's Bar on Angel Ridge.

Jared and I followed Ash's directions through another couple of rooms until we reached a large metal door with a blinking sensor pad on the wall beside it.

"I'm impressed," said Jared. "This is max-level security door with biometric access control panel, 15-point locking configuration incorporating a Leyton deadbolt system, and high-tensile internal hinges. One of the best on the market. Do we really think the Khans got through this?"

"They had full control of the security systems, and that's not to mention the King and Princess as well," Ash replied. "We've got to assume they did."

"Okay. So it would probably help if we could get through it as well," Jared suggested, with just the slightest hint of sarcasm.

"Hey, Captain." It was Ty who answered. "The system's still on full lock-down. I'm trying to reverse whatever the Khans' men did to it, but it's slow going. Give me five minutes."

Coms had been quiet for a while, and I was beginning to fidget when I heard Ash's voice. "Jake's team have just got to the King's office. They ran into some trouble on the way which delayed them... they're all okay, but no sign of the King so far. I'll keep you updated."

A few minutes later, a buzzer sounded, the light on the access panel switched to green, and with a faint slurp, the heavy door swung open. I raised my weapon and stepped through to a wide stairway, blinking rapidly to let my eyes adjust to the severe strip-lighting reflecting off whitewashed walls.

I followed Jared as we descended the surprising long staircase into the Palace basement.

At the bottom of the steps, we took a short, similarly clinical-looking corridor, which dead-ended at another set of security doors. In contrast to the previous ones, these were frosted glass with the words Decontamination Unit in large, bright letters. Below, a sign warning against unauthorised access was part obscured by an arc of dripping red.

A security checkpoint stood unoccupied and I moved

around the desk to get a better view of the monitor, skidding through a pool of congealing blood. A King's Guard was tucked out the way, several bullet holes punctuating his chest.

"See anything?" Jared asked.

"A dead guard," I replied.

"I meant on the monitor."

I scrolled through the camera feeds. "Nothing. But we know for sure someone came through here."

"Yes, but was it the Khans?"

"Guess we'll find out soon."

It took Ty a few minutes to switch the mocking red light on the biometric access panel to green. As soon as the door opened, we passed through in to a small tube-shaped room, just wide enough for us to stand side by side. The metal grated floor clanked underfoot, but every other surface was covered in millions of tiny bulbs – at least that's what they looked like to me.

We followed automated computer instructions while a string of decontamination protocols ensured we didn't compromise the protection of the artefacts. When the cycle was complete, it released another door leading out onto a balcony. Stairs led down to floor level on both sides.

"Holy crap!" I whispered, surveying the vast underground hangar that housed a series of smaller, climate-controlled glass pens. I stared, open-mouthed, but Jared looked just long enough to get his bearings.

"Shae, go left, eyes open for targets. I'll go right," he whispered. "We'll meet at the far end. Got it?"

"Copy that."

I moved cautiously past pens accommodating sterile looking equipment, flashing data-screens, and well-lit workstations. From the top of each glass box sprouted a variety of tubes and cables that fed into a sequence of boxed ducts in the high ceiling.

In one compartment, a heavy-looking book sat open

about a third of the way through. The left page had been restored, the ink bright and the pictures colourful, the right, in contrast, was dull and faded, the paper pocked with decay. I passed along to the next enclosure where a vase, almost as tall as me, stood on a small plinth, and after that, a statue of a woman sitting on a stool, naked except for a cloth which draped across one shoulder before cascading gracefully over her lap.

The Restoration Room was silent and eerie… and empty. As I got to the far end, I met Jared. "Anything?" he whispered.

I shook my head. "Clear." I was about to ask what he wanted to do next, when Ash's voice came over the com-channel, his tone urgent.

"Shae, Jared, we've got a problem."

9

"I've just heard from Jake. The King's safe was open and the Third Seal's missing," Ash said.

"Then we're too late; they've got what they came for," Jared replied, rubbing his temple vigorously. "Which also means they're probably long gone."

"Not necessarily," Ash countered. "Their ship's still on the landing pad and we can't locate them anywhere on the monitors. We know they hit the King's office first, but there's a strong chance they went to the Catacombs for more antiquities. Have you seen any evidence to support that hypothesis?"

"Someone's been through here," Jared replied. "Can't say for sure it was the Khans though."

"This doesn't make sense," I said, trying to smooth the frown lines from my wrinkled forehead. "If the Seal is the most valuable thing on this entire planet, why would the Khans come here rather than escaping with it? Why would they do that?"

"I've no idea," replied Jared. "Nothing about this whole thing makes any sense, but we need to put that aside and concentrate on getting the King, the Princess, and the Seal back."

"Agreed," said Ash. "The access to the Catacombs is through the Research Laboratory, which is halfway down the west wall."

Doubling back, we found the door to the lab slightly ajar, but the room was empty. A virtual copy of a candlestick rotated silently above a holo-table, and even though I knew it wasn't, it looked so real I put my hand out to touch it. The image fractured and distorted around my fingertips.

"There's the lift," Jared said, looking around the room before shaking his head. "Ash, are you sure this is the only way in to the Catacombs?"

"Afraid so, Captain," Ash replied. "Security reasons."

"Yeah well, security reasons or not, I'm not happy about this. We have no idea what we're walking into down there. We're going in blind... and we're about to announce our arrival in a god-damn lift with no protection once the door opens." He paused, thinking. "Maybe we should wait for back-up."

"As strategies go, I agree this isn't the best I've ever heard, but the lift is our only option," I said. "The Khans have to be down there, there's nowhere else they can feasibly be, and we don't have time to wait for backup. Besides, everyone else has got their hands full. We can do this, Jared... just don't get shot again, okay? Once today is quite enough."

"I'll try not to," he replied before addressing Ash. "We're heading down now. Feel free to send reinforcements as soon as you can."

"Acknowledged," Ash replied. "There's something else you need to know though. Sergeant Mollere's just informed me that coms don't work in the Catacombs."

"Great," I huffed. "Any more good news before I press the call button?"

"If the Khans are down there, it would explain why

they've been off-coms and haven't reacted to the chatter from their own people," Ash continued. "They won't know what's happened, which gives you the advantage."

"Oh, well that makes all the difference."

"Be safe," Ash replied, ignoring my sarcasm.

I tapped the call button and a slight hum indicated the heavy freight lift was ascending. A moment later, a short ping sounded, and the doors slid open. We readied our weapons and I took a deep breath before stepping in, my footsteps echoing around the vast metal box. The doors closed, the lift descended, and I checked my weapon for the tenth time.

"Remember," Jared said, "our priority is to get out of the lift and find cover... without getting shot." He smiled and that made me feel a fraction better.

As we slowed, I braced myself against the side and rested my finger lightly beside the trigger. Blood pumped in my veins, and I could practically hear the rush in my ears.

The lift gave one last judder as it came to a stop, the ping indicating that the doors were about to open. I took a deep breath and held it, calling on my Brotherhood training to calm myself. During those heartbeats, it was as though the air itself froze, and tranquillity washed through me.

The doors slid sideways with a light whoosh, and I felt the cold air from the Catacombs rush in. For a moment there was nothing but an eerie silence – then the shooting started. The distinctively rapid pop-pop-pop from the Seekers soon mingled with the deafening sound of splintering wood as a set of storage crates exploded. Metallic echoes rang through the cave as bullets whizzed past my head, burying themselves into the back wall of the lift. Other shots ricocheted off the cave walls producing high pitched cracks and whines.

A stack of crates, just to Jared's right, were still intact and he motioned towards them.

"You okay? You shot?" Jared asked, the pungent stench

of gunfire mingling with burnt wood.

"No, I'm good," I shouted over the noise. "You?" He gave me an okay signal before peering around the side of the crate. A volley of bullets hit the crates, and shards of wood flew randomly through the air.

"I can see muzzle flashes at eleven, one and two." He indicated the positions with his hand. "I think there are three… maybe four."

The thunderous pop-pop-pop of a new wave of bullets echoed around the Catacombs and I ducked down further. "There goes our element of surprise," I joked.

"Funny," Jared replied, not smiling, but before I had a chance to respond he leant around the side of the crate and fired back at the hostiles. I followed suit.

"I think I might have got one," I told Jared optimistically.

"Me too, but we can't stay here we're…" he paused to return fire over the top of the crate. When he crouched back down, his hair was full of tiny wooden slithers and he had a series of scratches across his left cheek. He continued as if there'd never been a gap in his sentence. "…sitting ducks. I don't think we have a choice." He held out a plasma grenade and I nodded my agreement. "On three."

I hunkered down as far as I could, feeling Jared's weight on top of me as the explosion rocked the cavern. Even though I'd covered my ears, the sound had been deafening, so when Jared shouted something at me, I couldn't barely hear anything over the high-pitched ringing. I understood enough to give him the okay signal before readying my Seeker and disappearing around the side of the crate.

The air was thick with wood smoke and rock dust and I coughed heavily, trying to clear my throat. My eyes stung, and visibility was so poor I practically ran in to one of the bad guys. He was bloodied and dazed, so I was able to disarm him easily, putting him down quickly.

I rubbed my eyes with the heel of my hand to try and

clear my sight before heading forward. I didn't so much see as sense the man who loomed out of the darkness, but I certainly felt the agonizing pain as he brought something hard down on the side of my head. A second later everything went black.

I struggled to open my eyes because they were stubborn and uncooperative, and I had a thumping headache. After a moment, I tried again, and that time, with concentration, I got them to flicker. I blinked several times until they remained open, and gradually focussed on my surroundings.

I lay on the ground in the foetal position, which explained the chill down my left side. Jared was propped against the wall a couple of metres in front of me, conscious but bloodied, his hands and feet both bound. I moved my head slowly so I could see more of the room.

"So, you're awake. 'Bout fuckin' time," a man grunted, the muzzle of his Seeker pressing hard against my cheek. "Don't even think 'bout doing nothing stupid or I'll end you. Got it?"

I peered around his legs to see the King and Phina leaning against a crate, their hands and feet bound like Jared's.

"Is everyone okay," I croaked, but before they had time to answer, the hostile flipped the Seeker and brought the butt of the weapon down on my temple. Not hard enough to knock me unconscious again, but hard enough that it hurt like a son-of-a-bitch.

"No talkin'," he yelled, spraying spit-bubbles on my cheeks. He grabbed my shoulders and hauled me to the wall by Jared. I was too dazed to put up a fight as he bound my wrists, but alert enough to realise he didn't bind my ankles.

It took a while for the double-vision to clear and my brain to un-fog, and I spent the entire time fighting the urge to vomit. When I was able to concentrate again, I realised there were two hostiles guarding us – the skinny, balding shit who'd hit me, and a man-mountain who lolled casually against the crate next to Phina and the King. No sign of Vanze or Blain.

The small bay was no bigger than six metres square, and it was empty except for us and the pile of crates Man-Mountain leant against.

Raised voices filtered in from the passageway outside our alcove. My ears still rang, so I couldn't make out what was being said, but I could tell from the tone of the conversation that the Khan Brothers were not happy. When the tall, lanky frame of Vanze appeared in the opening, his eyes were burning, and his lips were set in a tight straight line. His forehead quickly furrowed when he saw Jared and me.

"Who the fuck are they?" he grunted at Baldy, who shrugged unwisely. Vanze mimicked him, and for a second, I thought he was going to shoot him, but instead he turned towards us. Blain appeared behind them. "I take it you're the ones responsible for all the excitement a few minutes back?" Vanze's voice was calm, he was even smiling, but his eyes... a storm raged behind the green.

Neither of us said anything, which prompted Blain to crouch next to me, his Seeker ominously close to my kneecap. "I believe my brother asked you a question," he said, an unreadable look on his sweaty face.

I wanted to say, 'Of course it was us, meathead. Who else was it going to be?' but instead I said, "Who do you—"

"It was all me," Jared interrupted. "Nothing to do with her." I turned to him, my mouth open.

"Really?" Vanze replied. He sounded doubtful, almost bored. "And you are?"

"Marcos, Jared. REF Fleet Captain. Serial number: DB 466 687 896."

"I see." Neither Vanze nor Blain seemed particularly phased by Jared's credentials. "Why aren't you with the others in the Great Hall?"

Jared paused for a moment, his eyes flicking briefly

towards me. "I was at the ceremony, but it was dull and tiresome – you know how it is. Then I met this pretty young thing here and we… well, we decided to take the party elsewhere, if you know what I mean." He managed a roguish grin.

"That doesn't explain how you ended up down here shooting up our men," Blain said, his nostrils flaring.

"We were, how should I put it, getting acquainted in one of the conference rooms when some Spec Ops guy burst in and interrupted. He told us the King and Princess had been taken hostage, and as a Fleet Officer, I had an obligation to help find them."

"And find them you did," said Vanze. "Just a shame you couldn't save them."

"Doesn't explain why she's here," Blain pushed.

"I couldn't exactly leave her on her own without protection, could I? Thought it would be better if she stayed with me."

"Oh, yes. This is much better for her." Blain didn't hide his sarcasm, but he removed the gun from my kneecap.

"Enough!" Whatever patience Vanze had left was spent. He turned to Baldy. "Where are the others?"

"Thaxter, Kirtis and Caplin are dead. There's just us and Hoban left." As if on cue, the last man arrived, puffing.

Hoban's tanned, weather-warn face shone red from running, and I wondered just how big the catacombs were. Lighter wrinkle lines appeared around his eyes as the flush faded, and I couldn't help thinking he looked out of place amongst thieves and gun-thugs. I would've placed him in his mid-thirties, but the faded cargo pants and scruffy t-shirt, with its cracked Westchester Academy Archaeology Department logo, suggested he was much younger – late-twenties even. Years of working on dig sites under blazing suns had taken their toll. He whispered something in Vanze's ear.

"Are you sure?" Vanze replied quietly, taking a step

backwards. A cloud crossed his angular features.

"Yes, sir." Hoban shifted position, picking at the frayed bandana wrapped around his wrist.

"And you've looked in all the vaults?"

"Twice, Sir. It's not there."

Vanze's faced darkened further. "Look again. Use the RP scanner to check for hidden vaults or compartments. Don't come back till you've found it," he ordered, his tone threatening. Hoban disappeared quickly.

"I don't like this," Blain said joining the hushed conversation, his voice showing the first signs of concern. "It's taking too long, and we've left Vita much longer than we said. You know what she's like."

"She'll be fine," replied Vanze.

"What if something's happened? What about that Spec Ops guy this one was talking about?"

Vanze placed his hand on Blain's shoulder. "Vita will deal with it. Look, he said it wasn't going to be easy to find, brother. Everything's going to plan – be patient."

"Were they part of the plan?" Blain pulled away, pointed at us, his anger rising. "Was it part of the plan for them to kill our men? For a Fleet Captain to get this close to us? We have the Seal, we should—"

"Enough!" Vanze thundered so viciously that Blain recoiled.

"Your brother's right," said Sebastian. In an instant, all eyes and guns were on him. "You have the Seal. You've got what you came for. Why don't you just leave?"

Vanze started laughing. His whole body shook, and he had trouble gaining his breath. I caught Jared's eye and raised a quizzical eyebrow, but he shrugged his shoulders, looking as mystified as I felt. Eventually Vanze got himself under control and he wiped the tears from his cheek.

"You think the Third Seal is all that we want? How precious. No, that's just an added bonus. Neither we, nor our benefactor, have any interest in politics, Your Grace.

Although we will enjoy reaping the benefits from the chaos that will ensue following your family's forced abdication. We're actually after something far more important."

I didn't know what interested me more: the fact that the Khans where working with someone else, or that they thought there was something in the Catacombs more important than the Seal.

Vanze continued unfazed. "My family have been after something for a very, very long time, but not even we had the resources to attempt an assault on the Palace of Palavaria. So, when we found out that someone else, let's call him the Outsider for sake of argument, was after the same thing, we agreed to join forces and share information. Sensible really, especially as he had the unlimited funds we needed to pull this shit off. He was happy for us to take the lead, didn't want to get his hands dirty, so he probably won't see it coming when we double-cross him and keep it for ourselves."

The King's forehead creased. "Tell me what you want, and you can have it. Just take it and leave."

Vanze laughed again. "What I want," he crouched down directly in front of Sebastian, "is the Helyan cube."

The King looked stunned. "I… I have no idea what that is," he said, but the stricken look on his face, and the sudden panic in his eyes, betrayed him.

Vanze stood and took a step back, smiling triumphantly. "You could save yourself a lot of heartache and pain if you just tell us where the cube is. And then, like you suggested, we'll be on our merry way."

"I told you, I don't know anything about a cube."

Vanze wrinkled his beaked nose. "Get him to his feet," he ordered Man-Mountain, who obliged a little too enthusiastically. Sebastian winced in pain, and that was before Blain punched him in the guts. "I have no patience left, Sebastian. Tell me where the cube is," Vanze demanded.

"I don't know what you're talking about."

Vanze nodded briefly to Blain, who hit him again, and again.

"Stop," Josephina cried, tears streaming down her pale face. "He's telling the truth. We've never heard of this cube thing. Please… stop hurting him."

In contrast to her father, I believed the Princess truly didn't know about the object, but she'd attracted Vanze's attention and he moved towards her, his fists clenched.

"Wait," Jared said quickly. "Even if you get the artefact, do you really think you're going to get away?" I knew he was trying to take Vanze's focus away from Phina, but perhaps that hadn't been the best thing to say.

"We have the King, the Princess, a Fleet Captain and," Vanze paused, "whoever the hell she is." Charming. "And the rest of the palace is on lock-down. So, yes, I think we're going to get away – with the Helyan cube." He turned his attention back to the King. "Let's try this again, shall we? Tell me where the cube is, or I'll kill your daughter. Right here, right now." He grabbed Phina roughly by the hair and pulled her to her feet.

Sebastian sighed heavily and his shoulders slumped, pain etching his face as he looked at his daughter.

"I love you, Phina, with all my heart. I'm so very sorry. God forgive me." He turned back to Vanze. "There is no such thing as a Helyan cube." His voice was hollow and broken, but completely resolute. I was stunned. Whatever the artefact was, King Sebastian was willing to sacrifice his daughter, sacrifice all of us, to keep it a secret.

"So be it," Vanze said. Man-Mountain raised his gun towards Phina's chest. "No, kill her slowly; painfully. Let's give the King time to change his mind," he instructed.

Sebastian lunged at Vanze, but with his ankles bound he fell to the floor, where Blain delivered kick after kick to his abdomen and chest. Phina squirmed and wriggled, but Man-Mountain closed his fat, chunky hands around her delicate neck. Jared and I tried to get to our feet, but Baldy turned his gun on us.

Things only de-escalated when Hoban returned carrying a small wooden box.

"Stop," Vanze ordered Man-Mountain, but he was too engrossed in his task to hear, or perhaps care. "Enough," he grunted, physically pulling the thug away. Phina dropped to the floor next to her father, holding her throat and gasping for air.

"Is that it? It's much… smaller than I expected," Blain grumbled, but Vanze ignored him.

"Let me see it." Vanze held out his hand towards the light-coloured box, which almost glowed in the muted lights of the alcove.

He took the object carefully, like he was handling a live plasma grenade that could go off any second, and I hadn't realised he'd been holding his breath until he let it out in a long slow puff. He paced the room, looking at the item with a mixture of awe and triumph, finally coming to stop next to me. Once he was closer, I saw the fine, delicate engraving on the wooden case – swirling patens and symbols that I'd seen before. My stomached flipped with surprised anticipation.

The moment Vanze opened the box, something deep inside my chest began to vibrate. He lifted out a small, brushed-bronze metal cube and held it in front of him, an enigmatic smile pulling at his lips. "Just perfect," he muttered, studying the same symbols that were engraved on the case.

The trembling under my ribcage quickened and tiny bursts of energy pulsed through my veins, but I was too preoccupied to care. I was completely captivated by the object and couldn't take my eyes off it until Vanze put it back in the box and closed the lid.

The energy and vibrations dissipated as quickly as they'd started, and I felt like I was waking from a dream.

Excitement turned to fear; what the hell had just happened? I looked around to see if anyone else had noticed my reaction, but all eyes were on Vanze.

"Now we can go," he said cheerfully.

"About fuckin' time," huffed Blain, seemingly less impressed by the Helyan cube than his brother.

"Grab the Princess, Hoban, she's coming with us – as leverage," said Vanze.

"Me?" Hoban stuttered.

"Yes, you. Just get on with it. And you," he indicated to Baldy, "wait till we've gone, then dispose of these three. Join us at the ship when you're done."

"Yes, Sir," Baldy replied, grinning maliciously.

Phina resisted Hoban, who seemed hesitant to restrain her, but Blain grabbed her wrist, pointing the muzzle of the Seeker between her eyes until she gave in.

"Get up," grunted Man-Mountain when we were alone. With my ankles free, I was able to stand easily, but Jared struggled. Man-Mountain made the mistake of leaning forward to help him up, and in that split-second Jared lunged forward, catching the ape off guard.

With Baldy's attention diverted away from me, I was able to put my full weight behind the two-fisted punch I landed to his face. A quick kick to his hand knocked the gun away, and a second to his groin had him sinking to his knees groaning. I looped my arms over his head and used my bound wrists to cut off his airway. Using the same cal'tar move Ash had earlier, I broke his neck easily.

I grabbed his gun and turned towards the two men brawling on the floor. Jared had both hands around Man-Mountain's wrist trying to keep the Seeker pointed away from him. The gun fired, ricocheting bullets off the hardstone wall and I ducked automatically. I aimed my weapon but couldn't get a clear shot as they squirmed on the floor.

"Jared! Delta Charlie," I yelled. He looked up for no more than a second before letting go of the hostile and rolling to the side, covering his head with his hands. Bullets from my Seeker ripped through Man-Mountain's chest exposing shattered bones.

"Interesting weapon," I said, mildly impressed by the tight grouping of bullet holes and light recoil. "I can see why it's a favourite in close quarters combat."

"Delta Charlie? Duck and cover? That's the best you could come up with?" Jared said, but he was grinning as he pulled a knife from Man-Mountain's belt and cut the binding around his ankles.

"Worked didn't it? And you're welcome, by the way," I replied, holding out my hands towards the blade. "Just consider yourself lucky I'm a good shot." I put two fingers against Sebastian's neck. "He's still alive."

"Good, but we need to get to the Princess. Once the Khans find out their sister's dead, there's no telling what they might do to her in retaliation." Jared picked up the second Seeker before we headed out of the alcove and back through the passageways towards the lift.

The tunnels were longer than I expected and I was surprised at how big the Catacombs were, but I knew when we got close to the lift because rock dust and the smell of burnt wood lingered in the air. We slowed, moving cautiously, and when we reached the space in front of the lift, I flattened myself against the wall before peering around the corner.

The lift doors where open, Hoban and the Princess already inside, but Vanze stood out in the open, cradling the small wooden box like an infant.

I didn't stop to ask myself why they hadn't left, or where Blain was, and I certainly didn't assess the entire situation like Brother Benjamin had taught me. If I had, I would've noticed Blain stringing together a set of plasma grenades. If I'd used my head instead of my heart, I would've seen the danger. But I didn't.

Before Jared could stop me, I rounded the corner and

ran straight at Vanze. To begin with, I wasn't sure if it was really him I was after, or the mysterious object that was so important to him, but by the time I was on top of him, I was sure. Whatever else happened, I wanted that cube. I wanted to know why it affected me the way it had, and I wanted to know why the Khan family had been after it for generations.

I took Vanze by surprise as I bowled into him, knocking the box from his arm, and a guttural cry escaped from his lips. We both lunged for the object, pushing it further away, and it skittered across the floor and under a pallet.

I didn't care about Vanze anymore and tried to clamber after it, but Jared wrapped his arms tightly around me and lifted me clear off the floor. He pulled me backwards towards the tunnel and I struggled against his grip until I saw the blinking digital display taped to a string of small black grenades.

Forty-five seconds... forty-four... Forty-three...

I'd been injured in a grenade attack before and it wasn't something I wanted to repeat in a hurry. I stopped struggling and indicated to Jared that I understood. He immediate let go and we both headed back towards the passageway.

"There's no time! If we don't leave now, we'll get caught in the explosion," I heard Blain yell. I stopped in my tracks, turning back towards them. Blain had Vanze tightly around the shoulders and was physically manhandling him into the lift.

"I have to get the cube," Vanze cried, his eyes wide and his voice desperate. The doors closed on his continued protests.

I glanced at the timer, seriously contemplating whether I had time to get the box.

Thirty... twenty-nine...

"We have to go, Shae. Now," ordered Jared, but I hesitated. "Now!" he yelled, tugging at my arm. The urgent aggression was like a slap in the face and my brain finally kicked in. I let him pull me towards the rock opening before we broke into a sprint along the passageway, heading deeper into the Catacombs.

The blast wave took me off my feet and threw me into the wall opposite. I cried out in pain, but the echo from the explosion swallowed my voice. The tunnel filled with a hot, gusting wind carrying dust and debris and I covered my head with my arms, the fine rock particles like sandpaper against my skin. I held my breath until the wave of air slowed and the debris began to settle.

When I was sure it was safe, I stood up, coughed heavily, and looked around for Jared, but the explosion had taken out the chem-lights and it was pitch black. A moment later, the passageway gradually brightened − lit by the pale blue glow of my skin healing from the hundreds of tiny cuts and grazes I hadn't realised where there.

"Jared?" I coughed through the dust.

"Over here. You alright?"

"Yeah. You?"

"I think my arm's broken." The last of the light died as my skin finished healing and the tunnel blackened again. "Stay there," Jared continued. "I'm coming to you. Keep talking so I can find you." His disembodied voice sounded hoarse and scratchy in the darkness.

"Do you think they got away? Do you think Phina's okay?

"I don't know." His voice was close. "Let's hope so." I felt his hand brush my arm before it slid up to my shoulder. It was so dark that even that close I couldn't see him, but I felt his breath on my cheek as he pulled me into a one-armed hug. "We should try and get back to the King. Hold my hand so we don't get separated."

After a bit of groping in thin air, my hand found Jared's and we started down the passageway, but we'd only gone a few metres when it became obvious I was going to need both hands to find us a safe route. Jared seemed reluctant to let go, but he released his grip and placed his hand on my shoulder instead.

It was slow going with plenty of trips, cracked shins, and swearwords, and I even had a flashback to the creature-cave which left me feeling inexplicably claustrophobic. Eventually I came up with an idea I knew Jared would hate. Hell, I wasn't exactly keen on the idea myself, but it beat groping around in the darkness.

"Have you still got that knife on you?" I asked.

"Sure, here," Jared replied before he traced my arm down from the shoulder and placed the cold metal object in the palm of my hand. "Why?" he asked carefully.

10

The tunnel glowed silver-blue and Jared gasped. "Shae! What the hell?"

"Don't try this at home, kids," I tried to joke through a pained smile. A neat cut ran down my left arm from my elbow to my wrist, blood dripping from the blade I still clasped between my fingers. "I suggest we don't hang around. The cut's deep, but it won't take long to heal." I took Jared's good arm and pulled him along the passageway, ignoring the look on his face – which was somewhere between concern and disgust.

"Give me the knife, Shae," he growled. I gave it to him without argument because I thought he might actually wrestle me to the ground to take it from me if I didn't. "What the hell were you thinking?"

"I was thinking we were going to spend the rest of our days groping around this bloody labyrinth. Oh, don't look at me like that." I held my arm out in front of me, blood drips tickling my skin. "It's not like I make a habit of cutting myself just to become a human chemstick."

"I'm glad to hear it. I just... You think it's easy for me?" he asked, and I stopped to look at him, momentarily confused. "I love you…" Guilt stabbed my chest like a new knife wound. "But since we met, you've been stabbed, beaten, blown up and shot. Do you think it's easy for me to watch you go through that and not be able to do anything? To be completely helpless? I know you heal, but I see the pain on you face, in your eyes, before you do. It kills me every time."

"I'm sorry, I didn't think…"

He seemed to compose himself. "You know what? I'm the one who should be sorry. I shouldn't have said anything – you've made it quite clear you're none of my business."

"That's unfair! You know why I can't…" The tingling in my arm diminished and the blue shimmer began to fade. "Hurry," I said walking faster, glad of the distraction.

As the last of the light disappeared, I saw the entrance to the alcove maybe ten metres ahead. Jared took my hand, intertwining his fingers with mine, and it felt comfortable even after everything that had just been said.

Thrown into total darkness again, Jared stumbled and swore loudly. I couldn't help laughing. "You sure you don't want to give me that knife back?" I said.

"Don't even joke about it," he replied sternly.

It seemed to take us forever to go those last few metres and my eyes ached from trying to spot any point of reference through the blackness. I was so happy when we made it to the alcove, I completely forgot about King Sebastian and tripped over him, landing heavily on the floor. I don't know whose groan was louder, mine or his.

"I'm okay, just winded. At least we know the King's still alive. Ouch!" I added as Jared walked into me in the darkness.

"Sorry," he replied kneeling.

"Stop fidgeting and hold still," I said, taking the opportunity of our closeness to fix his arm. A couple of minutes later I heard him scratching around the floor. "What are you doing?"

"Earlier, while you were unconscious, that big bastard threw a kit bag against the wall over here and I'm sure… got it!" I heard fastenings open, then the crack of a chemstick, and in the luminous pink light I watched him rummage through the bag before pulling out a water bottle. I hadn't realised how thirsty I was until that first drop hit my throat. I gulped down a few mouthfuls before he stopped me. "Easy. We don't know how long we're going to be trapped down here."

I wiped my mouth and passed the bottle back. He took a couple of small sips and replaced the lid before delving back into the bag. "Now that's more like it," he said, setting a top-of-the-range Glow-Xtreme lantern on the floor. "For the Xtreme adventurer in you," Jared continued, mimicking the advert they played constantly on the Data-Net. A blazing white light lit up the alcove, and the boyish grin on his face made me smile.

Sebastian shifted position on the floor and groaned again, so I shuffled over to assess the damage.

"I really don't like the look of this," I said, feeling bones move that shouldn't. I glanced at Jared, who'd found a second kit bag. "It's pretty bad. I'm going to fix him – not sure he's going to make it otherwise."

"The last thing you need is for a member of the Tetrarchy to know what you can do," Jared said. "I'm just stating a fact, not suggesting you shouldn't heal him to keep your secret."

"I know, but I can heal him like I did with Harrison. Just enough to get him out of danger, but not enough that he realises what I've done."

While Jared catalogued our resources, I concentrated on mending Sebastian. When his eyes flickered, and he started to come around, I removed my hands from his chest and sat back. It took a few minutes for his eyes to focus and comprehension to sink in, and when he tried to sit, I leant forward to help him.

"Urgh, what happened?" he groaned, holding his head, but after looking around the alcove, his eyes widened and his hand dropped. "Where's Phina? Where's my daughter?" He looked desperately between Jared and me before trying to stand. I put my hand on his shoulder and added sufficient weight to sit him back on the ground.

Jared explained everything that'd happened. "So, we know Prince Frederick is safe, and we can only hope Princess Josephina was protected by the rock lift shaft," he concluded.

"But you don't know for definite?" The King's demeanour fluctuated between desperate and angry.

"No, there's no way to tell for certain," I confirmed.

"The lights and power were taken out by the explosion," Jared continued. "We only just managed to find our way back here. When was the last time you both ate?"

"I'm not hungry," I replied.

"Me neither. I just want to get the hell out of here and find my daughter," added Sebastian.

"I understand, but we need to keep our strength up. Here." He passed over high-energy protein bars he'd found in the packs.

"Oh, that's disgusting," I grumbled, after taking a bite.

"You're not kidding," said Sebastian as he forced himself to swallow. "They should come with a health warning."

"Now we've got light," Jared said, "I suggest we head back towards the lift and see what damage the explosion's done. It might give us an idea how long we going to be stuck down here."

Sebastian and I agreed, so after we'd eaten, we headed out of the alcove, making it halfway along the final passageway before facing a wall of fallen rock and debris.

"Damn it! That's not good," said Jared, summing up exactly what I was thinking. "I think we're going to be here some time." We turned around and walked back towards the alcove in miserable silence, but about halfway there, Sebastian peeled off to the side, indicating for us to follow.

"There's a communications panel down this tunnel," he explained, and a flicker of hope skittered through my brain. "No, no, no!" he shouted a moment later, kicking the wall. "It's totally dead."

"Let me take a look," Jared offered, stepping forward. He removed the shattered screen before rummaging through some wiring, pulling out the primary energy core. The normally white crystal was cracked with thick black lines running through it like spider's legs. "It's trashed," he said, and my flicker of hope died. "Looks like the explosion caused a power surge. Are there anymore stations?"

"Two," Sebastian said, his words resuscitating my hope, but two more broken energy cores later, we had to accept defeat and headed back to the alcove, disappointed and deflated.

"I'm sure Jake and Ash are on the case," said Jared as I settled myself on the floor. I appreciated his optimism.

Jared and Sebastian went through the resources and rations from the two kit bags, discussing how long we could last – worst case scenario. I rested my head against the wall and closed my eyes, only mildly aware of their chatter. Once I'd accepted there wasn't anything we could do to get out of the Catacombs, my brain stopped thinking of escape and moved onto other things that were equally important, at least they were to me.

I let my mind wander back to the moment Vanze had opened the wooden box, remembering the inexplicable vibrations in my chest, the warm, tingly feeling that swirled in my stomach, and the way it had all come to an abrupt stop the moment he'd closed the box. I pictured the cube in such detail, it was as if I was holding it right there in front of me.

Questions swam in my head. What was the Helyan cube? Why was it so important to the Khans? Why was

Sebastian willing to sacrifice us all to keep it a secret? And most importantly, why did it affect me physically?

The last thing I wanted to do was anger the King while we were stuck in such a confined space, but I needed answers. I'd practiced several sentences in my head, but none seemed adequate, so I was both surprised and pleased when Sebastian asked, "Did... did the Khans find what they were looking for?" His words were cryptic and reluctant, and he must've known that by asking the question, he was admitting to the existence of the mysterious object.

"The Helyan cube?" I clarified, almost mischievously, but I caught the flash of anger in the King's eyes. "Yes, they found it, but—"

"But what?" he demanded so intensely I was momentarily speechless.

"The good news is they didn't get away with it," Jared explained, stepping in. "Shae knocked it from Vanze's grip just before the explosion." The dark clouds in the King's eyes lifted and his lips broke into a relieved smile. He relaxed against the crate. "The bad news is it's now buried under tons of rock."

Sebastian's smile slipped. "But the Khans didn't get it? The cube is still here? In the Catacombs?" His words were deliberate.

"They didn't get it," I said. "It's still here... if it wasn't destroyed in the explosion."

"It wasn't" He seemed sure. "Thank God."

"About the cube—" I started.

"The Helyan cube does not exist," Sebastian interrupted, his fierce resolution taking me by surprise. "Do you understand?" He looked between Jared and me, nailing each of us with a long, hard stare. "As far as you're concerned, you've never heard of the cube, let alone seen it. You're not to tell anyone – hell, you're not to talk to me or each other about it. I want you to forget everything to do with the cube right now. Do you understand?"

"But..." I stammered. Was he kidding me? There was no way I was going to forget about it.

"Am I making myself clear, Shae? The-cube-does-not-exist." He stressed every word. "I can't stress how important my order is. And it is an order," he added ominously. I nodded my understanding, more out of shock than anything. He turned towards Jared.

"Of course, Your Majesty," Jared agreed, but a deep groove had settled between his eyebrows.

"Good. Then that will be the end of it." Sebastian winced and rubbed his ribs.

"You should rest," Jared suggested. "You took quite a beating."

"Don't I know it. Perhaps you're right though, wake me if anything changes." The King carefully lowered himself to the floor, using one of the folded kitbags as a pillow, and it wasn't long before his breathing changed to a slow, steady rhythm.

Jared went through the supplies again, and I was sure it was simply to give him something to do. After he'd lined everything up and re-ordered it for the fourth time he got up and paced the small alcove. "I'm going to take one of the lanterns and explore the caves, see if there's something we've missed," he said eventually.

"I'll come with you," I replied, starting to stand.

"No, stay with the King. Besides, you should try and sleep too. You look exhausted. How many people have you healed today?"

"Lost count," I replied truthfully. "Be careful. Oh, and don't get lost," I added as he left the alcove.

I settled onto the cold floor, wrapping my arms tightly around my body for warmth and comfort. The ground was stony and uneven and I kept shifting position to try and get comfortable, but when I finally did sleep, it was fitful and restless.

At one point I woke and realised I wasn't shivering. When I opened my eyes, I found that a thick, dusty tarpaulin had been draped over me, and the blazing white intensity of the lantern had been turned down to a warm glow. Jared lay on his back, close enough that I could touch him, and I felt better knowing he was there. I let my eyes close and slept deeply.

"Hey, welcome back, sleepyhead," Jared said the next time I opened my eyes.

I pulled back the tarp and stretched. My blood-soaked dress had dried and was crispy and rough against my skin. "What time is it?" I asked.

"Late afternoon," replied Sebastian.

"I take it you didn't have any joy on your walkabout last night?" I asked Jared as my stomach rumbled loudly.

"No," he said flatly, holding out another high-energy protein bar. "Eat." I pulled a face. "Eat," he repeated, peeling back the wrapper and forcing it at me again. "I know it tastes like crap, but you need it." I took it and forced myself to take a bite, chewing it for a long while before finally plucking up the courage to swallow.

"God-damn it," Sebastian bellowed so suddenly I almost choked. "My son's injured, my daughter's been taken hostage, the Third Seal's been stolen, and I'm stuck down here unable to do a god-damn thing!"

The frustration etched on the King's face bubbled up inside me as I got a hit through the temporary Link we shared since I'd healed him. He paced angrily.

"I apologise," he said after he'd calmed. "I just feel so helpless, and in my line of work, that doesn't happen often."

The hours passed slowly, but we tried to kill time by discussing the Khans and the mysterious 'Outsider', contemplating exactly what they planned to do with the Third Seal.

No one mentioned the Helyan cube.

Jared disappeared for a while to try and fix one of the communications stations, but he came back a while later looking beaten. He passed the lantern to Sebastian, who went off to check out the carnage caused by the explosion and assess the damage it had done to the artefacts stored in the vaults.

Later that evening, we were deep in discussion about who the Outsider could be, when a deafening explosion rocked through the Catacombs, shaking the ground violently. Moments later a warm breeze blew fine dust particles into the alcove. I grabbed up a lantern and sprinted down the passageway, closely followed by Sebastian and Jared, only slowing when the dust in the air thickened and I had trouble breathing.

Beams of light flicked through the gloom, but I couldn't tell who was approaching until Ash yelled, "Shae? Jared? Can anybody hear me?"

"Over here," Jared shouted back, the torch beams turning towards us in unison. Ash and Jake appeared through the dust.

"Is everyone okay?" Ash asked, visually inspecting each of us.

"Your Majesty," Sergeant Mollere added, stopping beside them. "You need to come with us, Sire."

Sebastian ignored him. "Colonel Mitchell, did you get the Khans? Tell me you have my daughter."

"I'm sorry, Your Highness. We had the Khans pinned down as soon as they came out of the lift, but they used Princess Josephine as a shield."

"Are you telling me she's gone?"

"Yes, Sire."

Even through the grey fog I saw the fire burning in Sebastian's eyes.

"I want to see everyone in my office in thirty minutes for a full debrief," he roared. "I want to know everything that happened: how the Khans took control of the Palace, how they managed to get away, and what you're going to do to get my daughter and the Third Seal back."

Any trace of the frustration and weakness he'd shown us in the alcove disappeared. Sebastian the distraught father was gone – King Sebastian the Third, ruler of Sector Three, was back in control. The change was palpable.

Mollere directed the King back towards the lift shaft and the rest of our rescuers followed. Jared coughed, clearing his throat of the cloying debris that still hung in the air.

"You okay?" Jake asked, handing him a bottle of water.

"Yeah." He coughed again, then smiled. "I appreciate the concern though. Didn't know you cared."

"Yeah, well... don't let it go to your head. What about you?" Jake asked, gently touching my cheek.

"About to choke to death. Can we get out of here?"

"Sure, follow me," he replied, taking my hand.

The King's office was already full by the time we got there. Sebastian, Prince Frederick and Mollere were gathered around the King's desk, while Francis, Kaiser, Connor and Ty stood together by the bookcase at the opposite end of the room.

"Before we get started, let me make one thing clear: whatever is said here is classified Alpha-Secure, top secret," Sebastian ordered. "Let's start from the beginning. Just how in the name of holy hell did the Khans take control of my Palace, Mollere?"

"From what we've ascertained so far, the Khans' pilot gave Flight Control a pre-authorised ident code," Mollere explained. "Further investigation has shown that prior to the party, our records were hacked and altered to show the Khans as legitimate guest, although the family name listed was Greystoke." Jake snorted. "What?"

"The irony." Jake paused. "Come on... Greystoke... Captain Horatio Greystoke – the most notorious thief in history!"

Mollere grunted as he got the connection. "The point is..." he said deliberately, "someone knew enough about our security procedures and systems to be able to get in and alter information. And believe me, that's not easy."

"An inside job?" Ash asked. Mollere bristled.

"It's impossible to say at this point. The Khans' men did a number on the entire data-network. It's going to take time to find out exactly what was done, when, and by whom. It could've been done locally, or it could've been an external hack, we just don't know at the moment. But I promise we will find out."

"Okay, so the Khans landed. They still shouldn't have been able to take the Palace?" Sebastian argued.

"It wasn't just the party guest-list that had been hacked, Your Majesty," Mollere confirmed. "As soon as the Khans landed, they crippled our security cameras and coms-channels. Within minutes, their men had locked down the palace, overrun most of the patrolling guards, and simultaneously taken Security Operations and the Great Hall. It was an extremely planned and well executed attack."

"So, what went wrong? For them I mean," asked the King.

"It's common knowledge you hold a post-Tetrad Summit party, Sire, but it wasn't common knowledge that it was going to include the ceremonial giving of the Order of Royal Battle," explained Mollere.

"It seems the only thing they hadn't counted on was us," Jake added. "Oh, and the fact that the *Nakomo* is falling to pieces."

"Hey," I grumbled, but Jake smiled.

"All I meant was, if you'd been on time, we would've been in the Hall when it was taken. Thanks to your delay, we were free to mount a counteroffensive."

After that, each of us went through our own version of events, and I listened with interest as Jake explained what had happened during the hours we'd been stuck in the

Catacombs. I let Jared tell our story, include what we'd found out about the Outsider, but he didn't mention the Helyan Cube.

Ash picked up from the point the Khans got out of the lift in the Research Laboratory. "Vanze was incandescent with rage," he said. Jared and I shared a furtive glance. "I thought it was because they'd heard about Vita, but they seemed genuinely surprised to see us."

"Do you know why he was so mad?" Sebastian asked casually.

"Not really. He said something like, 'I had it. I held it in my hands,' but we've no idea what he meant. We thought you might?"

"Actually, I think I do," replied the King, and my eyes shot to his face, trying to read his expression. "They were looking for an old painting, one they claim belonged to their family many generations ago. In reality, it was stolen from Earth and belongs here as part of the People's Legacy. They've wanted it back for a while now, but we've consistently denied their right to ownership." I couldn't believe how easily the lie left his lips. He sounded flawless. "The painting is irrelevant though. What I really want to know is why the Khans aren't in custody and the Princess safe and unharmed." An ominous tone had crept into his voice.

"That was my call," said Jake. "I take full responsibility. Whatever had made Vanze so mad was nothing compared to what happened after they found out about their sister. Blain was like a wild animal, and he wanted to kill the Princess there and then in retribution. Vanze was against it, but for a moment I wasn't sure whether even he would be able to control Blain."

"But he did?" asked the King. A brief flash of pain surfaced on his face, but it disappeared quickly.

"Yes," confirmed Jake. "But the situation was volatile, and I believe that if Vanze felt they had no chance of escape, he would've let Blain kill the Princess as a last act of revenge. She was being used as a shield, there was no way we could've taken both brothers out without risking the Princess' life. By letting them leave, there's now a chance we can get her and the Third Seal back."

"I see." The King sighed deeply, rubbing his ribs gingerly. "The father in me is grateful your decision was based on the welfare of the Princess... but as King, I cannot stress how much better it would've been for the Sector if you'd stopped the Khans and retrieved the Seal... regardless of the consequences. What happened next?"

"The plan was to let them leave, let them think they got away, then follow their ship's wake-trail in one of the *Defender's* Warriors," Jake explained. "Worked fine to begin with, but they must've realised we were pursuing because the Warrior was hit by some kind of altered teslax pulse that knocked out their sensors. When they got them back on-line, the Khans' signal had fractured into multiple trails and it was impossible for the pilot to know which one to follow. Commander Tel'an immediately dispatched a squadron of Hellfires to follow as many of the cloned wake-trails as possible, but the ship was long gone."

The room fell silent as the King digested Jake's words. His face was blank, his eyes unemotional, and it was impossible to read how he was going to react.

"Do you think my daughter is still alive?" he said eventually, the question posed to anyone who was brave enough to answer.

"It's impossible to say," said Ash. The King flinched. "We can't give you that guarantee, especially now they know what happened to Vita, but we will do everything we can to get her back."

"I appreciate your honesty, Brother Asher." Sebastian sighed, and then he sat up straighter in his chair, squared his shoulders, and cleared his throat. Even his face took on a hard resolution – his eyes clear and focussed, his lips set in a determined straight line. "Okay. The fact is, the Princess is not all the Khans have taken. They also have the Third Seal. And let me be totally clear: if news of its theft leaks out, the political ramifications would be disastrous for Sector Three. The fallout would be catastrophic. Without a stable ruling power, it will be impossible to maintain proper order without turning to the Military, and we all know how that ends." He looked purposely from Jared to Jake. "As Captain of the *Defender*, I'm putting Marcos in charge of Operation Fallen Star." Jake's nose wrinkled. "But I expect the full cooperation from all arms of the Military, and I hope the Brotherhood as well?"

Ash nodded. "Of course."

"To everyone, and I mean everyone outside of these four walls, your mission, Captain, is to find and return Princess Josephina. However, the true priority of Fallen Star is to retrieve the Third Seal," Sebastian ordered, holding up a hand to silence objections from the Prince.

"Understood," replied Jared.

"Good." The King turned his attention to the rest of the room. "I remind you all that what we've discussed is Alpha-Secure, and from now on, any reference to Operation Fallen Star must be restricted to the retrieval of the Princess only. Dismissed." As the collective group headed for the door, the King added, "Captain Marcos, I'd like to stay for a moment. Colonel Mitchell, Brother Asher, and you too, Shae."

Francis shared the same interested look as the Wolfpack, but they left the King's Office without word.

"Officially, as far as all formal channels are concerned, Captain Marcos is in charge of the operation," Sebastian said. "Unofficially, I'm putting your Guardian unit in command. I appreciate you haven't been legitimately assembled, and you've been given no terms of reference for your responsibilities... or credentials of jurisdiction for that matter... but I'm sure you'll muddle through. If there's ever any doubt about your authority, remember you report directly to the Tetrarchy of Souls, and we outrank... well, everyone." I couldn't help but smile at his flippancy. "Colonel, you said you lost the Khans, what? A little over twenty-four hours ago?"

"That's correct."

"So where do we start?"

"Most of the Khans' men were killed during the re-taking of the Palace, but the Guard managed to detain a few – eight, I believe. Two of my men have been interrogating them and it seems they were recruited from multiple locations throughout the Sector: Angel Ridge, Merron, Santorra, a couple of the GalaxyBases. Most of them wouldn't say any more than that, but Kaiser broke one of them."

"Do I want to know how?" asked Sebastian.

"No, probably not," replied Jake, the hint of a smile tugging at the corner of his mouth. "The guy told Kaiser they were taken to a compound on a Category Three planet, a rock world, but he has no idea where it is. They trained constantly for months to ensure everyone knew what they were doing as part of the assault. That means whoever this Outsider person is, he's extremely well-funded... and very connected."

"What do you mean connected?"

"The Khans knew the complete layout of the Palace and grounds in advance. They had access to your security protocols, and information on how to bypass your system firewalls – they had to have been given that information from somebody. Oh, and they also had access to restricted Marine-issue Seekers. So far, that's all Kaiser's got from the man, but with your permission I'd like to take all eight prisoners with us so we can keep interrogating them. No disrespect to Sergeant Mollere and his people, but my men are much more experienced in this area."

"Of course," agreed the King.

"Also, my tech specialist has been combing through your computer systems," continued Jake. "He hasn't been able to tell where the hack came from, but he's looked at the hardware they used to knock out our communications and reviewed the data from the Warrior that was hit by the Teslax pulse. The equipment is high-end – rare, specialist and expensive. Ty says there are only a few people outside of the REF who have the capability of putting something like that together. We've got a few leads to follow."

"Commander Tel'an has compiled the names of the Khans' known allies," Ash said, more to Jared than Sebastian. "It's quite the list of who's who amongst the Sector's delinquents, but it's a start."

Jared stood and paced behind the sofa, his forehead creased, and his hands rested on his hips.

"Say what's on your mind, Captain? This isn't the time to hold back," Sebastian said.

Jared hesitated for a moment then nodded. "The Khan Brothers have many allies, using bribery and brute force to ensure their total support and compliance. They have multiple hide-outs and are constantly on the move, never staying in one place for more than a few days at a time."

"Your point?"

"My point is, there's a reason we haven't caught them before. I just wanted to make it clear that this is not going to happen quickly. We won't stop until we've got the Third Seal... and the Princess back, but it's not going to happen overnight."

"I understand," said the King. "Unless word leaks out, there's no reason for the public to know the Seal is missing. That gives you time... up to fourteen days anyway."

"Why fourteen days?" I asked.

"That's when the next Sector Senate meeting occurs. The Third Seal is displayed as part of the proceedings. If it's not there... well, you get the picture."

"Okay, we have two weeks to locate people neither the

REF nor the Brotherhood have been able to catch in decades," Jake said. "No pressure then."

Sebastian rose from his desk and paced towards the window, where he watched the King's Guard continue to clear the mess left by the Khans' men.

"What's your plan, Captain?" he asked, his breath fogging the glass.

"From what Colonel Mitchell's said, I think we've done everything we can here," replied Jared. "I suggest we leave Sergeant Mollere and the King's Guard to deal with the aftermath of the attack while we head out and start chasing down leads before they go cold."

"Agreed," replied the King, turning back to face us. "Dismissed."

11

The deep, throaty roar of the Warrior's engines vibrated through my bones and I had to concentrate to hear what Ash was yelling to Jared. "Captain, we'll take the *Nakomo* back to the *Defender* and brief our Primus on the way. I'm positive he will commit the full resources of the Brotherhood to finding the Princess."

"I hope so," replied Jared, his eyes sparkling in the light from Decerra's waning moon. He rubbed his chin. "Jake, you said you wanted to keep hold of the remaining hostiles?"

"Yeah, I do. Kaiser?" Jake deferred to his second in command.

"The Khans' men are well trained, and most of the fuckers are resisting our questioning, but there's definitely more info to get. I just need to find the right… motivation," Kaiser replied, grinning.

"Okay. Jake, why don't you and the guys round them up and take them to the *Defender* in the *Veritas*? I'll get Tel'an to prepare the brig and put a security detail at your disposal. I'm assuming you'll need to brief your CO?"

"Already informed Brigadier Venning about the

kidnapping, but I'll need to update him on Operation Fallen Star. After that... we're all yours." The last words stuck in Jake's throat and he forced them out one at a time. He folded his arms tightly across his chest.

"Good," Jared replied. I caught a hint of a wry smile tug at his lips and I'm sure he relished the upper hand he had over Jake, even if it was just an illusion given by the King to keep the Guardians a secret.

"What about you?" Jake asked. "I guess you'll be catching a lift in the *Nakomo* with Shae while we're doing all the grunt-work?" It was clear his words were heavily loaded, but I wasn't exactly sure what he was intimating.

"Actually," Jared replied after a brief glance in my direction, "I'll be taking the Warrior back to the *Defender*."

Jake's eyes narrowed, a groove settling between his eyebrows as he looked between the two of us. "Whatever. You're in charge," he said sarcastically.

"Let's meet at ten-hundred," Jared suggested, looking at his com-pad, either oblivious to, or ignoring, Jake's tone. "That'll give everyone the opportunity to check in with superiors, grab a beat, and... take a shower." He looked purposely at Jake.

Ash placed his hand on my elbow to indicate we should leave, but I'd only taken a few steps when Jake grabbed my other arm, spun me around, and pulled me into a hug.

"I'm glad you're okay," he whispered, his breath tickling my skin and covering my body in goose bumps. "I didn't get the chance to tell you that before," he continued after letting me go. I had no idea what to say, but it didn't matter – he was already jogging to catch up with the others. Just before he reached them, he stopped and turned. "We still need to talk," he called back, his lips breaking into a wide smile. "God I've missed you, Babe."

Jake disappeared through an archway while I stood rooted to the spot, my mind in sudden panic. How on Lilania was I going to tell him about Jared?

I'd always held a bit of a romantic notion about love. Boy meets girl, they fall deeply in love, and life is happy-ever-after. Having been brought up by a bunch of celibate men, my education on the topic was generally confined to clichéd romantic novels and bad Data-Net soapellas, where the bad-guy always got their comeuppance, and the good-guy always got the sexy, but morally respectable girl.

Reality, I decided, was crap in comparison.

But then I'd never really entertained the thought that I would ever be in a position to fall in love. My whole life had been spent at the monastery, and I'd never thought of that changing. I certainly hadn't pictured myself as the 'girl' in the 'boy-meets-girl' equation.

I jumped when Ash put his arm around my shoulder. "Come on," he said in that soothing voice he adopts when I need cheering up. It's usually followed by a lengthy heart-to-heart and the biggest tub of Carmichael's Chocomel ice-cream we can get our hands on. I didn't see that happening though.

The trip to the *Defender* was so smooth and quick, we were still briefing Primus Noah as Francis powered down the engines.

"I understand," said Noah after Ash finished briefing him about the Operation Fallen Star. He didn't mention the Third Seal. "It must've been an exceptionally difficult situation," Noah continued. "It goes without saying that I'm delighted all three of you are safe. My prayers are with King Sebastian, and obviously the Brotherhood will offer its full support and resources to locating and retrieving Princess Josephina. I'll get things started from our end immediately."

"We have a meeting with Captain Marcos and the rest of the task force at ten-hundred," explained Ash. "I should be able to let you know what the REF mission plan is after that."

"Good. Keep me informed." Noah sighed deeply and

rubbed his eyes vigorously. "Ash, before you go, I'd like to speak to you in private."

Francis and I shared the same intrigued expression, but then he stood and said, "We'll unload the Ready Bags and meet you in the hangar." I only moved when Ash raised an eyebrow at me and nodded his head towards the exit.

"What do you think that was all about?" I asked Francis as I pulled a faded bag out of my locker.

"No idea," he replied.

A glint of bronze caught my eye and I stuck my hand back into the locker to retrieve my necklace. I held the brushed-bronze object in the palm of my hand, tracing the delicate swirling symbols with my fingertip. My thoughts instantly shifted back to the Catacombs, and to the Helyan cube which bore the same mysterious markings – the markings the Brotherhood and I had never found any reference to in any library or data repository anywhere.

"Everything okay?" Francis asked.

"Sure. Why do you ask?"

"You looked… you zoned out for a moment."

"I was just wondering what Noah wanted with Ash," I lied, unable to look at him. I tucked the chain into my bag and added my com-pad, earpiece and weapons. "Francis?" I chose my words carefully. "If you knew something… something that didn't make sense… and you really, really wanted to talk to someone about it but had been… forbidden…"

I knew I shouldn't have said anything as soon as the words left my lips, but it was too late, I couldn't stuff them back in. Francis stopped what he was doing mid action and stared at me, his mouth open slightly, his eyes narrow. He studied my face and I looked at my feet to avoid giving anything else away, but he took my chin gently in his hand and forced my head up so he had eye contact.

"What's happened, Shae?"

"It's nothing," I replied casually. "Just ignore me." I

took a step backwards and he dropped his hand.

"Shae?" That one word really meant, I know you're not telling me everything.

"Honestly, it's really nothing. Forget I said anything. You know a lack of food and sleep gives me jelly-brain."

"Don't I know it." He gave me a brief half-smile. "But you're right, I do know you. And I know you wouldn't say something like that unless—"

"Hey," said Ash as he appeared in the rear cabin, oblivious to the conversation he'd interrupted. "What's up?" he added looking between us.

"Nothing," I replied. "Just chatting." I raised an eyebrow at Francis, almost begging him not to contradict me. I hated putting him in that position, but the King, and my big mouth, had given me no other choice.

"Just chatting," Francis repeated, but I noticed the slightest edge to his voice and hoped Ash hadn't.

"So… what's going on with our new Primus," I asked, keen to change the subject.

Ash's face became serious and he crossed and uncrossed his arms, looking uncomfortable. Eventually he propped himself against a bulkhead, as if using it for mental support as well as physical.

"There's no other way to say this other than to just spit it out," he said. "The Primus wants Francis to take the *Nakomo* back to the monastery and—"

"What?" Francis interrupted. "Why? I don't understand."

"He wants you to supervise the Brotherhood's part in Operation Fallen Star," Ash explained, putting his hand on Francis's shoulder. "He's chosen you to coordinate the activities of all our people in Sector Three. You'll be in charge of the lot. It's a great responsibility, and a great honour."

"I know it is." Francis sighed heavily. "But what about Benjamin? Or even Andre? They're both capable."

"But they're not as good as you," I said before realising I should've kept my mouth shut.

"Shae's right," said Ash. "Francis, you know how much we want you here, but the Primus thinks you're the best person to represent the Brotherhood, and, well, I have to agree with his decision." Francis's head lowered. "Hey, cheer up." Ash's sudden change in demeanour made Francis look up again. "You might even make Ninth Degree... if you don't screw it up!" His face broke into a wide, lopsided grin and he started laughing. After a second, Francis's shoulders loosened, and he joined in.

Although he wasn't happy about leaving, after he'd thought about it rationally, Francis agreed that Operation Fallen Star's Brotherhood liaison was a worthy task.

Once I'd fixed up the injuries Ash sustained from his fight in Security Operations, we grabbed our bags and headed down the ramp into the hangar. We stayed there watching the *Nakomo* until Francis disappeared star-side.

"There's something you should know," Ash said quietly. "Noah knows about us, about the Guardians. The Supreme Primus briefed him on our status the moment he made him Primus."

"I guess that's logical," I replied. "He'll be the one covering for us when we get called on a mission. And on that subject, I feel super bad keeping this from Francis. He already suspects something's up."

"Don't worry about Francis. Turns out the Supreme Primus agrees with you. Isaiah's authorised Noah to brief Francis when he returns to Lilania. Things might change once the Tetrarchy decides how they're going to run the Guardian programme, but for now, you, me, Isaiah, Noah and Francis are the only ones who know. Within the Brotherhood, that is."

I looked around the empty hangar and frowned. "Do you think they're sending an escort?" I asked. Ash shrugged before heading towards a set of doors. They didn't open.

"What do you think?" I said, pointing to the ident pad.

"Only one way to find out," he replied, pressing his thumb on the sensor. The doors immediately whooshed open

"Welcome to the *Defender*, Brother Asher," said Grace. "We hope you enjoy your stay."

"Perhaps Jared's got fed up with giving us the VIP treatment," I suggested as we headed for the lift. Not that it mattered, all I wanted to do was to get to my quarters and get out of what was left of my blood-crisp dress.

I fastened my utility belt over clean cargo trousers, and holstered my Sentinel and Cal'ret, jiggling them slightly to get them into a comfortable position. I was just putting in my earpiece when a buzzer announced someone at the door.

"Open," I said, planting myself on one of the couches so I could put on my boots.

"Hey, Babe," said Jake. He stood on the threshold, muscular arms folded across a broad chest, an easy smile on his lips. He took a step forward then stopped, as if waiting for me to say something. But what could I say? I felt so bad it hurt in my guts. How was I going to tell a man I cared deeply for that I was in love with someone else?

I was a horrible person. I knew it. I was weak, and he deserved better – they both did.

"Hey, Jake," I said pathetically, paying more attention than was needed to tie my bootlaces.

"Shae?" His voice was unusually gentle, and I looked up into his pale, tired face, wondering if he'd slept at all since the Khans' attack. He dropped to his knees in front of me, and I hated myself even more as my body reacted to his closeness. A small flickering of heat started to glow inside me before ice-cold guilt extinguished it. He placed a hand on my knee, but I jumped up as if he'd touched me with a white-hot poker, moving quickly behind the couch, using it as a barrier.

When I'd slept with Jake, I'd known I wasn't in love with him, not in a boy-meets-girl, happy-ever-after, relationship kind of way. But as I was about to hurt him, I knew for certain that I loved him like a best friend. The kind of friend you cared deeply about – the kind you'd give your life for. He was one of the most important people in my life, and I was about to destroy everything we had between us. For what? It wasn't as if Jared and I were even together.

I was broken.

There was something very wrong with me, and for a second, I wondered if I could ever be fixed... or whether I even deserved to be fixed.

"I know what you're going through, Shae," Jake said.

My stomach flipped, and a wave of nausea made me light-headed. "You do?" I stammered. Had Jared said something? Had Ash?

"I know what Finnian meant to you, and I know you must be going through hell right now," he said gently. The tight knot in my chest loosened. "Just because I'm supposed to be some hard-arsed Spec Ops Marine, doesn't mean I can't identify with the pain of losing someone. Someone you love. You've got a lot going on, I just... I just want you to know I'm here for you if you want to talk. No pressure."

The self-hatred and guilt gave way to pain and heartache. Tears flowed, and I didn't back away when Jake wrapped his arms around me. He held me close, making 'shushing' noises, while I snuffled and shook, and when I'd composed myself, he let me go. I took a step back, wiping my eyes and nose with my sleeve.

"Oh, now that's attractive," he joked. I managed a weak smile. "I know I said we needed to talk, but it can wait... until you're ready."

Jake was a man of action, impulsive and instinctive, and

that's part of what drew me to him in the first place, but this was a side I hadn't seen before. He was so kind, so thoughtful. I couldn't stand keeping the truth from him any longer, even if it meant he'd never talk to me again. I took a deep breath and looked him straight in the eyes.

"Jake, I—" The door buzzer interrupted my sentence, but I ignored it. "I have to tell you—" The buzzer was relentless, followed by heavy thudding. "Open," I said reluctantly.

If Ash was surprised to see Jake, he didn't show it. "You need a moment to finish getting ready?" he asked, and I knew it was a tactful way of saying he'd noticed my red eyes and blotchy face.

"Thanks. I'll be ready in five."

Conner and Ty were finishing breakfast when we arrived at the Mess Hall. They stayed and had a quick coffee with us before heading off to install some new gizmo on the *Veritas*, which Ty hoped would protect the sensors from a teslax pulse.

Kaiser arrived just after, and Jared appeared moments after that. Jake raised an inquisitive eyebrow when Jared chose to sit next to Kaiser, even though there was a space on the bench next to me. He shot me a quizzical glance, but I ignored it, choosing instead to engage in Kaiser's speculations over where the Khans got hold of the Seeker weapons.

When we'd finished eating, Kaiser went to resume his interrogation of the prisoners, and the rest of us headed to our first official Operation Fallen Star briefing. I thought we were going to our usual conference room on Level Two, but as the lift doors closed, Jared said, "Bridge please, Grace."

I was surprised and excited. The Bridges on warships were strictly off-limits to even non-essential personnel, and it was almost unheard of for visitors to have access. From what I'd seen of the rest of the *Defender*, I expected something pretty damn special, and anticipation fluttered in my chest.

I held my breath as the lift pinged to tell us we'd arrived. I expected the door to open and for us to step straight into the busy operational hub of the ship, so I deflated when we were confronted by a plain, softly lit hallway. A med-tech lazed against the wall looking bored until he saw Jared, and then he immediately stood to attention.

"Wait," Jared said suddenly, holding his arm out across my chest to prevent me taking another step. His unexpected movement made me jump and I stopped so abruptly Jake walked into me. But when he slipped his arm around my waist and whispered, "Sorry, Babe," in my ear, I was certain he'd done it on purpose.

Jared coughed loudly, and Jake removed his arm, smirking.

"I didn't mean to scare you," Jared apologised. "But I had to stop you before you crossed the bio-sensor." He indicated towards a dark, glass band that ran the full circumference of the hallway, not half a metre in front of my boot. "Only authorised personnel have access to the Bridge for security reasons, and the only way to get to the Bridge is through this corridor. The sensors scan everyone for an authorised bio-tag, and if you don't have one... well, let's just say it's very, very painful." He looked at Jake, smiled, and narrowed his eyes before adding, "You could always give us a demonstration if you want."

Jake returned his smile, but it didn't reach his eyes. "I'm good thanks. I think we'll take you word for it."

Jared motioned for the med-tech to join us.

"These DNA tags are the latest thing in security. Top of the range," explained the man as he removed a small black case from the bag slung over his shoulder. "The old-style nano-tech's been replaced by some super-smart bio-engineering. The *Defender's* one of only a few ships to use it so far. Would you mind, Captain?" He passed the box to

Jared, who held it open so he could remove an injection gun and a small vial of clear yellowish liquid. My name was printed on the side in bold capital letters. "If I could have your arm please, miss?"

I hesitated.

"It's perfectly safe. Every member of the crew has one." A hint of irritation had crept into his voice.

"I'm not sure," I said, conflicted. "Ash?"

"I—"

"Pearce is right, Shae," Jared interrupted. "The biological tags are safe, I promise, and they'll degrade harmlessly within a month if not reactivated. It'll make life onboard so much easier for you."

"Really? How?" Ash asked.

"There are different types of sensors throughout the ship, you must've seen them. The most important are the security bio-sensors like this one," he pointed to the glass ring. "And based on the programming of your tag, they'll grant you entrance to certain restricted areas. There are other sensors that will unlock personal sleeping quarters, open lifts, dispense food in the Mess Hall, and even give access to workstations. No more thumb prints or waiting for one of the crew to allow you access to something. Your DNA signature will literally unlock the ship."

Ash nodded his head in agreement, so I offered my arm to the tech.

"All done," Pearce said a moment later, replacing the empty vial in the case and picking out one with Ash's name on it. "Actually, the bio-tags have many other applications," he continued to explain as he worked. "As the Captain said, they're predominantly used for security, granting crew members access to areas of the ship relevant to their work, but they can also track medical information, relaying real-time data directly to Med-Bay. The bio-tags alert us to health conditions at their early stages and send a warning if someone goes into medical distress. Very clever."

"Sounds like it," Ash agreed.

Pearce took out the remaining vial as Jake reluctantly rolled up his sleeve, but the tech chatted on, despite Jake's grumbling. "They can even act as locator beacons, so we know exactly where on the ship you are, and who's with you."

"Whoa! Hold up," said Jake, swiftly pulling his arm away. "There's no way I want you tracking where I am… or who I'm with." His comment was aimed at Jared, but I didn't miss the glance he flicked in my direction. "And where the fuck did you get my DNA from anyway?"

"Relax, Jake," said Jared, clearly irritated that something so simple had caused such drama. "We got your DNA during the last mission, after we were ambushed on the Planet of Souls. And the locater element of the tag is switched off as standard. Only a limited number of crew can activate it in emergencies: me, Commander Tel'an, Doc Anderson, and Lieutenant Commander Rodriguez, my Chief of Security." Jake's arm remained clamped to his side. "Let me put it this way: no tag – no bridge access. Simple as that," Jared stated bluntly.

Jake huffed loudly and offered his arm to the technician.

"Finally," Jared mumbled, taking a couple of steps down the hallway, but then he stopped and turned.

Ash, Jake and I stood at the threshold of the sensor ring. It was irrational, but I couldn't quell the fear that someone had programmed my tag wrong, or that my gift would somehow interfere with the sensor signal. I had images of searing pain, and lots of screaming, before falling to the floor in a particularly undignified and embarrassing heap.

"Here," Jared said, holding out his hand. "I promise you'll be fine." I reached out, took a deep breath, and stepped through the ring. When nothing happened, I puffed out a relieved sigh.

"See? Told you."

Jared's hand was warm, and his grip was both strong

and gentle at the same time. For a second, I didn't want to let him go, but Ash and Jake had followed me through the sensor and it was time to get on with things.

As we approached a set of seriously secure-looking doors, they slid open vertically, and the hallway immediately filled with the unmistakable sounds of activity.

I wasn't sure whether it was a reaction to the magnificence of the room, or because someone had just shouted, "Captain on the Bridge," and everyone had stood to immediate attention, but I couldn't help drawing in a loud gasp.

An instant hush had fallen, which made my gasp even more embarrassing, and I felt my cheeks pink. I offered an apologetic smile to Jared, who, by evidence of his own grin, seemed to think it amusing.

"As you were," Jared commanded. The crew returned to their activities.

"Impressive," said Ash, stepping around me so he could move further into the room.

"She is, isn't she?" Jared replied, pride creeping into his voice.

At first glance, the Bridge looked more in keeping with a Pleasure Liner – bright, roomy and pristine. The warm colour scheme, thick carpet, elegant smooth surfaces, and curved edges on every station, gave the impression of lazy comfort. But in contrast, the ships tactical operations were clearly state-of-the-art and more in-line with a Scorpion Class attack vessel.

"Let me give you the tour," Jared said. "At the back we've got Engineering." A few ensigns turned around and smiled politely before returning their attention to the screens against the rear wall. "To the right we've got the Science and Communications stations, and to the left are Security and Tactical." The two sets of desks sat on raised platforms, and from the Lieutenant Commander insignia, I guessed the man standing behind the Security station was

Rodriguez.

Jared ushered us down a set of four steps to a lower tier where three unobtrusive chairs with individual plexi-screens sat in a slight horseshoe. "Commander, Captain, and Officer on Watch," he explained before moving us on to the next tier, where images of our current star-system floated above holo-tables. "This is Navigation and Stellar Cartography, and finally, Flight Control on the bottom level."

In front of Flight was a large open space, and I noted the holo-projectors in the ceiling pointing to the centre, where Tel'an spoke to a waif-like female ensign.

I tried to take everything in, but there was so much it was impossible. I noticed a door to the right, which displayed a silver plaque with the words 'Stateroom of Captain Jared Marcos' engraved in large, bold script. Underneath, in smaller font, was written 'Commanding Officer', and below that was the eagle head and wings emblem of the REF Fleet Division. On the wall to the side was the *Defender's* dedication plate, polished and shining.

"This way," Jared said. I thought he would lead us to his stateroom, but instead he headed towards an identical door on the other side of the Bridge. The silver plaque was stamped 'Tactical Data Command', with the abbreviation 'TaDCom' below. I followed him through the door, trailed by Ash and Jake, and was surprised that there wasn't a room on the other side, but a set of stairs.

About halfway down, the dark glass band of another bio-sensor glinted. Although Jared continued down the steps unconcerned, I hesitated again before crossing it.

It didn't really surprise when nothing happened, but I turned around to smile at Ash anyway, as confirmation I was okay. He stepped through the sensor looking just as unconcerned as Jared, but the moment Jake passed the ring, he gasped and doubled over, groaning loudly.

12

I had no idea how the sensors worked, or how they were administering pain, but I knew I had to do something. I threw a panicked glance towards Jared, immediately furious that he hadn't moved an inch, or made any effort to come to Jake's assistance.

"Jared, do something," I begged, but he merely cocked his head to one side and rested his hands on his hips, looking irritated.

"Stop messing around, Jake," he said, clearly annoyed. I opened my mouth in disbelief, but then I felt Jake's chest rumble and heard his soft laugh.

"What the?" I let go and took a step away, stumbling on the step and only just keeping my balance. Jake straightened up, grinning like a schoolboy.

"Sorry, Babe. Couldn't resist." He casually ran his fingers through unruly hair before winking at me.

"Couldn't resist?" I shouted, part frustrated, part furious. "I thought... I can't believe... Not funny, Jake. Not funny at all." I punched him on the arm as hard as I could. He reached out to me, but I pushed his hand away. "Get the hell off me."

"Babe, come on," he called after me. "It was just a joke."

"Nice one, Jake," Jared said before following me to the bottom of the stairs. A door automatically opened, and we stepped together into another large, imposing room, the same size and dimensions as the Bridge. I guessed we were directly below. "Welcome to Tactical Data Command," Jared said when the other two arrived a few moments later.

"Okay, maybe that wasn't as funny as it was in my head… but you have to admit, it was a little bit funny," Jake said, resting his hand on my shoulder. I shrugged off his touch and nailed him with one of my best I'm still pissed at you stares. He held up his palms in surrender and mouthed, "Sorry, Babe."

"When you're quite finished," interrupted Jared, quietly agitated by the entire episode. "Under normally circumstances, TaDCom is used to gather and collate the *Defender's* internal and external sensor information. Summary reports are then sent to the TAO – that's the Tactical Action Officer – who operates the Tactical station on the Bridge." He ushered us down a set of gentle steps towards the centre of the room, clear except for an expansive operations table where a holo-screen displayed strategic data, maps and charts.

The room reminded me of a smaller version of the Summit area onboard the *Athena* – a lower area in the middle with the room sloping up on all sides towards giant screens posted around the outside walls. Various workstations sat on two tiers, circling above the central point, giving whoever stood at the operations table a clear view of every operator in the room. I counted at least five crew sat at screens, and a further eight watching displays, studying data-pads, or talking animatedly to each other.

The atmosphere was unlike its twin room above. Where the Bridge gave the impression of quiet efficiency, TaDCom had an energised, almost excited buzz to it. An air of anticipation.

Jared tapped the table and the holo-screen disappeared. "During times of war, or for the duration of large military operations and training exercises, TaDCom becomes the focal point for all tactical information relevant to the situation. Additional crew are drafted in to operate stations as required, and Lieutenant Commander Hale, the *Defender's* TAO, moves down here from the Bridge to take control. Talk of…" added Jared as a man descended one of the stairs towards us. For a person his size, he was light on his feet, taking several steps at a time.

"Captain." His voice was deep and rumbled slightly. "Colonel, Brother, err…" Hale paused, searching for the right word, finally deciding on "Ma'am." I think I managed to laugh and snort at the same time, which left me choking, unable to get my breath. Someone tapped my back as tears filled my eyes.

"You can call her Shae," Ash offered as I got my breath back. The tapping on my back turned to slow, rhythmic circles and it felt nice. Comfortable. "I'm Brother Asher," he continued, introducing himself. "Colonel Mitchell," he added, nodding in Jake's direction. Jake removed his hand from my back and offered it to Hale.

I hiccoughed loudly.

"You okay?" Hale asked, his deep chocolate-brown eyes showing concern.

"I'm fine," I replied through another cough. "Not your fault. It's been a long time since anyone called me Ma'am."

"You're lucky," said Ash. "That guy's probably still looking for his teeth." Hale's low, rumbling laugh stopped abruptly when Ash added, "I'm not joking." Then we all laughed, mainly because of the look on Hale's face.

I decided I was going to like him.

Once I'd composed myself fully, I noticed Hale studying me. He smiled, but shook his head slightly, as if trying to figure me out. Good luck with that one. He scratched at a greying temple then seemingly remembered why he was there in the first place. "Captain, I'm available to give the morning sit-rep as soon as you're ready."

"Understood. I'll let you know. Carry on," Jared replied.

"Of course, Sir." Hale excused himself.

Jared looked purposefully at Jake before continuing. "We've wasted enough time. I suggest we get on with things."

"Here?" I asked, glancing up at the other people in the room. "Don't we need to talk about…umm… secret stuff?"

Jared smiled and pointed to a mark on the floor which ringed the centre floor area, including us and the operations table. At first, I thought it was another bio-sensor, but looking closer, I recognised it as something completely different. When Jared tapped the screen on the table, the sound-shield activated, and an instant silence descended. It was weird to see people still talking outside of the barrier, but not be able to hear what they were saying.

"We're off the grid. Whatever is said within the shield is totally secure," Jared confirmed. "So this is the situation as I see it: the Princess and the Seal have been missing for approximately thirty-five hours, and we've no more than fourteen days to retrieve them."

"Thirteen now," I corrected. "The Sector Senate convenes at ten-hundred, exactly thirteen days from today."

"Okay, we have thirteen days to retrieve them," Jared amended. "We know they were both taken by the Khans, but we also know the Khans were working with someone they referred to as the Outsider. As we have no idea who this Outsider is, I suggest we focus all our efforts on the Khans, at least in the short term. If they still have the Seal, great, but if they've already offloaded it, we'll have to persuade them to tell us to whom."

"Agreed," said Ash. I added my support by way of a nod, but I noticed Jake took longer to offer his agreement.

"Jake? If you've got something to say, now's the time," Jared said.

"Nope. I'm good," he replied, but his tone was clipped.

"So, where do we stand now?" Jared continued. "Ash, I was informed by my Officer on Watch that Brother Francis departed in the *Nakomo* earlier this morning."

"That's correct. When we briefed Primus Noah on the situation, he put the full resources of the Brotherhood at your disposal and recalled Francis to act as liaison for the duration of the op."

"Good," said Jake, crossing his arms. "At least we can be confident one person knows what they're doing." He caught the look both Ash and I threw in his direction. "What I meant was, as Francis was in the thick of things at the Palace, he's fully up to speed with the situation."

"More than you realise," Ash said. "Supreme Primus Isaiah briefed Primus Noah on our status as Guardians when he was promoted. It was also Isaiah's decision to allow Noah to brief Francis. He already suspects something anyway. Plus, Francis will be an exceptional resource for us to draw on."

"That sounds logical," Jared agreed.

I didn't hear Tel'an enter TaDCom because of the sound-shield, but I felt her presence, glancing up to see her glide gracefully down the stairs. She crossed the shield, and for a second, I heard the hustle from the rest of the room.

"Perfect timing," said Jared. "As Commander Tel'an will effectively captain the *Defender* during Guardian missions, Commodore Northfield authorised me to read her in on the situation, for exactly the same reasons as Francis, no doubt."

Jake huffed loudly. "For fuck's sake! Is there anyone who doesn't know? Except the Wolfpack, that is?"

"About that," Jared said quickly, trying to defuse the situation. "When did you last speak to your CO?"

"I talked to Brigadier Venning early this morning." A

scowl settled across Jake's forehead. "Why?"

"Northfield told me that Venning's going to allow you to brief the Wolfpack."

"He is?" Jake looked momentarily surprised.

"You need to get it direct from Venning, but from what I understand, it will be your decision to make – depending on whether you trust them to keep it Alpha-Secure," Jared concluded.

I held my breath, preparing for the blast wave.

"Whether I trust them?" bellowed Jake, beyond insulted. "Whether-I-trust-them?" he repeated, spitting out each word with venom. His hands balled into fists.

"Whoa, Jake. That's not what I meant." Jared held up his palms, but he squared his shoulders and stood firm. "I'm just repeating what Northfield said. I know you trust your men... and so do I." Jake's shoulders lowered slightly, but he still bristled. "I've put my life in their hands before, and I'd do it again," Jared continued.

"We all would," I said. Then, trying to defuse the situation further, I laughed lightly and added, "Guess we're not exactly that covert anymore. I kind of liked having a secret that wasn't to do with my freaky healing abilities."

"Or the fact you can blast people across the room," Jake added. I was glad he'd calmed, but there was definitely something else simmering under the surface.

I also hadn't missed Tel'an's raised eyebrow at his comment. Although she knew about my healing talents, she didn't know that it had developed – what Ash had described as an 'evolution' of my gift.

At the time, it had been pretty damn scary. Jake and Jared were knocking ten bells of hell out of each other during our last mission, and all I wanted them to do was stop. Energy built up inside me, but instead of using it to heal like normal, the silver-blue energy wave blasted from my fingers, knocking them both of their feet and throwing them clear across the room.

On that occasion, I hadn't been in control. It had simply happened. None of us knew how, or why, and I promised Ash I'd tell him if anything like it happened again. Truth was, it had happened again — a lot — and I hadn't said a word.

The week after Finnian's death, the week I'd spent avoiding everything and everyone, I tried exhaustively to recreate the pulse. Gradually, through re-living the events of the fight, and my feelings at the time, I'd started to control the tug in the pit of my stomach and the energy radiating through my chest.

In my head, I was back on my tiny island, remembering how I'd moved small stones before eventually progressing to large rocks. I did it again and again, until calling up the pulse became natural. Admittedly I had to concentrate super hard, and the pulse wasn't nearly as powerful as the one I used on Jake and Jared, but it was a start. I remembered how—

"Shae?" Tel'an's voice pulled me back to the room. "Is everything okay?"

"Yes. Sorry, I was... never mind, it's not important," I replied.

"Captain, our Primus said to tell you that the Brotherhood will assist in whatever way it can," said Ash. "But he insists the lines of distinction between us and the REF remain clear and intact. People come to us for help because we're not the REF It's important they don't see those boundaries getting distorted."

"Of course, I completely understand. We certainly don't want to compromise the Brotherhood's position, and are glad of any support you can offer," Jared said.

Ash nodded his head in thanks before offering Jared a small data-disc. "This holds all the information your team needs to initiate secure communications with Francis."

Jake fidgeted. I couldn't put my finger on what was bugging him, but if there was one thing I'd learnt about him, it was that you'd hear about it eventually.

"Tel'an, where does Fleet stand at the moment?" asked Jared, purposely ignoring him.

Tel'an, who'd been standing at a discreet distance, took a step forward and addressed the group. "As soon as the Captain gave me notice of Operation Fallen Star, I activated TaDCom. Commander Hale has set up a team of specialists, who have been mining every REF data repository for any reference to the Khans and their known associates. All of that information is being routed through the Oracle."

"The Oracle?" Ash asked.

Jared laughed. "You walked into that one," he said, before giving Tel'an a wry smile.

"It's what we call TaDCom's central computer," she explained, raising a delicate eyebrow at her captain.

"Go on," he pushed. "Tell them what it's really called."

"I don't think it's of any relevance to the situation," she replied politely.

"Humour me... or don't you remember? Wait, you don't, do you?" Jared teased, laughing again.

"Of course, I remember," Tel'an said, feigning frustration.

I already knew the two shared a close working relationship, but I liked watching the light-hearted banter that flowed easily between them. Jared stepped to the side to give Tel'an centre stage, and she sighed, gave a look of mock-indignation, and took a deep breath.

"Advanced Self-Actuated Composite Processor for Hypothesis Investigation and Predictive Analytics... or Oracle," she said.

"I think we'll stick with Oracle," Ash suggested. Tel'an smiled and nodded wisely.

"TaDCom is the hub for all information pertaining to Operation Fallen Star," she continued. "At the moment, the Oracle is trawling through every piece of REF information on record, but when it's finished it'll move on to all other repositories we can get access to. Even the smallest, seemingly insignificant piece of information held on any open data-net anywhere, is fair game."

"Impressive," said Ash. "I won't ask you to repeat the full name again, but did I hear you say Predictive Analytics?"

"You did," Tel'an replied. I got the impression Jared was more than happy to let her take the technical questions. "The Oracle is one of the fastest super-predictors ever designed by Humans, processing at speeds of up to 1.2 zetta-fens. It can evaluate data for relevance, at the same time sorting and comparing it against every other piece of information held in its memory, looking for connections and trends. It'll look at static-data, but it can also review psychological profiles, as well as accessing vid-coms for body language and speech patterns. Everything it can get its virtual hands on.

"If it finds a connection, it'll follow that lead; when it finds another connection, it'll follow that one as well. At any one time, the Oracle can review millions of links to determine whether they're relevant. It'll report a summary of what it's found depending on the boundaries we've given it. Most of the time, we use it at a tiny fraction of its capability, accessing and reviewing the *Defender's* sensor information. But in extreme or exigent circumstances, like now, we can call on the Oracle to process large amounts of data. Once it has a sufficient amount of information to make a hypothesis, it'll provide predictions based on whatever parameters we've set."

"So at the moment the Oracle is... what? Looking for the Khans' current location based on historical data?" Jake asked. I wasn't sure whether he looked impressed or sceptical.

"Effectively, yes," Jared replied. "We've told the Oracle to predict where the Khans might go, and who they'll most likely turn to for help, based on previous behaviour."

"I see. So if you've had this fancy-schmancy equipment all along, why haven't you used it to find the Khans before now?" Jake pushed.

"Because it's actually relatively new. And because a super-predictor's power consumption is off the charts," Jared replied. "I need High Command's authorisation to use the Oracle at even a quarter of its potential, and at the moment it's working at near-on a hundred percent. They're normally housed in massive warehouses on Earth, consuming vast amounts of energy just to stop them overheating. The *Defender's* engines are at full capacity just to keep the Oracle from melting. I can only run it like this for twenty-four hours before I have to shut it down, after that I'm at risk of burning out at least one of the engine cores." Jared looked decidedly unhappy at the thought. "As it is, I'll have to take her to Carmare Station to have a complete diagnostic assessment and possible engine overhaul when all this is done. Besides," he added flippantly, "Predictive Analytics are inherently flawed."

"Excuse me?" Jake spluttered.

"Humanity, or more specifically, behaviour, is impossible to predict to exact certainty," Tel'an said, her slight melodic accent soothing the mood. "Most sentient beings – Humans, Santians, D'Antaran... even Rhinorians for that matter – have free will. The ability and the opportunity to make their own choices."

"Unless you're one of those people who believes everyone has an inescapable, predestined route through life, that is," Jared added. "Look, essentially it comes down to this: people will always do something unexpected – something we couldn't possibly expect." He looked purposely at Jake.

"So what you're saying is that the Oracle guesses?" Jake said, and I wondered if he was being argumentative because of whatever it was he was still stewing over.

"Effectively, but an educated guess based on all the information it has amassed," Tel'an explained.

"I know I'm just a simple Mud Monkey and all, but if the system's flawed, why are we relying on it?"

"The short answer is we're not," she continued. "We're using the Oracle mainly to centralise information – to help us plan what we're going to do next. The Predictive Analytics will simply offer additional data that we can use to base our decisions on."

"Let me put it this way, Jake," Jared cut in, clearly irritated. "If we have nothing more concrete to work on, and the Oracle predicts the Khans are most likely to trust a particular person, we might choose to follow that lead. And it may or may not take us anywhere. But it sure as hell beats sitting on our arses twiddling our thumbs."

"Okay, I get the point," Jake conceded.

"Information's been coming in since we activated TaDCom," said Tel'an. "We've already compiled a list of known associates and possible places the Khans might go to lay low, but these are based solely on what they've done before. Captain Marcos and I spoke with High Command a little while ago and they've dispatched a number of ships to lean on the Khans' past collaborators. We'll get copies of all live-action data, including coms recordings and After-Action reports as and when. And that's pretty much where we are at the moment," she concluded.

Jake looked like he was trying not to look impressed.

"What about the Wolfpack?" Jared asked him.

"Oh, it's my turn now, is it?" he said sarcastically. "Thanks."

Was that why he was so pissed? Because Jared hadn't asked him to brief first? No, it wasn't that; I knew he wasn't that petty.

"As I mentioned during our meeting with the King yesterday," Jake continued, "Ty reckons there's only a handful of scroats in the Sector capable of making the ultra-tech used by the Khans during the robbery. Factor in the altered teslax pulse, and he believes he's narrowed it down to two, maybe three. He's tracking their current whereabouts right now. They're tech-heads, not soldiers or gun-thugs, so if we can get our hands on the right one, I'm confident we'll be able to get something from them."

"About that teslax pulse," Jared said. "It took the Warrior's sensors off-line in an instant. Would it do the same to the *Defender*?"

"Ty said the *Defender's* shields will deflect the worst of the pulse. It shouldn't take your sensors down completely, but it'll probably fuck 'um up a bit. From what I understand, a full re-boot of the system's the only way to get them working at full capacity, and that would mean taking them temporarily off-line. Ty's reviewed the data the Warrior collected before their sensors were completely fucked, and he's designed what he calls a patch and pray defence guard for the *Veritas*. He and Connor are installing it now."

"Is it something our engineers can adapt for the *Defender*?" Tel'an asked.

"Don't see why not. I'll get Ty to send you his schematics, though I should warn you, he's a little... unconventional."

"Unconventional we can work with, Colonel." Tel'an smiled.

"Your guys should understand that Ty's fix is purely theoretical. There's no way of knowing whether it'll work without hitting the *Veritas* with the same converted teslax pulse… and before you suggested it, Marcos, there's no way in hell that's going to happen."

"I wasn't even…" Jared broke off as if he wasn't going to dignify Jake's comment with an answer. A short, uncomfortable silence followed before Tel'an put her hand to her earpiece to indicate an incoming call.

"Colonel Mitchell, Kaiser would like to speak to you,"

she said. Jake looked at his com-pad frowning. "Your coms won't work in high-security areas of the ship like the Bridge, TaDCom or the Engine Room," she explained. "You can take the call at one of the stations. I'll show you."

Tel'an held out her arm to indicate the way, before leading Jake through the shield towards a workstation on the first tier. As I watched him access the coms-panel, uninvited thoughts crept into my head. How would I tell him? How would he react? What would I do if he never wanted to see me again? If he hated me?

He looked up, and for a moment our eyes locked. I turned away, quickly engaging in a conversation with Ash.

"I've an update from Kaiser," Jake said when he returned to the group moments later. "He's got the location of the planet where the Khan's men trained for the assault on the Palace."

"Anywhere we know," I asked.

"A shitty little planet on the outer rim of the Sector," Jake replied. "You mind?" he asked Jared, indicating towards the data-table.

"Be my guest."

Jake entered a few commands, and a map of Sector Three's stellar configuration appeared on the desk. It focussed in, skimming through the Sector until it displayed a close-up of a small Category 4 planet. With a swipe of his hand, the image transferred to a holo-projection, and the planet rotated slowly above the table.

"Dennford," Jake concluded. "Stupid name for a planet if you ask me. Anyway, it's mostly uninhabited, except for a few self-sufficient settlements populated by a bunch of backwards folks who, in their great wisdom, have decided to separate themselves from civilisation. They've banned all but the most basic tech."

"People who choose to steer away from political and economic control are not always backwards, Jake," Ash said. "In many cases it makes the more enlightened."

"Whatever. The important thing is, they keep themselves to themselves. You could set up a whacking great militia encampment a few miles from a settlement and they won't have a clue it's there. It's the perfect place to train in peace," Jake clarified.

"Okay," said Jared, interrupting the tension building between the two men. "This is where we stand as I see it. One: thanks to Ty, we have leads on the expert who created the ultra-tech for the Khans. Find the expert – find the Khans. That's the theory anyway. Two: we have the location of the planet where the Khans trained their men. There may be someone or something at the camp that can point us towards the Khans… and if we're lucky, they might even be there themselves."

"We're never that lucky," I said.

"Perhaps you're right," he continued. "So… Three: we have a list of previous hideouts as well as known associates of the Khans. We hit every single one hard until we find them or find someone who'll give up their location. Everyone with me so far?" He looked around the group for acknowledgement. "Good. Then this is what we do. I'll—"

"Wait, hold up. Who the fuck put you in charge?" Jake interrupted angrily. So that was it. That was why he'd been antsy and unsettled. "Just because the King put you in charge of fake Operation Fallen Star, doesn't mean you're in charge of us, of the Guardians. Am I right?" He looked to Ash then to me for support.

To be fair, he was right. As Guardians we were equal, technically. I looked to Ash for guidance, who sighed and rubbed his temples. I don't think Jake and Jared noticed though; they were too busy arguing over the equality of their military ranks. Old resentments resurfacing at the worst time.

"Enough!" Ash said loudly to get their attention, and I felt his irritation smouldering through the Link. Tel'an tactfully removed herself from the situation, leaving to talk to Hale. "Jake's right. When the Tetrarchy of Souls put us together as a team, they did so with all of us as equals. But…" he added carefully, as a smug smile spread across Jake's face, "they made it obvious they hadn't agreed how each team should work, which includes who should lead each mission. And we do need a leader, gentlemen. You both know how the chain of command works, and you know how bad things can get when that chain breaks down. You saw what happened on the Planet of Souls during our last mission. At a time we needed one voice, we had four, and that almost cost lives." I shuddered at the reminder. "Look, Jake, we all know that no matter how equal things are, sometimes there has to be one person who has the final say, and on this occasion, given the circumstances, I believe that person should be Jared."

I thought Jake would object but he remained silent.

"The *Defender* is Jared's ship. All this," he waved his hand around the room, "is his. Besides, Fleet, the Marines, and the Brotherhood all believe he's in command of Operation Fallen Star, so it's logical. Even you have to admit that."

"Fine," Jake agreed after a moment's thought.

"Cheer up. You can lead the next mission… if we live through this one," Jared added, smacking Jake hard on the shoulder. "We're all in this together, remember. Till the end." I wasn't sure I like the finality of his comment, and I don't think Jake did either. He tugged at his collar and shifted his weight from foot to foot.

"We need you a hundred percent committed, Jake," I said, trying to get him to focus on someone other than Jared.

"I know," he replied, turning towards me, his tone gentle in contrast to how he'd been with Jared. "You don't need to worry, Babe. I'm totally committed," he continued, reaching out before realising what he was doing. He pulled his arm back and ran his fingers through his hair instead. I wasn't sure if his words had a double meaning, but my stomach churned anyway.

"So we're good?" Jared asked, signalling for Tel'an and Hale to re-join us.

"Yeah, we're good," Jake replied, but I got the impression he wanted to add, for now.

"Okay, let's finish this briefing and get to work then. Jake, how do you feel about you and the Wolfpack taking the *Veritas* and chasing down Ty's leads?"

"Sure, we can do that."

"Good. I'll stay with the *Defender* and tackle the leads the Oracle thinks have the highest contact probability. Ash, Shae, if I give you a Warrior, Lieutenant Harper, and Team Two, can you take the Dennford lead?"

"Of course," Ash replied.

"Excellent. What do you think? Anything I've forgotten?" The question was aimed at the full group, but I suspect it was a diplomatic way of giving Jake the opportunity to add anything.

"Well..." Jake started, and my heart sank a little. "Actually, that's exactly what I would've suggested," he concluded with a grin. "Maybe you're not so bad at this after all."

"I'll take that as a compliment."

"Whatever. Just don't let it go to your head, it's big enough as it is."

"Wouldn't dream of it."

The banter continued, but I wasn't listening anymore; my thoughts had drifted elsewhere.

I hadn't forgotten about the Helyan cube, and although I'd followed the King's orders and not spoken about it – not even to Jared – I couldn't ignore the fact that it existed, or the fact that Vanze knew what it was. Maybe he knew where it came from, and why my pendant shared the same markings.

Could Vanze give me the answers I'd been looking for?

Could those answers tell me where I came from?
   Or who my parents were?

13

Two hours later, Ash and I sat with Jared and Lieutenant Harper in Situation Room One.

"Let me be completely clear," Jared said to Harper. "You're in command of your team, but Brother Asher is in command of the mission. Constantine Agreement aside, whatever Ash – or Shae – says, goes. Treat it exactly the same way you would an order from me or Commander Tel'an. Am I clear?"

"Sir, yes, Sir," Harper replied, a flicker of intrigue in his eyes.

"This is the first mission for the new squad," Jared continued. "Do you foresee any problems?"

"Sir, no, Sir." I almost giggled at the military posturing. "As you know, we lost half the team during the creature attack on 758-C2. It's hit the remaining members hard, but the replacements are outstanding. The team's raw, but they're squared away. I have full confidence, Sir."

The door opened and a young woman with a buzz-cut entered, standing to immediate attention.

"At ease," Harper commanded. "Report."

"Sir, the Warrior is prepped and the team's ready to

deploy on your orders."

"Excellent. Tell the pilot to fire up the engines and load up the team. We leave in fifteen. If you'll excuse me, Sir," he added to Ash, "I'll collect my gear and meet you both in the hangar."

Ash nodded his agreement and the lieutenant left, followed by the trooper.

"What's the Wolfpack's situation?" Ash asked, folding up the sleeves on combat fatigues.

"The *Veritas* is prepping to depart. It seems Jake's taken it upon himself to requisition half of our weapons supplies – just in case, he said." I knew Jared was exaggerating. I'd seen the munitions store, and if Jake had taken even a hundredth of what they had, the *Veritas* wouldn't be able to get of the deck. "A little overkill I reckon," Jared continued, frowning. "Anyway, they're loading up now. I'd guess fifteen, maybe twenty minutes, and they'll be ready to leave."

"I need to check in with Francis," Ash said. "See where things stand with the Brotherhood. Shae, can you grab our kit and meet me in the hangar?" I nodded and he left, leaving me alone with Jared – a situation I wasn't overly comfortable with.

"I best get the bags," I said, hoping Jared would have more important things to do. I should've known better.

"I'll walk with you," he said.

"You don't need to."

"I know, but I want to."

We walked in silence and I took the opportunity to evaluate the three separate missions – assignments designed to locate the Khans, retrieve the Seal, and rescue the Princess. But as far as I was concerned, there was another objective: to find out everything Vanze knew about the Helyan Cube.

I was preoccupied with my own thoughts and hadn't realised Jared had hit the lift's emergency stop button until we juddered to a halt.

"Shae, I know you don't want to hear this, but please, please be careful out there. I know you can heal, but promise me you won't put yourself in unnecessary danger. You're far too reckless when it comes to your own safety."

"Am not," I replied quickly, with more venom than I'd intended.

Jared cocked his head to the side. "Do I need to remind you about the whole Human Chemstick incident?" Damn, I hated it when he was right. "You say you love me, then you tell me you can't be with me because you couldn't bear it if anything happened to me. Well guess what? That goes both ways, Shae. It would destroy me if anything happened to you, and that doesn't change because we're not together," he added deliberately. The ache inside my chest was almost unbearable. "All I'm asking is that you be careful. Can you do that one thing for me?"

I nodded my agreement, afraid that if I opened my mouth, I would tell him how much I really did love him, and that I wanted to be with him more than anything in the Four Sectors. I'd thought cutting myself off from him it would make things easier, but it hadn't. Jared tapped the emergency button and the lift started up again.

Ash was already in the hangar talking to Harper when we got there. "Ready?" he asked.

"Actually, I've been thinking," I replied. "Do you think you can handle Dennford without me?"

He looked at me carefully, one hand resting on his Brotherhood belt buckle, and a sure sign that he wasn't happy.

"You want to stay here?"

"No, I want to go with the Wolfpack," I said, keeping my voice steady.

Jared's eyebrows puckered into a deep V-shape. "Why do you want to go with them?" he asked, jaw set, lips tight.

"I… I have my reasons," I replied cryptically, thinking

of the Helyan Cube, but as soon as the words were out, I knew he would think it was something to do with Jake. To make matters worse, I felt a wave of anxiety through the Link from Ash.

"I don't know, Shae," Ash said. "You know the rule."

"I'll be fine. I know what I'm doing, I promise. Besides, it's a stupid rule, and I'm not a child anymore."

"Okay, but only if you're sure?" I nodded. "Be safe. I love you."

I watched Ash and Harper jog across the hangar and board the Warrior before turning to leave, almost walking straight into Jared who was stood right behind me. I detected disappointment and resentment on his face and a knot tightened in my stomach.

"It's not what you think," I told him.

"Oh? What am I thinking?" His tone was unkind.

"You… we…" I didn't know what to say without breaking a direct order from the King. "I think Jake's team has the best lead, and I want… I need—"

"You haven't told him, have you?" he interrupted, but he already knew the answer. "I've seen the way he looks at you – the hugs, the kisses. He still thinks you and he are—"

"We're not together." It was my turn to interrupt. "I don't love him. Not like that, anyway."

"I believe you," he said, putting his hand on my shoulder. "But he doesn't know that." I shook off his touch. "For God's sake, Shae. It's not fair on Jake." He paused and looked directly into my eyes. "It's not fair on any of us."

"I tried to tell him," I replied lamely.

"Then you didn't try hard enough."

"Now you're not being fair."

"What part of this is fair?" A flash of frustration crossed his face, but then his stormy-blue eyes lightened and his forehead smoothed. "I get that you still care for him, but you need to tell him the truth."

"I know." It was just easier said than done. "Jared, I've really got to go if I want to catch the *Veritas*."

"Okay, but be careful." I headed for the doors. "I love you," he shouted after me, but I didn't turn around or stop. I couldn't.

Instead of heading straight forwards towards the lift, I swung a left and sprinted for the adjacent hangar, only just managing to skid through the doors as they were closing. The *Veritas'* ramp was already secure and from the thunderous roar of the engines, they were ready to take off. I waved my arms wildly, trying to catch Connor's attention through the front screen, but I wasn't sure he'd seen me until a side hatch opened and steps descended.

Jake bolted down them, his expression confused and concerned as I met him at the bottom.

"What's the matter? Is everything okay?" he yelled above the engines. His hand was on my cheek and he was searching my eyes for clues. "Are you okay?" he continued, giving me a quick body-check.

"Everything's fine. I'm fine," I shouted. "Can I come with you?"

"What?" Jake yelled, moving closer.

"Can I come with you," I repeated. "I'll explain everything onboard."

Jake's face relaxed and he smiled before putting his hand on the small of my back to lead me up the steps into the main cabin. As soon as he sealed the hatch, the roar dropped to a low hum and I felt a slight jolt as Connor lifted the ship off the hangar floor.

"Hey, you," Kaiser said as he strolled back from the flight deck. "What you doin' here?"

"Good to see you too," I replied, throwing him a wounded look.

"You know that's not what I meant," he said hastily. "I meant…" He caught the smile I could no longer hide. "Oh, you're funny, Blue. Seriously, who did invite you?" he added.

"Kaiser's right, Babe," Jake said. "I'm really glad you're here and all, but what's up? And where's your keeper? I'm surprised he's let you out of his sight." I wasn't sure whether he was referring to Jared or Ash.

"I am capable of doing stuff on my own, you know."

"Oh, don't I know it," he said, grinning.

"It's really nothing exciting," I added quickly, ignoring the hungry smile twitching at his lips. "I just thought you guys had the best lead, and I wanted to be where the action is." I suppose that was technically the truth, even if I'd left a large chunk out.

"Admit it, Blue" Kaiser said. "You just wanted to be with the cool kids, not fucking about with those lame-arse, pansy, Fleet pussies. 'Scuse my language."

"Sure." I smiled. "You got me." I didn't think there was any point in trying to defend Fleet to the Wolfpack. It would've been completely pointless, and a waste of my breath. "That's the second time you've called me Blue. What gives?"

"Term of affection." He grinned. "In reference to that sparkly colour thing you do. Anyway, I for one am glad you're here – it's always good to have a super-freaky healer chick onboard. Every ship should have one." His grin turned to a broad smile and he rubbed his face where I'd healed a broken cheekbone during the previous mission. "I'll go let the others know."

"Sorry about the super-freaky thing," Jake said. "He didn't mean anything by it."

"I know, it's okay. So, what's the plan, Jake?" I asked, rubbing my shoulder from the friendly 'tap' Kaiser had given me before leaving.

"It's simple," he replied, sliding closer. I bolted off the bench and walked around the cabin, feeling his eyes follow me as I paced. "I've used my own super-predictor to narrow the list of potentials to one person," he concluded. I must've looked confused. "Ty," he explained, laughing. "He costs a lot less to keep, and uses up way less energy than the Oracle."

"That's funny," I said, relaxing slightly.

"When Ty studied the tech in more detail, he found a hidden signature specific to one man: Nathaniel Marshall. We put out some feelers and got his last known location from a kid called Hank, a cyber-hacker we busted a few years ago who turned C.I. rather than going to jail."

"You think his info's legit?"

"I'm as confident as I can be, given he's a low-life, scumbag hacktivist. But as scroats go, he's not a bad kid. Anyway, Hank says Marshall's got a lab somewhere on Independence."

"No way! Independence? I've always wanted to go there," I said, sitting back with Jake, but that time on the opposite side of the table and with my legs folded tightly under the bench. "I hate to question your C.I.'s intel, but what the hell would a tech-head be doing on a Frontier planet?"

"That was my first thought as well, but if you think about it, it's genius really. Who'd look for one of the Sector's foremost developers of ultra-tech on a planet colonised by farmers and cattle wranglers? People who've chosen a simple existence, one without any sophisticated tech."

"You sound like you admire them."

"Perhaps I do. Don't you occasionally wonder what it would be like to live an uncomplicated, peaceful life? One where you're not getting shot at half the time?"

"I'd be lying if I said I didn't." I paused, thinking. "I don't get something. You don't judge the people of Independence, but you thought the settlers on Dennford were backwards and uncivilised. Haven't they've both effectively turned their back on technology?"

"It's different, and it's not so much about the tech. The

people of Dennford have cut themselves off. They've no order, no discipline – no regard for the Crowns. But Independence still chooses to be part of the Empire. They may skirt on the periphery of our economic, political and military boundaries, but they've got a democratic system. They still have law and order, even if they are a little too egalitarian for my liking. The point is, they haven't removed themselves from humanity. They trade off-world and allow off-worlders to visit and settle."

It was interesting and surprising to see this different side of Jake.

"Fair enough," I commented, not knowing enough about Independence to get into a debate. Ash and I had always wanted to visit when we were younger, just to see what all the fuss was about. But contrary to Jake's insistence that they were open to outsiders, the locals had made it evidently clear that the Brotherhood, like the REF, were not welcome. "What's our eta?"

"Mid-day tomorrow, give or take, and that's pushing the engines the entire way," he replied. "Make yourself at home. There are spare quarters downstairs, second door on the right – I believe you know the way," he added, winking, then he leant forward and lowered his voice. "Or you can always bunk with me."

"Jake!" I said, almost choking on the word. My stomach flipped, and I know I must've blushed fiercely because I felt a rush of heat to my cheeks.

"Relax, Babe, I don't want to push you into anything. You can dump your bag in whichever room you want… whenever you're ready." He sniffed the air. "Smells like dinner will be ready soon. You're in luck; we raided the *Defender's* food stores, so it might actually be something edible for a change."

"I heard that," said Ty, strolling into the cabin. "About twenty minutes," he added as he continued past us towards the flight deck.

The five of us sat down to dinner not half an hour later. Ty had laid the round table next to the small kitchenette with warm, baked breads, and fresh Nikolov olives from the Western Agricultural Region. I was impressed by his culinary skills, finishing off a large bowl of spicy 'pasta a la Ty' in record time. According to him, it was all down to Mamma's secret ingredient, which he was only going to pass on to the woman he married. Or if he didn't marry, he'd take it to his grave, which he decided, shrugging, was probably more likely.

The first time I'd met Jake, he'd told me the Wolfpack were the best team he'd ever worked with. While I'd never questioned that opinion, the more time I spent with them, the greater I began to appreciate his sentiment. Kaiser, after seeking Jake's approval, decided to make me an honorary member of the pack, although as I wasn't a hairy-arsed marine, expert in guerrilla warfare and counterinsurgency – his words – I couldn't be full-wolf. He decided I could hold the title of 'pup', much to the other's amusement.

I forced away the urge to correct him in his assessment of my battle readiness. I mastered both covert and overt military tactics while I was still in my teens, and having trained in unarmed combat since I was old enough to carry a wooden staff weapon, I was probably better trained than he was. I would give him the hairy-arsed bit though, that was something I had no intention of disputing.

Jake and Connor got up to clear the dishes, and when they returned, Jake placed a large pink and cream tub in the middle of the table.

"See, Babe? I pay attention," he said as he took the top of the Carmichaels Chocomel ice-cream. "It's even your favourite flavour."

"But you didn't even know I was coming when you stocked up."

"True. But I knew you wouldn't be able to stay away for long," he replied, smiling.

After we'd demolished the entire tub, we decamped to the lounge chairs in the main cabin, and the rest of the evening passed quickly as the Wolfpack regaled me with stories of past exploits – both operational and personal. Some of the latter made me blush, and Jake had to step in on a couple of occasions to cool them down. It was wild at times, but always entertaining, and I felt happy and relaxed, even sharing a few non-classified stories of my own.

Jake, lounging back with his hands folded behind his head, was content to let the other three take the lead, only chipping in to clarify details or correct some of the more outlandish stories. He seemed happy and relaxed, and when he turned and caught me watching him, he smiled and winked. Guilt prickled in my chest and I had to force myself to concentrate on Connor's tale.

When my eyes started to droop, I decided it was time to say goodnight.

"Guys, it's been... umm... educational, but I'm going to head to my crib. See you in the morning."

"Night little pup," Kaiser said, to another round of raucous laughter.

I'd just rested my head on the pillow when there was a knock on the door.

"Who is it?" I asked, knowing damn well who it was.

"It's me. Can I come in?" Jake asked. Panic ran through me like a chill, but when I didn't reply he knocked again. "Babe?"

"Come in, Jake," I conceded, sitting up and propping the pillow behind my back. I pulled the covers up to my chest and drew up my legs, crossing them so he could sit on the end of the bed.

"In case I hadn't made it clear, I'm really happy you're here," he said, reaching out to touch my foot. I pulled it up closer to me and even in the dim light from the table chem-lamp, I could see creases spread across his forehead. "So much has happened in such a short amount of time," he continued. "I still can't get my head around it... around us."

"Jake—"

"Let me finish, please. I know Finnian was like a father to you, and losing him must've..." He paused, trying to find the right words. "That last night on the *Defender* – the one after our last mission – all I wanted to do was hold you, tell you I was there for you, and that I'd do anything I could to make it better." His eyes turned sad. "But you had Ash and Francis. And Ash... well, he made it clear I had to stay away. So out of respect I tried to give you space, even though it killed me. The only thing that made it bearable was knowing that Ash wouldn't let Jared near you either." He laughed sadly. "I came to you though."

"You did? When?"

"In the morning. I came to your quarters, but you'd already gone."

"I didn't know."

"Why would you? I understand why you left without saying goodbye, you had other things on your mind, but I sent you messages, several of them..." He trailed off, studying his fingernails, and my heart physically ached in my chest. "Babe, I know it's none of my business, but what's going on between you and Captain Annoying?" His sudden direct question startled me. "Come on, I'm not blind. Back at the Palace, even before the shit hit the fan, things were hinky between you two."

"Hinky?"

"You know? Strange. Weird. Have you been fighting again?"

"No, it's nothing like that." I thought about what Jared had said back in the hangar, and he was right. I wasn't being fair. "I need to tell you something, Jake."

"Wait, before you do, before you say something you'll... I need to tell you something. I think I love you."

"Oh, Jake," I gasped, completely thrown. That wasn't supposed to happen. He didn't love me, he couldn't. I didn't know what to say that wouldn't hurt him, so I said the only thing I could. "I love Jared. I'm sorry. I'm so, so sorry."

Jake's shoulders slumped, but he didn't take his eyes off mine. I expected him to be angry, to rant, to swear, to do something, but he was calm, like he'd been expecting it.

"When did you work it out?" There was resignation in his voice, and plenty of pain, but no rage. His question confused me. "I knew you felt something for him, and I suspected... but I hoped you wouldn't realise... When did it happen?"

"After the creature attack," I said quietly. "After he was so close to death."

Jake got up and I thought he was going to leave, but instead he paced the small room, raking his fingers through shaggy, uncontrollable hair. He looked like he was thinking, working through something, then he sat back down on the bed. "No," he said, his face set with determination.

"No?"

"No," he repeated. "You were grieving for Finnian, then you thought Jared was dying as well. Your emotions got mixed up, that's all. It's not real. What we had, that was real – is real."

"What we had was extreme," I replied, tears beginning to well. "But it isn't love, not in that way."

"I think it's love." Jake's voice wavered slightly.

"Do you though? I'm not denying there was something. I've never had that kind of immediate intense reaction with anyone but you." I smiled weakly. "There was certainly passion... and more than a little lust... but you don't love me, Jake."

There was a flash of anger in his eyes. "You can't say that, Shae. You can't know what I'm feeling."

"I'm sorry. I didn't mean—"

"But if you want to play that game," he interrupted, "fine by me. Because I know there is something between us, and it's more than lust. I believe you love me as well."

"I do, Jake, but not in the way you want me to. I love you the way people love someone they really care about."

"But you do love me?" he clarified.

"Like a best friend."

"I don't believe you."

"You think I'm lying to you?" I asked, stunned.

"I think you're lying to yourself." He got up and paced the room again. "So, have you and he…?"

"Have we what?"

"You know."

"What?"

"Been… intimate?"

"No," I said, shocked. "We're not even together."

Jake looked astonished, then confused, then happy. A smile crossed his lips and his eyes crinkled. "You haven't told him," he said, echoing Jared's words from earlier. "That means, deep down, you don't really believe it yourself."

"I do believe it, and I have told him. I kind of blurted it out by mistake," I said. Although the smile remained, confusion crept back into Jake's eyes. "It's complicated," I concluded.

"So that's why things were so strained back at the Palace – because you told him you loved him and he, what, knocked you back? The man's a fucking idiot."

"No, Jake, that's not what happened at all. Jared told me he loved me before I told him how I felt. I never intended on saying anything… it's just made things more difficult."

"I don't understand."

"You were right about Finnian's death hitting me hard. It nearly destroyed me, literally." Jake opened his mouth, but I continued before he could say anything. "It brought all the feelings of losing my biological parents to the surface and I... It was too hard." Tears began to fall. "I can't afford to get that emotionally involved with anyone again. My heart can't take any more loss." I wiped at the tears on my cheek. "So I told Jared we couldn't be together. End of story."

I was drained, both emotionally and physically. I knew telling Jake about Jared would be hard, but I'd had no idea just how bad it would be.

Without saying another word, Jake sat on the bed next to me before gathering me up in his arms, and I let him even though I knew I probably shouldn't have done. I rested my head on his chest and listened to the slow, solid beat of his heart.

When I woke the following morning, I was still in his arms. I tried not to move because I didn't want to wake him – he looked so peaceful – but a moment later he stirred and opened his eyes.

"Morning, Babe," he said casually, as if waking up with me was the most natural thing in the Four Sectors.

"Morning," I replied, surprised that his behaviour showed no signs of the previous night's discussion. He unwrapped his arm and stretched languidly before yawning and standing. "Jake, I—" He held up his hand to stop me.

"I heard what you said last night, but I'm not prepared to give up on us. You and me? We've always been good together, even you have to admit that. You and Captain Courageous? Let's just say even I know it's been a bumpy ride. The last month has been emotional, and I don't believe you're thinking straight." He held up his hand to silence me again. "I'm not going to walk away from what we have, and if that means I have to fight Jared for your affections, then I will." He caught the horrified look on my face. "Not literally fight him, Babe – been there, done that," he added with a roguish smirk. He looked at his com-pad. "Get dressed, breakfast's in twenty," he said cheerfully before bending down and placing a light kiss on my forehead. He'd left my room before I could comprehend what'd happened.

After breakfast, I decided it was time to put Kaiser and the others straight about the standard of my combat-readiness. We eventually got into a debate about whose style was better, discussing the differences between military unarmed combat training and the Brotherhoods. They were interested to see what I was capable of, so I showed them how to execute a few key Tok-ma sequences, including the neck-breaking Cal'tar manoeuvre. They were quick to learn and equally as ruthless as the Brotherhood's Warrior Caste.

"So how does that thing work? Can I have a go?" Connor asked, pointing to the Cal'ret holstered at my thigh. I handed over the baton and he held it carefully, studying the small runic carvings that covered the shaft. He gave it a shake, but nothing happened.

"Give it here, you're doing it wrong," said Ty, shaking it vigorously. Again, nothing happened. In the end he passed it to Kaiser who had the same amount of luck.

Jake watched their progress, chuckling and shaking his head in disbelief. "You guys are morons. Only Shae can work her Cal'ret. It's how they're made, idiots."

"Jake's right," I said. "The monks wear gloves during the forging and engraving processes, so the first contact a baton has with skin is when it's presented to a monk by their Primus. At that point, the Cal'ret bonds with its new owner on a cellular level, allowing only them to use it. It's all to do with the fact that the Stidium metal is fused with a bio-fission organism on a molecular level, or something like that."

I gave the Cal'ret a quick shake, and it seamlessly extended to a full-length fighting staff. The guys looked impressed. I guess they hadn't really been paying much attention to it when I'd used it on them back on GalaxyBase4 during our previous mission.

"So how does it actually work?" asked Ty.

"Beats me," I said honestly. "What I just told you? Sounds good, right? Sounds like I know what I'm talking about? Straight out of a textbook," I clarified, laughing. "Look, all I know is there's a mental connection between user and the baton. The stronger the connection, the more powerful the Cal'ret."

"From what I remember, yours is pretty powerful," said Ty. "Is that something to do with your freaky supernatural shit?" Jake glared at him. "What?" he said, "You can't tell me what she can do ain't weird?"

"That's enough, Ty," Jake warned.

"It's okay," I said, interrupting the tension. "Ty's right. It is to do with my gift, but I'd rather not be called a freak."

"Sure, sorry." Ty's cheeks darkened and his skin glowed. I could almost feel the heat from where I stood.

"No harm, no foul," I replied. "Why don't I give you a demo? Everyone grip the staff."

Kaiser grabbed it instantly, but Connor and Ty hesitated. "In your own time, ladies," he goaded. "Jake?"

"No thanks. I've already had first-hand experience of what that thing can do."

"Don't worry, I'll be gentle," I teased as I sent a mental signal to the staff. The three marines let go immediately, shaking their hands and swearing profusely. "Come on! It wasn't that bad. I just gave you a little buzz."

"Fuck me! If that was a little buzz, I'd hate to be on the receiving end of its full power," moaned Connor, rubbing his fingers. "Talk about pins and needles."

"You're such a girl," Ty mocked, though I noticed he was massaging his hand vigorously.

"Right," Jake said, standing and flexing out his muscles. "Back to work. Con, how long till we arrive at Independence?"

"Two hours. That puts us in orbit at approximately thirteen-twenty, with boots on the ground by fourteen-hundred – as long as we don't have any problems with local traffic control."

"Good. This mission is going to go by the book," Jake continued. "Hank says Nathaniel Marshall drinks at a bar called The Lone Tree Saloon in Wishbone Creek."

"Seriously?" Connor laughed loudly. "How the hell do they come up with names like that?" Jake nailed him with a look. "Sorry, Boss. Carry on."

"Wishbone Creek isn't huge. Its footprint's no more than a couple of miles across, but I don't want any surprises." He accessed the data-net on one of the large screens and drew up a detailed diagram of the area. "This map is old, and probably out of date, so after we land, I want a full tactical analysis of the town before we even approach the saloon, especially these areas here and here." He pointed to two regions on the map. "They could be potential choke points if we run into problems. Ty, Shae, and I will enter the bar to locate Marshall. Connor, I want you covering street level on this corner. You'll have clear line of sight to these roads here, here and here, and the front entrance of the bar here. Kaiser, I want you on the top of this building with an AG59."

"What's an AG59?" I asked.

"Long range sniper riffle," explained Kaiser. "Uses fifteen-millimetre armour-piercing rounds. Explosive tips. Nasty shit. Very effective."

"Take an RPG as well," Jake suggested. "Better to be safe than sorry. Once we have Marshall, we'll bring him back to the *Veritas* and interrogate him here. Any questions?"

"What if we encounter local resistance?" asked Connor.

"I know we're going in undercover, due to their mistrust of authority, but this is a fully-sanctioned REF mission. I know that's a bit of a change for us, but it means we play it by the book. Securing Nathaniel Marshall is the priority, but if anyone stands in our way, you know the drill. Let me make it clear: nobody starts anything unless you have no other choice. Understood? Good. I want weapons and Rover prep completed by thirteen hundred. Get to it."

14

The blistering sun shone high in a cloudless blue sky, and the heat seared my lungs as I stepped out of the climate-controlled comfort of the *Veritas*. My first step on to the planet of Independence puffed up tiny swirls of bone-dry, copper-coloured earth.

When we'd arrived in orbit, Jake had introduced us to traffic control as merchants looking to trade. Much to his disgust, we'd been charged an off-worlder's levy before being given authorisation to land – non-refundable, even if we didn't manage to trade, so the controller told us. Once Jake had stopped griping and paid the man, we were authorised to land on a large plateau to the north-west of Wishbone Creek.

A heat-haze shimmered over cracked earth, shrouding the base of the mountains in the distance, and making them appear like they floated above the ground. I was already starting to sweat, and I wiped my forehead with the back of my hand.

The copper terrain morphed to a deep, murky brown as I held the dark-tinted Ranger scope to my eyes, scanning the horizon. According to the telemetry display, Wishbone

Creek sat exactly 3.24 miles in the direction of the sun. I focussed in on the town, using the three-storey outline of the Courthouse as a reference point.

Our map was outdated, and most likely incorrect, so Jake had decided to leave finalising our egress strategy until after the on-the-ground tactical analysis of the area.

A warning klaxon signalled the underbelly of the ship was about to open and I took a few steps to the side, even though I knew I was already out of the way. The hydraulics groaned and creaked as the ramp descended, hitting the ground with a hollow thump. I covered my eyes with my arm as a cloud of hot air and rock dust blew over me like sandstorm and coughed to clear my throat.

Through the settling dust I watched Ty walk down the ramp, his tinted goggles glinting in the sun. I heard him laugh through the scarf wrapped across his face.

"There are spare goggles in the locker by the primary ramp controls," he said, lowering the bandana briefly.

I nodded my understanding as I headed past him, only just managing to dive out of the way of the Rover as Connor drove it from its docking clamps. He screeched to a stop at the top of the ramp and jumped out.

"Fuck. Shit. Bollocks! Are you okay?" he asked, helping me off the floor. "I'm so sorry, I didn't see you."

"I'm fine," I replied, wiping myself down. "Just a scratch." I held up my elbow to show him raw flesh turn to pink skin.

"You know, I'm never going to get used to that shit."

"I hope you don't have to."

"We ready?" Jake asked as he slid effortlessly down the ladder behind us. "What's going on?" he added, eyeing Conner suspiciously, but to be fair, he did look extremely guilty.

"Nothing," I relied easily. "All good here."

"Are we good to go then?"

"The *Veritas* is locked down and the Rover's charged

and loaded. We're good to go," replied Conner, but Jake didn't move.

"Con?" he said questioningly. "As if the heavy-duty plasma cannon and side-mounted machine guns aren't going to make us stand out enough, what's wrong with this picture?"

"Oops," Connor replied, looking at the matt-black carapace of the all-terrain buggy. He grabbed the data-pad resting on top of one of the massive wheels. "One moment... and... all sorted." The Rover shimmered for a second then transformed into hues of reddish-brown.

"That's better. Load up," ordered Jake, pulling himself up into the driver's seat.

I grabbed a pair of goggles from the locker then hesitated, not exactly sure how to get into the back seat of the Rover until Kaiser appeared. "Put one foot here," he said pointing towards the rear of the buggy, "and the other one here."

"You want me to stand on the fully-loaded machine gun?" I asked sceptically.

"Sure." He grinned. "It's perfectly safe, we do it all the time," he added, hauling himself into the front passenger seat. I thought he was taking the piss, until Connor strode past me and did exactly what Kaiser had instructed. Satisfied it was safe, I hopped up behind him, practically falling into my seat as Jake gunned the engine and sped down the ramp. He didn't even stop to pick up Ty, only slowing enough for him to clamber on the rear as we passed.

Ty tapped me on the shoulder to get my attention before passing me a khaki bandana. I shouted my thanks and tied it around my neck before pulling it over my face. My goggles were already blurry from the sand, and I wiped them clear with my fingers.

The Rover bucked and bounced, throwing me around in my seat as Jake drove at break-neck speed towards the town. I held the roll-bars tightly the entire time to stop myself from careening into Connor in the seat next to me. Jake only slowed when we approached the outlying buildings, finally parking the buggy next to a simple single story, adobe-brick building.

"You okay back there, Babe?" he said turning to face me.

"That was awesome," I said, a stupid grin plastered across my face. Jake raised his eyebrows and shook his head before jumping down from the vehicle.

"You're awesome," he said as he appeared next to me. "Here," he added, wiping sand from my cheeks before turning his attention to the Pack. "Okay, you know the drill. You have your orders, and you've got your routes. I want coms open at all time, and everyone's to keep in touch. Got it? We rendezvous at Point Alpha at sixteen-hundred, and I expect a full tactical analysis of your quadrants at that time. Remember, we're here to trade whisky for animal pelts, and if anyone asks what you're up to, you're just getting your bearings around town. We stick with that story unless I say otherwise. Clear? Good. Connor, deal with the Rover."

The carapace of the Rover flickered before camouflaging itself against the ruddy earth and the building beside it.

"Sixteen-hundred," Jake reminded the team as we split off in different directions.

As he and I walked in from the edge of the town, we passed more of the same type of modest single-story homes. The people were reserved and unassuming, but they were friendly. They smiled and said hello, but were clearly wary of the armed newcomers, gathering children to their sides as we approached. I wouldn't say they were living in poverty, but it was clear from the patched clothes and worn shoes, that Independence didn't live up to the equality for all hype it advertised off-world. I remembered Jake's comment about egalitarianism, and I wondered what he was thinking.

The nearer we got to the centre of Wishbone Creek, the more things changed. The buildings became extravagant, grandiose structures built with white and light-brown timber. No doubt brought down from one of the mountain regions at a time when the river was still deep enough to enable trade ships in from other settlements.

In stark contrast to the folks we'd met on the outskirts, the people were affluent and well dressed. Most were indifferent to our arrival, but some were just plain rude. I decided that the fabled generous hospitality of the locals was hugely exaggerated after the third person had spat chewing herbacco in our direction.

"Clearly it's not just the Brotherhood that isn't welcome," Jake said, sidestepping the glob of green-grey slime that splattered the road in front of him. He put his arm around my waist and pulled me into his side, and I didn't protest because I'd seen the way people were watching us.

Main Street was the commercial hub of the town, one long road running through the centre. To begin with, we passed several run-down supply stores, but the closer we got to the heart, the better kept the buildings became. Washed windows, clean, bright paintwork, and fresh flowers welcomed potential shoppers.

The Courthouse, whose splendour and magnificence separated it from the buildings around, was build dead centre, and had a small well-tended square out front. Directly opposite sat an ominous looking building, with thick bars on blacked-out windows. I was bothered by the sturdy wooden gallows erected right outside, and I tried not to look at them, even though my eyes kept being drawn back to the man pulling on a noose to check if it was secure.

We strolled past the Courthouse and the General Store, coming to the Lone Tree Saloon towards the far end of the strip. "Nice place," I said, taking in the peeling paint, cracked windows and broken decking. Even from the street I could smell stale liquor and cheap herbacco.

We used the time we had left to survey the area, identifying locations, buildings or roads which differed from our original map. Laughing and hugging occasionally to look as inconspicuous as possible, we checked out alleyways and potential evac routes. Just before sixteen hundred we made our way to the rendezvous point, and within minutes the entire team had assembled.

"Ty, where's the map?" Jake asked.

"Here," he replied, pulling a data-pad from his backpack.

Each member of the Wolfpack gave Jake a tactical analysis of his quadrant, pointing out differences and danger points on the map.

"Okay, the main plan hasn't changed," Jake said. "Ty, Shae and I will go in the Saloon and get Marshall, or at least get information on where we can locate him." He turned to me and continued, "Ty and I will use aliases we back-stopped a few years ago. They should still be valid."

"Should? That doesn't instil much confidence," I replied, but Jake laughed.

"It'll be fine, Babe."

"Before we go in, you need to understand something," Ty said, scratching his shaved head before replacing his cap. "Tech-heads are, by nature, extremely paranoid and secretive... and they trust no one. These guys stay in business because they live and work off the grid. Some of them, like Marshall, are ghosts – more legend than actual person. Half the time we don't even know what they look like. My point is, you spook them, they rabbit, and you'll never find them again." He paused to check we were taking him seriously. "We'll probably have to get past a Blocker first, someone who'll assess whether we're genuine or not. To even get to see Marshall we're going to have to be completely believable as buyers. Jake, I need to lead on this if it's going to work."

Jake didn't hesitate. "It's your call, Ty. Shae and I will follow your lead."

"As far as I can tell, our aliases are intact, and the backstories I put in place are watertight." I think he said that more to me than to Jake. "We may have used trading as a ruse to get on the planet, but in the bar, we're going to be thieves looking to purchase some sensor jamming equipment."

"That's pretty fucking lame, Ty," Kaiser said, a frown puckering his weathered forehead. "You can pick that shit up anywhere. Even I'd be suspicious."

"It's not lame if the sensors you want to jam are the ones at the First Federal Bank on Tertia Nova," Ty explained.

"Come on!" Kaiser snorted. "That's even more suspicious. No one can crack that place. It's got more security than a Max-Five prison and a Royal Palace put together."

"And there's the challenge." Ty wasn't put off. "Trust me, I can sell this. If Marshall is the person who created the ultra-tech used by the Khans, and if he believes we're going to make a run at the bank, I guarantee you he won't be able to resist meeting us."

"Okay, so Ty's got the lead in the bar. Conner, Kaiser, your positions haven't changed, but I'm shifting our primary egress. I'm not liking this area," he pointed to the map, "so we'll take this road and join up with the original route here. Remember, coms open at all times."

Ty, Jake and I headed back to Main Street. A nervous excitement began to vibrate in my chest, but Jake stopped and gripped my arm, pulling me around so we were face to face.

"I want you to stay close to me. Whatever happens, you don't leave my side. Understand?" He studied my eyes.

"I can handle myself," I replied, irritably.

"I know you can." He smiled. "That's not what I meant. Not totally anyway. Look, Ty and I… we've worked together for a long time. We know how each other will react to situations, you don't, but if you stick with me, do what I do, you'll be fine."

"Okay."

"Okay?" he repeated, still watching me carefully.

"Okay, I'll stick to you," I clarified. "You can let go now." He rubbed my arm where he'd gripped it, and we continued down the street, past the Courthouse and General Store.

When we got to the Lone Tree Saloon, Jake opened the door, but he held me back to allow Ty in first. I followed directly behind but stopped the instant I crossed the threshold.

The bar wasn't busy, but every one of the gamblers, well-armed gunslingers, and barely clothed entertainers, had stopped what they were doing to stare. The room was pin-drop quiet.

"Afternoon," Ty said, removing his cap.

Grimy, shuttered windows let in little natural light, but the few shafts of sun that made it through, highlighted the swirls of herbacco smoke and dust motes which hung in the air.

Ty didn't move until the bar gradually fell back to business. The musicians in the corner started playing again, and the gamblers went back to their tables. The noise rose until it hit an even plateau of chatter and laughter.

Most of the patrons were Human, but I spotted a few Others dotted around, and several of the entertainers were most definitely not like us. Even though most had taken to ignoring our group, there were a few who watched every move we made. A balcony ran around the bar, and I clocked at least four men leaning against the balustrades, scrutinising us.

I followed Ty to a round table to the right of the bar, which at one time would have been stylish and well cared for. Now it was faded and pocked with gouges and... bullet holes? The engraved mirror behind was cracked and cloudy.

The floor, sticky from spilled bear and herbacco, was strewn with nut shells which crunched under my boots. The moment we sat, we were approached by a pretty waitress wearing a strapless bodice, cut low over her breasts, and a brightly coloured ruffled skirt which skimmed her thighs as she moved. The tassels on her kid boots were ostentatious, designed, no doubt, to try and hide the pistol tucked down the side.

She took an instant like to Ty and moved in closer, touching his shoulder and arm as she swished her skirt and picked at the frilly garter holding up net stockings.

"It's nice to see new people for a change," she said sweetly, her smile bright. "What can I get you nice folks?"

"Three whiskies," Ty said, returning a dazzling smile that was just as practiced as hers was.

"Three whiskies it is," she almost sang. "Coming right up."

Ty watched her as she walked back to the bar. She stopped halfway, turned, and blew a kiss in his direction. I didn't like her. The pretty makeup, brightly coloured clothes, and frilly boots didn't fool me. Under that girly, kitten exterior was a cantooa with claws. Ty winked back at her.

"All part of the cover," he whispered to me, grinning broadly.

It wasn't long before she returned with our drinks. "The name's Tara," she purred, sitting herself on Ty's knee before draping her arm around his neck.

"Ty Reston," he replied, slipping his arm around her impossibly slim waist. "Jake Elliott, my business partner," he added, nodding in our direction. Normally I would've been pissed at not being introduced, but as I didn't have an alias or back-story, we'd decided to keep me as low-profile as possible.

"So what brings you folks to Wishbone Creek?" Tara asked casually. She was good, I'd give her that, but the almost imperceptible flick of her eyes to the two men at the next table, and the practiced timbre of her voice, indicated an ulterior motive.

"Business," Jake said simply.

"Oh?" She smiled sweetly. "What business would that be, Mr Elliott?"

"The none-of-your kind of business," Jake replied, the friendliness of his voice incongruent with the words.

"I see," Tara said. She got up, her expression hurt.

"Actually, perhaps you can help us, sweetheart. We're looking for someone," Ty said smoothly, caressing the back of her thigh with his hand. She seemed momentarily appeased, and it impressed me just how seamless Jake and Ty's routine was.

"Anyone I might know?" she asked, her attention on Ty. Clearly Jake had annoyed her.

"You might. We were told he drinks here. His name's Nathaniel Marshall."

The sharp intake of breath betrayed her surprise, but she recovered quickly, shrugging her delicate, tanned shoulders before saying, "I've not heard of him. Perhaps you've been misinformed, Mr Reston."

"I don't think so," Jake said bluntly. "We came here to see Marshall, and we're not leaving till we do."

"We have a… a proposition for him," Ty interrupted quickly as the two men from the next table got up, gripping the handles of their still-holstered weapons. The few patrons sitting at other tables in the vicinity quickly moved away.

"What kind of proposition?" Tara asked tersely, the girly sweetness gone.

"That's between us and Marshall," Jake replied.

"We'll see about that."

"Look," Ty soothed. "We just want to talk to Marshall about a bit of business we believe he has the talent to help us with. If he's not interested, we'll leave. No big deal."

Tara studied us for a moment then indicated for the two men to sit.

"Enjoy your drinks," she said, the kitten purr back in place. "I'll be back shortly." She left to a swish of skirt and a blur of colour.

I downed my drink in one shot. As soon as it hit my stomach, I had to fight the urge to bring it back up again. A hot flush surged through my body and I wiped the sweat off my forehead, continually swallowing to stop myself being sick. The Fire Whisky I'd had with Jared was strong, but at least it was smooth – what I'd swallowed tasted more like Rover fuel. When the cramps subsided, and I could talk again, I suggested to the others that they might want to avoid the liquor.

After a few minutes, an ape of a man pulled up a chair, which creaked and groaned in protest as he sat between Ty and me. The buttons strained on his waistcoat and he had to re-arrange his gun belt so he could sit properly. He didn't bother to introduce himself.

"It seems you're quite the legend in the Thieves Guild, Mr Reston," the man said. "You have an interesting reputation."

"I couldn't possibly comment," Ty replied humbly, but a dry smile lingered on his lips.

"Come now," he continued, "a man of your talents shouldn't be so... modest."

"You say modest, I say careful. Bragging brings attention, and attention brings the law. Wouldn't you agree?"

"Of course, of course." I expected a booming belly-laugh from such a huge, brute of a man, but his was more of a high-pitched titter. I had to work hard to hold in my own laughter. "And you, Mr Elliott, your right hook is almost as well-known as Mr Reston's talent for... how should I put it... acquisitions."

"Thank you," Jake said simply, watching the man carefully. I wondered whether Jake's fake reputation was why the man had chosen to sit on the opposite side of the table from him.

"So, is that why you here?" he asked. "To acquire something that isn't yours?"

The men at the next table had gripped the handles of their guns again, and a quick glance around the room told me there were several more people watching, waiting, gun hands poised.

"We're here," Ty said quietly, "because we're planning a job and we need some highly specific tech."

"You came here for tech? Look around you," he said loudly, waiving his arm around the bar and drawing attention. "Wishbone Creek is a Frontier town, Mr Reston, not a hub of technological advancement. There's nothing for you here – I suggest you finish your drinks and leave." He stated to rise but Ty grabbed his arm.

"I know you're Marshall's Blocker," Ty hissed before dropping his voice to barely a whisper. "Tell Marshall we'd like to discuss an interesting article we read the other day. It was about the First Federal Bank of Tertia Nova and how, allegedly, it's impenetrable."

"Go on," the man grunted, intrigue filtering into his voice.

"We think they're cocky and arrogant, and it wouldn't surprise us if someone robbed them just to... I don't know... prove them wrong. If you get my drift."

The man's mouth fell open. I don't think he knew whether to be impressed or sceptical. "Stay here," he said before pulling his arm from Ty's grip. The wooden floorboards bounced slightly as he stalked off.

Jake yawned openly and stretched before pulling me

closer and kissing me on the temple. "I think it's going well," he whispered in my ear.

I turned and hugged him. "You call this going well?" I whispered back.

"We're still alive, aren't we?" His breath was warm on my neck and the inevitable goose-bumps spread across my skin. Jake sighed happily then removed his arm.

It was a good half-hour before the huge man returned from somewhere out the back. I didn't like the expression on his face, or the way he walked, like he was trying to look too casual. A knot tightened in my stomach and I began to get that feeling, the one I got right before a situation went hideously bad. Scanning the room, I noticed a slight but perceptible change to the atmosphere; a hint of anticipation or readiness – but readiness for what?

Jake tapped my foot with his and used a flick of his eyes to indicate the two men who'd taken up flanking positions by the front door.

"Well this isn't good," he said, leaning in so Ty could hear him.

The man approached the table, but this time he didn't sit. "Mr Marshall's not interested in having any discussions with you gentleman." I know I was supposed to be unassuming, but I wasn't used to being completely ignored. "Leave immediately, and don't come back... not if you value your lives," he added loudly.

It was as if the whole bar had taken a deep breath and held it. In a repeat of our arrival, everyone stopped what they were doing and watched in anticipation. The only noise in the entire room was the pinging of a slot machine in the far corner.

"Was I not clear?" the man asked when we hadn't moved.

"Wait," said Ty standing, but his unexpected movement spooked one of the men at the next table, who drew his weapon. In a cascade of overreaction, every armed person in the room followed suit.

A fraction of a second later, I was stood with my own Sentinel un-holstered and ready to fire. I caught the big man by surprise, swiftly kicking him in the side of the knee so he dropped heavily to the floor, grunting. I had one hand gripping the back of his hair and the muzzle of my gun pressed against his temple before he even knew what had happened.

His biggest mistake was underestimating me.

Jake flipped the table out of the way with one hand, and in an instant, I was back-to-back with him and Ty. On the upside, the three of us had managed to draw our weapons without being shot, but on the downside, we were surrounded and totally outgunned. And the worst of it was that Marshall was probably long gone.

I wasn't even sure having the Blocker as leverage was going to get us out of the situation in one piece.

"Con, check the bar's rear exit," Jake said over the jumble of shouted orders for us to lower our weapons and release Balcombe. So that was his name. "If Marshall splits, you need to pick him up. Copy?"

"Copy that. But I've got eyes on the back now and no one's left since you guys got there," Connor replied.

"What's going on?" Kaiser added. "You need me in there?"

"No. Stand firm," Jake said. "Hold for orders."

There were way too many loaded weapons in the bar for my liking, and it was clear our cover hadn't worked. Even if they still believed we were who we said we were, Marshall had chosen not to see us.

I had a plan.

It was risky, but I figured things couldn't get much worse for us. Besides, perhaps a radical solution was exactly what was needed.

I let go of Balcombe's greasy hair and kicked him in hard in the centre of his back, so he fell forward on to his face. He turned and looked at me with pure hatred in his eyes before scuttling away as quickly as his bulk would allow. I holstered my Sentinel and raised my hands in the air.

"Marshall," I shouted. "Nathaniel Marshall. I know you can hear me. You're an intelligent man. I know you don't want a bloodbath any more than we do, and let me tell you, it will be a bloodbath. We're not who we said we were." I paused to let another round of yelling die down.

"I hope you know what you're doing, Babe," Jake said over his shoulder.

"Me too," I replied to him before readdressing the bar. "We're not thieves and hitters, Nathaniel, we're REF." There were several gasps, and some of the crowd slowly lowered their guns. "Our mission is one of utmost importance and urgency, sanctioned by King Sebastian himself. We're not looking to arrest you, or take you in, we just want to talk to you about some ultra-tech we believe you may have created. We really don't want this kind of trouble."

"And why should I believe you?"

I snapped my head around in the direction of the voice. The crowd parted so I could see an older man, possibly in his sixties, turning slowly on his stool, a cane propped against the bar next to him.

"Nathaniel Marshall?" I asked sceptically, looking to Ty for confirmation. He shrugged.

"I prefer Nate," the man replied, struggling to stand. Tara hooked her arm under his and helped him, passing him his stick when he was steady. "I asked why I should believe you?"

"My name's Colonel Jake Mitchell," Jake said, but the man held up a gnarly, wizened hand.

"I wasn't talking to you," he said calmly, taking a few, unsteady steps. "I was talking to her. You're not REF, so you've lied already. Why should I believe anything else you said, young lady?"

"You're right," I replied. "I'm not. But they are." I indicated to Ty and Jake. "Everything else I said was the truth. We just want to talk to you."

"Hmm." Nate looked like he was thinking through something. "If you're not REF, then who are you? And before you answer, I suggest you think about the consequences of lying to me again."

I did think about the consequences, but I also thought about all the times I'd told people the truth and they didn't believe me. "I'm Brotherhood," I said, my voice strong and confident, but the room erupted in disbelief.

"Quiet," Nate said to silence them, and I couldn't be sure, but I thought I saw a brief smile cross his lips. "She's telling the truth."

"Impossible," grunted Balcombe.

"Improbable: yes. Impossible: no," Nate continued.

I wasn't sure why he'd believed me until his gaze dropped to my Cal'ret. Of course he would've recognised it, even if no one else had.

"Show's over people," he said. "Get back to your business, there's nothing more to see. Colonel? I don't believe those are necessary anymore." He pointed his stick towards the guns Jake still pointed around the room. "Come. We'll talk in the back; it'll be more private."

15

I settled Nate into an armchair by a holo-fireplace in the backroom and Tara placed a drink in front of him before she left. He struggled to grasp the handle with swollen, crooked fingers.

"BJS," he said without looking up, still concentrating on the glass. He took a sip and retuned the drink carefully to the table. "That's what I've got. Bryson Jacomb's Syndrome. I picked up a family of nasty little parasites on a trip to Sector Two about five years ago. Hardy little blighters, and resistant to everything the doctors threw at them. They attack the synovial tissue between all the joints in the body, releasing poisonous toxins into the bloodstream and causing this." He held up a twisted hand. "Fatal in the end. Doc says I've probably got two, maybe three years left… if I'm lucky."

"So that's why you didn't want to discuss work with us," Ty said.

"You're very astute, young man," Nate replied with more than a hint of sarcasm. "I couldn't build a toaster, let alone hold a plasma scalpel, even if I wanted to. May I?" He nodded towards my Cal'ret. I gave it to him, and he took it carefully with both deformed hands, his eyes widening like a child as he studied the markings.

"How long have your hands been like this?" I asked.

Nathaniel Marshall looked up from the baton and smiled at me with unexpectedly kind eyes. "Too long," he replied. "I shut down my workshop about three and a half years ago when it became obvious I couldn't provide the quality my clients expected. And trust me, the kind of clients I had, were not the kind of people you wanted to let down." His eye's narrowed. "Ask me what you really want to know."

"There was a—" Ty began, but Nate cut him off.

"Her," he said simply.

I looked to Jake, who nodded for me to take lead. "Three days ago, the Khan Brothers led an assault on the Palace of Palavaria."

Nate looked amazed. "A coup?" he asked, running his fingers along the markings of the Cal'ret. "That doesn't sound like the Khans." There was distaste in his voice, which surprised me.

"No, a robbery," I explained. "But things didn't go well for them. They took a hostage when they left."

"Who?"

Jake, who'd taken up a position by the door to the bar, shook his head slightly.

"That's not important," I replied, picking up on his cue. "What is important is that we find the Khans and get that person back."

"To be honest, I didn't think the Khans had the balls, or the resources, to take on a Crown. They should've stayed under a rock, where they belong."

"You sound like you've no love for them," I said.

"Vanze and Blain are exceptional at what they do, I'll give them that," he replied, his eyes glistening with disgust. "But what they do is tasteless and repugnant. They like to think they're royalty amongst criminals, but in my opinion, they're no better than back-alley thugs. They're uncivilized, loathsome creatures... and don't even get me started on that sister of theirs. Does that answer your question?"

"I think you've made your point. You don't like them, I get that, but have you done any work for them in the past?"

"Believe it or not, there's a hierarchy amongst criminals, with codes and disciplines. The Khans... they ignore all of it. They live by their own rules; rules I find morally disagreeable, to put it mildly. I may have created some minor equipment for their old man back in the day, but nothing since."

"So nothing recently?" Jake asked, leaning casually against the wall.

"Isn't that what I just said," Nate snapped.

"I'm sorry, it's just we've got to be sure," I soothed, hoping to pacify him. It must've worked because he returned his attention to my Cal'ret. "Mr Marshall—"

"Nate," he interrupted.

"Of course. Nate, the Khans used state of the art ultra-tech to knock out REF encrypted communications and hijack the palace security system. That level of sophistication means it had to have been created recently, and by someone highly skilled. The list is very short – if you didn't make it, then who did?"

Nate's smile returned. "I may have been out of the game a while, young lady, but I still keep my ear to the ground. I know exactly how advanced Palace security systems are, and I also know that REF rotating encryptions are almost impossible to hack. What I don't know is why you thought I created the tech."

"Well, umm, to be honest, this is where I'm going to have to defer to Ty; he's our tech whiz."

"Really?" Nate said, raising a sceptical eyebrow before turning carefully towards Ty.

"I'm sure the idea was to remove all the equipment when they left," Ty explained, pulling a data-pad from his pack. "But as Shae said, things didn't exactly go to plan for the Khans and they ended up leaving some of it behind. I've been able to study it extensively."

"Is there a point somewhere," Nate said impatiently.

"There's a signature in the tech," Ty continued, unfazed. "It's buried real deep in the coding, and it's slightly different from the reference samples we have on file, but there's no question the fundamentals are the same. It's your signature."

"Impossible. Let me see."

Ty slid the pad across the table, and we waited patiently for Nate to review the information. The two of them discussed the data and schematics for almost an hour, agreeing at times, disagreeing at others.

"I'm impressed," Nate concluded eventually, sitting back in his chair. "The signature was well hidden; I'm amazed you found it at all. Listen, I'd love to take credit for such an extraordinary work of art, but like I said, I didn't build it. I'm loath to admit it, but even if I did have working hands, I wouldn't have been able to create that."

"I don't understand," I said. "Ty say's it's your signature. Are you saying he's wrong?"

"Yes… no… well, not exactly. Your man here's right, to a point. There's no denying the basics of the signature are mine, but it's a bastardised version. There's enough there to bring you to my door, but it's different enough to belong to someone else."

"Do you know who?" I asked.

"Hmm, now there's the rub," Nate replied ambiguously, looking thoughtful.

"An apprentice," Ty suggested. "Someone who's advanced beyond your teachings. That would explain why the signatures are similar, yet different."

"Gold star to the young man," Nate said laughing, but it was a hollow laugh that didn't reach his eyes. "It's true I've had a few apprentices, but they were a long time ago. When you're the best at what you do, you expect the best from others. You expect them to have the same work ethics you do, to put in the same amount of effort and dedication, and when they don't, it's soul destroying. You've put in all that time and effort to teach them, and it's for nothing. Nowadays the young have no pride in their work, wanting to learn how to mass-produce commercial shit rather than concentrating on the craft. What I do… did," he corrected before sighing heavily, "was art. Most of my apprentices failed to live up to my expectations, so I cut them loose. None of them would be remotely capable of creating this tech." He tapped the data-pad with a swollen finger.

"You said most failed to reach your expectations," I pushed.

"There was one who may be able to produce this level of ultra-tech now. Jesper was the last trainee I had, with me for about eighteen months maybe ten years ago. Far more advanced than anyone else in his peer group, and interested in creating custom-built, individually crafted tech. He was a technical genius, but he was also sloppy and impulsive. At first, he seemed happy to learn the fundamentals of the craft. We concentrated on code scanners, sensor jammers, communication overriders, biometric cloners – standard stuff really, but it gets more complex depending on the level of security you're trying to bypass."

"So what happened," Ty asked as Nate paused to take a drink. He looked tired, his movement slow and deliberate.

"Jesper got the hang of the fundamentals quickly. I was impressed, especially after the other dross I'd taught, so it wasn't long before we moved on to more intricate work. After a while he became impatient, always pushing on to the next thing, and when I wanted him to concentrate on something he wasn't interested in, he became temperamental and argumentative. Eventually his mood swings became unpredictable and he started working on private projects he wouldn't tell me about, keeping his lab locked. One day he left it open by mistake and I went in – turned out he'd been creating weapons prototypes. That was the end as far as I was concerned. I confronted him and made him leave immediately."

"And that's it?" I asked.

"'Fraid so."

"No, there's something more, something you're not telling us," Jake prompted, eyeing him suspiciously.

"Well, there was something else, but it's not something I particularly like talking about," Nate mumbled. "Kind of embarrassing to be honest."

"Nate, please. Anything you can tell us might help," I added.

Nate sighed deeply and shifted in his chair. "About a week after Jesper left, I noticed my secure data-network had been accessed. Yes, I get the irony. Top hacker gets hacked by pupil, like I said, it's embarrassing. Anyway, he'd copied everything: my entire work history, back catalogue of tech, notes, ideas, schematics, the lot. After that I vowed never to have another apprentice."

"So, this Jesper? You think he could be the one who created the ultra-tech?" I asked.

"Ten years ago, I'd have said no, he wasn't disciplined enough, but a lot can happen in ten years, and as I said, Jesper was a technical mastermind. This tech's beyond even me, but if Jesper continued to learn and develop the way he did when he was my apprentice, I'd say it's more than likely he's your man."

"Is there anything else you can tell us about Jesper, like where he is now?" asked Jake.

"About the time I picked up these nasty little buggers in Sector Two, I heard a rumour he'd set up a workshop in Dome Two on GalaxyBase5, but like I said, it was just a rumour."

"Do you have any records of work he did, or any photos, background history, family details. Anything that could help us track him down?" I asked, hoping to jog a memory.

"Sorry." He shrugged wearily. "After I found out he'd hacked my life's work, I was furious. I erased every trace of him ever working with me. Besides, he wasn't exactly forthcoming with personal information. All I can tell you is he went to Westchester Academy. That's where I first met him."

"What is it, Babe?" Jake asked, catching a look on my face.

"I'm not sure. That name: Westchester Academy. It sounds familiar." I searched my brain briefly but couldn't dredge up anything further. "Probably nothing," I concluded.

Jake turned his attention back to the old man. "And there's nothing else you can tell us?" he pushed, but Nate simply shook his head.

"In that case, we won't bother you any further," I said. "And we appreciate that you didn't let things get out of control back there."

"You're welcome, but I suggest you don't hang around. The locals can be a little... twitchy."

"Nate?" I said after a moment.

"Hmm?"

"I'm going to need that back." I pointed to my Cal'ret.

"Oh, of course." He handed it over with a grin. "I'd hoped you'd forgotten."

As Jake reached for the saloon door, Nate added, "Jesper's an unstable sociopath with an off-the-chart IQ. Whatever you do, don't underestimate him."

I nodded my thanks for the warning, and we left the bar, all eyes following us until we were out on the street.

"Well that was intense," joked Ty. "Never a dull moment with you around," he added looking straight at me.

"Hey, if I remember rightly, you were the one that spooked them. I was the one that calmed it all down."

"The way I remember it—"

"That's enough, children," Jake waded in before adding, "Kaiser, Con, we're done here. Standard egress protocols. I'm not expecting trouble, but keep your eyes open."

Connor stepped out of the shadows as we rounded a corner and a few moments later Kaiser appeared from a side ally, a canvas bag slung casually over his shoulder.

"I'm gutted I didn't get to use the RPG," he grumbled.

"I know, dude. It's just not the same when you don't get to blow shit up," Connor quipped, smacking him hard on the arm.

Forty minutes later we were back in the *Veritas*. While Ty described Tara's attributes in every minute detail to the other two, Jake and I headed to the flight deck to contact the *Defender*.

"I'm sorry about the guys, they can be a little boisterous at times," Jake said, letting me through the hatch first.

"Don't be, I think they're great."

"You're incredible, you know that, right?" he continued, resting his hand on the small of my back.

"Don't, Jake." I wasn't sure whether I was referring to his touch, or his comment. Perhaps both.

"It's a fact. A compliment," he said, perching on the arm of the pilot's chair. "They like you too, by the way… and they don't normally take to outsiders tagging along."

"Tagging along?" I raised an eyebrow to indicate mock offence.

"You know what I mean. They don't like outsiders joining the team, even temporarily. They say it destroys their equilibrium. Seriously, the last person High Command insisted join us for an op ended up in hospital. The official report said he got himself on the wrong side of an argument with the target, but unofficially… let's just say Kaiser and I had to have strong words and leave it at that."

I giggled because I could picture the conversation

exactly.

"God you're beautiful when you laugh," he said.

"Jake…"

"Okay, okay." He held up his hands in defeat before sitting properly in the flight chair. I took the navigator's seat beside him.

"So, I guess our next step is to find Jesper," I said, my voice an echo of the frustration I felt inside.

I'd hoped it would be easy: Nate would be the one who'd supplied the Khans with the tech, he would lead us directly to them, and we would get the Princess, the Seal and my answers.

Deep down I knew life was never that simple. I don't know why I felt so disappointed.

"This Jesper character's definitely our new target," confirmed Jake. "But I'm not taking the *Veritas* all the way to GalaxyBase5 on a rumour. It would take us two days to get there and two days back – I can't risk it without more up to date intel. As much as I hate to admit it, we need the *Defender* and that god-damn Oracle thing. Why are you smiling at me?"

"Because you pretend to be the moody loan wolf, the guy who doesn't play well with others, but it's all an act."

"No, it's not," he said in an exaggerated deep, tough accent, but he couldn't stop the corners of his mouth from twitching. "Okay," he said in his normal voice. "You got me. I'm a secret good guy. Just keep it to yourself, I don't want to ruin my reputation. You ready?"

I nodded as Jake hailed the *Defender*. The view of silhouetted mountains through the *Veritas*' front screen disappeared and was replaced by the activity of TaDCom. Hale appeared on screen, juggling three data-pads.

"Colonel Mitchell, Shae, good to see you," he said politely. "One moment." He called over a short female ensign and passed her the pads. "Sorry about that. As you can see, things are a little crazy here."

"Is Captain Marcos available," Jake asked, getting straight to business. Hale took no offence.

"The Captain's on his way back from the planet." He didn't say which one. "He should land in approximately ten minutes, but I can patch you through to the Warrior if you'd like."

I opened my mouth to say yes, but Jake got there first.

"No, it's okay. Our mission was a bust anyway. There's not much to report, he can read it in my After-Action account later. It's actually you we want, Commander."

"Of course. What do you need?"

"Nathaniel Marshall didn't create the ultra-tech, but he thinks an old apprentice of his might have," I explained. "Unfortunately, we've got almost nothing on this new guy."

"Tell me what you have, and I'll see what we can do."

"The man's name is Jesper. There's a rumour he was on GalaxyBase5, Dome Two, five or so years ago… oh, and I'd guess he's late twenty's early thirty's because he was studying at Westchester Academy about ten years ago," offered Jake.

That name again. Something niggled at the back of my brain.

"We'll get on it straight away, cross-referencing Jesper with the Khans, Marshall, GB5 and Westchester—"

"Hoban!" I almost shouted as the blurred half-memory burst into focus. I turned to Jake. "In the Catacombs there was man working for the Khans, his name was Hoban. He escaped with them. You remember?"

"Yeah, scruffy little fucker if I recall correctly. But what's the relevance?" Jake looked amused by my excitement.

"That's where I recognise the name from. Hoban wore a Westchester Academy t-shirt, and I'd put him about the same age as Jesper. But it could just be a coincidence," I decided, my enthusiasm waning once I'd listened to my own feeble case.

"You know we don't believe in coincidences, Babe," Jake said, offering a reassuring smile.

"No, it's all good," added Hale. "The more information we can give the Oracle to work with, the better. I'll throw this Hoban character into the mix and see what happens. Do you know anything else about him?"

"Just that he's an archaeologist," I replied without thinking.

"What did the Khans need with an archaeologist?" Jake's forehead creased. Crap. I'd walked straight into that one.

"No idea." I shrugged, trying to sound convincing.

"Not to worry, we'll get the Oracle on the case," Hale said. "It'll take a bit of time, but we'll get back to you as soon as we have something."

"Okay. Tell Captain Marcos I'll submit my After-Action report later this evening," Jake said.

"You can tell him yourself." Hale smiled. "He's just arrived."

"Oh, great. Must be my lucky day."

Jared appeared on screen wearing full tactical gear. "Hey, any luck with Marshall?" he asked, undoing the clips on his breast plate.

"No," Jake replied bluntly.

Jared stopped what he was doing and looked up, an enigmatic smile on his face. I sighed and lent forwards in my chair.

"We have a new lead, but we'll let Hale fill you in," I said. "What about you?"

"Nothing. We've crashed a few places, but none of them have given us anything helpful." He passed his armour to someone off-screen. "Is everyone okay there?" he asked, looking at me.

"Everyone's fine," huffed Jake. "Not even a hangnail," he added lazily.

"Are you all right?" I asked. "And your men? Is

everyone all right?"

"We're all good." Jared smiled, and I couldn't help returning it. I glanced sideways and caught Jake watching me.

"What about Ash?" I tried changing the subject. "Any news?"

"They arrived at Dennford several hours ago but no update since they left for the planet."

"When he checks in, could you ask him to contact me?" It had only been twenty-four hours since I'd spoken to Ash, but I needed to see him, to hear his voice – make sure he was alright. "It doesn't matter what time it is."

"Sure," Jared replied.

"Okay then," Jake said loudly, standing up. "You'll get my mission report later this evening, and we'll wait to hear from Lieutenant Commander Hale about our lead."

"Wait—" Jared started, but Jake cut the signal off.

"That wasn't necessary," I huffed.

"What wasn't, Babe?" He looked innocent, eyes wide and bright.

I was annoyed, but I didn't have the energy to get into another discussion with Jake about Jared. Instead, we walked back to the main cabin in silence.

Later that evening, Jake brought the Pack together for a briefing.

"Connor, we'll save the fuel cells and stay on land tonight, but I want the ship prepped and ready for departure as soon as we have a location on Jesper." Connor nodded. "Kaiser, I don't want any surprises from the locals. Take Ty and set up a perimeter of AG42's. I know it's a little overkill, but I don't want anyone getting within a hundred metres of the ship."

"On it," Kaiser replied.

"I also want all mission reports in my inbox by twenty-two-hundred. That includes yours," he added to me. "Dismissed."

With Connor on the flight deck, and Kaiser and Ty outside setting up the automated weapons stations, I decided to take to my quarters to complete my report. I tried to tell myself it was for the peace and quiet, but if I was truthful, it was because I didn't want to be alone with Jake.

He hadn't mentioned our 'talk', but perhaps that was because we hadn't been alone since. Part of me thought it was for the best, but part of me knew it was just a pause in the conversation. Jake had said he loved me, and no matter how hard I tried, I couldn't get those words out of my head.

I'd finally told him how I felt about Jared, but instead of being hurt and angry, he'd told me I was confused, mistaken even.

But I wasn't. Was I?

I loved Jared… but I also loved Jake.

I threw the data-pad on the bed and pulled the pillow over my head in a ridiculous attempt to block everything out.

A knock on the door made my stomach flip.

"Come in," I said, surprised to see Connor open the hatch.

"Expecting someone else?" he teased with a mischievous grin. "Thought you might like this." He held out a steaming mug and I took it gratefully, breathing in the distinct Goldflower perfume.

"Tea?"

"You drink too much coffee," he said, shrugging. "It's not good for you last thing at night."

"That's so thoughtful," I replied. His eyes narrowed. "I'm serious. Thank you."

"Yeah… well… umm…" He cleared his throat. "I was making one for everyone else, so it was no bother. I'll leave you to it."

The tea was good and I drank it while I finished my report, finally sending it off to Jake with an exaggerated press of a button. I hated paperwork. As far as I was concerned, it was somewhere between scraping lunar arthropods off the *Nakomo's* hull, and ironing monk's robes. I forwarded a copy to Francis for our Brotherhood files and was just setting the data-pad on the desk when it beeped loudly.

Connor's face filled the screen. "You've got a call," he said before disappearing. A moment later, Ash appeared.

"You could've com'd half an hour ago and given me an excuse not to write my After-Action report," I moaned.

"Hello to you too," he replied, a lopsided grin appearing. "What's up?"

"I've missed you."

"It's only been a day," he said laughing, but I knew he understood, even if I couldn't feel him through the Link. "You okay? Jared said you wanted to talk."

"Oh, you know, I just wanted to see your ugly mug. See for myself you're okay. Now I'm satisfied, you can go."

"Funny. I'm glad to see you're all right as well."

"We're all fine here. Except Marshall wasn't our guy."

"Yeah, Jared told me. He's not happy with Jake about something though. What happened?"

"Just Jake being Jake. Nothing to worry about," I replied. "Hey, where are you?" I didn't recognise the background.

"Still on Dennford. We encountered a small amount of resistance when we got here, but we took the compound without casualties. We've got six prisoners, all mercs and gun-thugs, but they haven't given us anything we didn't already know."

"Nothing at all?" I was disappointed

"We did learn one thing. The Khans had a lieutenant with them called Deakes. You said you saw him in the Great Hall with Vita."

"I remember him."

"Well, he was responsible for rounding up the militia

and bringing them to Dennford. The mercs had no idea they were working for the Khans. As far as they were concerned, Deakes was the boss. Incidentally, Sergeant Mollere has confirmed that Deakes wasn't left on Decerra, either dead or alive, so we have to assume he got away with the Khans."

"Using Deakes as a proxy was a smart move on the Khans' part." I sighed and sat back. "I'm not liking our odds, Ash."

"I hear you, but we've still got time."

"I'm not giving up, it's just…"

"I know. How's things with Jake," he asked.

The sudden change of topic threw me for a second. "It's complex. We're okay…" Ash looked sceptical. "Honestly, we're okay. I told him how I felt about him, and about Jared, but things… they didn't exactly go how I expected."

"What do you mean?" Concerned furrows etched his brow.

"I'll tell you everything, I promise, but it's not the kind of conversation to have over a com-link."

"I understand. As long as you're okay?"

"I'm fine. You don't need to worry about me."

"But I like worrying about you. So, tell me more about your mission. I hear you had more excitement than we did."

16

The morning came too quickly, and I was woken by a thudding on my door, followed by Kaiser yelling that breakfast was ready. My heart raced from being roused from such a deep sleep, and it took my brain a while to catch up. I yanked on a pair of combats and a t-shirt and made my way to the kitchenette.

"Holy shit!" Connor exclaimed as I sat. "You look like the dead walking."

I threw him a look before resting my head on the cool tabletop.

"She looks like you do after a night on Santian Vodka," I heard Ty say.

I didn't know who he was talking to until Jake replied, "It was only that one time. And I swear it was spiked."

"Hmm, that's what you say," Ty replied. Everyone laughed, even Jake.

The deep, rich smell of fresh Shatokian coffee made me lift my head off the table, and as Jake pushed the mug closer, I picked it up, inhaling the intense aroma.

"We acquired some from the *Defender*," he explained. "For emergencies." He smiled, but didn't take his eyes off me, watching my every move.

"I've never pretended to be a morning person," I grumbled, taking a large mouthful and feeling instantly better.

Halfway through breakfast, the com-panel beeped, and a holo-screen appeared above the table.

"You got something for us?" Jake asked Hale.

"Yes, Sir, but I have to say, it's not much. The Oracle has found fragments of information on Jesper, but it seems he's worked very hard to scrub most traces of who he is from the data-nets. We haven't been able to find one photo of him, not even from his Westchester days."

"So we've got no idea what the dude looks like? Great!" Jake was frustrated and impatient. "Tell me there's some good news?"

"The Oracle predicts there's a fifty-two percent chance that Jesper's on Genesis."

"Fifty-two percent?" I said. "Is that all?"

"I know it's not much," Hale replied. "But all indicators point to him owning a tech repair shop in the Beta District."

"A shop owner?" Jake snorted. "You're saying Jesper runs a repair business? You're kidding me, right?"

"No, Colonel. That's the intel we have... although I would suggest the shop is simply a front." There was just a hint of reciprocated sarcasm in his voice, enough to make me smile anyway.

"And that's it?" Jake pushed.

"That's all we've got. Your guy's basically a ghost, we were lucky to get this much. I'm sending you the information now. Is there anything else I can do for you, Sir?" Jake shook his head. "Then I won't keep you further."

The holo-screen dissolved.

"Great. Genesis of all places, now my day's complete," I grumbled, downing the last of my coffee. "I hate that shitty little planet."

"I take it you're not a big fan, Babe. What's the story?"

"How do you know there is one?"

"Because there's always a story," Ty said, eagerly leaning forward.

"It's not that exciting." I hoped my bland tone would put them off. It didn't work.

"Come on," added Connor beseechingly.

"Yeah, come on, Blue. You've got us all interested now," Kaiser said.

The entire Wolfpack looked at me with expectant faces, but my stomach froze over just thinking about the place.

"Okay." The word came out as a sigh as I resigned myself to the fact that they weren't going to let me get away without explaining. "Have any of you actually been there?"

"I have," Connor said, but he was the only one.

"Then you'll agree it really is a shitty little planet?" He nodded emphatically. I turned to the others. "Picture a quaint Category Two planet with some cute little indigenous critters and a few interesting species of flora. Then add a smattering of small settlements, basic but sufficient... you got it?" They nodded. "Now picture the arrival of Scientia Corp, with promises of a better, easier life. Guaranteed jobs, good wages, nice homes... who wouldn't want that, right? But don't forget this is Scientia we're talking about. What they really wanted was for the people to hand over their mineral rights. They threw credits and tech at the planet, defining and structuring it as they wanted. Affairs of state, law enforcement, mines, hospitals, schools, all the major organisations... they had a hand in the lot. Eventually everything was owned by the Corporation, including the people."

"I can see why you're not so keen, Babe," Jake said.

"You think that's bad? Fast-forward a thousand years and what you've got now is a planet that's literally imploded. The pits are dry and the Corporation's moved on to some other unsuspecting planet. There are no more mining jobs, and tech has replaced a lot of the work once done by people... so now they have no work, no wages, and no future. They can't afford to leave, so they're stuck in a system that doesn't give a shit about them."

"Sounds like a great place," Ty said.

"I haven't got to the best bit yet. Huge, sprawling metropolises now cover almost the entire surface of the planet, run by a small elite of the rich and powerful who lord it over everyone else with force and oppression. It's a miserable place full of hopeless Humans and Others; people who've simply given up. It's what happens when accelerated industrialisation is allowed to run unchecked," I concluded. Just talking about the place made me feel depressed.

"So why were you there?" Connor asked.

"I was sixteen when I tagged along on a Brotherhood mission. We'd been pursuing a guy named Loka, a trader. Big in people trafficking, Human and Other. Eventually we tracked him to Genesis, and I was allowed to go with the team as part of my training. As an observer only. We went in hard and fast and took him down, persuading him to take us to his 'stock' as he called them. It was hideous. They'd kept them in the worst conditions I'd ever seen – cramped, filthy and full of disease. They hadn't even moved out the bodies of the poor people who'd perished in their cells. We helped as many of them as we could and closed down a number of other sites as well, but it was impossible to get them all. I've got no doubt there were many more, probably worse." Jake rubbed my arm gently. "You know what it's like when you're young and idealistic. I thought I could change the Sector, but Genesis taught me what evil people were truly capable of. It was a hard lesson."

"I'm sorry," Jake said.

"Why? It's not your fault."

"We shouldn't have pushed you to tell the story."

"It's okay. As Finnian used to say, every lesson we

experience becomes a part of who we become." I swallowed the lump in my throat. "You know what I could really do with now?"

"It's got to be either coffee or ice-cream," Ty said.

"How about both?" Jake offered. "Who cares if it's breakfast time." He stood and flexed his shoulders. "Kaiser, you and Ty need to bring in the AG42's asap. Con, plot a route to Genesis. Struts up in thirty. Looks like we're going to Hell."

About an hour out from Genesis, we received coms from Hale. "Captain Marcos asked me to contact you—"

"Where is he? Is he alright? Is he hurt?" I interrupted, afraid something had happened.

"No, ma'a... umm... the Captain's about to go on a mission, but he wanted me to let you know that a ship's been dispatched to rendezvous with you in orbit. For assistance."

"Well, you can tell Captain Marcos that we didn't ask for assistance, and we certainly don't need it," Jake said, bristling. "You can also tell the ship to stand down."

"I would, Colonel, but she doesn't belong to us. The *Nomad* was dispatched under the instruction of Brother Francis. I have no jurisdiction."

For a moment, Jake seemed lost for words. "Fine," he said eventually. "We'll catch up with them in orbit." He terminated the com-link with more force than necessary. "Tell me about the *Nomad*," he asked as we left the flight deck. "What can I expect?"

"Well, to start with, she's a Wanderer."

"Aren't they those hippy-ships that go around preaching the word of the Brotherhood? The whole 'we'll be saved from hell by glowing, golden gods' thing."

I frowned at him. "Not exactly. As you know, the Brotherhood is split into two distinct disciplines: the Warrior Caste, who look after physical needs, and the

Doctrinal Caste – teachers and scholars – who look after the spiritual side. The Wanderers are a small fleet of ships that literally roam space, making themselves available to anyone who needs our help. It doesn't matter whether that's spiritual or physical."

"Like a first line response team?"

"Something like that." I liked the analogy. "The exact contingent of each Wanderer depends on ship size, but if I remember correctly, the *Nomad* has a crew of six. Three Warrior, three Doctrinal."

"And the Captain?"

"Unless it's changed, that would be Brother Cassius. Seventh Degree, Doctrinal. He's a good man."

"Great," Jake said, puffing out an exaggerated breath. "He couldn't be Warrior Caste, could he? No. That would be too helpful. He had to be a bloody scholar."

"These are my people, Jake. My family," I said, immediately defensive. "They're coming to help us, the least you can do is be civil."

He lowered his head, running a hand through his shaggy hair before looking up through his lashes.

"Babe, I'm sorry. I didn't mean… I'm not used to all this… support. The Wolfpack has always been an independent unit, surviving on our training and each other. I guess I'm just taking longer to adjust to all this team stuff than I thought." His eyes told me he was telling the truth, so I didn't pull away when he put an apologetic arm around my shoulder.

"You're right though," I conceded with a cheeky smile. "Cass may skipper the *Nomad*, but in matters like this, he would always defer to the highest-ranking Warrior Caste onboard."

When we arrived in orbit, the *Nomad* was already there. During a brief com-link, Cass introduced himself to Jake before presenting Brother Riley, a Sixth Degree Warrior Caste monk.

Jake was on his best behaviour, and after a brief update on the situation, we agreed that Riley and the two other Warrior Caste monks on board would meet us at coordinates slightly to the north of Jesper's supposed repair shop.

As we were gearing up, I noticed the others tucking weapons out of sight and looked down at my own belt, the Cal'ret and Sentinel in full view. Jake noticed.

"You want my opinion, leave the Cal'ret here and hide the gun," he suggested. "Genesis isn't the place to draw attention."

Connor brought the *Veritas* in to land, navigating it down a narrow shaft surrounded by dangerously decaying buildings hundreds of stories high. "Good job I'm an exceptional pilot," he bragged as we touched down on our designated landing coordinates.

It was early evening, but already dark. Grey, aging buildings, with plain, muted shop fronts introduced a depressing and harsh world. Persistent, torrential rain bounced off the sidewalks, turning mounds of rubbish into soggy mulch. People scuttled towards unknown destinations, heads down or covered with hoods and shawls, all in equally dismal colours.

I sloshed through a good five centimetres of water, my boots creating little tidal waves that rippled across the street. I was already soaked to my skin and irritated by the unrelenting rain. I tugged the collar of my jacket up around my ears, but it didn't stop the cold trickle of water that ran down my back.

As we approached the rendezvous point, Kaiser lent over and whispered, "I thought they'd be wearing robes."

I gave him my don't be ridiculous look. "Not on a mission like this. Don't you know anything about the Brotherhood?"

"Always tried to steer clear before," he said apologetically.

We huddled together under a battered shop canopy to escape the worst of the weather, but out of the rain the smell of rotting waste burnt my nostrils.

Jake held out his hand to Riley and the two men shook firmly. "These are Brothers Elias and Peter," the monk said.

"Thanks for coming at such short notice," Jake replied graciously. "That's Kaiser, Connor and Ty. I believe you know Shae?"

Elias and Peter looked a little awestruck, but Riley didn't hesitate to step forward and give me a hug. I was accepted by the Brotherhood, but that didn't mean I wasn't an oddity amongst the collective. Especially with the monks who didn't see me that often.

"How can we assist you this evening?" asked Riley, getting straight to business. Something I knew Jake would appreciate.

Jake held out a data-pad so everyone could see the displayed holo-map. "Ty, Shae and I will go in the shop after Jesper, but we could do with extra back-up around the perimeter. I'd like one of your men to go with Kaiser to this building, and another to go here – ground level, next building over from Connor. I'd like you to take the rear of the building here, to stop anyone who heads that way. You okay with that?"

Riley nodded.

A block from Jesper's we split, small parties heading in different directions. As our group approached the shop front, Jake said, "We've done this once, we can do it again. Smooth and easy."

"Smooth and easy," Ty repeated slowly. "Just how I like my women."

I laughed. I couldn't help it, even though Jake pinned both of us with a withering glare.

The shop windows were lit, displaying different items of low-level tech, each in various states of repair. Jake opened the door, and that time I knew to let Ty in first. The three of us stood just inside the entrance, letting the thermo-vec dry our clothes almost instantly. The good thing about unendingly bad weather was that people learnt to adapt. I felt better once I was warmed to my insides.

A young woman with bright purple hair sat on a stool behind the counter, and behind the dark, heavy make-up, she looked bored and indifferent to our arrival. She continued to stare into a mirror on the counter, applying grey eyeshadow, until Jake banged on the counter. She looked up and give each of us an annoyed once-over.

"What you want?" she enquired lazily. "You here to collect something?"

"Something like that... Justine," said Ty, reading the embroidered name on her cheap, overly tight shirt. He fell seamlessly into the same routine we'd used on Independence, but when he mentioned that Nathaniel Marshall had sent us there to talk to Jesper, she held up her hand.

"Ramirez," she screeched at the top of her voice. "Ramirez, get your fat, lazy arse out here."

An Other, who had more than a few Rhinorian genes in him, stormed through a door, knocking a stack of old data-pads flying.

"What the fuck do you want, bitch?" he growled. "You know I hate being disturbed when I'm eating."

"They're looking for Jesper," she said, seemingly used to his manner.

"Then you're mistaken, there's no one of that name here," he grunted, placing a bowl and chopsticks noisily on the counter.

Ty ignored his comment and introduced us anyway. At least he introduced Ty Reston and Jake Elliot. The purple-haired girl turned her attention to a data-pad, her black fingernails clicking quickly on the screen.

I thought Ramirez was going to physically throw us out of the shop, until Ty used the same line about the First

National Bank of Tertia Nova.

"So if, say, hypothetically, someone was going rob the bank, just to prove they could… then, hypothetically, they'd need the best ultra-tech credits could buy. Rumour has it, Jesper's the best tech artist in these parts. And I can promise you, money's not an issue."

The Other looked at Ty with beady eyes, clearly trying to decide whether to believe him or not.

"Oi," Justine said, poking him in the side before sliding the data-pad towards him. He studied it briefly then looked back at Ty, and I might have been imagining it, but he looked slightly more… respectful? His gaze returned to the pad before rising to Jake. He nodded approvingly.

"I'm impressed," Ramirez grunted. "It seems if anyone can prove those cocky little shites wrong, it's you, Reston."

"You know what they say," Ty said. "Pride comes before a fall."

Ramirez barked out a deep, gravely laugh. "Stay here," he rumbled before turning his attention to the girl. "Well don't just sit there, bitch. Lock the door. Shop's closed."

Justine slid off her stool and headed towards the door, mumbling curses under her breath, while Ramirez picked up the data-pad and thudded towards the back of the shop.

"And pick up these fucking pads," he yelled. "The place is a fucking shit-pit." He disappeared through the door, unaware of the hand gestures the girl was giving him.

She locked the front door before scanning her handprint into the sensor pad on the wall. Thick metal shutters closed on the street-side of the smeared windows, and on the inside, bright orange lasers crisscrossed the shopfront from floor to ceiling.

"Jake, what's going on," Kaiser said over the com-link. "Clear your throat if you're okay."

Jake coughed lightly.

"What are we looking at if we need to breach?" Kaiser continued.

"That's interesting security you've got there," Jake said to the girl. "What is that? A Maxwell Two-Fifty armour plated shutter?"

"Close, it's the Two-Sixty," she replied.

"Right. Two-Sixty," Jake repeated.

"Damn, that's tough shit," Kaiser commented.

"And I've not seen that internal laser configuration before," Jake pushed.

"It's one of Jesper's own designs, from his darker collection. Damn thing's hotter than the sun. I'm convinced it's going to take my bloody hand off one of these days." She turned serious and lowered her voice. "The man's a legend when it comes to ultra-tech, but he's got a sick, twisted side to him. Some of the shit he creates is just downright inhuman. If you want my opinion, the guy's wrong in the melon. You can see it in his eyes. He's not playing with a full deck, if you know what I mean. If I were you, I wouldn't do anything to piss him off."

"What the fuck are you gabbing about, woman," Ramirez grunted from the back of the room.

Justine jumped and turned ghost white. "Nothing. Just passing time, right?" She looked pleadingly at me.

"That's right," I said. "Just passing time."

"Hmm," he rumbled. "You could always pass the time... clearing up those fucking data-pads like I told you too," he bellowed. He straightened his shirt and turned his attention to Ty. "Jesper's intrigued by your proposal and will be with you shortly," he added at a reasonable volume.

Justine was on her knees collecting up pads when the door opened. A short, emaciated man appeared, his long, lanky hair hanging over his pasty face like ribbons as he studied a data-pad.

Jesper took a few steps into the room before he looked up. His mouth fell open, his eyes widened with recognition, and he turned quickly, bolting back through the door.

"Bollocks," Ty exclaimed before taking off after him.

Jake and I were close behind, but when I passed Justine she reached out and grabbed my arm, pulling me back.

"You don't want to go down there," she pleaded. "Let him go." I pulled away from her grasp.

I'd only been delayed a moment, but already the others were out of sight, and the door on the far side of the storeroom swung shut. I pushed on, through an office and into a stairway, barely noticing the rusting signs, strewn garbage, or the overpowering stench of urine.

After a few levels, I'd nearly caught up, and could hear Jake talking quickly to Kaiser as we chased after Jesper. But after another floor down we lost coms. For a fleeting moment I wondered whether it was because we were underground, encased in metal and concrete, or because some kind of jamming-tech was involved. It didn't matter, and I had other things to worry about. The thought vanished a second later.

We closed in on Jesper, but then he veered away from the stairs and headed down a long corridor, using something in his hand to remotely unlock a hatch at the far end. The lights on the access panel turned from red to green and it swung open, allowing him to go through without even slowing. I watched it starting to swing closed again.

Ty got there first. The gap was too tight for him to get through, but he got his fingers around the edge of the hatch, groaning with the effort to pull it open again. It was futile. The hydraulics were stronger than the three of us combined, and in the end, I had to snatch my hands away so I didn't lose my fingers. Over heavy breathing I heard the mocking, metallic clank of the deadbolts shifting back into place.

"Damn it," Jake shouted, punching the hatch. "Ty, get us in there. And will someone please tell me what the fuck happened back there?"

"It's my fault, Boss," said Ty as he worked on the

keypad. "We've met before, he knew I was military."

"What the?"

"I didn't know the guy was Jesper," Ty continued quickly. "I interviewed him after a heist years ago, before I was Wolfpack. He used a different name, and his ident-report said he was a lawyer or some shit. We didn't have a picture of Jesper. How was I supposed to know?"

"Okay, okay," Jake said, pacing. "It's not your fault. Just get the damn hatch open." As the words left his mouth, the lights flicked, and the deadbolts retracted. "On three: Shae, open the door, Ty, go right and low. Got it?"

As instructed, I placed a hand on the cold, slightly slimy lever, waiting for his countdown. When he'd checked we were ready, he held three fingers in front of his chest, then two, then one. A heartbeat after the one count, I yanked the lever down and pulled the door towards me as hard and fast as I could, stepping out of the way so the others had clear access.

I'd expected a room of some sort, but another hallway lay ahead of us – two metres across and maybe fifteen or so in length. The hatch at the far end swung shut with an echoing metallic clang.

I stepped into the dim hallway behind Ty and Jake, the only light coming from three air processing fans that swirled in the metal ceiling, casting intricate patterns on the floor. I pulled out a torch from one of my trouser pockets.

"Let's hustle. Shae, stay behind me. Ty, you've got the rear. This bastard's not getting away," Jake said, striding forward. His torchlight glinted off metal shavings on the stone, but the second the beam of light swept over the thin reflective strip on the floor, just in front of his boot, I knew.

"Stop," I shouted. At the same time, I reached forward, catching the collar of his shirt with my fingers. I yanked backwards, pulling him with me as I heard a light swish followed by a dull thud. The combination of our momentum, plus Jake's weight, toppled us over backwards, and I hit the floor heavily, the back of my skull bouncing off the hard stone. A white-hot pain ripped through my brain, my vision blurred, and I felt instantly nauseous.

I was pinned to the ground by Jake's bulk and couldn't move – could barely breath. I heard Ty shouting, but my brain was still muddled from the blow and I couldn't understand what he was saying. The torch lay at my side and I stretched to reach it, just getting my fingertips on the rubber shaft. I tilted my head backwards and turned the torch in Ty's direction.

My heart stopped.

His gun lay discarded on the ground by his feet, and his hands were clasped to his head. Horror and disbelief flicked over his face in waves, and his eyes were wide and white in the torchlight. At first, I thought something terrible had happened to him, but then he opened his mouth and words just came tumbling out.

"No! No! This can't be happening. Fuck. Shit. What are we going to do?" He paced frantically, never taking his eyes from Jake and me.

Correction: never taking his eyes off Jake.

I'd been so worried that something had happened to Ty, I'd hardly noticed that Jake hadn't moved. That he hadn't rolled off me and stood up cursing, like he normally would have. But once my concentration was solely on him, and with Ty finally quiet, I heard the ragged breath and the low, pained growls escaping his lips.

And there was something else… a burnt, acrid smell that made me want to heave.

I tried to move, but Jake was like deadweight.

"Help me, Ty," I implored, panic exploding inside me. He didn't move. "Help me now," I shouted, pushing on Jake to try and move him. His pained cry ripped through, but suddenly he became lighter and I realised Ty had rolled him to the side so I could shimmy out.

I stood up and looked down on him, scared and confused.

My torchlight skimmed his grey, contorted face, and his clenched teeth couldn't stop the choked groans from breaking free. I moved the beam down his chest, his stomach, pelvis and legs. I didn't know why he was in such pain until my light found the bloody stump of his right leg, severed just above the ankle. Wisps of smoke still danced in the air.

His booted foot lay half a metre away, just on the other side of the line, where moments early a razor-sharp blade had swung up from the floor and embedded itself in the wall.

"What happened?" Ty asked, confusion mixing with fear.

"Booby-trap," I explained urgently. "Don't move further than that line." I noticed the unfocussed look in Ty's eyes. "Ty!" I shouted, slapping his face hard. "I need you to concentrate." It must've done the job because he came back to me.

I sank down next to Jake, studying the cut flesh and bone that ended his leg. The wound was straight and clean, and there was hardly any blood oozing from the cauterized flesh. Even the material of his trouser leg just… stopped. No tagging or fraying, just a straight, even line with a hint of burnt fabric.

The smell was sickening, and my hand automatically rose to cover my nose and mouth.

Don't panic, I told myself. Do not panic.

"How…? His foot…? I don't understand," Ty babbled.

"I think, when I pulled him back, his right foot must've come up, breaking the sensor for the trap."

My hands shook as I took the end of the hard-wearing trouser fabric and folded it up out of the way, but after a couple of seconds I switched to autopilot.

"Ty, I need you to check the trap, and if it's safe, get

Jake's foot." The words sounded surreal as they left my lips. "It's okay, I can fix this," I said, more to myself than him. "I can fix this. I can. I mean… I've never actually re-attached anything, but how different can it be to mending a gaping chest wound, right?"

I looked to Ty for confidence, but his scared smile didn't help at all.

"Jake? Jake, listen to me. You're going to be fine," I said. His eyes were scared, his face damp with sweat. I took a shot of Oxytanyl from one of my trouser pockets and jabbed it into his thigh. "Something for the pain," I told him, and he blinked slowly, nodding his head a little. "You're going to feel better real soon, but I need you to stay very, very still. Do you understand?" He blinked again, his teeth grinding in pain. I pushed his sweat-damp hair out of his eyes with shaking fingers.

I held back the urge to vomit when Ty handed me Jake's foot, still encased in the black, military boot. The end of the ankle was just as precise and surgical as the end of Jake's leg, and weirdly I took that to be a good thing. I tried to roll what was left of the trouser leg out of the way, but in the end, it was easier to yank it from out of the boot and discard it to one side.

For a moment I froze, staring between the leg and the foot. It wasn't the time to be squeamish, I knew that, but I couldn't help it. Another wave of nausea and doubt crashed through me before I could pull myself together.

"No different from a gaping chest wound," I repeated to myself.

I placed Jake's severed foot right up against his leg, forcing the two together. He flinched, and I had to grab him to pin him down. Unable to keep it in any longer, Jake let out an agonised howl.

"I'm sorry," I said, not relieving the pressure. "Ty, you have to keep him still."

I took a deep breath and tried to focus, but a battle

raged inside my head. Half of me knew I could do it – knew he wasn't going to die because he was important, vital… and not just to me. Somehow, I understood that, but I didn't know why.

Unfortunately, the other half of me was petrified. Paralysed by fear and shock.

"Better not attach it wonky," Ty said with a scared half-smile. "He won't be happy if his foot sticks out to the side for the rest of his days."

"Ty!" I gasped, but his moment of humour had brought my thoughts into focus. "Just point the torch here. And feel free not to add any more helpful comments."

I pushed past the fear until the deep tingly sensation filled my chest, turning the hallway a bright silver-blue. I pressed the two raw edges together and closed my eyes until I felt the energy flow between my hands and Jake's leg. I opened my eyes and watched the silver stands dance between us, slowly knitting together bone and muscle.

Blood flowed again, seeping from flesh onto the ground beneath, and for a second I was distracted, the connection between us fading slightly. His skin, iridescent with my energy, came together in a red-raw line, eventually fading to the shiny silver of a new scar before disappearing completely.

The silver-blue glow refracting off the metal walls dissipated, and the skin on Jake's leg turned pink under the torchlight.

When I moved my hands away, I noticed concrete debris and small slithers of metal stuck to my palms by Jake's blood. I wiped them on my trousers, desperate to get rid of the evidence.

At first, I prodded his leg lightly, watching the skin pale and then pink up again. But then I pressed it harder, rubbing it, making sure it wasn't going to split apart again at any moment.

"Hey, Babe," Jake said, sitting up, his words slurred

from the drugs. He looked down at his leg and smiled stupidly. "Wow. Great job."

The trouser material, which stopped abruptly just above his ankle, was the only reminder of the horror.

"Can you stand?" Ty asked.

"I'll try," he replied drowsily. Ty and I scooped our hands under his armpits and helped him upright. He held all his weight on his left foot, holding his right above the floor. "Here goes nothing," he said, tentatively placing it on the ground. Gradually he added more weight until he'd transferred it all, and I watched his face carefully, studying it for any sign of pain or distress. He took one wobbly step, and then another.

"Feels like new," he slurred. "Not even a twinge." Jake threw his arms around me and I staggered under his weight, wondering how long the drugs would take to wear off. "Babe, you're... remarkable... and beautiful. You're... beautifully remarkable." He sounded drunk and was unstable on his feet, but I don't think that had anything to do with the injury. Ty and I helped him back to the ground, where he sat studying his leg for a moment. "Let's go get Jesper," he almost sang as he tried to get up again. I put my hand on his shoulder and easily forced him back to the floor.

"It'll be a while before the effects of the painkiller wear off," I told Ty, thinking that in any other situation it would've been funny to see Jake like that.

"The mission objective was to find and detain Jesper, but Jake's in no fit state," said Ty. "We can't go forward, we can't stay here, and we have no coms to call for backup. I hate to say this, but our only option is to go back."

The sensible part of me agreed with him, but the stubborn part didn't want to give up on the mission, or our lead. I wasn't about to let Jesper get away.

I looked down the hallway, the next hatch was maybe ten metres away. "Ty, take Jake and retrace our steps back up through the shop," I said.

"What about you?" he asked.

"I'm going after Jesper."

"That's madness," Jake grunted. "I may be high, but I can still recognise a suicide mission when I hear one."

"We need him," I protested.

"We'll track him down some other way."

"But—"

"All of us will head back up through the shop. Regroup with the others and make a new plan. That's an order."

"You heard the man," Ty said. "Orders are orders."

My mind raced through options.

"I know what you're thinking, Shae," Jake said.

"Oh, you do, do you?"

"I do. Don't even think of pulling that you're not the boss of me Constantine Agreement crap. This is my mission. I'm your Commanding Officer, and you will follow my orders. Or I'll get Ty to put you in cuffs and drag you out of here kicking and screaming if necessary."

"Fine," I conceded.

And maybe, if I was being brutally honest with myself, I was glad he'd stopped me from running the gauntlet of booby-traps.

17

I picked up my Sentinel and turned my torch towards the hatch, ready to retrace our steps back up to the shop, but the lever was stuck solid.

"Umm, I think we've got a problem, guys," I said, tugging harder. Ty got his kit out and started working on the access panel, but a moment later he put it back in his pack.

"The control crystal's fried," he said. "Don't know what Jesper's done to it, but the tech's destroyed. There's no way I can open it with the equipment I've got here."

"Can we blow it?" I enquired.

"Connor's the explosive expert, but I'd say in these confined quarters, and with these walls…" he pounded the metal with the side of his fist, "the concussion wave would probably kill us, even if the explosion didn't." He offered an apologetic shrug of the shoulders. I holstered my gun and swung the torchlight back down the hallway towards the hatch at the far end.

"Looks like we're pushing forward after all," Jake said, wobbling and reaching out to the wall for support.

"Ty, what else have you got in that bag of yours?" I

asked, formulating a plan, even though it wasn't a very good one.

Ty dragged his pack from his shoulders and opened it, pulling out a large water bottle followed by a red plastic med-kit. "Guess I should've got this out sooner."

"I don't think a can of synthetic protein polymer and a band-aid would've cut it," I said, grimacing at the reminder. "But the container and the water bottle might do." I took the kit and tipped the loose contents back into the pack before inspecting the red-speckled blade that was part imbedded in the wall. "Is this safe?" I asked Ty.

"That one is… or at least it was when I retrieved the foot."

Jake shuddered and almost lost his balance.

"Let's be sure." I tossed the med-kit over the barely detectable thin line on the floor. Nothing happened. "I'll take point. Ty, bring up the rear. Jake, you stay right behind me, do you hear?" He nodded and grinned like an idiot. "I need you to promise me you'll tell me if you don't feel right. Okay?"

"I love it when you get all bossy, Babe," he slurred, but he caught my look of exasperation. "Yes, I promise," he added, trying to sound serious.

I stepped cautiously through the first trap, and then stooped to pick up the red container. "Here goes nothing." I threw the box, recoiling as the silvery-grey blade sprung through the air no more than a metre in front of me. The med-kit lay in two pieces, the plastic smoking at the edges, and I swallowed heavily. "I'm okay," I said, but my voice wavered.

I retrieved the two parts, throwing the biggest piece forward, and that time I barely flinched as the blade shot up. I moved on, using the water bottle to spring two more traps, until I was within three metres of the hatch. Given the spacing of the previous traps, I didn't think there would be another one, but I wasn't about to bet my life on it.

The med-kit box and water bottle were now in small pieces, but I tossed the largest bit and listened to it bounce of the hatch with a light metallic twang.

I took a step forward but felt an arm loop around my waist, pulling me back.

"Wait," Jake whispered in my ear. He threw his torch forward, the blur of metal making both of us flinch.

"How did you know?" I stammered when my heart kicked back in.

"Didn't, not for sure, but that box of yours was getting mighty small. Look…" He pointed towards the floor, where a small rodent scuttled along the concrete. "I wasn't sure how sensitive those sensors were."

"You saved my life."

"Just returning the favour, Babe," he slurred.

"Umm, hate to interrupt, but…" Ty said, indicating towards the hatch. We moved out of the way to let him past. He dropped his pack by the base of the door, pulled out some tech I didn't recognise, and started to run it slowly around the edge of the hatch.

"I can't be sure, but it looks clear," he said after a minute.

"Okay, stand back. Just in case," I said, un-holstering my Sentinel and stepping forward.

"No, I'll take this one." Ty replied. "Besides," he laughed quietly, "if it is booby-trapped, it'll most likely take us all out anyway."

"Oh well, in that case… be my guest," I half joked, moving out of the way.

Jake and I flattened ourselves against the wall. I held my breath as Ty pressed down on the lever and slowly opened the door, and when nothing happened, I let out a long puff of air.

The hatch opened to a large open space and I peered in, not crossing the threshold. It looked strangely out of place in the bowels of the city, more like the kind of lounge you'd find in a superior hotel. The walls were painted pale cream, with several picture-screens displaying images of Old-Earth art. The furniture looked new and unused, and a real-flame fire crackled in a cast-iron hearth.

"Clear," Ty said, taking a step inside. "But don't go too far until I've swept the rest of the area," he added, moving slowly across the floor. The room was surreal. Fine china tea sets sat next to what looked like torture instruments in glass cabinets, and blue animal-skin rugs lay on the floor. Ty barely noticed, too occupied with the sensor he carried. He walked cautiously towards a second hatch, the dark opening punctuating the wall directly opposite.

I took the opportunity to check on Jake.

I'd healed his leg, but he'd gone through one hell of a trauma, and the drugs I'd given him were pretty strong. I turned to him, noting the pallid skin and slightly vacant look.

"You okay?" It seemed weird to ask. Normally it was him asking me that very same question.

"I'm fine, Babe, I—"

"No!" I cried, lunging past him towards the hatch, grabbing at the metal as it swung shut. "Shit. Shit. Shit." I hammered on the sealed door, pulling at the immovable handle. "Shit!" Even kicking it didn't help, not that I really expected it to.

A dull clank from the other side of the room told me the second hatch had also closed, and when I turned, I saw Ty tugging furiously at the handle.

"Let's not panic just yet," he said, working on the access panel with some piece of kit he pulled from his pack. A few moments later he mumbled something inaudible, and then came to check on my hatch. "Both panels are fried," he said, before pulling the sensor back out of his pocket, tapping and scrolling vigorously.

"What is it?" Jake asked.

"Jesper used an incredibly complex remote signal to

close the hatches before overloading the control crystals, but I was able to isolate and identify both the coding and the frequency. Most people wouldn't have the skill, but then I'm not most people." He looked up from the sensor and smiled proudly.

"Apart from giving you the opportunity to be annoyingly smug, is there any other reason you're telling us this?" asked Jake, frowning.

"Of course." Ty grinned. "Once you know the coding and frequency, it's just a matter of building an echo-cipher and creating a piggy-back com-signal. And before you know it…" He tapped the sensor enthusiastically. "Instant jammer."

"Fantastic!" I said with fake enthusiasm. "What does that mean?"

"It means Jesper won't be able to remote-activate any more doors or traps. At least not locally to our position. I don't have the power to cover more than our immediate vicinity, and it won't last forever, but it's a start."

"I take it back, Ty. You can be as smug as you want," said Jake.

"Thanks." The smile broadened. "For information though, I'm not picking up any traces of explosives or incendiary devices, but I'm buggered if I know how we're going to get out of here."

"Well, that's just peachy," I replied, suddenly overwhelmed by a wave of exhaustion. It took me a second to realise it was Jake's fatigue I felt through the Link, and it was the first hit I'd had from him since I'd healed him. "I'm worried about you," I said, putting out my arm to steady him.

"I'm okay. I'm functional."

"Let me look at you. Follow my finger."

His eyes moved left and right but they were sluggish, and his pupils were dilated. I moved closer so I could get a better look, but he blindsided me with a kiss. It took a couple of heartbeats for me to find the wherewithal to pull away. His eyes sparkled.

"Blame the drugs," he suggested innocently. I shook my head disapprovingly, but deep down my body had reacted to his kiss, to his lips – remembering moments of intimacy I'd tried to file away. Feelings of guilt rose in my chest and I began to panic.

"Well, isn't this nice?" I recognised the voice immediately and was glad of the distraction. Jesper's face was part obscured by the metal grate covering an access hole in the ceiling directly above the large dining table. "Three rats trapped in a maze. My maze. How do you like it so far?" He didn't wait for an answer. "What? You thought it would be easy? That you could just walk into my crib and take me out? Typical. I'm so much smarter than you, it's laughable. You're everything I detest about the regime. Mud-monkeys mindlessly following orders given to you by arrogant, stupid men in suits, who no more understand the revolution than they understand quantum physics."

"Bored now," Jake mumbled, yawning, but that wound Jesper up further.

"Whatever happened to the notion of free will, huh? I'm just following my right as a human to make a living at what I'm good at. But you," he blustered, "you're nothing but oppressors of artistic technical creativity."

"Is that how you see yourself? As an artist?" Jake grunted sluggishly. "Because I've got to tell you, what I see is a short fuck with an inadequacy complex... and seriously bad fucking hair." Jesper let out a hollow bark. "I bet your mama told you size doesn't matter, but trust me, it does," Jake continued, sneering.

"We'll see who can still make cheap jokes in a few minutes," Jesper spluttered with rage. "But then again... maybe we won't... because I'll be long gone, and you'll be... oh yes, you'll be dead."

"Bring it on," Jake taunted.

"Oh, I will," Jesper replied.

Given our situation, I thought goading the dangerous sociopath wasn't exactly the best tactic Jake could've used. Damn drugs.

"Nice knowing you... or not," Jesper continued before his face disappeared and I heard footsteps crossing the floor, heading back in the direction we'd come. I gave Jake my *was that really necessary* look.

"What?" he said, shrugging his shoulders. "He was pissing me off."

"And you think riling him up was going to make things better?"

"Sure as hell wasn't going to make things worse. You seriously believe some jacked-up little scrotum like him is going to give a rat's-arse about what happens to us at this point?"

"No, but I... what's that noise?" I tried to locate the origin of the deep grinding sound, but it seemed to be coming from all around us. Picture screens on all four walls slid upwards, revealing small round grills that slowly twisted open.

"What the hell now?" Ty said.

Viscous, pearlescent-grey fluid seeped in through the holes, flowing down the walls like slate lava, pooling before spreading across the floor. I stepped backwards towards the centre of the room as the liquid oozed towards me.

"Is that...? Get off the floor. Get off the floor now!" ordered Ty.

The urgency in his voice encouraged me to climb on top of the dining table. By the time Jake had clambered on top of a coffee table, and Ty was balanced precariously on the back of a sofa, the floor had been completely engulfed in shimmering pinky-grey.

"Whatever you do, do not let the liquid touch you," Ty said. "Not even a drop."

"What is it?" I asked, spinning on the table to keep an

eye on its progress as the levels started to rise.

"It's Diothodine. A solvent," Jake answered, carefully moving from the coffee table to an armchair.

"That doesn't sound so bad."

Jake laughed humourlessly and shook his head while traversing to another chair. "Except Diothodine dissolves organic matter. Us," he clarified.

"Oh." It was all I could think to say. "Why would someone create something like that?"

"It was during the early wars," Ty explained, shuffling along the sofa. "When they needed to dispose of large numbers of the dead."

"That's awful. Wait, Ty, I thought you said Jesper couldn't set off any more traps."

"I said he couldn't set them off remotely. This one looks like it was manually activated."

"Remote, manual, who gives a crap? Ty, can you get to the dining table?" Jake said.

"Yeah, I'll make it. Even if it kills me."

"Do you guys ever stop with the jokes?" I asked.

"Nope." Ty grinned. "Kinda takes your mind of the whole imminent death thing, don't you think?"

I held out my hand and pulled Jake on to the large table, noticing how quickly the tide had risen in only a few minutes. It was already a third of the way up the legs of the table, and dangerously close to the top of the unit Ty was moving along.

As the liquid breached the top, he leapt towards us. One foot made the tabletop, but the other slipped off the edge and he started to topple backwards. Jake and I both lunged for him, grabbing at the front of his jacket and pulling him upright to safety.

"Thanks," he said, rearranging his clothing and looking nervously at the sea of Diothodine. "Now what?"

Jake glanced up. The ceiling grate, which only minutes earlier had part hidden Jesper, looked black and mocking.

"You're kidding me." Ty looked doubtful. "You know it's going to be sealed."

"Maybe, but there's only one way to be sure. You up for this, Shae?"

"If it gets us out of here, hell yes," I replied.

Jake seemed to have rallied himself somewhat, and I wondered if a surge of adrenaline had countered the effects of the painkiller. The two men stood side by side, their shoulders almost level.

"Don't drop me," I joked.

"Never," Jake replied, and I got a hit of something through the Link. It was muddled and unclear, but it took my breath for a moment.

"You okay?"

"Yeah, sure. Let's do this," I replied, strengthening my mental roadblocks.

Jake interlaced his fingers and held them out for me to step into. I pushed myself up until I had one foot on each of their shoulders and I felt their hands on my legs, steadying me.

"You ready for this?" I asked.

"Go for it," Jake replied.

"You'll catch me if this goes wrong?"

"You know it."

I bent my knees and focused on the grate, feeling Ty and Jake preparing themselves. I jumped as high as I could.

The fingers on my left hand slipped through the holes in the grate, allowing me to close my fingers and gain a secure hold, but my right hand hit solid metal. I swayed from my one-handed grip, hearing a sharp intake of breath from one of the men below me, but managed to steady myself. I switched hands, using my dominant right to hang by while using my left to feel around the edges of the grate with my fingertips, searching for some kind of catch or release. The surface was smooth and unblemished.

I grasped the grate with both hands and used my weight

to tug down, but again, there was no movement.

"Ready to catch me?" I asked.

"All set," Jake replied. I let go of the cold metal and immediately felt the safety of his arms closing around me as I dropped. I thought for a second he was going to kiss me again, but he didn't. He simply stood there, quiet and motionless, and my mental roadblocks vibrated as they held out his feelings. I blinked, re-focussing, and he unwrapped his arms from my waist. "It's not budging," I confirmed.

Ty peered over the edge of the table. "There's not much time left," he said. "Whatever we're going to do, we better do it quick."

"We could shoot it?" I suggested.

"We've only got plasma-based weapons with us," Ty replied. "And I certainly wouldn't advise using them with all this highly flammable Diothodine about. Probably do us more harm than good."

"More harm than flesh dissolving super-goop?"

"Ty's right, Shae," Jake said.

"Are you suggesting we don't even try?"

"No… at least not yet." Jake rubbed the stubble on his chin, his eyes darting backwards and forwards as he thought.

While Jake paced, and Ty sat cross-legged on the tabletop, I did some thinking of my own.

"What about an energy pulse?" I suggested.

"Might work, if it was powerful enough," Jake replied. "But as we don't have any pulse-weapons with us, it's a moot point. I'm beginning to regret my suggestion that you leave your Cal'ret on the *Veritas*." He smiled weakly.

"But what if we did have a pulse-weapon?" There must've been something in my tone because he stopped pacing and cocked his head to one side. "What if… what if I was that weapon? You said it yourself, Jake. You said if I could control the energy, it could be used like a weapon."

Jake looked stunned. "Are you saying—"

"I'm saying I've been practicing. I haven't been able to produce anything like the power I used on you and Jared, but…" I looked around the room, "if anything's going to motivate a girl…"

"You can do it, Babe, I know you can," he encouraged. "What do you want us to do?"

"Stand behind me. I've no idea how this is going to go."

I shook my arms out and stretched the muscles in my neck. I let my mind travel back to my small island, remembering the tiny reef cabbles I used to move across the sand before advancing to rocks. I tried to convince myself the grate was just one step up from that.

Concentrating on the memory, I began to feel the tug inside – the swirling energy coming together in a writhing mass under my ribcage before flowing down my arms. I raised my hands up, palms towards the grate, and released a bright shimmering pulse. The metal shuddered, and tiny paint chips fell like soft snow, but the grate remained in place.

"I believe in you," Jake said behind me, but his voice seemed a million miles away.

The Diothodine was only centimetres from the tabletop. If I couldn't get us out of there, we were all going to die: Jake…Ty… me. There was no way on Lilania I was going to let that happen.

I summoned up all the energy I could. My chest vibrated, my vision blurred, but then the swirling mass in my chest suddenly come together in a ball of pure, cohesive energy. I only just had time to lift my arms before the blast ripped from my fingers, tearing the grate from its frame and leaving a gaping hole.

I dropped to my knees and everything went black. I felt hands on me and I heard voices, but none of it seemed important until a sharp pain burst across my face, forcing me to open my eyes. My cheek stung like a son-of-a-bitch.

"Sorry, Babe. You can kick my arse later, but we've got

to go," Jake said, pulling me to my feet.

Ty stood under the hole in the ceiling and Jake used his clasped hands as a springboard to his shoulders. Ty swayed under his weight, but he steadied himself, allowing Jake to jump up to the ceiling and grasp the ledge with his hands. He pulled himself up, spun himself around and lent back through the hole, his arm stretched out.

"Your turn," Ty said urgently, trying to focus me. He held out his hands and I had to concentrate hard to get an uncooperative boot into them.

"I don't know if I can."

"I'll help you. All you need to do is reach for Jake, he'll do the rest. We won't let you fall."

"You promise?"

"I promise. On three: one, two, three..."

I tried hard to push off from his hands, but it wouldn't have mattered if I'd made no effort at all. Ty propelled me upwards, and Jake's fingers closed around my wrist, pulling me into the safety of the room above.

I looked back through the hole and watched Ty bend his legs before pushing off the table towards Jake's grasp. Their hands weren't even close. He tried again, that time closer, but it wasn't enough. The viscous, pearlescent fluid seeped over the table edge and started closing in on him.

"Grab hold of me," I ordered Jake, pushing myself through the hole. I felt him seize the back of my waistband and lowered myself further, confident I was safe in his hands. I looked directly into Ty's eyes, reaching out to him. He bent his legs and his feet left the surface just as the tabletop disappeared below an ocean of Diothodine.

His hands gripped around my right wrist and he swayed precariously. My shoulder dislocated, and beads of sweat sprung up on my forehead, but I didn't cry out. The pain was excruciating, but there was no way I was going to let him go.

Jake tugged at my trousers, pulling me upwards. With

one hand still on my waistband, he held out the other to his teammate. Ty released one hand from my wrist to grab it, and I heard Jake grunting with the effort of pulling us both up.

We lay on our backs around the hole in the floor, shattered, out of breath, but laughing. At least I was half laughing, half crying in pain, until Ty helped me pop my shoulder back into place.

"I didn't know. I'm sorry," he said.

I grinned and rubbed his shaved head. "I wouldn't let you fall," I replied, echoing his earlier words.

"Let's get out of here," Jake suggested after giving us a moment to rest. I didn't need telling twice, but I worried about him. His face was ashen, his eyes heavy, and when he spoke, his voice lacked its usual strength and command.

But then, who was I to judge? I felt worse than he looked.

Healing Jake, and then the whole freaky pulse business, had left me wiped-out. It felt like every cell in my body was exhausted, and even healing my shoulder took way longer than it should have. My legs wobbled, and my arms were weak, and although I wanted out of that place as much as the next person, I wasn't even sure I could get up off the floor. In the end, I didn't have a choice. Jake put his hand out and dragged me to my feet.

He surveyed the room, which had the same dimension as the one below, with two hatches in exactly the same places.

"We'll go that way." He pointed to the door heading back in the direction of the repair shop, the way I'd heard Jesper walk. He rubbed his bloodshot eyes with the palms of his hands. "There could still be traps, so you know the drill: slow and steady."

"I thought Ty's jammer thingy would make everything safe," I said.

"It only jams a signal to activate or deactivate a trap," Ty explained. "It doesn't send a signal to deactivate ones that may have already been set. Get it?" I think I did, but I was too tired to question it further.

Ty checked the hatch before announcing it was clear, and like the floor below, it opened up into a long hallway. Only halfway down this one, Jesper's lifeless body hung pinned to the wall by thick metal spikes, killed by one of his own booby-traps. The irony amused me.

We approached carefully, the iron-salty taste of his blood lingering in the air. A vertical line of six stakes crossed the width of the hallway, skewering his body like a Santian kebab. The top one pierced his skull, causing his eyes to bug out of their sockets.

Ty struggled to prise a remote from Jesper's hand.

"I'm not denying this couldn't have happened to a nicer guy," I said, "but… how? Why? He knew the traps were here. I can't believe he just walked straight into them."

"I think that's exactly what he did. Take a look." Ty tossed me the remote.

The clear glass remote displayed a list of zones down one side, with the word 'Active' next to each one – except Zone Four. Next to that one, the words 'Warning' and 'Error' flashed alternately.

"You're going to have to help me out here, Ty" I said.

"It's just speculation, but I'm betting this is Zone Four. When Jesper came through, he would've used this remote to deactivate the traps in the hallway. It probably didn't even cross his mind that his signal could've been jammed. We'll never know for sure, but I'd bet he pressed the deactivation code and carried on up the hallway without realising the traps were still active."

"Shame," I said with false sentiment. It didn't even bother me that we wouldn't be able to interrogate him for information on the Khans. He'd got what was coming to him as far as I was concerned.

Ty retrieved a data-pad from a bloodied bag by the tech-head's feet and tucked it into his own pack. "I might be able to get something useful off it," he said optimistically. I wasn't going to hold my breath.

"Can you deactivate the rest of the traps, Ty?" Jake asked, looking down the corridor.

"Sorry, no can do. At least not any time soon. The remote's locked, and it would take me ages to de-code it without my equipment."

"Fine. Looks like we're doing this the hard way then."

Jesper's body jiggled and shook like a marionette as I climbed the stakes like a ladder, jumping down on the other side, careful not to move further down the hallway than absolutely necessary.

Using a couple of large, ugly wooden statues he'd picked up back in the room, Jake triggered each of the 'kebab' traps, and we moved steadily towards the end of the hallway.

Climbing over the spikes took all the effort and energy I had left, and by the time we got to the last set, Ty had to sit on the top stake and pull me up. On the other side my legs gave way and I collapsed.

I wasn't the only one the stakes took their toll on. Jake looked pale and unstable, but he tugged me off the floor again. I propped myself against the wall and closed my eyes. Big mistake. The swirling tendrils of sleep spread quickly through my brain and I had to force my eyes open before it took me completely.

"I know you need to rest after what you've done, Babe, but we've got to get out of here first. Just a little longer and then you can sleep as long as you like, okay?" He placed his palm on my cheek before kissing my forehead, and a warm, comforting wave flowed through the Link.

"I'll help her," said Ty. "She'll be okay with me."

Past the next hatch was the stairway we needed. Ty slipped his arm around my waist and pulled me closely into him for support as we staggered up the steps.

After a few floors, my earpiece crackled, and I heard Kaiser's broken voice. "At last!" He actually huffed. "We were about to launch a search and rescue. What happened to you guys?"

"That," Jake replied, stopping to look at his cropped trouser leg, "is a long fucking story. I want everyone to converge on the shop entrance, but do not attempt to enter until we disengage the security measures. Brother Riley, don't try to come in the rear exit, it's probably booby-trapped."

"Booby-trapped? What kind of booby-trap?" Connor asked.

"Just do what I ordered, Con," Jake snapped, exhausted and in no mood to have to explain himself.

We were only one flight of stairs from the shop, but I couldn't take another step. My legs gave way and Ty had to hold me even tighter to stop me ending up in a heap. He passed his weapon to Jake before bending down and scooping my feet off the floor. The sudden feeling of weightlessness made my head spin, and swirling grey fog seeped through my brain again. I felt my head falling and I jolted it upright, taking deep breaths to try and revive myself.

The light swaying movement of Ty carrying me up the last of the steps did its best to lull me back to sleep, and it must've succeeded because it was only a split-second later that I opened my eyes and we were back in the shop. Ty sat me on the high stool behind the counter while Jake ordered Justine and Ramirez to their knees, hands on their heads.

I leant forward, resting my arms on the counter for support, and my breath faltered as my brain finally registered the red-stained skin and jacket sleeves soaked in blood. My stomach churned.

Ty took his gun back from Jake. "You," he said to Justine. "You're going to turn off the security and open the doors. And you're going to do it quickly and without fuss.

Ain't that right?"

"Don't you even think about it, woman," Ramirez rumbled dangerously.

I don't think she knew who to be more scared of, but Jake cracked the bones in his neck, and glared at both captives before bringing his gun down hard on Ramirez's head.

"Let me make this simple for you," he said to Justine. "I just lost a foot, and it's made me kinda cranky, so I suggest you do what my friend asked."

She had no idea what he was talking about, but she was terrified, and terrified people tended to do whatever the man with the gun wanted them to do.

"Don't you—" started Ramirez again, but he was silenced by another blow from Jake.

"After you, miss." Ty waved his gun towards the keypad, and the girl with the purple hair got up quickly, tapping in a code with shaking fingers. The bright orange lasers shut down, the shutters lifted, and the shop instantly filled with Marines and Brotherhood.

Voices merged into each other and I wasn't exactly sure what was happening. Riley started to ask Jake something, but when his eyes fell on me, he stopped mid-sentence, his mouth open, his eyes wide. I knew I was exhausted, and probably looked pale, but nothing that should've caused such a strong reaction.

I pulled over Justine's mirror from further down the counter and glanced at my reflection, finally understanding Riley's reaction. Jake's blood was smeared across my forehead and down my right cheek, and in stark contrast to my bone-white skin, my eyes were bloodshot with heavy black circles.

Jake stood between the three monks and the counter, arms up, blocking their advance. Riley's shock had morphed into anger, and he tried to duck around him to get to me. Kaiser and Connor waded into the fray, and I opened my mouth to try and defuse the situation, but no words came out.

My brain fogged over, clearly deciding that enough was enough, and I felt myself swaying. Ty spun the stool until I was facing him, and although we locked eyes and he rubbed my arms vigorously, he couldn't stop the encroaching darkness.

18

The next time I opened my eyes, my surroundings were in near darkness, but I knew exactly where I was. I just didn't understand how I'd got there. I sat up, stretched, and breathed in the distinctive smell of roseberry and vanilla that always filled my quarters on the *Defender*.

"Shae?" A sleepy voice floated through the darkness.

"Lights," I called, pulling back covers before jumping out of bed and throwing myself at Ash, who was getting out of an armchair, rubbing lazy eyes.

"Whoa! Easy," he said as we both staggered backwards.

"What happened? When did I get here? When did you get here? How long have I been out? Is Jake okay?" So many questions came out of my mouth in one long sentence.

"Take a breath already," he suggested, a lopsided grin pasted on his face. I threw my arms around him again, burying my head in his chest.

"I'm so glad you're here."

"Me too. Come, sit, and I'll answer your questions." He patted the bed and I shimmied back under the soft, silky covers, propping a pillow behind my back. "To start with, you've been asleep for…" he looked at his com-pad, "thirty-two hours straight."

"Thirty-two?" I said, amazed. "Oh no, that's too long. What about—"

"It's okay," Ash soothed. "You haven't missed anything. Contrary to popular opinion, the Sector doesn't come to a grinding stop just because you happen to take an extended nap." I took the pillow next to me and swatted him with it. "Seriously though, it sounds like you needed it." His eyes searched my face, and I wondered how much he knew about what had happened. I felt guilty for not having told him I'd been practicing my human-pulse-weapon skills.

"Ash, I…" I didn't know what to say, how to explain, so I changed the subject. "What happened?"

"I can tell you what I know. After you passed out in Jesper's shop, the mother of all property battles erupted. You being the property in question."

"Really?"

"Brother Riley said Jake got aggressively possessive, and adamant he was going to take you back to the *Veritas*. Jake said Riley overreacted, and that the monks became overprotective, demanding that he hand you over to them. Apparently neither side would back down. Riley placed a call to Francis, who eventually managed to agree a compromise with Jake."

"That he could take me back to the *Veritas*, as long as he brought me back to the *Defender*. To you."

"Spot on. Jesper was dead, and there was nothing further for the Wolfpack to do on Genesis, so it was logical to recall them anyway. Harper and I were just finishing off on Dennford when Francis contacted me to let me know what had happened. We returned to the *Defender* immediately. Riley and his team stayed on at the shop to search for any information on the Khans, but they didn't come up with anything. Now they're dismantling Jesper's traps with the help of a local security contingent." He caught the look on my face. "Don't worry, they're being careful. Jake warned them what to expect."

"Did he... did Jake tell you what happened?"

"You mean, did he tell me about the Diothodine? Or that you reattached his foot? Impressive by the way, even by your standards." I nodded. "Or are you referring to the fact that you blew a hole in the ceiling with an energy pulse?"

My heart sank. "He actually told you about that?"

"Yes, though I got the feeling he was torn about it, if that makes you feel better."

"Not really. Does Jared know?"

"Yes. Jake briefed us together, but he didn't put it in his After-Action report. According to that, the metal was fatigued, and you were able to break through without the use of weapons. Ty had already told the rest of the Wolfpack what you'd done, but Jake has sworn them all to secrecy. Ty's also used the same line about the rusted grate in his report, and neither of them has put in anything about a severed foot. In case you were wondering."

"That's something, I suppose. Ash, it wasn't that I was purposely keeping it a secret from you, it's just... I still don't really understand what this evolution of my gift is all about. My whole life, everything about me has been an open book to the Brotherhood. It was nice to..."

"Have something to yourself for a change," he finished for me. "I understand. I just worry about you."

"I know. I'd like to say you don't need to, but I kinda like that you do." I smiled. "So you're not mad?"

He looked like he was thinking hard, but then the lopsided grin appeared and I hit him with the pillow again.

"Is Jake okay?" I asked.

"He needed a plasma transfusion and some forced rest, but he's fine."

"Forced rest?"

"It seems he wouldn't leave your side during the journey

back to the *Defender*, and refused to let you out of his sight, even when you arrived onboard. Eventually, Doc jabbed him with a sedative when he wasn't looking, just so he could treat him properly. Jake was... let's just say he was a tad mad when he woke up, but by that point I was here and thought you needed uninterrupted rest."

"You always did know me better than anyone else in the entire Universe."

"That's true. Do you want to tell me what happened when you told Jake how you felt?"

"I suppose now's as good a time as any. Let me start by saying it didn't exactly go as I expected," I explained before telling him the whole story.

"Interesting," he commented after I'd finished. "But I suppose, in a way, I can understand Jake's reaction."

"You can?"

"Sure. If he really does love you, why should he give you up to Jared without a fight?"

"But I'm not even with Jared," I replied in frustration.

"I know that, but—"

"Why does everything have to be so complicated?" I moaned. "And talking of complicated, how is Jared?"

"As you'd expect. Worried... anxious... pissed at Jake... annoyed I'm not letting anyone near you while you recuperate. Come to think of it, I think Doc might've given Jake the sedative just to prevent Jared from punching him out. When I got here, he was still livid with Jake for getting you into trouble."

"Jared does know it was Jake's foot that got cut off and not mine, doesn't he?" I said sarcastically.

"I'm sure he does. But like it or not, you were in trouble, and he feels guilty he wasn't there to protect you."

"There was nothing he could've done."

"And that's what makes it worse for him." Ash fell silent and I knew something wasn't right. I couldn't put my finger on it, but he seemed more pensive than usual.

"What's up," I asked eventually.

"Huh?" It took him a moment to focus. "Oh, it's nothing. Just thinking about the mission, I guess." He looked at his com-pad. "Zero-six-thirty. You need more sleep, or are you ready for an early breakfast?"

"Are you kidding me?" I asked, sliding out of bed.

The Mess Hall was busy, with a constant stream of crew coming and going, but our usual table was empty.

"What's going on, Ash?" I asked, after he'd pushed a sausage around his plate for a couple of minutes. Both his eyebrows raised and a creased formed between them. "There's something you're not telling me," I pushed.

"It's nothing."

"It's definitely something."

"Look, it's—" He seemed relieved by the distraction of Jared and Jake's arrival.

Jake arrived at the table first and Ash stood to shake hands. I wasn't sure what I was supposed to do: stand, stay seated, shake, nod graciously? The question was answered for me when Jake put his tray on the table and pulled me up into a tight hug.

"You smell edible, Babe," he whispered in my ear, sending goose bumps scurrying across my skin.

"Um, thanks," I replied, extricating myself from his arms.

As he sank on to the bench beside me, Jared approached hesitantly. I don't think he really knew quite how to greet me either – especially after Jake's enthusiastic display – so I waited for him to put his food down and then stepped forward to embrace him. Granted it wasn't as affectionate as Jake's had been, but it was warm and genuine. I breathed in sandalwood and musk, and for a moment I was back in his quarters, sitting on the overstuffed, brown-leather couch. Jared sat opposite me, next to Ash.

"How you feeling?" I asked Jake. "How's the foot?"

He grinned. "I'm fine, Babe. All thanks to you. It's like it never happened. And you? After everything... are you okay?"

"I'm fine. Like it never happened." I returned his smile then laughed. "It was kind of funny, looking back on it."

"Getting my foot cut off was funny?" he asked in disbelief.

"No, silly. Not that bit, the bit after. When you were all doped up and, well, dopey."

"That's still not funny," he moaned.

"Come on, it was a little bit." I turned to Jared. "He was worse than you were after that night on Fire Whisky. All wobbly and slurring... and saying daft stuff."

"Man, you must've been bad," Jared said, laughing, his blue eyes sparkling.

"Yeah, well... so would you've been if she jabbed you with that... whatever the hell it was. I've got to say though, it did give a good buzz – after the excruciating pain had gone away, that is." Jake shuddered at the memory.

Jared ordered more coffee for us and we discussed the missions that had been going on throughout the night. Apart from the obvious frustrations of not being any closer to the Princess, and therefore the Third Seal, the conversation was natural and easy, at least between the two military officers. Ash, on the other hand, was quiet and reserved, only joining the conversation to add an occasional thought or opinion.

After a large gulp of coffee, Jared asked, "How was your call with Supreme Primus Isaiah, Ash? Anything we need to be aware of, mission wise?" But when he caught the brief, but unmistakably anxious glance Ash shot at me, he added, "I'm sorry, have I put my foot in something?"

"No, not at all," he replied, clearing the creases from his forehead. "He was simply checking in on the operation. First-hand update, that's all."

That definitely wasn't all. He may have been able to smooth over the physical signs of whatever was bothering him, but he couldn't mask the feelings that were coming through the Link loud and clear.

"What's the plan for today?" he asked, changing the subject.

"We've got a couple of targets to concentrate on." Jared tactfully ran with the new topic. "Jake and the Wolfpack are going to take one; I was going to take the other if you'd like to join me?"

"Sure, count me in," replied Ash.

"And me," I added.

"Not you," Jared replied. "You need to rest."

"Rest?" I blurted in amazement. "I don't need to rest, Jared, I've just slept for thirty-two hours straight. That's probably more than all of you put together. What I need is to get involved, to do something useful before I go crazy worrying about what the Khans might've done to Phina." I felt heat rising in my cheeks. "Don't side-line me, please. Not now."

"You know you've always got a place on the *Veritas*," Jake said. "Regardless of what Captain Ungrateful says."

"Shut up, Mitchell." Jared scowled across the table, but his face softened as he turned to me. "I only meant... Shae, I just want to make sure you don't overdo things. If you really feel you're ready to get back in it—"

"I am."

"Great," said Jake. "Then you can come with us."

The tension growing between the two men was overshadowed by Ash's sudden anger, and the maelstrom of feelings busting through the Link made me dizzy.

"Shae is not some *thing* you two can fight over like a piece of meat... or a weapon for that matter. She's a person – with her own thoughts and opinions... and feelings. You'd both do well to remember that."

I was both touched and surprised by his unexpected outburst, and from the stunned look on both Jake and Jared's faces, I would say they felt the same. He took a breath and composed himself.

"I'll make things simple for both of you," he continued. "Shae is Brotherhood, and Brotherhood stays together. We'll both go with Captain Marcos."

I nodded my agreement, but after a moment of confusion my brain unscrambled, and everything fell into place.

"I'm sorry. It's all my fault. I shouldn't have gone with Jake," I said.

"What? Wait now. Is this because of what happened on Genesis?" Jake asked, defensive and belligerent. "Is the Brotherhood mad because they think I put Shae in jeopardy?"

"Why wouldn't they be mad at that? I am," waded in Jared.

"Stop it," I warned. "This has got nothing to do with either of you."

"Then what's going on?" Jake asked. "I hate to pull the Guardian card here, but we need to know what this is." He waved his hand between Ash and me. "What's your fault, Babe?"

Ash sighed heavily. "Nothing's Shae's fault," he said eventually. "It's mine."

"It's not. It was my decision to go with Jake," I argued.

"I'm the senior representative. I should've said no."

"Isaiah thinks you should've said no, more like." I paused, feeling guilty for putting him in that position, and for disrespecting the Supreme Primus. "I've said it before, and I'll say it again: I'm not a child anymore, and it's a stupid rule."

"Look at it from their perspective, Shae. You went off on your own, and you were put in a position where you nearly died."

"Hey, I could take offence at that," Jake said.

"Maybe you should," Jared replied, pouring oil onto the fire. "You were the one who almost got her sliced, dissolved and skewered."

"You think you could've done any better under the circumstances?" Jake argued back. The two men squared off over the table.

"Actually, yes. I—"

"Enough," Ash hissed. "This is neither the time nor the place."

They glanced quickly around the room, and then forced themselves to settle. The little vein on Jake's temple began to flatten out, and after a moment, he said, "If I can ask, Babe, exactly what rule have you broken?"

"The stupid rule," I huffed.

"I agree," Ash soothed. "But regardless of what we think about it, the Brotherhood has decreed it. It was only right that Isaiah remind me of my obligations."

"Decreed what?" Jake pushed.

"Under no circumstances am I to go off-world without being chaperoned by a senior level Warrior Caste monk. And at no time, within reason, am I to leave the protection of the accompanying monk." I quoted the rule.

"That's ridiculous," Jake snorted.

"I'm only going to tell you this because we're a team – Guardians – otherwise this would be none of your business," Ash explained, but I hadn't heard him sound so blunt in a long time. "As you both know, Shae was accepted as part of the Brotherhood when she was a baby, but clearly she is different from us, and I'm not just talking gender. As soon as she started travelling off-world she began to draw attention, and not all of it welcome." It was strange to hear him talking about me like I wasn't even there. "Shae understood not to use her gift in front of outsiders, but just the fact that monks were travelling with a young girl seemed of undue interest to some. There were concerns for her safety, so the rule was put in place."

"I get that," said Jared. "But I've seen first-hand what she's..." he seemed to remember I was actually there, "what you're capable of. And that's way more than most highly-trained military people I know." He smiled proudly and my chest warmed. "I can see Shae's point though. The rule does seem obsolete now."

"Like I said, I agree. And I made just that point to Supreme Primus Isaiah—"

"You did?" I interrupted.

"Of course I did." He smiled and took my hand. "Not that it made any difference. I'm afraid, as far as Isaiah is concerned, we – the Brotherhood in general – have been careless in our obligations towards your safety."

I thought about all the times I'd been off-world with lower level Warrior monks, and even Doctrinal monks. Why was the Supreme Primus so adamant the rule be reinforced all of a sudden?

"Okay," I said, rubbing my temples with my fingertips. "There's no point arguing over this now. Isaiah's orders are for us to stay together," I waved a hand between Ash and me, "and that's easy enough to achieve. We," I indicated to the two of us again, "can deal with this issue after we get the Princess back. Agreed?" Ash nodded. "Agreed?" I looked between Jake and Jared. They nodded, albeit more reluctantly. "Good."

"It's sorted then," Jared concluded. "Jake and the Wolfpack take one lead, the three of us will take the other."

"Fine," Jake grunted.

"I need to grab my kit. Where are we meeting?" I asked.

"Situation Room," Jared replied. "We'll go quickly through the mission brief and aim to be star-side by zero-nine-hundred."

"Cool. I'll see you there in a couple of minutes." I downed the dregs of my coffee as I stood up and stepped over the bench. Waiving my thanks to the kitchen crew, I headed out of the Mess Hall and down the hallway towards the lift. I was halfway there when Jake caught up with me.

"Shae, wait up. I just wanted to say I'm sorry," he said,

raking his fingers through unruly hair.

"Sorry? For what?"

"For all the trouble I've caused you... and Ash."

"This isn't your fault, Jake. You didn't force me to come with you, I asked if you recall." I absentmindedly moved a piece of disobedient hair that was about to stick in his eye, then realised what I'd done and quickly removed my hand.

"It's okay, Shae. I'm not going to suddenly leap on you because you happen to touch me. Well..." his eyes turned mischievous, "I guess it would depend where you touched me."

"Jake!" I scolded, but my heart wasn't in it.

"It pains me to say it, but Jared was right," he continued. "I should've been looking after you better."

"I'm not getting into this again," I moaned. "Was it your fault for letting me come with you, or my fault for asking you? Was it Jared's... or Ash's? After all, they both let me go. Perhaps, and this is way out there," I did a big, exaggerated sweeping movement with my arm, "it was Jesper's fault for setting those damn traps in the first place." I was getting grouchier by the second. "You and Jared have got to stop treating me like some china doll that needs protection. I get enough of that from the Brotherhood, I don't need it from you two as well. I can look after myself." Hearing the words out loud, I realised how ungrateful and sarcastic I sounded. "Jake, I'm sorry," I gasped. "I didn't mean..." The rest of my words were said into his chest as he put his arms around me.

"I know," he said gently. "I know."

I let him hold me longer than I should, because whatever else was going on in my life, I always felt safe and calm when I was close to him.

"I've got to go," I said when he released me. "Jared and Ash will be waiting."

"Okay, but one last thing..." He lifted his foot off the ground and twirled his ankle around in big circles. "Thanks again for the fix. Losing it would've sure put a dampener on things." His hazel eyes sparkled, and his lips spread into a wide, genuine smile.

"Get out of here," I said, playfully punching him on the arm.

"I'll see you after the mission. It'll be interesting to see if Captain Extraordinary has better luck controlling your impulsive side than I did."

"Ha bloody ha. You're a funny man. Say 'hi' to the guys. I kind of miss their incessant banter… which is something I never thought I'd find myself saying."

"Will do. They'll be gutted you're not coming back out with us."

"No, they won't. They'll be glad to have their equilibrium back."

"You don't get it, do you? You're part of the pack now, Little Wolfpup." He winked before turning and jogging back up the hallway.

"Be careful," I yelled after him. "I'm not going to be there to fix things."

He didn't stop, or turn, he simply raised an arm in acknowledgment.

We took Team One with us on the mission and it was good to see Lieutenant Grainger and Trooper Roberts again, both of whom Ash and I had met on Angel Ridge during our previous mission. As for the assignment itself, things went from less than hopeful, to total bust. After a lengthy, and ultimately fruitless, cat-and-mouse chase around half of down-town New London, Jared eventually came to the conclusion that the targets knew nothing about the Khans' whereabouts. Something I could've told him three hours previously. We'd wasted the entire day and were no closer to finding Phina.

That evening in the Conference Room, Jake's After-Action report was almost a mirror image of ours. He was relaxed and joking, but I knew him well enough to know it was his way of masking his frustration. We knew that to find the Princess, we'd have to find the Khans, but there was no guarantee they still had the Seal. There was the chance they'd already passed it on to someone else, who would take even more time to track.

Jake wasn't the only frustrated person in the room.

When we were done with the debrief, Jared suggested hitting the bar. Ash and Jake agreed, but I decided to head back to my quarters.

"You want me to come with you?" asked Ash.

"Thanks, but I'll be fine. What kind of trouble can I get into in a VIP suite? Besides, I've got crappy paperwork to do. Guess I can't put it off any longer."

"As long as you're sure? I'll see you in the morning. Sleep well." He kissed me gently on the temple. "Love you," he whispered.

I spent the next couple of hours writing my After-Action report for that day's wasted mission, and for the failed operation on Genesis which I hadn't done because of the whole extended-nap thing. When I got to the bit about Jake's foot, I stopped and picked up a second pad which displayed his own report, to make sure I didn't contradict it. As a work of fiction, it wasn't half bad.

I finished writing my report and re-read it carefully for inconsistencies before submitting it to Jared and Francis. After that, I scanned old mission files to see if there was something we'd missed. Not that I really thought I'd find anything, but there was no harm in looking.

I was about to call it a night when there was a knock on the door. "Open," I instructed, not getting up. Jared was propped casually against the doorframe, and I smiled when he held out a hand, two beer bottles clinking gently together.

"Thought you could do with one. Can I come in?"

"Sure," I replied, my stomach doing that little flippy

thing it always did when he was close. I moved a stack of data-pads off the sofa so he could sit. "You okay?"

"I should be asking you that."

"You know me. Sleep and food, and I'm good to go. A beer's always an added bonus though," I said, nodding towards the unopened bottles.

Jared sat sideways on the other end of the sofa before opening one of the bottles and handing it over. He picked up the data-pad displaying Jake's AA report.

"Quite the work of art by all accounts," he said, taking a swig of beer. "I was going to buy him a drink to congratulate him on his creativity, but I was afraid he'd get legless."

"Oh my Gods, that's so bad!" I groaned but couldn't help laughing.

"I've got more," he continued, smiling mischievously before launching into a series of cheesy jokes. It was the relief I needed, and I laughed until tears rolled down my cheeks.

"It's really not that funny," I tried to chastise through a hiccough.

"It most definitely is," he replied, his eyes twinkling.

"Please don't tell him we did this. He'd be really pissed," I begged when I managed to stop laughing, but Jared just cocked his head to one side and looked roguish. "I'm serious. Promise me."

"I promise... but only because it's you asking."

"Thank you."

"You're welcome."

I took another sip of beer and lent lazily against the back of the sofa, no longer nervous. The room fell silent as we drank, but it wasn't awkward... until his face changed, and I knew he was trying to find the nerve to say something I wouldn't like. Which meant it had to be about Jake.

"Why haven't you told him?" he asked, after taking a large swig from his bottle. "Is it because you want to be with him? Because I think I have the right to know if that's how you feel."

"Jared, you have it all wrong," I stammered after recovering my voice. "I did tell him. I told him everything."

He looked confused. "You have? But he's still… the way he looks at you… the hugs, the kisses… I just assumed…"

"Well, you shouldn't assume things," I snapped. "And perhaps you should've brought more beers, because the situation is far more complex and confusing than you can possibly imagine." Tears welled, and I felt embarrassed for getting emotional.

Jared studied my face carefully then tapped his com-pad and ordered a pack of chilled beers to be delivered. He lent forward and took my hand.

"You can tell me anything. You know that, right?"

"I do. It's just not that easy," I replied, wiping at my eyes before trying to explain what had happened, pausing briefly for him to accept the drinks when they arrived five minutes later.

I don't know how I expected him to react to Jake's response, but I certainly wasn't expecting him to laugh. He added his third empty bottle to the growing collection on the coffee table, before opening another and passing it to me. I took it, waiting anxiously for him to comment on Jake's behaviour, or at least offer some explanation for his own.

"You can't blame the man for wanting to fight for you," he said eventually.

"That's what Ash said."

"Ash is a wise man," he commented. "Do you think you're mistaken?"

"About choosing not to be with anyone?"

"No, about loving me. Do you think Jake's right? That you only think you're in love with me because things got mixed up back with the creatures. Because you thought you were going to lose me so close to Finnian?"

"No! Of course not. If there's one thing in all of this mess I am sure about, it's that."

I watched his face lighten as a little voice in my brain said, 'Tell him you want him. Tell him you've always wanted him.' But then another voice chipped in, 'What if something happens to him? Could you live with that? What if he dies like Finnian?' I closed my eyes and pushed both voices to the very back of my brain.

"What is it?" Jared asked.

"I..." I fell silent, not trusting myself to say anything.

"Shae, I can't pretend to understand your crazy logic. Either you love someone, or you don't, but not being with that person isn't going to change what happens to them. We are who we are, and we all have dangerous jobs."

"You make it sound so simple."

"Isn't it? I love you, and you love me. How much simpler could it be?"

I didn't reply, but looked intently at my beer bottle, picking obsessively at the label.

After a moment he sighed, took another swig of beer and changed the subject. "What about all this chaperone business?"

"Oh yes, this is a much better topic." I said sarcastically. "What about it."

"You're capable of looking after yourself, so—"

"I'll remind you of that next time you get overprotective."

"I love you, it's my job to be overprotective, but what I was going to say was why force the issue now? You said yourself the monks had been more relaxed about it recently, and I know you, Shae, I can't believe you're happy to be put on a leash."

My immediate instinct was to jump to the defence of the Brotherhood, as I always did when someone criticised them, but he was right.

"I don't know why Isaiah is pushing the rule now, and no, I'm not happy about it, but it's Brotherhood business, Jared. I'm sorry."

"I understand," he said, then he grinned. "Besides, my overprotective side is quite happy you'll always have a Warrior Caste monk to look after you when I'm not around."

I swatted him playfully with a data-pad, noticing the time displayed on it. I hadn't realised it was so late.

"So, what now?" I asked. "I feel like time is running out on us."

"I know what you mean. I'll be able to dial up the power on the Oracle tomorrow to get an update on its predictions, but it feels like we're going nowhere fast."

"How are the engines holding up?"

He looked pleased I'd asked. "I'm concerned about the number four engine core, but Chief Hannigan's keeping an eye on things. They're all taking a bit of a hammering."

"I know how they feel."

As if that was his cue, Jared drained his bottle and stood. "Get some sleep. I'll see you at breakfast," he said.

19

The whole of the following day was a tedious repeat of the one before. We were clearly scraping the bottom of the barrel when we raided an illegal weapons depot on a planet not too far from Angel Ridge.

The intelligence report said we should encounter ten to fifteen people at what they called a 'soft' target, but the information was way off. There must've been thirty, maybe more, and we came up against heavy resistance – but it certainly made things more interesting. There was a lot of shouting and chasing... but more importantly there was fighting.

I don't think I was the only one who used the opportunity to burn off a little frustration.

We may have been outnumbered, but we were faster, stronger and better trained. I took out four bad guys without having to draw my weapons, and I hadn't even broken a sweat. I was disappointed when Ash confirmed the area had been contained, and I was even more disappointed when the targets weren't able to get us closer to the Khans. Not that I was surprised.

When I'd finished writing my After-Action report that

night, I tossed the pad on the table in annoyance. It clattered loudly, skidding off the other side and ending up on the floor. I brought my feet up on the sofa and rested my head against the cushions, running through possible 'what next' scenarios.

I jumped and my eyes shot open, burning from the lights still bright in my quarters. My heart pounded heavily, and I wasn't sure what had woken me until a loud thudding continued on my door.

"Open," I said, jumping up from the sofa, confusion replaced by fear and anticipation. Jake strode straight into the room, not waiting to be invited. "What's happened? What time is it?"

"Zero-three-thirty. We've had a... have you not been to sleep?" he asked, distracted by my clothes and the data-pads spread across the coffee table.

"I must've fallen asleep on the sofa. What's going on?"

"Gear up. We've got a lead on Deakes, the Khans' Lieutenant. Remember him from the Great Hall? Anyway, the intel's solid and Jared wants to jump on this immediately. One thing we actually agree on for a change."

The hallways of the *Defender* were practically deserted, but we still turned a few heads as Jake and I double-timed it towards the hangar where we found Ash and Jared waiting for us at the ramp. The *Veritas*' engines were already roaring and impatient, and we were star-side within minutes.

"It seems we've stumbled across some good luck for a change." Jared began his briefing. "The REF has a Spec Ops team working up intel on a narcotics cartel along this part of the Sector. It's a standard four-man team running a deep undercover mission."

"That sounds great, but what's it got to do with us?" asked Kaiser.

"They're based on a planet called Lexin, not too far from here," Jared continued, ignoring him. "Due to the long-term nature of their mission, they weren't included as active assets to be used in Fallen Star, but during their last scheduled check-in they were given 'look out' orders for the Khans, Hoban and Deakes. Approximately one hour ago, we received word from their CO to say they had eyes on Deakes. He's at an twenty-four hour dive-bar called Carpe Noctum."

"Who's the CO?" Jake asked.

"Captain Durrand. You know him?"

"Yeah, Scotty. I heard he got promoted. Haven't seen him since he did a couple of jobs with me back in the day. He's one of the good guys."

"Understandably he doesn't want his team to blow its cover, but they've managed to get one of their guys close. Last report had Durrand's guy, Logan, palling up to Deakes in the bar. Apparently Deakes is waiting for somebody, some kind of breakfast meeting, but Logan says he's being tight-lipped over who it is."

"You think it could be the Khans?" Ash asked.

"We can hope. At the moment it's anyone's guess," Jared replied. "We're set to rendezvous with Durrand outside the bar at zero-five-thirty. The plan is to cover the inside and outside of the bar and wait for the meet. If it is the Khans, we take them down. If it's not, we'll pick up Deakes separately. And…" Jared added purposely as I opened my mouth. "If for some reason Deakes decides to leave before then, Durrand's team will tail him."

"What if they lose him… or he works out who they are?" I asked.

"They're a good team, Babe. They won't lose him, and he won't make them, I promise," Jake said. "If it makes you feel better, think of them like another us." He indicated to the Wolfpack.

"God help us all," Jared quipped. "Ty, can you access the floor-plans for Carpe Noctum, then superimpose the surrounding buildings, streets, and sub-structures?" he added, tapping the holo-table.

"Easy peasy." Ty worked his magic until a green-tinted three-dimensional plan of the bar materialised just above the table. "How much of the surrounding area do you want?"

"Let's try a mile to start with."

Blue-tinted buildings and roads, and red-tinted substructures and tunnels appeared on the map.

Ash lent closer to study the detail. "There's only one underground access point to the bar, here." He touched the door on the map and it instantly glowed. "So we can get rid of all this other clutter and just keep anything connected to that door. Agreed?" Jared nodded. Ty punched commands into a remote pad and ninety percent of the red disappeared from the map, leaving only a trail of underground maintenance and supply tunnels snaking out from the bar.

"Connor, I want you to stay with the *Veritas*," Jared said, pausing as Connor shot an enquiring look towards Jake.

"This is the Captain's mission," Jake said stiffly. "His orders are my orders. That goes for all of you," he clarified. Connor screwed up his nose.

"I need you on the *Veritas* co-ordinating the environment," Jared continued. "Hack into whatever surveillance and communications systems they have and work the ship's sensors for additional observations. I don't want any surprises, so I'm counting on you as overwatch to keep track of everything that's going on in and around the bar, including the locations of every team member. I want continuous threat-level assessments and immediate evac-readiness should things go south. Understood?"

"Understood," Connor replied.

"Kaiser, you head towards the bar from this direction and take up position here," Jared advised.

"Outside?" Kaiser questioned, his tone halfway between amazed and pissed. "I thought we were all going in?"

"Firstly, I need eyes and ears outside," said Jared. "From your position you'll be able to cover the rear exit and gain access to the supply tunnel through this hatch here should that be necessary. But secondly, and more importantly, Deakes knows what you look like from back in the Great Hall. I'm not prepared to risk your safety, or that of the mission."

"Of course," Kaiser replied, comprehension clearing away the frown-lines. "If I can suggest though, this elevated point here would cover all the areas you mentioned before, but also here and here." He pointed to two other, smaller pathways.

Jared lent forward to get a better view of the area. "Good observation. That will be your primary position. Ty, you'll approach the bar from this direction and cover the front. Where do you want to set up?"

"I'd say this is the best place," Ty replied, pointing.

"Excellent. The rest of us will meet with Durrand outside the bar, here." Jared indicated towards a vacant lot a block away. "Once he updates us on Deakes, we'll enter the bar in two teams: Shae and Ash, Jake and me."

"Wait, Jake can't go in," I said.

"This is no time to joke, Babe," Jake reprimanded, his hands resting on his hips.

"I'm not joking. When you pulled your little diversion stunt back at the Palace, Vita sent Deakes after you."

"So?"

"So... Jared and I saw you on the security monitors. The monitors the Khans had control of," I explained. "It's a clear bet Deakes used them to track you, and if we saw you..."

"She's right," Jared said.

"Come on," Jake pleaded. "It's a long shot he'll recognise me from a blurred image on a camera."

"We can't take that chance. Sorry, Jake, but you're outside with the others."

"But—"

"Decision's made. End of discussion," Jared concluded.

"So, that leaves Ash, Shae and me going in together. Like I said before, we'll keep an eye on Deakes. If his meeting is with the Khans, Vanze and Blain are our main targets, if it isn't, we take Deakes. Okay, that's it. Gear up."

Connor landed the *Veritas* half a mile from Carpe Noctum. We paused briefly on the landing pad for a coms-check, and to confirm Connor could pick up our individual locator signals, before Kaiser and Ty sprinted off to take up their perimeter positions. The rest of us headed to our rendezvous point.

We only had to wait five minutes before our contact arrived.

"Scotty," Jake said as a fearsome-looking guy strolled casually down an ally towards us, his dark skin and clothes camouflaging him against the shadows.

"Jake Mitchell," he replied, grinning broadly – the wide, ragged scar on his cheek flexing as he spoke. "How the fuck are you? Thought you'd be dead by now. Shit, thought we'd all be dead by now." He laughed loudly, and the two men shook hands.

"Captain Jared Marcos, Brother Asher, and Shae," Jake said, introducing us.

"Welcome to Lexin," Durrand replied, his vest-top flaunting muscles the size of the Rover's tyres. He scratched at his goatee and looked quizzically at Jake. "So, full Colonel now I hear. Congrats. I'm surprised High Command still lets you run with the cool kids though. Thought the rank came with a desk and a pair of fluffy slippers."

Jake laughed. "You know how it goes... save the right person from the wrong situation and suddenly you get to choose your next command... I was never a fluffy slippers kind of guy anyway."

"I hear that."

"What can you tell us about Deakes?" asked Jared, getting us back on track.

"He's still in the bar with my man, Logan. They're sat ground floor, far south-east corner. Not great location wise, he's got easy access to the door leading to the sub-basement."

"Has Deakes said anything more about who he's meeting?" I asked.

"No, nothing. Jake, I don't know your full mission, but I got two other guys in that bar, and I'd really like to avoid blowing their cover if at all possible."

"Of course," Jake replied. "This shouldn't involve your people at all. Just tell them to keep their heads down, avoid trouble, and they'll be fine."

"Cool. Appreciate that, man."

"Is there anything else we need to know?" Jared asked.

Durrand glanced at me briefly. "I'd keep an eye on her, if I were you. The dudes in the bar… not exactly gentlemen. A pretty little thing like her will get eaten alive."

"I can handle myself," I replied, but he laughed.

"I don't doubt that," he said. "That's all I can offer you, Captain."

"Appreciate your help," Jared replied.

Durrand turned to leave, but he stopped. "Hey, Jake, perhaps we'll stay alive long enough to do another mission together."

"Maybe," Jake replied. Durrand smiled, waved, then melted into the darkness of the alleyway. Jake caught the look on my face. "Just a little Spec Ops humour, Babe. Doesn't mean anything."

"If you say so," I replied, trying not to read too much into it.

Jake reluctantly left to take up his position, and the rest of us headed to the bar. We approached the black-brick building, navigating around rows of tricked-out drift-bikes and leather-clad gang members chatting to scantily dressed waitresses. I felt the heat from the blazing white flames spelling out 'Carpe Noctum' on the roof.

Why couldn't bad guys ever hang out in nice areas?

Jared stooped to tie a bootlace that was already securely fixed. "Overwatch, this is Team Leader. I need a go, no-go on the mission."

"Overwatch has the ball on all surveillance and communications. Your locater signals are five by five. Chatter is clear. You're good to go. I repeat, you're good to go."

"Copy that," Jared whispered before standing.

The brutish doorman stopped us at the entrance, looking me up and down with a shameless leer. "You're always welcome at Carpe Noctum, sexy lady," he said directly to me. "But you two…" He glanced at Jared and Ash. "Bar's full."

"Perhaps this will free up some space?" Ash said, discreetly offering the man a wad of credits.

"You know what? Perhaps we could squeeze in a couple more after all," he said, taking the money with large, beefy hands.

The doorman hadn't been kidding. Even though the bar was far bigger than it looked from the outside, it heaved with a mass of spirited women, and sweaty, smelly men. All of whom seemed to possess the meat-head gene. Heavy, pounding music blared so loudly I could barely hear Jared when he shouted we should head towards the bar.

I tried to follow, but the swell of people grinding and pushing against me made it almost impossible. Jared turned and slipped a strong, warm hand into mine, pulling me to him, and I stuck close as he forced his way through gyrating bodies.

Someone grabbed at me, but Ash snatched their hands away. I was sure he broke one or two fingers, but it was impossible to know for sure because the man had already been swallowed up in a wave of ravers.

Jared fought his way to the bar and ordered three beers, which we then took towards the south-east corner so we could get eyes on Deakes. I recognised him immediately and it took all my effort not to go straight over and punch him in the head.

Away from the bar and the dancefloor, the room thinned-out, and it became easier to talk. "You can let go of my hand now," I said.

"Oh, yes, of course," Jared replied, as if he'd forgotten he was. He glanced quickly around the bar before propping himself against a plain, concrete column about ten metres from our target. "I suppose the good thing about it being so busy is that nobody's taking any notice of us."

"Speak for yourself," I complained. "My arse is probably black and blue from all that pinching. I swear to the Gods, if I could've got hold of some of those handsy bastards, I would've broken some damn fingers of my own."

"I'll kiss it better for you later, Babe" Jake said over coms.

Jared's face darkened. "Coms silent except for emergencies," he hissed.

"You're the boss," Jake replied casually. Jared shook his head wearily.

"There are too many people in here to make a clean grab," Jared continued. "We'll wait until after Deakes has his meeting and snatch him when he leaves."

"What if he spooks and bolts? What if we lose him in the crowd?" I asked.

"If he bolts, and if he gets past us, the Wolfpack will pick him up," Jared said confidently, but I wasn't so certain.

I scanned the room, the people, the exits – including the one to the sub-basement – and came up with several possible escape plans. Granted some were more elaborate and less plausible than others, but the possibility was too substantial for my liking.

"We can't run the risk he'll escape," I pressed. "But I've got an idea." I unzipped a pocket in my trousers and took out a small tube of pale pink lip-gloss before looking to

Ash. He smiled and nodded his agreement, so I pulled my Sentinel from my waistband and passed it stealthily over to him. He tucked it under his jacket.

"What's going on?" Jared asked.

"Contingency plan," I replied, taking off my shirt so I was left wearing a strappy vest top. I pulled my trousers down slightly so my waistband sat a little lower on my hips and folded up the bottom of my vest, so a provocative band of skin was on display.

"I've no idea what's going on, but I'm not sure I like it," Jared said, his lips tightening.

"It's okay," Ash replied. "She knows what she's doing."

I carefully unscrewed the top of the gloss and used the Santian vodka branded mirror to apply it to my lips, pressing them firmly together.

"We'll be right here if you need us," Ash continued, but I gave him my nothing's going to go wrong look. "Just be careful."

"You know I will," I replied.

I picked up my beer bottle and headed into the crowd. When I was closer, I started to weave and bump into people, deliberately drawing attention. I purposely didn't look at Deakes until I was practically on top of him, by which point I had both his, and Logan's, interest.

As soon as I caught his eyes, I forced my face into a drunken grin. "Arkie!" I cried. "Arkie, where have you been, you old dog?" I slurred drunkenly, throwing myself into his lap and kissing him full on the lips. He didn't seem to mind though, kissing me back with more enthusiasm than I was prepared for.

I pulled away and stared dreamily into his eyes. "I can't believe…" I paused, letting my eyes focus. "Hey, wait a minute. You're not Arkie." I giggled drunkenly then using an arm around Deakes' shoulder to anchor myself, I swung around towards Logan. "Oops." I giggled again. "He's not Arkie."

"No, he's not," Logan replied, clearly amused by the drunk girl with the bad eyesight.

I swung back to Deakes, who took the opportunity to lean forward and kiss me again. "Shh, don't tell Arkie," I slurred, putting a finger to my lips, "but you're a much better kisser than he is. I… umm, I should really leave you two gentlemen to your… whatever you were doing." I tried to stand but his arm tightened around my waist.

"Stay," he said. "I may not be this Arkie character, but you and I could have some fun."

Great. Just what I needed.

"That's quite the offer. Shame I've got plans," I replied, giving him an exaggerated sad face. I stood and added a wobble for effect. "It was nice… umm… kissing you," I slurred as I turned and meandered away, dancing to the music until I was swallowed up by the crowd.

I looped around the bar and ended up back with Jared and Ash.

"Here," said Ash, passing me my shirt and weapon. "Good job. He didn't suspect a thing."

"While I'm impressed by your acting skills, Shae, how does getting up close and personal with Deakes stop him from running?" asked Jared, his tone clipped and unhappy.

"It doesn't."

"Then what the—"

"Have faith, Jared," I interrupted, before accessing files on my com-pad. "Overwatch, I'm sending you the formula properties for a complex bio-chem compound. Re-programme the *Veritas*' external sensors to scan for the unique marker."

"On it," Connor said. "File's coming through now. I'll let you know when I have something."

I waved the tube of gloss at Jared. "Not so much girlie accessory as harmless chemical tracer," I explained. "Wears off after a couple of hours, but its distinctive signature will allow us to keep tabs on Deakes. Think of it as a temporary locator beacon."

"And you couldn't just tell me that before," Jared said, deep frown-lines settling across his forehead. "Did you have to kiss him on the lips?"

"Whoa, someone's jealous."

"Shut it, Jake," I warned.

"Hey, that was uncalled for, Babe," he replied, feigning offence.

"Enough," Jared growled. "Coms silent. That's an order."

"Yes, Sir," Jake replied.

I ignored him. "In answer to your question, Jared, I could've kissed him on the cheek, but the tracer gets into the system quicker via the mouth, and the signal is stronger."

"Okay, but—"

"This is Overwatch," Connor interrupted with perfect timing. "I'm getting two pings from the ground floor, south-east corner. One is in sync with Shae's locator beacon, the other is nine-point-three metres away towards the rear wall."

"Excellent," I said. "The second ping is Deakes. That's the one to keep an eye on."

"Will do. Overwatch out."

Half a beer bottle later, Ash said, "Something's happening. Looks like Deakes is trying to get rid of Logan."

"Perhaps his meeting's about to start. Any sign of the Khans outside?" Jared asked. Silence. "Perimeter, any sign of the Khans?" he repeated.

"Oh, are we allowed to talk now," Jake said sarcastically. "No, there's no sign. Just ugly bikers and pretty waitresses."

"Fine. Just keep your eyes open," Jared ordered.

Moments after Logan left Deakes, three men joined Deakes at his table.

"Okay, so not the Khans then," Ash said. I felt a wave of disappointment through the Link.

There seemed to be a great deal of discussion and disagreement, but eventually, after about half an hour, Deakes and the mysterious men exchanged a duffel bag for a case.

"Here we go," said Jared. "Everyone get ready."

The men, and their newly acquired duffel bag, melted into the throng of clubbers, who were still going strong, even at that time in the morning. Deakes, on the other hand, stepped away from the table, stretched, called to the waitress for another drink, and sat down again.

"You have got to be kidding me?" I groaned as Logan re-joined him. "Is he ever going to stop drinking?"

"It's too great a risk to take him here," Jared commented, looking around us. "We'll just have to wait him out."

"Maybe not," Ash said. "Shae, remember Cinterhouse? You think Deakes would bite?"

"He's already propositioned me, so I don't see why not. It's worth a try."

"What the hell is Cinterhouse?" Jake said over coms.

"Not what, who," Ash replied as I shrugged out of my shirt again.

"Are you being particularly vague to piss me off?"

"Steady, Jake," Jared warned.

"Easy for you to say. You're not stuck outside having to guess at what the fuck's going on in there."

"Cinterhouse was a sexual predator we were after a few years back," I explained. "We caught up with him, but he was surrounded by innocent, vulnerable women who didn't have a clue what was going on. We were concerned that if we tried to take him down, he would hurt one or more of them. I went in undercover and persuaded him to leave with me."

"You persuaded him? How?"

"Oh, Jake." I laughed, surprised by his sudden bout of naivety. "Use your imagination."

"You're talking about a honey-trap, right? You are not going to give yourself to him," Jake roared, each word exaggerated over coms. "Jared, if you let her—"

"It's not a honey-trap… well not exactly," I interrupted.

"What the hell does that mean?" He wasn't appeased.

"Nothing physical's going to happen. I promise. You'd be surprised what a simple suggestion from a drunk girl can achieve when the target's a complete sleaze. All I'm going to do is get him out of the bar. As soon as we're clear, you guys can intercept."

"I wouldn't have suggested it if I didn't think it was safe… and morally acceptable," added Ash.

"That's a matter of opinion," countered Jake. "And I can't believe you're being so quiet on the subject, Jared."

"She'll be okay," Jared answered, but his eyes told me he wasn't happy. I touched his arm gently before disappearing around the column.

I slipped easily back into my drunken routine and was glad when Deakes reacted well to my re-appearance. "Hello again, man-who's-not-Arkie." I hiccoughed and slid my way into his lap, draping my arm lazily around his shoulder.

"Hello again," he replied, running his hand up my thigh. "I didn't expect to see you again."

I picked up his drink and downed it in one before moving closer so I could whisper in his ear. "Turns out, you're not only a better kisser than Arkie, but also the loser I came here with. Better kisser, better looking, and better…" I lowered my hand and felt the strain against his zipper. "Let's just say, better all round… so I ditched him."

"Really?" Deakes seemed pleased. There was nothing like stroking the male ego after all. "So you've decided to join me for a drink after all?"

"Not exactly," I said, stroking his chest. "I was kinda hoping to join you for something, but the something I had in mind is a bit more intimate than a drink. It's a little crowded here for my liking, if you know what I mean." I swung around and touched Logan's leg before adding, "No offence."

"None taken," he replied, looking bemused.

I moved back to face Deakes and kissed him on the cheek while running a finger lightly along his jaw. "I'm more of a one-on-one party-girl."

"I get what you're saying," Deakes said, moving his hand further up my thigh. "I've got a place not far from here."

"Sounds perfect," I purred. "Lead the way."

"Shae, you're doing great," Jared said over coms, his words forced. "Take him straight out the front door and we'll pick him up as soon as you're away from the bar. Perimeter, prepare to follow as soon as she's out. Overwatch, keep eyes on Deakes' tracer signature at all times."

I shielded my eyes from the sudden glare of the morning sun and glanced casually around the square. I couldn't see any of the Wolfpack, but I knew they were there.

"I've got eyes on the target, Blue," said Kaiser. "If he makes one dodgy move, I'll blow his fucking head off."

Deakes guided me passed the mass of people still crowding the outside of the bar and down a road to the right, which was almost as busy. His hands were all over me and I had a horrible feeling he wasn't going to wait until we got to his place before he made his move.

"Say the word, Shae, and I'll take him out in a heartbeat," said Jake in my ear. I was surprised how much I appreciated the offer, and how close I was to taking him up on it. But no matter how uncomfortable I felt, I knew we couldn't lose Deakes as a source of information.

"How much further," I slurred, weaving gently.

"Not far," Deakes replied as we took another right onto a smaller, almost empty side-street.

"This is much more like it. Hardly anyone around," I said for the team's benefit.

"This is it then. Shae, we're taking him down in sixty seconds. Be prepared," Jared said, but before the team could get in place, something unexpected happened.

"Deakes!" The angry voice came from somewhere behind me and I felt Deakes remove his arm. I turned slowly, raising my hands the moment I saw the weapons. From the furious looks on their faces, the men from Deakes' meeting earlier meant serious business.

"You think you can play us and get away with it?" the middle one said, his voice venomous.

"Fellas, there must be some mistake," Deakes said, putting his arm back around my waist and pulling me in front of him like a shield. He sounded calm, jovial even, but his body tensed as he held me closer.

"There's no mistake, Deakes. You should've known not to fuck with us."

"Come on, guys. Let's talk about this rationally." Deakes' voice was breathy and held a hint of fear.

"Time for talking's over. You're a dead man, Deakes," the one on the left said, raising his weapon.

"Shae, get down," Jared yelled, a fraction of a second before bullets started flying. I did as ordered and fell deadweight to the floor, slipping through Deakes' arms. I buried my head in my arms and screwed myself up into the smallest target I could manage while bullets whistled past, splintering and cracking as they hit stone cobbles.

When everything finally went still and silent, I lifted my head and peered through the light-grey gun-smoke filling the narrow lane. The three men lay in bloody, broken heaps on the floor, with Kaiser checking each one for a pulse.

Jake reached me first, pulling me off the floor, his hands searching my body for bullet holes.

"I'm okay. What happened to Deakes?" I asked, urgently scanning the ground for his body. "Overwatch, where's Deakes? Tell me you have him on sensors."

"Affirmative. I've got him moving quickly through a

maze of side-streets," he replied.

"Directions, Connor. Which way did he go?" Jake asked as Durrand's bulk appeared through the smoke.

"Need some help?" he said. "I know the place pretty well."

"Appreciate the offer, Scottie, but what about your cover?" Jake replied.

"I think I'm safe for the moment."

"In that case, sure. The more help, the better."

Connor began giving directions and we sprinted after Deakes, leaving the three bodies in a lake of blood.

"Little bastard sure can run, but he can't outrun the sensors," Connor said after he'd taken us directly to the target. "He's twenty metres directly in front of you, behind some kind of large container. Happy hunting."

By the time we'd surrounded him, Deakes had no choice but to give himself up.

"We're using an old warehouse not three blocks from here as our base," Durrand said. "You're more than welcome to take this piece of shit there to interrogate him. It's completely private; no one around for blocks."

"Thanks," replied Jared. "We might just take you up on that."

"Hey, you," Deakes yelled to get Jared's attention. "You the one in charge here?"

"You could say that."

"Do you even know who I am?" he continued coldly, looking at the cuffs pinching the skin around his wrists. Given his predicament, it unnerved me that he was so cool. "The people I work for are going to have your balls for paperweights for this. And you," he glared at me, "you're dead, whore. You hear me?"

"For fuck sakes, will someone shut him up," Jake ordered.

"With pleasure." Kaiser punched him out cold.

20

The vast, rectangular warehouse was perfect for what we needed. Thick, brick walls added soundproofing, while large blacked-out windows circled the entire building just below the high roof, avoiding the possibility of anyone wandering past and looking in.

Durrand's team had some equipment and cots set up at one end of the room but the rest of the area was bare, lit by orange chem-lights that hung by long cords from the rafters. Kaiser strapped an unconscious Deakes to a metal chair he'd placed right in the centre of the room, and Ty placed a table and a couple more chairs in front of him. It wasn't bad for a makeshift interrogation room.

"He still out?" I asked knocking his lolling head roughly from side to side. "How hard did you hit him?"

"It was just a tap," Kaiser replied, a playful grin on his lips.

At the opposite end from Durrand's equipment, Jared and Jake were engaged in an animated disagreement. I walked over, the dull thud of my boots echoing gently around the vast room.

"...if she'd been hurt," was the tail-end of Jake's

sentence. "Don't even think about side-lining me like that again."

"Are you done?" Jared replied. "You know I had no choice. Don't tell me you wouldn't have done exactly the same thing if the roles had been reversed."

"And you'd have been just as unhappy about it as Jake is, Jared," I said, adding my opinion whether he liked it or not. "What's done is done. Now we concentrate on Deakes."

"You're right, Babe." Jake looked over at the prisoner. "Someone bring that son-of-a-bitch round."

Ty removed a vial from one of his pockets and snapped it under Deakes' nose. He came to, coughing and spluttering.

"You want to give it a go, Ash?" Jared asked.

"Don't mind if I do," he replied, folding up his sleeves neatly as he strolled over and took one of the seats in front of Deakes. The rest of us stood behind him, far enough away so we weren't a distraction to Ash, but close enough for Deakes to feel our presence.

I watched our prisoner closely for signs and clues – the involuntary, tell-tale give-aways that accompany lies and misdirects – but Deakes was calm and composed, his eyes expressionless, his thoughts unreadable.

"I'm going to make this easy for you," Ash began.

"No," Deakes replied quietly, his face impervious. "I'm going to make this easy for you. Whatever you think I can give you, I can't. I'm not going to tell you anything, so you might as well save us all some time and just let me go now."

"Hmm," Ash replied, unimpressed. He stared at Deakes in silence until the Khans' Lieutenant shifted position.

"Let me tell you how this is going to go… and I'll make it simple, so you can keep up." A hint of cockiness vibrated in Deakes' steel-cold voice. "If you don't let me go immediately, my employers are going to hunt you down. When they catch up with each and every one of you, they're going to kill you slowly and painfully. And when they're done with that, they're going to locate every member of your families and kill them as well." He smiled maliciously, but it slipped when Ash shook with laughter.

"Wow. I've got to say that's… graphic. And I think I speak for all of us when I say thanks for sharing, but you still don't get it, do you? It's the Khans we want, not you. You mean nothing to us. But if killing you brings them looking for us… well, that saves us the bother of searching. We were keeping you alive because we wanted you to give up the Khans, but now it seems you've made yourself expendable."

"You're bluffing."

"Am I?" Ash turned and pointed to Jake. "Colonel Jake Mitchell, Marines." He moved down the line. "Captain Jared Marcos, Fleet. Shae, Brotherhood. Wolfpack Special Operations Team." He turned back to face Deakes again. "Brother Asher, Ninth Degree Warrior Caste, Brotherhood of the Virtuous Sun," he concluded, looking dangerous. "What? You didn't think King Sebastian would do everything in his power to get his daughter back? That he wouldn't afford us the freedom to do whatever was necessary?"

Deakes snorted, but his eyes flicked up towards the ceiling and he blinked a couple of times before saying, "If it's the Princess you're after, you're too late. She's already dead."

"He's lying," I cautioned.

"Let's try this again, shall we?" Ash said, with an exaggerated sigh. "And I'll make it simple, so you can keep up. Option A: you give us the Khans' location, and we'll let you live out the rest of your miserable life in a Max-Five High Security Prison. Or… Option B: we kill you here and now and wait for the Khans to find us. How's that for clarity?"

Deakes forced a laugh but he slumped slightly in his

chair. "I'm never going to give you the Khans' location. And you know why? Do you think I was bluffing when I told you what they'd do to you if you hurt me? I wasn't. And if that's what they'd do to complete strangers, what do you think they'd do to one of their own crew who narked on them? Here's the simple truth: you can't do anything to me that Vanze wouldn't do ten times worse. So do whatever," he concluded. "I'm not going to give them up. Ever."

Under the false bravado he was petrified, but it wasn't of us. Deakes was going to be much harder to crack than I'd imagined.

Over the following few hours, the guys used pretty much every non-physical tactic they could think of, working on him solidly like a tag-team, never letting him rest or relax. After Ash tried the calm, rational approach, Jake had gone in strong with threats and intimidation, but that hadn't worked either. Jared switched tactics and tried to appeal to Deakes' honourable side, but as he didn't have one, that had failed too. It was my turn.

I pulled the hunting knife from my boot and grabbed one of Deakes' arms, slicing through the masking tape binding it to the metal chair.

"Eat," I said, pressing a half-unwrapped sandwich into his hand.

It was my job to try the friendly approach, after all, what was the harm? Everything else had failed. I opened a bottle of water and placed it on the table in front of him. Deakes studied the sandwich, then the bottle.

"How do I know you haven't poisoned them or something?" he asked.

"Would it matter?" I replied. "You don't seem to care what we do to you, so what would it matter if we had poisoned one of them? But if it makes you feel better..." I leant forward and took a sip from the bottle of water. "You want me to take a bite of the sandwich as well? Trust me, if we'd got to the killing part, it wouldn't be as easy and painless as poisoning." I crossed my legs and sat back in the chair, watching him as he ate in silence.

After a couple of mouthfuls, he leant forward as much as his restraints would allow.

"I still think you and I would be good together," he taunted quietly. "What do you say we ditch that lot and go back to mine?"

"It's a tempting offer, but I don't think so. Look, Deakes, these guys mean business, and they're getting impatient. If you don't give them something soon, I'm afraid they're going to try something... more physical. I know you were at the Palace on the Khans' orders, and I agree with you, they're pretty scary people. Help me now and I'll put in a good word with the judge – tell him you were under duress when you committed the crime. If you tell us where the Khans are, I'll tell the court you cooperated. It could mean the difference between death by lethal injection and life in a Max-Five."

Deakes smiled, but his eyes were empty. "Nice try. And I gotta say, your interrogation tactics are much more agreeable than the others, but you can't change my mind. You won't find out the Khans' location from me. Give up now and find some other poor bastard to intimidate. You can tell the others I'm done." He placed the half-eaten sandwich on the table.

"As you wish," I said before leaving him.

At the far end of the room, Jared pulled everyone together. "Okay, what are our options?" he asked.

"Let me have some time with him," said Kaiser. "You might want to step-out though, Captain. I know how fragile Fleet sensibilities are."

"That's enough, Kaiser," Jake warned. "He does have a point though, Jared. Being Wolfpack means we have the leeway to do things not exactly by-the-book. You know that."

"Doesn't mean I have to like it... or agree with it," Jared replied. "I appreciate the offer, but we're not there yet."

"Threats aren't working," Jake pushed, but Jared was resolute.

"I've been watching him," Ash said. "I believe he's willing to die rather than give up the Khans. I don't think he fears death."

"He may not fear death, but perhaps he's not so keen on pain," Kaiser added.

Jared rubbed the stubble on his chin. "I don't want to lay a finger on Deakes if we can help it." Kaiser puffed out a frustrated sigh. "So, other than torture, what other options are there?"

"What about Cruillian?" Durrand suggested.

"Irrelevant... unless you happen to have some lying about?" Jake said.

"Colonel, this is me remember. With all due respect, would I have suggested it otherwise?" While the words were borderline insubordinate, Durrand's devilish smile and easy-going attitude allowed him to get away with it. "We keep a dose around... for emergencies."

He sounded so much like Jake, it was scary.

That time Ash provided the voice of reason. "It's too risky to use Cruillian without med-support. Of course there's a forty percent chance it will work and he'll tell us everything, but there's also a sixty percent chance it'll kill him."

"Is there anything you can do about that, Shae?" Jake asked. I knew what he meant, and I also knew he was being purposely obscure because Durrand was there.

"Dead is dead," I replied cryptically.

Eventually Jared decided to let Jake give it one more go. "Without torture," he ordered.

Jake put on a good show and even I was impressed by the fierceness of his interrogation, but Deakes remained unyielding. Ty and Kaiser took up flanking positions next to him, weapons hot, while Jake continued a spectacular exhibition of dominance and force, but nothing. He even through in a few punches, which Jared bristled over. I'd never seen someone remain so impassive and resistant.

When Jake finally returned to the rest of us, his voice was gravelly from shouting, and he was frustrated and angry at his lack of progress. "I was going for shock and awe," he croaked.

"I could see that," I replied.

"Do you think it worked?"

"Not a chance in hell. He's just not scared of you," I said, giving him a reassuring smile, but the words triggered a thought in the back of my mind.

"I know that look," Ash said. "What's up?"

"He's not afraid of Jake or the Wolfpack," I said, thinking out loud.

"Thanks, Babe. Rub it in why don't you," Jake replied.

"Knives and guns don't scare him, and nor does dying," I continued, ignoring him. "He has no morals or compunction, so we can't appeal to them, and Jared had no luck with threatening jail. The only thing that scares him is the Khans."

"What's your point," Durrand asked.

"We need to make him more terrified of us than them."

"I thought that's what we'd been trying to do all this time."

"We have. But when someone's not afraid of the possible, maybe they're afraid of the impossible."

"Is she always so cryptic," Durrand asked Jake, who shrugged his shoulders before winking at me.

"He said it himself," I explained. "He can't imagine us doing anything to him that the Khans wouldn't do ten times worse. So, let's show him something he couldn't imagine in a million years. People fear what they don't understand, and he sure as hell isn't going to understand me." Durrand looked even more confused.

"You think you can do it, Babe?" Jake asked. "It won't be easy; you'll have to be convincing."

"I know, and it may not even work. Plus, it might also mean getting physical. You're in charge, Jared, it's your call."

"As long as you're not in any danger, go for it. We've got nothing left to try."

Our lack of progress was so frustrating, it was easy to call on the energy inside me, in fact, I barely had to think about it. I let it swirl gently in the pit of my stomach, ready to be called upon at a moment's thought. I approached Deakes, the metal table and chairs now strewn haphazardly in front of him following Jake's last interrogation attempt. I stopped a few metres behind an upended chair and folded my arms tightly across my chest.

"Seriously?" Deakes said, a weary edge to his voice. "Haven't you given up yet?"

"Actually, we kind of have," I replied. Confusion shadowed his face. "We've pretty much accepted that you fear the Khans more than Captain Marcos, Colonel Mitchell and the guys." I nodded over my shoulder towards the men before pausing for effect. "But out of everyone, including Vanze and Blain, the person you should be truly afraid of is me."

"You!" He laughed cruelly. "What are you going to do? Kiss me to death? Coz I gotta tell you, on my list of ways to go, that's got to be right up there as one of the best."

"Kill you?" I said, feigning surprise at the suggestion. "I'm not going to kill you. What purpose would that solve? I've got something more... unique in mind."

"Then bring it on, Bitch, I'm totally scared." He shook for affect but froze the moment I sent a metal chair clattering across the warehouse floor with a small flick of my wrist. His eyes widened, and I knew exactly what he was thinking: had he seen right? Had that really just happened? The rational side of his brain would tell him that what had occurred was impossible, and a split second after that, logic would've convinced him his eyes were playing tricks on him.

I sent the other chair flying.

His face blanched, sweat prickled his forehead, and he pulled anxiously at the tape binding his wrists.

I straightened the table in front of him and looked directly in his watery eyes. "You scared of me yet?" I questioned, my voice casual and confident, nonchalant even. The tingling swelled in my tummy and the air around me practically sizzled with energy.

I'd always directed a pulse using my hands, but somehow, I just knew I was capable of more. I slammed my fists down hard on the table, and at the same time, released energy from my whole body, directing it upwards towards the roof. Every window in the warehouse shattered in a deafening symphony of splintering glass. Sunlight bathed the room in a warm glow as shards from the orange chem-lights sprinkled to the floor around us.

Panic and incomprehension filled Deakes' eyes.

I turned to Jake. "Now that's shock and awe," I said before returning my attention to Deakes. "You like that little trick?" I asked, moving behind him. I put a hand on his shoulder, feeling him stiffen. "Because I have a lot more up my sleeve." I circled back around in front of him, moving the table out of the way with another small pulse from my hand.

Deakes was speechless. He kept opening and closing his mouth like a big, sweaty, pletta fish. I almost had him.

"That was nothing," I said, flicking my wrist gently towards him. I had no intention of releasing any energy, but he flinched anyway. "I have another little trick, which is much more useful in this particular situation. So far, Captain Marcos has vetoed torture, mainly because the paperwork is a total bitch, but also because he doesn't want you to up and die on us, taking the Khans' location with you. But what if I told you I could bring you back from the brink of death as if nothing happened. Heal your wounds so no one would know what we'd done to you?"

"You're lying. It's not possible," Deakes said, trying to sound in control, but I saw the terror behind his eyes.

"Really? Is it possible for someone to move furniture and shatter windows with a mere thought? Perhaps a small demonstration will convince you just how possible it is." I took the knife from my boot and pressed the point against the pale, smooth skin of my forearm, but before I could apply any pressure, Jared grabbed my wrist.

"My turn this time," he said as he took the knife. Before I could object, he dragged the blade across his own skin. Bright red blood oozed from the neat, straight line, falling to the floor in fat droplets. The only indication of pain was a slight flicker in his eyes.

Deakes looked on in amazed disgust.

Silver-blue light briefly flickered between my hand and Jared's skin before I used my sleeve to wipe away the blood. Jared showed Deakes his flawless arm before handing me back the knife and re-joining the rest of the team.

"So you can sit there, all the big 'I am', holding on to the false notion that the Khans are scarier than us, but not even Vanze can hurt you like I can," I said calmly. "Imagine the worst physical pain he can cause you before it becomes too much, and you die – then multiply that by infinity. We're going to take you to the point at which every cell in your body is screaming out to give up – and at that point I'm going to bring you back, make you whole. Then we're going to do it again, and again… and again. I can go on as long as it takes for you to give up the information we need. Now, I can't tell you exactly how long that's going to be, but I can tell you…" I paused and glanced behind me. "Ash, how long has the longest person held out?"

Ash ran with the bluff without hesitation. "That guy on Merron lasted seventeen minutes, twenty-three seconds. He was a big bugger though."

"Think you can beat that?" I taunted Deakes, pulling up the sleeve on one of his arms to reveal soft flesh. On the outside I was cold steel, but inside my stomach was churning. I wasn't sure whether Deakes was quite ready to bite. Could I go through with hurting him if I had to? Sure, I'd hurt, even killed, people during fights, but only when it was absolutely necessary. I'd never cut into someone in cold blood. I prayed Deakes wouldn't call me on the con.

"Ash, start the clock on my mark," I said, glad that my voice sounded confident. I expertly manipulated the knife in my hand, twisting it backwards and forwards, the blade glinting in the sunlight flooding through the broken windows. I placed the tip of the knife on his skin, pressing just hard enough to prick the flesh. A single drop of blood ran down the side of his arm. "Ready, Ash? Three... two... one... ma-"

"Wait," Deakes spluttered. I pulled the knife away and used the tip of my finger to seal the small hole. It was so quick I don't think he even realised I'd done it.

"Well?" I asked, glad he'd had the sense to stop me. But instead of opening up with information, he laughed – albeit a scared, anxious bark.

"You can't torture me," he said, holding my gaze. "You're not capable. I can see it in your eyes."

I was completely thrown. Deakes had called my bluff, and I had no idea what to do next, but then Jake materialised at my side.

"You're right," he said. "But look into my eyes and tell me I'm not capable. Kaiser, take his arm," he added as he cut the tape holding it to the chair. Kaiser grabbed the flailing arm, holding it out so Jake could get the knife to the fleshy underside. "Ash, you said the longest someone's held out was what? Just under seventeen and a half minutes?"

"That's right."

"What's the shortest time?"

"Hmm." He pretended to think. "Fifty-three seconds. You going for the record?"

"Oh yeah," Jake replied. "Shae? You ready?" I held up my hand and let it shimmer in a haze of silver-blue light that reflected in Deakes' wide, petrified eyes. "Start the clock on my count. Three... two... one... mark." He dug the knife roughly into Deakes' arm just below the crook of his elbow and dragged it through the skin towards his wrist. My stomach lurched.

Deakes clenched his teeth and sweat sprung up on his ghost-white face, but he didn't cry out. Jake pulled out the knife and wiped it on Deakes' trousers to get the blood off. I stepped forward and healed the wound, unable to look him in the eye.

"That," Jake said, pointing at the arm, "was just a minor demonstration. Now we get serious." He used the knife to tear through Deakes' shirt, revealing his bare chest. "As long as you don't technically die, Shae can bring you back, which gives us quite a lot to work with. But we are on the clock here, so we'll have to jump ahead a few levels."

Deakes' breath faltered, and it looked like he was about to pass out.

"Tell us where the Khans are," I demanded.

"Go to hell."

"Tell us, or things are going to get a whole lot worse for you."

"Go... to... hell."

"Well, you can't say we didn't give you a chance," Jake stated. "Where do you reckon we start, Kaiser?"

Kaiser thought for a moment. "Between the third and fourth right rib," he finally concluded. "Go in at an upwards angle, puncturing the lung. That's got to be pretty painful."

"Sounds good to me," Jake said, feeling Deakes' chest, counting to find the right ribs. Deakes thrashed and bucked, but Kaiser was strong and held him tightly. Jake used his finger to guide the point of the blade to the right place. "Last chance," he said.

"Go to hell," Deakes repeated.

The knife, my knife, slid in and upwards with hardly any effort, and Deakes howled in pain as Jake twisted the blade.

"Stop, okay, stop," he gasped.

Jake pulled out the blade and I healed him instantly, glad that I didn't have to watch any more. A wave of nausea caught me by surprise, so I left the others to finish the interrogation.

As soon as I was outside, I doubled over and threw up the sandwich I'd eaten for lunch, and I was still heaving when I felt a hand rubbing my back. Jake passed me a bottle of water and I took a sip, rinsed, and spat.

"I'm sorry you had to go through that," he said. "I know it wasn't easy."

He sat next to me on a low brick wall, and we both squinted in the bright sunlight. I drank half the bottle of water in one go.

"Say something," he said when he couldn't take the silence any longer.

"Say what?"

"Anything. Just talk to me. I don't like it when you're this quiet. Tell me how you feel, tell me how awful that was, hell, tell me how much you hate me right now."

"Hate you?" I said, turning to look at him, but he didn't take his gaze off the building in front. "Why would you say that?"

"I just assumed..." he broke off. "What I just did made you physically sick. I disgust you."

"No, Jake, you've got it wrong." He finally turned to face me. "I can't pretend what we did sits well with me, because it doesn't. I honestly didn't think he'd hold out. I thought he'd give in before we..." I paused. "I know it was necessary, and you did what we needed you to do. Why do you think I would hate you for that?"

"It's the first time you've seen that side of my job."

I put my hand to his cheek. "That's just it, it's your job. I know what you do, but I also know who you are. You're a good man, Jake, and even if you question it sometimes, I never will."

He shook his head, the feathery crinkles reappearing around his greeny-brown eyes. "When are you going to realise it's me you love, and not Captain Annoying?" he asked.

"Jake!" I punched him lightly on the arm.

"I know, I know." He smiled, rubbing his arm as if I'd hit him with a fighting staff. "We're good though?" he pushed, concern drifting across his face again.

"We're good."

"Promise?"

"Promise." And to prove it, I hopped off the wall and stepped in front of him, wrapping my arms around him. "I mean it," I whispered into his neck.

"Everything alright out here?" Durrand asked. I unwrapped myself from Jake and took a step towards him, but he backed away, looking uneasy.

"Everything's fine," I said as he continued to study me carefully.

"What's up, Scott?" Jake asked, his tone hinting at irritation.

"Didn't mean to… umm… interrupt, Colonel," said the big man, regaining his composure. "Captain Marcos wants you inside. Deakes is starting to talk and he wants you both there, something about not wanting to go through it twice. Grumpy bastard, isn't he?"

Jake looked at me, grinned, and raised an eyebrow as if to say, told you so. I held out my hand, took his, and pulled him reluctantly off the wall.

21

Someone had righted the table and picked up the chairs, putting them back in place. Deakes was unbound, but Kaiser stood close, his weapon un-holstered, and a mean look on his face. Deakes sipped casually at a bottle of water, but he recoiled when we approached so I kept my distance.

"Okay, let's go back to the point the Khans came up from the Catacombs," Jared said, taking one of the metal chairs and flipping it around before straddling it. He folded his arms casually over the backrest as Deakes put his bottle of water on the table.

"The Khans knew they'd lost control of the Palace as soon as they were back on coms."

"How?"

"I told them everything had gone tits-up and to get back to the ship for immediate evac. From what Blain told me later, they thought it was all over the moment they were surrounded by the Wolfpack and the King's Guard. When they were allowed to leave with the Princess, they knew it was too easy. There had to have been some plan in play and assumed it had something to do with the Vanguard Cruiser in orbit. It was obvious you'd try and follow us, but the

Teslax pulse solved that particular inconvenience."

"We know all of this," Jake grunted. "Tell us something new."

Deakes crossed his arms tightly. "The Khans were crazy-mad. At first, I thought it was because of Vita, but then Vanze started on about something he'd lost in the Catacombs. Blain wanted to kill the Princess there and then in retribution for Vita, but Vanze kept saying she still had worth, and that the King may still trade her for whatever it was he'd lost."

"So she's still alive?" I asked from the back of the group, making both Deakes and Durrand flinch.

"She was when I left them."

"What the hell does that mean?" Jake grunted.

"It means what it means. She was alive back then... but what suits Vanze one minute, doesn't always suit him the next."

I looked around our group to gauge their reaction to Deakes' information and caught Durrand staring at me. When he realised, he coughed, shifted position, and returned his gaze towards Deakes.

"Okay, we'll work on the assumption she's still alive," said Jared. "What happened after the Teslax pulse took out my Warrior?"

"We used a signal modulator to send out multiple wake-trails to fool your sensors, then hit the FTL engines and got the hell out of Dodge. We took a round-about route to Angel Ridge, which is where we parted company. Vanze and Blain were going to lay low for a while, let the dust settle, so they didn't need me. Besides, after what went down on Decerra, I felt I'd earned a little down time. I hopped a shuttle and came here to deal with some personal business."

"We all saw how that went," Jake mocked.

"Yeah, guess I won't be doing any more business with those guys."

"You won't be doing business with anyone, for a very long time," Jake added with a tight-lipped smile. "Unless it's with other prison inmates."

"Let's stay on topic," Jared suggested, giving Jake a warning glance. "So, you left the Khans at Angel Ridge. Who else was onboard? Who stayed with them?"

"Apart from Vanze, Blain and the Princess, there was Fletcher, the Khans' pilot, and some brainiac nerd called Hoban."

"What about the others?" Jake asked.

"What others?"

"Don't play games, Deakes. Reports tell us there were at least three other people on that ship."

"Oh yeah." Deakes' eyes widened with recognition. "There were four mercs who made it back to the ship before we took off, but Blain killed all of them and blew the bodies out of an airlock. No loose ends he said. When the ship left Angel Ridge, the only people onboard were Vanze, Blain, the Princess, Hoban and Fletch. That's it, I promise."

"Why didn't Hoban get off at Angel Ridge as well?" Ash asked.

"No idea. I'm not his fucking keeper. Perhaps it's got something to do with Tartaros."

"Tartaros?" Jared repeated. "Why there?"

"Because that's where the Khans are laying low," Deakes said deliberately, as if we should've known.

"That's impossible," Jake growled. "Tartaros is a Cat-Five rock planet with a toxic atmosphere, completely uninhabitable. Shit, not even Santians could live there. Stop wasting our time." He approached the table, fists clenched. Deakes tried to get up, but he was forced back into his seat by the heavy weight of Kaiser pushing on his shoulders. Jared put his arm up to stop Jake's advance.

"Hey, I promised to tell you what I know," Deakes grumbled. "It's not my fault if you don't believe me."

"An REF Geo-team did a survey of Tartaros decades

ago. It's a dead world," Jared said.

"It's true that nothing can survive on the surface—"

"Stop fucking around and make sense," Jake shouted.

When Deakes picked up his water, his hand shook, and when he spoke, his voice wavered. "If you'd have let me finish, I was about to say that nothing can survive on the surface... but under the surface is a different matter."

"That's impossible. The planet's solid quartzide," I said, remembering a long-ago lesson.

"Look, I can only tell you what Hoban told me. When he was at Westchester he came across an old text which described a secret ancient site, abandoned some millennia ago by a race he called... shit, what the fuck did he call them?" He massaged the nape of his neck. "The Architects, sure, that's it. Anyway, he wrote a thesis on the Architects and the site, claiming to have found clues on how to discover its location. He was obsessed with finding the place and pressed the Academy for a grant, but they turned him down flat, refusing to give out money for something that was no more than myth and legend."

"Bored now," Jake grumbled, but Deakes ignored him.

"Apparently Vanze had read his paper somehow and offered to sponsor him. No clue why, he's not exactly the archaeologist type, but Hoban said he seemed fixated. Regardless, with the Khans' resources, Hoban found what he was looking for on Tartaros. Or more precisely, under Tartaros."

"You're kidding, right?" I snorted. "This is a joke. It has to be. I've never even heard of these... Architects. You guys?" I looked to the others, watching them shake their heads in answer, but the hit I got from Ash through the Link made me glance back to him. He shook his head again.

"Vanze wanted Hoban to find that place bad," Deakes continued, pulling my attention back to him. "And he's worked hard to keep it quiet since. That Outsider character wanted it kept quiet as well. If the Khans even suspected

Hoban had told me anything, we'd both be dead."

"I'm still not convinced," I said, earning a groan from Deakes. "Are you really telling us that someone has cut a bolthole into one of the hardest rocks known to man?"

"I'm only telling you what Hoban told me."

"Okay," Jared said, rubbing his temples. "What else did he tell you about this place?"

"He said the Khans have a crew that stays there permanently. They don't know where they are, and they never leave the compound – it's not like they can stick their heads up above ground for a look-see, is it?" he added sarcastically. "As far as I can tell, the only people who travel to and from the planet are the Khans, Hoban and the pilot. Anyone else who goes, never comes back. I've heard the tunnels are filled with the bones of people who've fucked them off."

"So, to clarify, you've never been there yourself?" Jared said.

"No."

"You expect us to believe that you, the Khans' Lieutenant, has never been to their super-secret hideout?" Jake pushed.

"I'm one of their Lieutenants, and I don't really give a shit what you believe. Whole thing creeps me out if you ask me. Got a touch of claustrophobia just thinking about the place."

"Okay." Jared scratched at the stubble on his chin. "So the Khans and Princess Josephina are on Tartaros?"

"Yes."

"In an underground lair?" He failed to hide his scepticism.

"Yes." Deakes sighed. "How many different ways can I say the same thing?"

"And you know this because the Khans told you that's where they were going?"

"Have you been listening to me at all?" Deakes shouted,

trying to get up again, with equal success. He scowled at Kaiser. "No, the Khans didn't tell me; I'm not supposed to know about the place, remember? Hoban told me they were going there. For all I know, the whole story could be total horseshit."

"Easy, Deakes," Jared said. "I was just making sure you weren't lying."

"Oh." He relaxed a little and took a sip of water.

"Can you tell us anything about the layout of the complex?" Ash asked.

"No." He pinched the bridge of his nose, thinking. "Hoban mentioned caves and tunnels, but I can't tell you more than that. Wait, he also said that the way in was impossible to find."

"And there's no one else who might know it?" Ash pressed.

"No one who's not already there. Like I said, apart from the Khans, Hoban and Fletcher, no one leaves…"

"What is it?"

"Maybe nothing. Hoban told me that about a year ago one of the prisoners tried to escape, but he was killed by a guard in the process."

"And you're telling us this because?" Jake glared at him.

"You know what? I don't like you very much." Deakes glared back. "And if you're going to be such a dick, perhaps I won't tell you anything else."

"That's enough, children," Jared interrupted. "Jake, back off, Deakes, continue."

"Thank you," Deakes said, overly gracious. "The way Hoban told the story, it sounded like there was more to it. And I'd say it was pretty convenient the body was unrecoverable after falling into a bottomless rock fracture."

"You think the prisoner got away? That the guard lied?" Ash asked.

"Couldn't say for sure, but that's the impression I got. Vanze or Blain would've killed their man for sure if he'd admitted to losing a prisoner. If I was that guard, I'd have lied. Wouldn't you?"

"Did the prisoner have a name?" Jake asked.

"Fuck me, do I have to do all the heavy lifting for you?" Deakes grunted, but Jake took a step forward. "Okay, okay, I was kidding. The guy's name was Angel or Angelo, no, wait... there was something before it..."

"D'Angelo?" Jake offered.

"Yeah, that's it."

"Ethan D'Angelo? You're sure?" Jake pushed.

"You know this—" Jared started, but Jake cut him off with a raise of his hand to let Deakes continue.

"Ethan, yeah. Don't know what he did to piss the Khans off, but whatever it was, it must've been pretty bad for them to take him to Tartaros."

"Do you know where he is now?" Jake asked.

"Nope. Can't even be certain the dude actually made it out. He could be at the bottom of that fissure, just like the guard said."

Through the high windows, the light from the early evening sun began to wane.

"What about the Outsider?" Ash asked.

"What about him?"

"What do you know? What can you tell us about him?

"Fuck all. I don't know shit about him, other than he has deep pockets. Never met him, never spoke to him."

"And you didn't hear Vanze or Blain talk about him?" Jake asked.

"Nope. The only thing I know is they called him the Outsider, and that he funded the assault. In fact, I couldn't even tell you whether he was a he, she, or it."

"Okay, is there anything else you think we should know?" Jared asked.

"Only that if you are planning on going to Tartaros to take on the Khans, you better plan on killing them before they kill you."

"I don't think that'll be a problem," replied Jake with a cocky grin.

"Maybe," Jared added, momentarily distracted by the automatic floor lights powering up. "But I think we have more pressing problems, like finding D'Angelo... if he's still alive. Kaiser, Ty, please escort Deakes to the *Veritas* and secure him for transfer to the *Defender*?"

"My pleasure," Kaiser replied, pulling the prisoner roughly from his chair.

"Captain Marcos," Durrand said. "If you don't need me anymore, I've got my own business to get back to. Good luck with your mission."

"Thanks. And we appreciate the hospitality," replied Jared, nodding his gratitude.

"About that," Durrand added, eyeing me carefully. "Thanks for aerating our warehouse."

"Yeah, umm, sorry. Guess I got a little carried away," I said, trying not to show how disappointed I was that yet more people knew about my gift. Nobody would believe Deakes if he blabbed, but a decorated and respected Marine... that was a different story.

"About that," Durrand began.

"I've got this," offered Jake, leading the big guy away.

"What's the story with D'Angelo?" I asked Jake once we were back on the *Veritas* and there was just the four Guardians together.

"D'Angelo," he mused. "What I'm about to tell you is classified eyes-only, but I guess it falls under the purview of our Guardianship, so what the hell. A few years ago, High Command decided that enough was enough as far as the Khans' activities were concerned, but as we know, they're not the easiest of families to track down. We've all been one step behind them: Marines, Fleet, even Brotherhood. Which either makes them exceptionally lucky—"

"Or they have someone inside the REF on their

payroll," Jared finished. "That's not exactly a secret, Jake. Rumours about a spy have been doing the circuit for years."

"People may think it's just a rumour, but the spy is very real. Which is why, just over two years ago, High Command sanctioned a top-secret mission to put someone deep undercover inside the Khans' crew. At the time, only a handful of people knew about the assignment and the identity of the operative – for his safety, and for the success of the mission."

"The operative was D'Angelo?" I asked.

"Yes. Ethan D'Angelo was the cover alias used by Marine Lieutenant Callum McCray. His assignment was to infiltrate one of the Khans' businesses and advance up the network until he got close to the family. Then he had two mission objectives: discover the mole, and identify every arm of the Khans' business empire."

"Take down the Khans, the mole, and their entire network at the same time," Ash said. "I can see the logic."

"That was the plan."

"So if the mission was so top secret, how do you know about it?" Jared asked.

"Because it was my mission."

"Your mission?"

"High Command approached me for the op," Jake explained. "I was supposed to be the one going undercover, not Cal. Ethan D'Angelo was an alias created for me, and a back-story was fashioned accordingly to fit my character and skills. The mission was green-lit, but just before I was due to go in, the shit hit the fan on a previous op the Wolfpack and I'd been working on. One where my cover had already been established. They didn't have time to put in a new agent, so I was pulled from the Khan mission. They asked me who I'd recommend to replace me and I gave them Cal. He'd done a few missions with me previously and was an exceptional Marine. Plus, he's similar enough to me to pull off the alias and back-story." He stuffed his hands in his pockets, shifting his weight from one foot to the other.

"There's more to it than that," I said, studying him.

Jake looked at his feet for a moment before continuing. "Cal's older brother, Jim, and I were tight back in the day. When Jimmy took four bullets during the Geminus Uprising, I promised him I'd look out for Cal. Great job I did."

"Whatever happened to Cal wasn't your fault," I said.

"No?" he barked. "Wait, I'm sorry, Babe, I didn't mean... I know it wasn't my fault I got pulled from the mission, but that doesn't stop me from feeling guilty for what happened to him."

I felt the faintest hit of anguish through the diminishing Link we'd shared since I'd healed him on Genesis.

"Technically, I was off the mission," he continued. "But given my original involvement, I managed to keep updated on Cal's progress over the months. Things seemed to be going well. He'd managed to assimilate himself into one of the Khans' narcotics businesses and was working his way up the ranks. His last report had him working directly with the Khans, on the verge of becoming one of their Lieutenants. Pretty much most of the information we have on those fuckers came from Cal."

"Then what happened?" Ash asked.

"No one knew for sure. Coms stopped about a year ago, like he'd dropped off the grid... or been killed. Officially the REF has him listed as MIA, but I guess now we know he ended up on Tartaros. The Khans must've found out who he was." Jake was agitated, shifting his weight again.

"But Deakes thinks McCray escaped from Tartaros," said Jared. "If he did, why didn't he check in with his handlers?"

"Would you?" said Ash. "Assuming Jake's right, and Lieutenant McCray's cover was blown, he had to assume the mole was responsible. The Khans thought he was dead, and by default, so did the spy. If Cal had contacted High Command, chances are the information would've gone straight back to the brothers, who would've hunted him down and killed him for sure. It would've been safer for him to lay low and let everyone think he was dead."

"Same as Phina, let's assume he is alive," I said. "How are we supposed to find a man who doesn't want to be found?"

"We get the Oracle on the case and keep our fingers crossed," said Jared, but Jake wasn't the only one who looked sceptical. "Is there somewhere we can brief Hale?"

"This way," Jake said.

Ash waited for them to leave then patted the seat next to him. "Before the others come back, we need to talk."

"Do we have to?" I groaned, knowing what was coming.

"Yes, come sit. Shae, you're getting stronger, and your gift is developing. If it was just that one-off incident with Jake and Jared during our last mission, I wouldn't be so concerned, but it's not. The grate back on Genesis... now the windows in the warehouse..."

"I know. Don't you think it scares me too? I don't know what's happening to me anymore. I never wanted to be different," I said in barely more than a whisper. "I never asked for any of this... and I certainly never wanted people to look at me like I was a freak." The constant buzz of Ash's fear thrummed through the Link. "I'm sorry," I said.

"Oh, Shae, don't be sorry. Never be sorry." He put his arm tightly around me. "You have a great gift. My worry is how other people are going to react. Not everyone is as enlightened as we are. You saw how Durrand was. We need to be careful," he concluded, rubbing the tears from my cheeks with his thumb.

"I know."

"I didn't report the first incident to the Brotherhood because I thought it was a one-off, but we can't keep it from them now. We have to tell them before they find out from another source."

"I know," I repeated.

"We should tell Noah as soon as Operation Fallen Star is over."

"Sure. You can tell him at the same time I complain about that stupid, outdated chaperone rule," I suggested, but rather than reprimand my rebelliousness, Ash looked pensive again. There was definitely something I was missing. "I'm sorry you got caught in the middle of all this."

He looked at me, his face flicking through emotions so quickly it was difficult to get a clear read. "Whatever happens, never forget that you're my family, my sister," he said. "I love you. You will always be the most important thing to me, and I will always look out for you."

A peaceful warmth radiated through my chest at his words, but I was still worried. There was an unreadable undercurrent through the Link that frightened me.

"Ash—" I stopped as Ty walked into the cabin carrying a large platter of food, big enough to feed the entire crew. He placed it on the table in front of us. "Wow, Ty, don't tell me you just knocked this together?"

"Mamma always said, if you can't rustle up a virtual feast in less than ten minutes, you don't deserve to set foot in a kitchen," he replied, smiling. "I'll get the drinks."

"Eat." Ash pushed one of the plates towards me. "All you've had today is a sandwich, and you didn't keep that down by all accounts."

"Damn Jake," I moaned. "Can't keep his mouth shut for a minute."

"He was worried about you. Besides, you need to replace all that energy you've used." His lopsided grin made an appearance. "All seriousness aside, that windows thing was pretty dramatic. Did you see the look on Deakes' face? It was all…" He did an impression and I howled with laughter. "I'll be careful never to get on your bad side." He pulled the face again and I laughed even harder.

"What's funny," Jared asked, walking into the cabin with Jake and Ty. I wanted to tell him, I wanted Ash to do the impression for them, but I couldn't breathe. Tears rolled down my cheeks, and Ty banged on my back until I had enough air in my lungs to protest.

"Thought I could smell coffee," said Kaiser strolling into the cabin. "Don't worry, Deakes is totally secure," he added, catching Jared's glance.

Connor also appeared from the direction of the flight deck. "We'll reach the *Defender* in three hours, give or take… was someone going to tell me there was food?" he grumbled. "Figures. Got left out of the op, why wouldn't I get left out of dinner as well."

"Moan, moan, moan," said Ty.

"I'm going to punch you in a minute," replied Connor.

"I'm going to punch both of you if you don't shut up," Kaiser waded in, putting an instant stop to the argument.

The following morning, I met Ash at his quarters on the *Defender* and we walked to the Mess Hall together. I wanted to ask him about what he'd said the night before on the *Veritas*, but the moment had passed, and I had no idea how to broach the subject again. Besides, Jake and Jared where already sat at our usual table. It still amazed me they were being civil, even friendly towards each other, after everything that'd happened.

I ate in silence, listening to Jared's update on what had happened since we'd been with Deakes. I'd just got my second cup of steaming coffee when an ensign entered the Mess Hall and headed straight to our table.

"Captain Marcos, Lieutenant Commander Hale asked me to inform you that he believes he's found what you're looking for."

I put down my mug so quickly, coffee slopped over my fingers, burning them slightly. In no time, Jared had taken my hand and was wiping off the hot liquid with a napkin, hiding the inevitable silver-blue glow. It was gone in seconds.

"Better?" he asked, studying my fingers.

"Yes, much," I replied, feeling the warmth of his own hand against my skin.

"Well, what do you expect from your hero?" Jake said sarcastically, rising and turning away from the table before I had a chance to respond. I caught Jared's smirk and pulled my hand away.

By the time we got to TaDCom, a frosty silence had settled between the pair, which Ash and I had chosen to ignore

"It's not a hundred percent certain," said Hale once we'd gathered around the centre table. "But we think Lieutenant Callum McCray, a.k.a. Ethan D'Angelo, is now Hunter Blade." He looked impressed... and so did Ash. Or more actually, Ash looked half impressed, half sceptical.

"Hunter Blade is Cal McCray?" I said, failing to keep the cynicism from my voice. "This is what the Oracle and its 1.2 zetta-fens of processing power came up with?"

Hale nodded.

"Babe, you sound like you know this Hunter Blade character?" Jake said.

"I don't know him, but I've heard of him," I said, receiving a frustrated frown in response. "Come on, Jake. Don't tell me you haven't? You must've heard of Throwdown Requiem, surely?"

"The underground fight network? Of course. I'm just surprised you know about them, Babe."

"Why? Because I'm Brotherhood... or because I'm a girl?"

"I didn't mean... you know what I meant. Tell us what you know," he said magnanimously.

"Okay, so for starters, Throwdown is a network of quasi-legal fight clubs throughout the Four Sectors, run by an unknown syndicate – but I'm sure you know all of this."

"The REF closes them down when we can," said Jared. "But they don't stay closed for long, or they just move to a new location. They're not in my purview… and it's not exactly my thing."

"Figures," Jake mumbled under his breath.

"There are five that we know about in Sector Three, but there are probably more," said Ash.

"So why doesn't the Brotherhood shut them down?" asked Jared.

"It's like you said, they'd just spring up elsewhere, and anyway, why should we? The Brotherhood doesn't consider them a threat, in fact, they're now pretty much considered a prestigious sport. It's not minority-trash hoods anymore but trained and highly-skilled athletes."

"It's all got kind of official now," I added, though I thought Jake would know that. I suspected he'd been to more than his fair share, and not all of them for work. "Don't get me wrong, it's still brutal, and the death rate is way too high for my liking, but they choose to take part, fully understanding the consequences. The fighters sign contracts and wavers, and they fight of their own free will and volition."

"What's Hunter got to do with Throwdown?" Jared asked.

"The best fighters are adored like celebrities," I explained. "And Hunter Blade is the new rising star."

"So why did you sound so cynical when Hale told us Hunter was McCray?" Jake asked, but he didn't wait for me to respond. "You know what, just show us a picture and I'll tell you whether it's Cal or not."

"That's just it," I replied. "Hunter fights in a mask – it adds to the mystique apparently. Nobody knows who he is. There's speculation all over the data-nets about it, I'm surprised you haven't seen it, Jake. What I was sceptical about is how the Oracle made the leap from escaped prisoner to top Throwdown superstar. I don't see it's possible."

"I can answer that," said Hale. "It's actually quite simple when you have the power of a super-predictor that can pull together threads you and I would see as totally random. Sometimes it's not what you find, but what you don't find, that builds the connection." He sounded proud of the damn thing. "All you need is a starting point. Short story: not long after a prisoner escaped the Khans, an unknown man was found beaten, dehydrated and unconscious on a world not too far from Tartaros. They've no records of who he was, and he left before they could ask him, but his physical characteristics match our target."

"The target's name is Callum McCray," Jake grunted.

"Of course, Colonel, my apologies. The Oracle followed Lieutenant McCray's movements as he used aliases and stolen identities to traverse the Sector, eventually ending up on GalaxyBase4, Dome Two – at exactly the same time Hunter Blade appeared on the fight scene."

"That could just be a coincidence," Jared said.

"That's true, Sir, but I have more. Wearing the mask prevents us from using facial recognition, but the Oracle has processed all McCray's post mission debrief tapes and training discs. He's put on a few pounds of muscle, but… well take a look for yourselves."

Two separate 3D images appeared above the holo-table. One side showed McCray running through training manoeuvres, the other showed Hunter Blade fighting in Throwdown. Various lines and equations superimposed the two bodies before the word Match appeared in bold green letters.

"I take it back," I said. "That looks pretty conclusive to me."

Jared leant forward and accessed the coms panel. A moment later, Commander Tel'an appeared on the holo-screen.

"Set a course for GalaxyBase4. Maximum speed." He

turned to Hale. "Take the Oracle offline immediately. I need to save the *Defender's* FTL engines."

"Yes, Sir. One more thing though, Hunter's due to fight tonight. Twenty-three hundred. It's the headline fight."

22

As we approached GalaxyBase4 in the *Veritas*, Jake followed me through to the small galley. "Looks like we're going back to where it all began," he said quietly, his arm out against the wall to block my path.

His words unlocked memories I'd tried to bury, and I remembered his touch, his kiss, the way he'd traced little circles on my tummy after we'd made love… I edged away from him and tried to rebury the thoughts, but I guess something gave me away. Jake smiled, removed his arm, and let me past.

Each of the six, huge metal domes that made up GB4 replicated a different environment. Dome Five, where I'd taken down Frampton Edge, met Jake, and been arrested by Jared – long story – simulated an Earth environment: a metropolis of skyscrapers hundreds of stories high, walkways, lakes and real grass parks. Dome Two, however, was an eclectic mix of ancient Earth and modern D'Antarus Prime.

Technologically advanced, the D'Antaran were much like us. They were generally peaceful, but like any race, they had their troubles. A few decades ago, we'd had an awkward standoff when they objected to our colonial advance into their territories. But the outcome was a peaceful treaty, where the Tetrarchy of Souls agreed to limit our expansion to their borders. Since then, apart from minor skirmishes, we've pretty much got on together.

Some D'Antarans had ventured into neighbouring Sectors Three and Four, which was why places like GB4 provided suitable accommodation, but most stayed on their side of the border. I have to admit I kind of like them, but their over-politeness and incessant acquiescence got on my nerves after a while.

To minimise the chance of spooking McCray, Jared decided to leave the Wolfpack on the ship while we went to pick him up, much to their disgust. Hale had managed to get us the location and access details of the fight club, but as we walked through peaceful streets, passing discreet bars and restaurants, I wondered whether we were in the right place. Delicious smells wafted from patisseries, and people nodded and smiled as we passed, some even wishing us a pleasant evening.

It was nice to be somewhere where I wasn't being spat at, shot at, or groped for a change.

We followed Hale's directions towards an old-style picture house. Humans, Others, and D'Antarans were queued, waiting to buy tickets before being ushered towards large concertina doors to the right of the kiosk. When it was our turn, Jared discreetly passed the cashier a large wad of credits and told her that Vittoria had recommended we see the show. The cashier flicked through the credits and looked at each of us in turn before nodding towards a single, unremarkable entrance to the left. Jared thanked her, and we headed through the door and down an exceptionally long, winding staircase.

As soon as we entered the venue, I felt the excitement and euphoria.

It was almost time for Hunter Blade's fight, and the

mass of revellers surged towards the cage in the centre of the room. An over-excited compare told us there were only five minutes until the fighters were coming out, and the energy and anticipation was almost tangible. Screams of support for each opponent fought their own battled against each other, reaching a deafening crescendo.

As he'd done in Carpe Noctum, Jared took my hand and led me through the arena and up some metal stairs, my boots sticking to the floor with every step. He pushed and shoved his way through the crowd, ignoring the grunts of complaint, until we were at the front of the first balcony overlooking the cage. The air was thick with the smell of liquor, sweat, and topical muscle balms.

"There's Hunter," Jake yelled over the up-swell of cheers. I watched the masked man enter the cage and take up position across from a huge Human-Rhinorian hybrid. The referee, small in comparison, stood between the pair, reading out a worryingly short list of rules before hastily exiting the cage.

The second the bell rang, the Other charged at Hunter, or McCray, or whatever the hell I was supposed to call him. Both fighters had some good moves, and to begin with they looked equally matched – McCray's skills compensating for the Other's bulk – but by the end of the third round, the punches and kicks were taking their toll.

McCray was pinned against the cage, and I flinched every time the Other's plate-sized fists pounded his body. Blood poured from a split eyebrow, but he managed to get in a surprise upper cut which sent his opponent staggering backwards. McCray saw his opportunity and went in for the kill. A roundhouse kick to the head, followed by a stamp to the side of the left patella, brought the Other to his knees. McCray landed multiple punches to his rival, not stopping until the bell rang and the referee re-entered the cage.

Clearly the crowd's favourite, I could barely hear myself think above the cheering as the referee lifted McCray's arm to proclaim him the winner. I felt a hand in mine and assumed it was Jared's, but it was Jake who led me back down the stairs towards the cage. We arrived at the gate just as McCray was leaving. A couple of bouncers held back eager fans, but Jake managed to get us to the front. I was almost swept to the side by a surge of girls trying to get to their hero, but he didn't let go, pulling me closer instead. Jared and Ash arrived behind us.

"Hunter Blade," Jake bellowed above the screams. McCray's face might have been covered, but he couldn't hide his reaction the moment he saw us. "We need to talk," Jake continued. For a moment I didn't think McCray had heard him, but then he motioned towards a door and indicated to the bouncers to let us all through.

When we were alone in the locker room, McCray removed the mask.

"It's good to see you, Cal," Jake said, conflicting emotions flicking across his face – the happiness at seeing his friend's kid brother again tarnished with guilt. For a moment there was an awkward silence, then McCray stepped forward and the two men embraced.

When Jake was done introducing us, he asked Cal to give him a full mission debrief from the point he'd gone coms-silent with High Command, until the day he'd escaped Tartaros. At first, he was reluctant, quoting the Alpha-Secure status of the mission, but after Jake explained our position, he began.

"I never found out who the spy was," Cal said a little later, confirming what we'd already suspected. "But I'm positive it was him, or her, who told the Khans about me. I only just got away from them with my head still attached to my body, I wasn't about to stick it back out on the chopping block by contacting the REF It would've been like sending up a red flag to the Khans. How the hell did you find me anyway? And why?" he added threateningly.

Jake filled him in on Fallen Star while he changed into

street clothes.

"No way," Cal said, pulling his hair back into a short ponytail before yanking on a khaki beanie to keep the loose bits under control. "Not interested. I was tortured on that planet, there's no way in hell I'm going back."

"We need you, Cal."

"Forget it, Jake. It's not happening."

"Look, Lieutenant—"

"What? You're going to pull rank on me now, Colonel? That's how it's going to be?"

"I'm sorry, Cal." Jake looked reluctant. "I know these are exigent circumstances, and I'd rather you agreed to come of your own free will, but like it or not, you're still a Marine and we need you. I don't want to make this an order, but if you leave me no other choice—"

"This is my life now, Jake," Cal shouted, indicated towards the door to the arena. "Lieutenant Callum McCray is dead. He died over a year ago. I'm Hunter Blade now, Throwdown fighter. Surviving the cage is what I do—"

"Okay then," said Ash, stopping Cal in his tracks. He stood and started to unbutton his shirt. "If it's all about the cage, let the cage make the decision."

"What?" Cal and I asked in unison.

"We fight. You and me – in the cage. You win, we walk away and leave you to be Hunter Blade. I win, you come with us and tell us everything we need to know. We take down the Khans, and you get your life, Callum McCray's life, back."

Cal looked him up and down, assessing the competition. Ash wasn't wearing Brotherhood kit, and Jake hadn't introduced us as such, so there was no way Cal would've known about his fighting skills. If he took up Ash's offer, I was confident Ash could take him. That didn't mean I had to like the idea. In fact, I hated it.

"You're on," Cal said.

I took Ash's arm and pulled him to the side. "What the

hell are you doing?" I hissed, but he merely laughed.

"What? You think you're the only one who can put themselves in harm's way? The way I see it, this is the best solution for everyone."

"And you figure that how exactly?"

"It's obvious Jake doesn't want to order McCray to come with us, but he will if he has to. And I believe McCray would follow that order, because even after everything that's happened to him, he's a stand-up Marine. But Jake will feel bad, and Cal will resent him. Neither of which is conducive to a successful mission outcome."

"Okay, I get it. Challenging Cal under fight club rules leaves his relationship with Jake intact, while forcing him to come with us under the same rules he respects. I just don't want you to get hurt."

Ash shrugged, a lopsided grin appearing. "I tell you what, I'll let you patch me up after I win. How about that?"

I scowled at him. "I've got a good mind not to. Just make sure you do win."

We left the changing room and re-entered the arena, which was empty except for the janitorial crew. The cage door stood open and the floor glistened, slick with blood and sweat. I guess they hadn't got around to that yet. My stomach knotted but I forced myself to remember how good Ash was.

The two men entered the cage and Jake shut the gate. The cleaning crew stopped what they were doing and gathered around, intrigued by the impromptu addition to the evening's entertainment.

I wondered who was going to ref, but Cal wasn't waiting to find out. He lunged forward, swung around, and landed a roundhouse kick to Ash's face. Ash collapsed, but rather than going in with another blow, Cal stepped-off, allowing him to get up. Ash's lip was split open, and he spat out blood before wiping his mouth on his t-shirt.

Considering Cal had just fought a match, he looked on

top of his game – and he was good. I could understand how Hunter Blade had made such a name for himself in a relatively short amount of time. The cleaners were shouting and hollering for both fighters, no idea that one of the men in the cage was Hunter.

Cal attacked again, but that time Ash was prepared, ducking to the side while landing a body-blow with his fist. Cal grunted but recovered quickly, slamming Ash against the cage wall. I knew Ash wouldn't let himself get pinned and cheered as his head-butt left Cal momentarily dazed.

Ash didn't wait for his rival to recover, pummelling his stomach with both fists before delivering a series of vicious head blows. Cal managed to swing his arm up and land a hefty but awkward strike to Ash's jaw. The unmistakable sound of cracking bone splintered the air, and I didn't need to see the pained look behind Cal's eyes to know he'd broken his hand. He pulled it back to protect it, but didn't stop his assault, kneeing Ash several times in the torso.

Ash ducked out of Cal's reach and the two men circled each other like predators. Cal's hand was already swelling, and the cut in his eyebrow had reopened, the side of his face smeared red. One of Ash's eyes was closing, and blood trickled from a broken nose.

They were out of breath and clearly in pain, but neither was going to back down. They both had good reason to win.

"Come on, Ash. What are you waiting for? Put him down!" I shouted. Jake raised an eyebrow. "What?"

"Nothing," he replied, grinning. I returned my attention to the fight.

Swelling and bruises were now clearly evident on both men. I knew I could, would, heal them after, but it didn't change the fact that every punch Cal landed on my brother was like a blow to my own chest.

Up until that point, Ash's fighting style had been pretty traditional, pedestrian even – just enough to hold his own –

but he obviously decided it was time to end things, throwing in a series of Tok-ma moves. When Cal's vision cleared, he looked surprised and impressed.

"Brotherhood?" he asked.

Ash continued to circle the cage, but he lifted the sleeve of his t-shirt to show his tattoo.

"Makes sense," Cal continued through heavy breaths. "I wondered why you were so confident about getting in the cage with—" He jumped back to avoid an uppercut, but Ash followed it up with a second punch to the ribs that landed successfully. Cal groaned, crumpling slightly, giving Ash the opportunity to duck around and grab him from behind. He kneed Cal in the leg causing him to lose balance and he went down. Ash swung his arm around Cal's neck, falling with him, using his weight to pin him to the deck. Ash had Cal's face pressed hard to the mat, his arm around Cal's neck in a chokehold, cutting off his blood circulation.

Just as Cal's eyes unfocussed and his muscles relaxed, Ash let him go. The fight was over.

Cal rolled on to his back, gasping for breath, but after a moment, Ash leant over and helped him up.

"I'm officially impressed," said Cal, studying his broken hand with glassy eyes that suggested a concussion. "I suppose a deal's a deal. Give me a moment to get my kit and I'll come with you. But I'm not going underground on Tartaros."

"Agreed," said Jake, slapping him on the shoulder. Cal winced.

There were too many cleaners lurking about to risk healing the fighters at the club, so it took a while to get back to the *Veritas*, especially with Cal's dodgy knee and Ash's swollen ankle. When we got there, I don't know who the Wolfpack were more in awe of McCray for being the infamous Hunter Blade, or Ash for beating him in the cage.

"Cal, I know your brain's a little fuzzy right now," Jake said. "But what you're about to see is Alpha-Secure. You can't tell anyone. Do you understand?"

Cal's forehead creased, re-opening the split above his eye. "Sure," he decided, pressing an icepack to his knuckles before wobbling a loose tooth with his tongue.

I healed Ash while Cal looked on, stunned, and Jake had to convince him his concussion wasn't making him see things. I expected him to be wary of me, like Durrand, but instead, he was fascinated.

"Are you for real?" he asked, prodding me. "No joke?"

"Yes, I'm real. No, it's not a joke. And ouch, that hurt."

"Sorry, I just… this is like… I don't even have words for it."

"Just keep it that way," Jake warned.

"My lips are sealed." He mimed locking his lips and throwing away the key. "This is awesome! It's like meeting the Tooth Fairy, Santa, and the Bon'daris all rolled in to one… only better," Cal slurred.

"I think that concussion's getting worse," Jake said.

"I think you might be right. Umm, Lieutenant…" I wasn't sure how to say what I wanted.

"Yes?"

"When you changed in the locker room, I noticed your scars from the… from when you were with the Khans." He looked instantly uncomfortable. "It's just I can get rid of them for you. Make it like they were never there."

"You can do that?"

"If you want me to."

He traced a wide, ragged scar on his arm with his fingertips and I wondered how bad the torture must've been.

"Get rid of them," he said categorically.

The silver-blue glow filled the cabin again, and when it dissipated, Cal was perfect. He studied his arm where the scar had been. "They're all gone?" he asked cautiously.

"All of them."

He flexed his mended hand and tried to wiggle his solid

tooth with his fingers. "How do you do it?"

"Don't ask," said Jake. "Just accept Shae's gift and don't mention it again. Seriously. Don't ever mention it again."

"I get the message, loud and clear, Sir. Do not talk about secret healer-girl… but she might not be enough," Cal said cryptically.

"What do you mean?"

"I mean, if you're really going after the Khans, you've got a serious death-wish, Colonel."

"That's why we need your help. We need you to get us in the complex on Tartaros without getting dead."

"So, to make things crystal-clear: Vanze, Blain and Vita are holding Princess Josephina captive on Tartaros, and you want me to tell you how to get her out," Cal said. Jake nodded. "You know they won't let her go without a fight." Jake nodded again. "And if you think Vanze and Blain are bad, their sister's worse. She's psychotic, by the way."

"She's dead, by the way," I said.

Cal's face broke into a wide grin and his brown eyes sparkled. "Who? You?"

"No, Jake."

"Good on you, Sir," Cal said, punching him on the arm. "I owe you one. That bitch deserved to die."

The journey from GalaxyBase4 to the *Defender* was short, but Cal talked non-stop about Tartaros, seemingly encouraged by the knowledge of Vita's demise.

"What's the underground bunker like?" I asked, still sceptical about the whole possibility.

"To call Tartaros a bunker, is like calling the *Defender* a shuttle," Cal explained.

"Hey!" Jared grunted.

"No offence, Captain," he added quickly.

"What would you call it then?" I asked.

"To be honest… I haven't got a clue. It's not like anything I've seen before. I mean, for starters, the place is massive, and the whole thing is cut into quartzide like it was nothing more than sandstone. Then there's a weird energy residue we could never quite get a read on, suggesting there was superior tech there at one time, but now... nothing. There are shells of structures, possibly living quarters, possibly meeting areas, and there's even carved rock channels that could've been aqueducts. If you want my best guess, I'd say it was home to an advanced species a long time ago, but when they moved out, they took everything, and I mean everything. Apart from cut rock, there's not a trace of their civilisation left – who they were, what they were doing there... except for the carvings."

"What carvings?" I asked, my pulse quickening.

"Symbols and patterns scratched into the lower chambers, but like the energy trace, I've never seen anything like them before." He thought for a moment. "Vanze seemed real interested in them, though."

I contemplated showing Cal my pendant, to see whether they were the same markings, but Connor announced we'd reached the *Defender* and I lost my opportunity.

Tactical Data Command was practically empty when we arrived, but Hale stood at the centre table reviewing statistics on a holo-display. As we approached, he cleared the information and replaced it with an image of Tartaros. The pale creamy-beige planet rotated slowly above the table.

"Captain, this image of Tartaros was captured during the last geo-survey of the planet. As you can see, it's completely comprised of quartzide: no water, flora or fauna, and..." He pressed a few buttons on a small data-pad. "The atmosphere is toxic. It's a dead world." A list of air quality and climate information appeared beside the image as evidence.

"This is your show, Lieutenant McCray," Jared said. "Let's start with the easy stuff. Where exactly is this complex, bunker, ruins – whatever you want to call it?"

Cal leant over the holo-table and spun the representation of Tartaros until he found the location he was looking for. He double-tapped the spot and the image zoomed in until topographical features were clearly detailed. He moved the landscape backwards and forwards as he searched.

"There," he said eventually, using both hands to stretch the image and home in further. "How do I get the image horizontal?"

"Let me," Hale said. He tapped the pad and the image flattened out above the table.

"That's better," said Cal as he surveyed the landscape, his fingertips skimming a three-dimensional mountain range. "Here," he concluded, pointing to nothing exceptional.

"I don't see anything," said Jake, leaning forward from the other side of the table.

"Precisely. That's why your surveys have never recorded anything but a dead planet. See this here?" Cal pointed to a jagged outcrop of stone, stretching out over a deep but narrow valley. "The entrance to the… umm… let's just call it a complex to keep life simple, is under there."

"I'm no pilot," said Jared, bending down and twisting his head to the side to get a closer look, "but how the hell do you even get in there."

Cal laughed. "I researched Fletcher's history while I was on mission. Turns out he's an ex-Hellfire pilot, posted to the *Vigilance*. One of the best apparently, but he busted up his spine pretty bad punching out mid-atmo during a dogfight. The docs did their best, but Fleet decided he wasn't fit for Hellfires anymore. They offered him a couple of other commissions, supply ships mainly, but he turned them down. Took medical discharge instead. Wasn't happy by all accounts, guess that's how he ended up with the Khans. Point is, he's an exceptional pilot, which is just as well because he has to bring the ship between these two mountains," he used his hand to show the route, "drop sharply down into this ravine here, do a virtual ninety-degree turn, without hitting the walls, and take her under this protrusion before bringing her in. The valley's so tight, there's maybe a metre's grace each side of the ship."

"Connor could do that," Jake said confidently.

"Doesn't matter," Cal said, tucking his hair behind his ear as he stood up. "We can't go in that way. Look, the Khans are cocky little bastards, and they're convinced no one else knows about the planet, but that doesn't mean they're not careful. They don't want to draw attention to Tartaros, so they don't use any equipment whose signature could be picked up outside the atmosphere. What they do use is localised intrusion sensors linked to some ultra-tech defence grid created by a sadistic little fucker on Genesis." Jake and I shared a meaningful look. "What?"

"He won't be creating anything else. He's dead," Jake said, grinning.

"Is there anyone you've met on this mission you haven't killed, Sir?"

"To be fair, Jake didn't kill him. He kind of killed himself," I explained.

Cal raised an eyebrow but didn't press further, instead he turned his attention back to the map. "The sensors will pick up anyone approaching, but there are no security measures inside the complex. I guess they made the assumption that no one would get past the external defences."

"How do you know all of this, Lieutenant?" asked Hale.

"I wasn't a prisoner on Tartaros to begin with. Came and went with the Khans. But when I was there, I made it part of my mission to check out the place: the cells, the control room, even some of the lower structures. That's where most of the carvings and symbols are. Spooky shit if you ask me. It's like a bloody ghost town... like everyone and everything just up and disappeared one day."

Jared scratched his chin. "So how, exactly, are we supposed to get in without getting blown out of the sky, or alerting the Khans?"

"I recommend you tuck the *Defender* behind Tartaros' third moon. Near enough that she can step in, or deploy Hellfires if necessary, but far enough that she won't be picked up on sensors. Then we take the *Veritas* from there to the planet."

"We?" Jake questioned.

"The deal was I'd come with you, Sir. I just wouldn't go underground."

"Right," Jake replied, the hint of a smile surfacing.

"Like I said, we take the *Veritas* to the planet, but we can't go anywhere near the main entrance or we'll be picked up on sensors, so instead..." he scrolled the map a distance to the left, "we come in this way. I hope Connor's as good as you say he is, Colonel, coz this is going to take some rock-star piloting. He's going to have to hug the rock, coming in low through here before ducking below the sensors in this ravine. He can land on this plateau, but you'll have to hump it on foot the rest of the way."

"But that's miles from the entrance," said Ash.

"You forget, the complex is vast." Cal made the image smaller, so a greater area was displayed. "The Khans' entrance is here, but it's effectively just a hangar. There's a tunnel that leads to the main part, which pretty much covers all of this area." He used a spinning motion with his hand to indicate an area several miles in diameter. "We're going to enter from the opposite side. The atmosphere on the surface is toxic, so you'll need rebreathers, but the air in the complex is filtered and re-circulated so you can ditch them once you're inside."

"I'm going to ask the question one more time," said Jared, pinching the bridge of his nose. "How are we getting in?"

"Through here." Cal tapped a small shadow on the map,

enlarging the view. The rest of us simultaneous lent forward and peered at the tiny crevice. "The Khans are sadistic, power-hungry thugs, but archaeologists they ain't. Vanze was interested in the symbols and carvings, but they didn't care about the rest of the place. Before my cover was blown, I did some exploring with Hoban. Below the main area is a series of passageways which Hoban said would've originally been utility tunnels for water and power, that kind of thing. One day I got restless and headed down there just for something to do. I found, and by found, I mean fell through, a shaft to a lower tunnel that hadn't been explored. I followed it for a while, going up and down, but it eventually hit the surface at one of the valley walls."

"At that tiny shadow," I said, looking at the map.

"Affirmative. Nearly choked to death from the surface atmosphere seeping in, but there's something about the tunnel formation and internal air pressure which kept most of it out."

"And that's how you escaped?" I asked.

"Yeah. I thought maybe one day it would come in handy, so I stashed a rebreather down there, just in case. Man, I'm glad I did. After I was out, I walked and crawled my way to the main entrance, hid on the ship, and waited until Fletcher did a supply run. I can't tell you how long I waited. All I know is it took everything I had left to get off the ship. Woke up in some hospital god-knows how many days later without a clue how I got there. Anyway, the Khans know nothing about it, so that's your ingress point."

"What about once we're in?" Jared said.

"Surface sensor sweeps wouldn't normally penetrate the quartzide, but I'm going to use the *Veritas*' sensor array to scan for that weird energy signature I was telling you about. It's faint, but at that proximity, and with a deep penetration pulse, I should be able to map the complex."

"Should?" Jared's forehead creased.

"I can't give you a guarantee, Sir. Quartzide is a dense

rock, and the energy signature is weak, but I think there's a good chance. If you place a transmitter booster at the mouth of the tunnel, then drop additional boosters as you move through the complex, I should be able to keep coms open and provide real time information on targets."

"There's that should again," Jared commented.

"Best I can offer you at this stage. If it works, I can review sensor telemetry from the *Veritas* and talk you towards the most likely places to find the Princess and the Khans. You'll have the element of surprise, but the rest is up to you, Sirs."

"Okay, this is what we're going to do." Jared took a deep breath and let it out slowly. "The Wolfpack can deal with the Khans' crew. Ash and Shae go after the Princess, Jake and I will deal with the brothers."

"No," I blurted, surprising myself as well as the others. I looked at Jared, my mind scrambling to think up a plausible reason for disagreeing with his order. "We all know how bad the Khans are. It would be prudent to have me... my gift... handy when you take them on."

"It's more likely the Princess will need you, Babe," Jake said. "But that's not the real reason, is it?" He huffed loudly.

"Okay, cards on the table," I lied. "Jared and I have a score to settle with the brothers. They did try to blow us up in the Catacombs, remember?" I looked at Jared, my eyes pleading.

"Fine," he agreed to a chorus of complaints from both Jake and Ash. Jared held up his hand. "I've made my decision. Shae and I will take the Khans, you two get the Princess." He looked at the com-pad on his wrist. "Get some sleep and report to the Situation Room at eleven-hundred for a final brief. Uniform is light combat armour. Ash, Shae, I'll have some Fleet-issue armour delivered to your quarters. Dismissed," he added as Jake objected again.

When we walked back to our quarters, Ash made it clear

he wasn't happy.

"I know they're dangerous, Ash, which is why Jared needs me," I explained.

"No, there's more to it than that," Ash countered. "I know you too well, Shae, and you're forgetting about the Link." When I didn't reply, he took my arm and turned me so I faced him. "Shae? What happened in the Catacombs?"

I wanted to tell him, but King Sebastian's orders had been clear. "Ash..." I was torn. "You're right, something did happen, but I can't tell you about it now. I'll tell you everything as soon as I can, I promise. You'll have to trust me. I need to do this."

"Okay," he said eventually. "I just want you to be safe."

"I know."

23

Ash and I were the last to enter the Situation Room, the anticipation and adrenaline thick in the air. Cal was discussing Tartaros' terrain with Connor, explaining that he'd have to manually pilot the *Veritas* in due to the landscape. I was glad Connor looked confident and unconcerned.

Apart from Jake expressing his concerns over task allocation once again, the brief was straightforward and quick. Cal had sketched a rough map of what he could remember of the structure, highlighting the area most likely to be occupied by the brothers, and the position of the cells. After advising us all to review the information, Jared released the Wolfpack and Cal to ready the *Veritas* for departure. He kept the Guardians behind.

"I don't need to tell you we're almost out of time," he said. "If we're not on our way to Decerra by midnight, there's no way we're going to get the Seal back in time for the start of the Sector Senate meeting tomorrow morning."

"What if the Khans don't have it?" I asked. I knew I sounded pessimistic, but it was a valid question. "What if they've already passed it on to someone else?"

"We'll have to cross that bridge if we get to it," Jared replied. "We know Deakes was with them up to Angel Ridge, and he said they came straight to Tartaros. Unless they met someone along the way, we have to assume they still have it and work on that premise. I suppose keeping your fingers crossed as well wouldn't hurt." He forced a grin. "Okay, let's do it."

Compared to the atmosphere in the situation room, the mood on the *Veritas* was pensive; everyone preoccupied with their own thoughts and preparations.

Following Cal's instructions, Connor took us around the dark side of the planet, bringing us in low and slow through a deadly mountain range. When we descended to only a few metres off the ground, I went up to the flight deck. Jake and Jared were already there, staring out the front screen at the lethal rocks passing way too close for comfort. I gasped as we dropped suddenly into a ravine.

"As much as I appreciate the cheer-squad," Connor said, without taking his eyes from the narrow valley, "this isn't easy. And an audience isn't helping. With all due respect…" A red button flashed, and the computer loudly repeated the words Proximity Warning interspersed with a blaring alarm. "Someone turn that fucking thing off," he grunted. Jake leant across Cal, accessed the automated safety systems, and disengaging the proximity sensors. "Thanks," Connor said, risking a quick glance in his direction.

The ship jolted violently, and I lost my balance, stumbling into Jared. A metallic screech vibrated in my chest and I put my hands up to cover my ears.

"A metre to the right, Connor," Cal shouted, having got up to look out of the window at the wing. "To the right! Watch out for that outcrop."

"I see it," mumbled Connor. The *Veritas* shuddered, then rocked fiercely as dislodged boulders hit the port wing. More warning alarms blared, but one by one they ceased as

Connor levelled us out and brought the ship back under control.

"Phew. That was close," he joked, wiping sweat from his forehead.

"You cause any more damage to my ship, Connor, and you'll be paying for the repairs out of your wages," Jake replied.

The rest of the trip was relatively uneventful, but I was still grateful when we landed on the plateau. We gathered in the hold of the ship where Ty handed each of us a mini holo-pad attached to a wrist strap. "Once Cal has mapped the complex, he'll send it to these. We'll be able to see the layout of the tunnels and know exactly where our targets are located."

"If it works," Jared said with an off-putting amount of pessimism.

"Have faith, Captain," said Cal, sliding down the ladder railings just like Jake.

I strapped one of the pads to my wrist while Jared helped me shrug into my oxygen rebreather. I put on the mask and displayed the unit telemetry on the inside of the clear plastic visor. The oxygen levels, cooling system and power-packs were all in the green.

Cal did a quick visual inspection of everyone's kit and then checked coms were up and running. "You're good to go. Good luck," he said before disappearing back up the ladder. Once the hatch was shut, the ramp descended, filling the hold with toxic gasses. My visor flashed a warning message, telling me not to remove my rebreather under current atmospheric conditions, then a small caution symbol appeared in the bottom left hand corner of the screen.

"We're covering some tough terrain," Jake said, standing at the top of the ramp. "Keep your breathing slow and regular and watch the person in front of you. Move out."

We headed down the ramp and I immediately felt the

heat on my skin, but it didn't feel as uncomfortable as it had on Independence. My boots crunched the creamy-beige quartzide particles covering the flat rock table, but as soon as we reached the edge of the ravine, the terrain became uneven. Rocks were larger and sharper, making climbing treacherous. A top layer of stone debris made getting a secure foothold difficult, and at one point I slipped, putting my hand out to stop myself falling. Quartzide ripped through my skin, and bright red blood oozed around the edge of the shard still imbedded in the flesh.

"Hold still," Ty said, grabbing my wrist before pulling out the stone.

"Thanks."

"No probs. Just be more careful."

I continued to climb the side of the ravine, concentrating hard to make sure I didn't slip again, but a muffled cry made me turn. Connor was sliding back down the steep rock face, frantically trying to grab on to something. Half a metre from the ledge to a yawning chasm, he managed to grasp a rock – stopping his fall – but it didn't look stable.

Kaiser and Ash scrambled to get to him, but before they could, the lip crumbled, and he fell out of sight. I held my breath, fearing the worst, but when Ash peered over the edge then quickly pulled a rope from his pack, I knew there was still a chance. He threw one end from the ledge and it went taught just as the outcrop below disintegrated into a rockslide. Connor dangled precariously over thin air, but Kaiser and Ash heaved on the rope, slowly hauling him up to safe ground.

"That was an adventure," Connor said when he got his breath back, but his bravado was betrayed by the shake in his voice. I let out a deep, thankful breath.

The whole group took the climb way more seriously after that and the rest of the way was spent in silent concentration until we reached the opening of the fissure.

We paused to allow Ty to set up the primary sensor booster.

"Rescue team, this is McCray." Cal's voice crackled in my ear. "The *Veritas*' sensor array was able to scan for the energy trace and has started to create a virtual schematic of the complex. I'm sending it to you all now, but more should appear as you move through the complex and drop additional boosters."

I looked at the holo-pad on my wrist, where a detailed line diagram appeared bit by bit. Passageways, rooms and halls, some vast like caverns, displayed on a multiple level, three-dimensional map.

"Fuck me," said Kaiser. "This place is huge."

As I watched, a cluster of little blue dots appeared at the edge of the diagram. Each had one of our names attached to it.

"Your locator beacons will show blue on the map," Cal said. "The Khans' men will show red."

"I don't see any red dots," Jake said.

"There's too much interference at the moment to give you reliable data," Cal explained. "The more boosters you drop inside, the stronger and clearer the readings will get. Be advised, the sensors can't distinguish between targets, the Khans, the Princess, or prisoners."

A few metres into the crevice, the little symbol in the bottom corner of my visor turned from red to green and a brief message told me the ambient air was breathable. We removed our rebreathers and stacked them against the wall for later use, including the extra one Kaiser had carried for Phina.

Following Cal's instructions, we headed up the small fissure until we came to a shaft. Connor dumped his backpack on the floor and removed climbing equipment before disappearing up the hole. A few minutes later a rope dropped down and Jake handed the end to me. "Ladies first."

"You just want to look at my arse," I said quietly.

"Babe, I'm wounded," he said, holding his hands over his heart like I'd just stabbed him in it. "I was being gentlemanly," he added, but his eyes sparkled mischievously in the torchlight and he couldn't hide the smirk that tugged the corner of his lips.

"Somehow, I don't believe you," I replied, grabbing the rope and heaving myself up into the shaft. I could practically feel his eyes on my backside.

When I reached the top, Connor had already lit a couple of chem-lights and was setting up another sensor booster. Little red dots began to appear on the map, but as no one was in our proximity, I used the time it took the others to climb the shaft, to have a look around. I ran my hand along the smooth, unblemished walls, marvelling at the precise corners and perfect edges.

When the last of the team emerged from the shaft, we crouched on the floor around Jared. "You've all got your assignments," he directed. "Take it slow and quiet, we don't want to alert the Khans to the fact that we're here before Shae and I have them in our sights. Keep coms open but maintain radio silence, and don't forget to drop boosters at regular intervals. As soon as we have the Seal and the Princess, I'll give the fall-back order. We meet at this location and head back to the *Veritas* together. Agreed? Good. Let me be clear: if it comes down to the Princess or the Seal, the Seal takes priority. King's orders. Do you all understand?" He looked at each member of the group in turn.

I wasn't happy, but I understood why the Seal was important, so when Jared got to me I reluctantly nodded my agreement.

He checked his com-pad. "It's just gone eighteen-hundred, so we've not got much time. The *Defender* needs to leave for Decerra no later than midnight with the Seal, which means you need to be back here by twenty-two-thirty at the latest or you're finding your own transport home. Clock's ticking."

Jared and I headed down the tunnel, with Ash and Jake not far behind, but on Cal's suggestion we separated off from them and turned down different passageways. After a few hundred metres, we came across a set of flawless stone steps leading upwards. The archway at the top was a doorway to a vast, man-made cave – no, not man-made I had to keep telling myself – and not just a cave either. It was something else entirely, something more like a Council Chamber or Ceremonial Hall, and its ethereal beauty took my breath from me.

Jared took a booster from my backpack and placed it on the floor next to one of the enormous, elaborately carved stone columns that literally grew out of the floor to the high, vaulted ceiling above. Creamy-beige sculptures of creatures I didn't recognise extended from giant stone plinths, covered in delicately swirling symbols. My stomach knotted, and my hand automatically pressed against my chest where my pendant rested next to my skin.

Jared was saying something, but I wasn't listening. I was hypnotised by the carvings, hardly daring to breathe for fear they would crumble into dust, or simply disappear altogether.

"Shae?"

I touched the patterns with the very tips of my fingers, hesitant at first, then more firmly to check they really were really there.

"Shae?" Jared was at my side. "What is it?"

"Don't you recognise them?" I asked.

He studied them for a moment. "Should I? Wait, actually…" He dredged up a memory until his eyes showed recognition. "Are those…" Jared tapped his earpiece. "Rescue Team, this is Marcos. Shae and I are going off-coms for a couple of minutes."

"Why? What the hell?" Jake immediately responded.

"What's going on?" added Ash

"Nothing to be concerned about. Carry on with your objectives, we'll be back on-coms momentarily."

"What are you play—" started Jake, but Jared cut us off from the rest of the group.

"Let's make this quick. We were given a Royal Order not to discuss…" Jared smacked himself on the side of the head as realisation dawned. "I get it now. I'm such an idiot. This is why you wanted the Khan bit of the mission."

"It's part of the reason."

Jared gave me his I don't believe you for a minute frown.

"Okay, yes, you're right. But aren't you a little bit intrigued? I know you saw the same symbols on the Helyan cube – an artefact we were strictly forbidden to even acknowledge exists. Don't you think that's strange? And then there's this." I pulled the chain from under my breastplate.

"The pendant from your mother?"

"Look closer."

Jared took the brushed-bronze disc and flipped it over, drawing in a breath. He looked between the object and the plinth several times to compare them, then he let it go and I tucked it back against my skin. He rubbed his chin, his eyes wide, almost ultramarine in the chem-light.

"I want answers, Jared. I don't know what these symbols mean, or why my mother had this jewellery, but it's driving me crazy. I need to know what Vanze knows about the cube and the carvings. I thought I'd come to terms with who and what I am, but all this…" I glanced around the hall. "Now I feel like I don't know anything anymore. I'm lost."

Jared turned me towards him before cradling my face in his warm hands, his thumbs stroking my skin. "I can't possibly understand what you're going through, but I promise you, when this is over, I'll do everything I can to help you get answers. Right now, though, we've got a mission to complete."

"I know."

"I need you five-by-five if you're going to go up against the Khans," Jared said, not taking his eyes from mine. "I mean it, Shae. If you're not one hundred percent with me, I'll reassign you."

"I'm with you, Jared. I promise."

"Good, then we need to get back in the game. Okay?"

I shook myself out, forcing thoughts of the disc, the cube, and the symbols to the back of my mind. At least temporarily.

"Just give me one second," I said, pulling a data-cam from one of my pockets. I took a close-up recording of the symbols on the plinth before panning it around the hall, capturing the statues and the columns right up to the high arched ceiling. "Hello... what are you?" I added, looking at the data-cam screen. I zoomed in on a shadowy object ringing one of the columns just below the roof. I couldn't make it out and I showed it to Jared.

"No idea," he said. "And we haven't got time to hang around. You good to go?"

I pocketed the data-cam and Jared reconnected us to group coms, fending off a few pointed questions from Jake before reminding him about his radio silent order.

After a quick look at the map to get our bearings, we headed towards another set of stairs leading up from the far wall. We navigated several hallways and rooms, using the location of the red dots on the map to avoid confrontation, and dropped sensor boosters as we went. Occasionally, I glanced at my wrist, watching little red dots blink out of existence as the blue, Wolfpack dots advanced through the complex.

We arrived at a blind, ninety-degree turn in a rock hallway and paused so I could check the map. It flickered and distorted sporadically, but there were no dots.

"Clear," I whispered. In hindsight, I should've realised that no dots meant just that – the sensors hadn't picked up our locator beacons, and they certainly hadn't registered the three hostiles we ran into just around the corner. The only advantage we had was that they were as surprised to see us, as we were of them.

They tried to un-holster weapons, but we were too quick. Jared slammed the head of one against the wall, before punching a second hard in the throat. I brought my knee up solidly into the groin of the third, and as he bent over in agony, I twisted behind him to get a good grip before snapping his neck. As Jared finished off the hostile he'd punched, I took the blade from my boot and slit the throat of the last man, who was unsteadily attempting to get up off the floor. I wiped the knife on his trousers and put it back in its sheath.

"McCray? Mitchell? This is Marcos, can anyone hear me?" Jared asked. "All teams report." Silence.

I glanced at the blank holo-pad on my wrist. "Looks like we've gone dark."

"We're on our own," Jared replied. "According to McCray's memory-map, we can't be too far from the Khans' quarters. This way."

We continued on our mission, passing through rooms and hallways, but our progress was slower and more cautious once we didn't have sensors to rely on.

Halfway down a hallway, we came to the entrance of a large room. Jared stopped and peered in, and I leant around him, noting the tiered rows of stone benches rising up the two longer walls.

"Some kind of meeting place?" I asked.

"No idea, but I don't like it," he replied. "It's too open, and there's no cover."

"Do we have a choice? Cal's map takes us this way, and without sensors we've no way to determine whether there's a suitable detour."

"Guess we're going this way then."

I readied my weapon and stepped cautiously into the room, keeping my eyes firmly on the only other doorway to the room.

We'd just reached the middle when a group of bad guys swarmed through the opening, all with state-of-the-art weapons and deadpan expressions. I froze, finger on the trigger. There was no shouting, no orders to lower weapons, just an eerie, silent standoff between us and them.

Jared and I were outnumbered and outgunned.

One of the hostiles lowered his weapon and took a step towards us. Jared countered by putting a hand across my chest, edging us back a step.

"Put your weapons on the floor," the man said eventually, his voice echoing gently.

I felt Jared tense and we edged further back, but the sound of footsteps, and the unmistakable metallic click of weapons being primed, made us both turn. We were flanked, and both exits were blocked.

"Let me put it another way," the man continued. "Put your weapons down... or die where you stand."

My gaze darted around the room, assessing the amassed group for possible weakness that we could exploit, but there weren't any. Not that I could see anyway. I felt the swirling, tickly sensation in the pit of my tummy and for a moment I considered using an energy pulse, but there was no way I could risk it in what was effectively a stone vault. If the concussion wave didn't kill us, the chance of taking out all the hostiles without one of them getting off a lucky shot, was too slim.

Jared and I exchanged a brief look. I saw from his eyes that he was also working through options in his head, but in truth there were only two – and they'd already given them to us: surrender or die.

Jared took his finger of the trigger and let the TK70's barrel lower before he slowly bent and placed it on the floor, kicking it out of reach as instructed. I reluctantly followed suit, the assault rifle clattering noisily as it skittered across the smooth stone.

"And the rest," the man ordered. I unfastened the clips around my thighs and undid the buckle, releasing my utility belt, the plasma pistol and Cal'ret still holstered. Jared removed his two Sentinels and added them to the growing collection. "Don't make me ask again," the man pushed. I added the knife from my boot to the pile.

As soon as I straightened up, a man grabbed me from behind, pinning my arms to my side, while a second searched me for further weapons. The objections to my left told me Jared was being subjected to the same routine. I turned to check on him, just catching the blur of a gun butt out of the corner of my eye before everything went black.

24

My eyes flickered, and a wave of nausea turned my stomach. My head felt like it was on fire. I lifted my hand, but the other came with it, and through a foggy haze, I felt the binds bite at my wrists. My fingertips found rough materiel instead of soft skin, and when I finally managed to open my eyes, I realised there was some kind of sack or hood over my head. I could just about make out shapes through the coarse weave.

I tried to sit up, but my stomach turned again, and I was further hampered by the fact that my ankles were also bound. With effort, I made it to a kneeling position.

"Jared," I whispered.

The force of the unexpected blow to my head knocked me over and my head bounced off the stone floor. I'd just made out the shape of someone's boots in front of my face when a second blow, maybe even a stamp, knocked me unconscious again.

It felt like an earthquake. Every bone in my body objected to the shaking and the growling in my ear demanding that I wake up. I'd just started to centre my thoughts when the sack was ripped from my head and rough hands pulled me back to a kneeling position. My head pounded, and my eyes were unfocussed, but none of that mattered because Jared was right there next to me.

As soon as his hood was removed, he scanned the room with blinking eyes, and when he found me, I saw the relief.

"Are you okay?" he asked, looking bilious. I winced even before the butt of a gun came down on his head.

The seeping cut added more colour to the various shades of angry red and bluey-purple that covered his face. I wondered if they would realise that mine wasn't bruised at all.

My coms and holo-pad had been removed. Not that it really mattered, given they weren't working, but without them I had no idea what the time was. I'd been knocked out twice, unconscious anything from minutes to hours, and had no idea how much time we had left – or even if it was too late.

I scanned the chamber, looking for some kind of plexi-screen or clock that would give me an idea, but nothing. I did, however, see our weapons and equipment on an interestingly engraved metal desk that seemed incongruous against the pale natural stone.

Could Jared and I take out our two guards to get to them? I caught his attention and flicked my eyes to the desk, but he shook his head, freezing the moment Vanze stalked into the room. He was trailed by Blain, Hoban and two further guards.

It didn't seem like they recognised us from the Catacombs. Though, to be fair, Jared's face was so swollen he was almost unrecognisable, and Vanze was more interested in getting an update on the incursion.

"You've found no one?" he shouted in disbelief, his voice shaking with rage. "These two didn't come alone. There's no way they could've taken out all those men by themselves. Find me the others, or I'll drag you to the surface myself and watch your lungs explode. Are you reading me?" he blasted.

The two guards who'd entered with the Khans scuttled back out, promising immediate action. Vanze sighed wearily, cracking his neck from side to side before finally acknowledging our existence.

"You two," he said, his face finally showing recognition. "I know you, don't I?" He crouched in front of me, his face darkening. A storm raged in his eyes and he stiffened with palpable fury. I knew what was coming. "You cost me the Helyan cube, and for that alone, I'm going to enjoy hurting you. Payback's a bitch, as they say." His voice was steel cold.

As he stood, he backhanded me across the face, and I toppled sideways, a sharp burn stinging my cheek. Jared's immediate objection earnt him several kicks to his ribs, turning his words to groans.

I tasted blood and knew my lip had split open, so I hid the slight silver-blue shimmer under my arm, hoping the Khans were too preoccupied to notice. I groaned for effect, and when the glow had dissipated, I wiped my mouth on my sleeve and tried to sit.

Vanze stood by the desk inspecting my Cal'ret, but Blain towered over Jared, flexing his fist with a malicious grin. One side of Jared's face was smeared with the blood oozing from an angry gash across his cheek. Blain laughed and smacked his head roughly before going to join his brother, while Hoban hovered anxiously on the periphery.

Vanze perched himself on the edge of the table. "Make no mistake," he said coldly. "You're both going to suffer greatly for what you've cost me. But before that happens, I'm curious…" His voice lightened slightly. "How did you find us? I mean, no one even knows about this place. And then there are our defences…" He picked idly at his fingernails, feigning indifference.

"That's easy," replied Jared, his voice hoarse. "Deakes told us."

"That's impossible," Blain roared, rushing forward, fists clenched.

"Wait," I cried, surprise stopping him in his tracks. "He's telling the truth. Deakes did give us this location."

"I have to agree with Blain," Vanze commented more reasonably, waiving his brother away from Jared. "Deakes doesn't know anything about Tartaros." He sighed dramatically. "And here I thought we were all playing so nice together." He picked up one of the Sentinels and primed it. Hoban edged quietly towards the exit.

"Neither of us is lying," Jared said. "Deakes does know about Tartaros because Hoban told him."

"What?" Blain wheeled around to face Hoban. The weather-worn archaeologist had rooted to the spot and turned death-white. He didn't need to say anything, the panic in his eyes and slack jaw told the brothers Jared was telling the truth.

Without missing a heartbeat, Vanze turned the Sentinel on Hoban, firing two shots into his chest and sending him sprawling backwards against the wall.

"Shame, I kind of liked him," he said humourlessly, replacing the gun on the table. "Well, that's one question answered, and relatively painlessly I might add. Answer the rest as cooperatively, and I might just kill you quickly."

Jared snorted his disbelief.

"Blain, tell Fletcher to ready the ship. We're moving out as soon as I've dealt with our guests," Vanze said. Blain grunted and stalked from the room as his older brother turned his attention back to us. "Well, I suppose it's obvious why you're here, although I have to say, I'm impressed you found us. How did you get passed the external detection grid, by the way?" He seemed distracted for a moment. "I thought our defences were comprehensive, but I guess I was wrong," he mused. "It's irrelevant though. You're going to die here, and the King will never get his precious daughter back. Not in one piece anyway. Wait, that sly old dog! He didn't send you for the Princess, did he? He sent you for the Seal. This Seal," he added, picking up a flat rectangular box from the desk.

Somehow, I felt better knowing it was right there, that they hadn't offloaded it, but I hadn't exactly planned on being a prisoner.

"Well, the King's not getting either back," Vanze continued, the viciousness back in his voice. "This little beauty's going to the Outsider. Hopefully getting this will be enough to appease him – after all, he's expecting the seal and the Helyan cube... not that we were going to give that to him anyway. That was our little secret, see? He thought he was using us to do his dirty work, when all along, we were using him for his money. No way we could have got near the cube otherwise."

"Who is the Outsider?" I risked asking. My guard raised his gun, but Vanze stopped him with a wave of his hand.

"Because I'm feeling magnanimous, I'm going to tell you, at least what I know." Vanze paused, a wry smile appearing briefly. "Which isn't much – other than he's very, very wealthy, and has been searching for the same thing we have. A common goal, you could say. Actually, we've never met him... could even be a her I suppose. We always dealt with a third party, a female Other called Breen. I can tell you that the Outsider is independent though, not part of ARRO or any other dissident movement. Not that we know of, anyway."

"What's he going to use the Seal for?" asked Jared.

"Didn't ask. None of my business. But if I had to guess, he's going to use it to destabilise the Sector. Undermine one and you weaken the whole. Simple really. Wish I'd thought of it."

"But why?" I said.

"Who cares? I certainly don't. The only thing I cared about was his money, which allowed me to acquire the army and equipment I needed to take the palace."

"Didn't exactly turn out like you planned though, did it?" Jared mocked.

Vanze's unfriendly eyes darkened further. "Maybe not, and you'll pay for that with blood. But before you do, answer my question," he barked.

"Oh, I'm sorry, was there a question in there somewhere?" said Jared, baiting him, and sounding more like Jake by the second. "I didn't catch it amongst all the pretentious bullshit." The guard kicked him hard in the ribs and I flinched.

Vanze knelt on the rug in front of me, his eyes almost completely black. "How did you get in the caves without us knowing?" he asked slowly.

"Go to hell."

"Hmm," he pondered. "I probably will, but you'll be getting there a lot sooner than me. Answer my question." When I didn't, he nodded to the guard next to Jared, who booted him in the ribs again. "Answer my question," he repeated calmly.

"Don't tell him," Jared grunted through pained breaths, prompting Vanze to reach over and backhand him across the face.

"Okay, let's try a different one. How many people came with you?" Silence. "What does the REF know about this location?" Silence. Vanze sighed deeply. "How many ships do you have in orbit?"

Jared's ragged laugh surprised us both. "Save your breath, shithead," he said. "Neither of us will tell you anything."

Vanze's smile was evil. "Is that so?" he said, standing up and going to the table. When he returned, he held my knife, stained brownish-red from the hostile I'd killed in the tunnels. He knelt between us. "Eeny meeny miny... moe." The blade pointed at Jared. "Take off his protective vest," he ordered the guard.

"Whatever happens, don't tell him any—" Jared's words

were cut off by a punch to the head. He swayed and his eyes unfocussed. The guard tore off a length of tape and slapped it over his mouth.

"That's better," Vanze said. "Now, where were we? Oh yes." He turned his head towards me. "You were about to answer my questions, or your friend here and this knife are going to become intimately acquainted."

I looked desperately at Jared, but he shook his head forcefully.

"Tick tock," Vanze taunted.

"I won't tell you anything," I said, my insides churning.

"Your choice." Vance drew the blade tip down Jared's cheek, opening up a deep, red cut, and I tugged at my bindings, wanting to kill him more than anything in the Four Sectors. "How many more of you are there?" he asked as my guard restrained me.

Jared continued to shake his head, his eyes telling me everything. My heart physically hurt as Vanze drew the blade across Jared's chest. Dark blood instantly oozed from the wound, staining his t-shirt. "Last chance," Vanze drawled.

Uncontrollable tears welled in my eyes, but I said nothing, just like Jared had told me to do. But when Vanze drew the knife back and prepared to plunge it into Jared's chest, I couldn't help myself. "Stop! Please don't hurt him."

"Oh," Vanze said, moving so he was directly in front of me. A tear slipped down my cheek. "You care for him, no?" he mocked. "Isn't that interesting?"

"You bastard," I said coldly, but he laughed.

Blain reappeared, puffing slightly. "Fletcher says the ship will be ready to depart in twenty."

"Good," Vanze replied. "You're just in time to find out whether this one," he pointed to Jared with the knife, "cares for her, as much as she does for him." A brief, malicious smile crossed his angular features. "Take off her body armour."

Hands gripped me, pulling at clips and tags. "You're a sadistic bastard, Vanze. You won't get away with this," I growled.

"But I already have." He laughed in my face before turning towards Jared's guard. "Take off the tape," he ordered. "You know the drill, Captain was it? Answer my questions or..." He placed the tip of the knife on my left cheek, just below my eye.

"Don't you do it," Jared roared. "I'll kill you, Vanze. Don't hurt her." His words were desperate, and they cut straight through my chest to my heart. He made a lunge towards Vanze, both of them bowling into me, toppling all of us over. There was a short scuffle, but the guards stepped in, separating off Jared and putting me back in a kneeling position.

I thought Vanze would go ballistic after Jared's assault, but he just sat in front of me, slack-jawed, eyes wide. His gaze was drawn to my pendant, which must've slid out from under my t-shirt when I'd fallen. Slowly he moved closer, edging the tip of the knife under the chain and lifting the two discs closer to him. Discarding the Brotherhood medal with a dismissive grunt, he studied the pendant my mother had given me with child-like awe.

Jared struggled with one of the guards, breaking Vanze's trance. "Gag and bag him," Vanze said.

The guard reapplied the tape and put the sack over Jared's head.

"What is it, brother?" Blain asked, but Vanze ignored his question.

"Take that one away. See if you can't get him to talk," he said instead, indicating towards Jared with a casual wave of his arm. He never once took his eyes off the pendant he cradled carefully in the palm of his other hand.

Blain and one of the guards hauled a struggling Jared from the room, and I tried to protest, but Vanze held the knife to my chest as a warning.

"Where did you get this?" he asked, his voice breathy with anticipation.

"You think I'm going to tell you?" I forced a hollow laugh.

"We'll see." He yanked the chain and I felt it pull on my neck before it snapped. "Give me your stunner," he said to the one remaining guard, who passed it over without question. Before I had a chance to protest, an excruciating pain shot up my arm and exploded into my brain.

I came to, coughing and spluttering, shaking water from hair. My guard stood over me, empty cup in hand, sneering. For a second, I wondered how long I'd been unconscious for that time, but my thoughts immediately turned to Jared and I frantically searched the room. He wasn't there. The chem-lights had been lowered so that dark shadows obscured most of the room, but I could make out Vanze sitting in an armchair by the desk.

"Let's try and be a little civilised, shall we," he said. My guard pulled me to my feet and dragged me across a rug to the chair opposite. "What do you think of the place? Interesting, yes?" he asked amiably.

"If you say so," I croaked. "Where's Captain Marcos?"

"In good time. He's still alive though, if that makes you feel better?" It did, but I tried not to think about what Blain had done to him. "Where did you get this?" he asked again, holding up my pendant.

"It was my mothers," I replied, thinking there was no harm in him having that information, and hoping that by being helpful, I could get him to let his guard down.

"Who are you?" he asked bluntly.

"I'm nobody," I replied. "What's the Helyan cube?"

Vanze's eyes crinkled and he smiled, making his angular features even sharper in the shadows of the room. "What do you know?"

"I know you wanted it badly. And I know the symbols on it match that disc and the carvings in the caves below us.

What do you know?"

"You seem to be under the misconception that this is a two-way interrogation," Vanze said, his voice betraying a hint of impatience. "But in the interest of cooperation, I'll tell you this: the cube is power. Pure and simple. Rumour has it, whoever controls the cube has access to unspeakable energy. Have you any idea what a person like me could do with that? Where did your mother get the disc?"

"I don't know. What power could the cube possibly contain?"

"Enough!" Vanze shouted, suddenly agitated. He stood and paced. "You're hiding something, and I want to know what it is right now. How did you really get the disc?"

"I told you, it belonged to my mother and she left it to me when she died. I was only a baby. I never knew her." A different pain burned through my chest.

"What does it do?"

"What did you mean, what does it do?" I was confused. He seemed to be as ignorant as I was.

"What does it say? Have you translated the writing?" he pushed.

"Writing? I didn't even know it was writing."

"You're lying."

"I'm not. I can't answer your questions because I don't know anything."

"You will tell me now, or your captain, partner, lover, whatever the hell he is to you, will suffer."

"How can I tell you what I don't know?" I stammered, fearful of what he would do to Jared.

"I don't believe you." He picked up a communicator. "Blain, bring the other one in."

"No, please," I begged. "He has nothing to do with this."

"I think you're holding out on me. I think you want the cube's power all to yourself, in fact…" Vanze's eyes suddenly widened and his cheeks pinked. "You know where the Amissa Telum is, don't you? That's what you're hiding from me." He practically shivered with excitement.

I froze, surprised by the additional information, but Vanze must've mistaken my pause as recognition.

"You do know," he gasped, running his fingers through lank, greasy hair. "You know exactly where it is, and this disc has something to do with it. You will tell me now." He moved towards me, knife in hand, but Blain's arrival interrupted his advance.

Through the shadows, I watched Blain and a guard drag Jared in and dump him brutally on the floor over the other side of the room. He had the sack over his head, and from the muffled cries I assumed he was still gagged, but he was alive, and the knot in my chest loosened a little. Between the shadows and the dim light, I could just see the dark stain on his t-shirt from the wound Vance had given him earlier, but thankfully he didn't look nearly as bad as I'd expected.

I tried to get out of the chair to go to him, but my guard put heavy hands on my shoulders, forcing me back into the seat.

Vanze sighed wearily. "I'm getting tired of having to repeat myself. Tell me everything you know."

"I have."

"You're lying."

"I'm not, I promise. You have to believe me," I pleaded. "I came here to get answer from you because I saw the cube's symbols matched the ones on my pendant." I spoke quickly, trying to sooth his rage. "I wanted to know what was so important about the cube. That's all."

Vanze ignored my words. "Perhaps a little persuasion is needed, yes?" He put down the knife and picked up a Sentinel, priming it to fire as he walked across the room to where Jared was kneeling. "Tell me, or he pays the consequence."

"I told you, I can't tell you what I—" The sound of the

plasma shot reverberated around the room. "No! Please, stop! You don't have to do this." I couldn't take my eyes off Jared's mangled arm. Tears flowed out of pain and fear, and I could hardly catch my breath to speak. I tried to get up again, but the guard stopped me.

"Last chance," Vanze grunted, moving the gun to Jared's head.

"I don't know anything," I gasped.

"Three."

"I promise." I was frantic and desperate.

"Two."

"Please," I cried, openly sobbing, my whole body wracked by violent shaking.

"One."

"I'm sorry." It was barely more than a whisper.

Vanze pulled the trigger.

I watched in horror as the back of the sack exploded in a mist of blood and gore. Jared's body slumped backwards to the floor, a dark pool expanding from beneath the sack.

Vanze had put his hand inside my chest and ripped out my heart. In that shattered second, I died inside.

"Fuck it. Maybe she didn't know anything after all," Blain mumbled. "Get this piece of shit out of here," he added to the guards. They bent down and lifted Jared's shoulders off the floor before dragging his lifeless body from the room, his covered head lolling from side to side.

I couldn't move, couldn't even breathe, and then I leant over the side of the chair and puked my guts up. The guard stepped sideways, grunting with disgust.

I'd lost Jared. Nothing mattered anymore.

No, something did matter. Rage bubbled up through the pain, replacing the ice inside me with a raging fire.

The Khans were going to die for what they'd done. That was the only purpose I had left. Not the Seal, not even the Princess, and certainly not those damn symbols that'd cost Jared his life.

I would bide my time, lull them into a false sense of security, and then I'd take my revenge. I didn't have to force the tears that fell freely, but I played on the distraught grieving, hoping they'd underestimate me.

Vanze looked disappointed as he placed the Sentinel back on the desk. "Guess you were telling the truth after all," he said coldly, perching on the edge. "Pity. For a moment there, I thought you might've been important, but you're not. You mean nothing. I'll take this though," he said, pocketing my necklace. An hour previously, I would've been furious that he'd taken it, but I didn't care anymore. "Maybe it will help me find the Amissa Telum, or fully decipher the codex."

The codex? What codex? And what was the Amissa Telum he kept referring to?

Revenge dispelled the thoughts; they weren't important to me anymore.

I watched Vanze pick up the rectangular box holding the Third Seal and tuck it into a backpack. He added a few other items from one of the desk draws then turned to Blain. "I'm going to get some things from my quarters. Deal with this," he glanced at me, "then meet me at the ship. We're leaving."

Blain nodded, a dangerous, sadistic lust in his beady eyes.

"It's just you and me now," said Blain, doing an exaggerated look around the room to prove his point. He was heavyset and strong, but he wasn't the smartest kid in the class. I'd use that to my advantage. "Looks like we've got time for a little fun," he added, openly groping himself.

"No, please, don't…" I cried, forcing myself to bide my time. My wrists and ankles were still tied, and that would cause a problem. I slithered out of the chair and dragged myself to the wall, whimpering and shaking for effect. It worked. Blain looked disgusted as he gazed down on the pathetic, simpering girl curled up against the wall for comfort.

He undid the clips on his gun belt, and as soon as he turned away from me to walk towards the desk, I grabbed a shard of jagged rock and started to saw at the tape binding my ankles.

"When I'm through with you, you'll be begging me to kill you," he growled. As he turned to sneer at me, I hid the shard behind my leg.

"Please don't hurt me," I begged, but he laughed and turned to place his guns on the table. As soon as he did, I went back to work on the bindings. The rock was sharp, and it only took a couple more seconds for the tape to cut.

Blain had his back to me, describing in detail what he was about to do. My hands were still bound, but with my feet free I could stand easily, and with the plush rug as soundproofing, I was able to cross the room silently. The idiot didn't even know I was behind him.

It would've been so easy to plunge the rock shard into his back, and he'd never have seen it coming... but I wanted him to know. I wanted to see the look on his fat, smug face. He was still talking when he turned, but the words stuck in his throat when he saw me. His eyes widened, and the sneer disappeared as I plunged the jagged rock-knife through his chest without hesitation.

He toppled back over the table, his hands grabbing frantically at my shirt, but all he did was pull me closer so that I could put all my weight into pushing the shard further in. Pain ripped through my palm as the serrated stone bit into my skin, but I didn't care. I looked deep into Blain's scared, desperate eyes, and watched the light drain from them. His chest heaved sporadically under me as I twisted the makeshift knife.

"For Jared," I said as his final breath escaped him. His muscles relaxed, and his arms dropped to his sides.

As I stood, taking my weight off him, Blain slipped from the table, landing in an undignified heap on the floor. I already knew the result, but I checked for a pulse anyway. Just to be sure. I was cold and indifferent to his death, and the only thought I had left was one brother down, one to go.

I grabbed my knife from the desk and cut the tape around my wrists before tucking it back into my boot. I noticed blood on the handle and vaguely registered the bleeding cuts on my hand but ignored them. I picked up my belt and quickly fixed it around my hips, securing the weapons to my thighs.

A thought of the others – Ash, Jake, the Wolfpack, the Princess – briefly entered my mind, but it was pushed aside by the rising tide of revenge.

I picked up my com-pad and looked at the time: just gone twenty-two hundred. I thought about securing it to my wrist, but it didn't even work. And besides, it didn't matter anymore. I went to put it back on the desk, but at the last moment changed my mind and stuffed it into my backpack instead – adding my earpiece and data-cam. I unholstered my Sentinel and grabbed one of Jared's for extra firepower.

My resolve wavered for a second as I caught sight of the blood pool on the floor where Jared had died. Grief pierced my chest, constricting my lungs so I couldn't breathe, but cold determination cleared my brain and I focused again. Scrolling backwards and forwards through Cal's memory-map of the complex, I found what I was looking for: Vanze's personal quarters.

Stepping over the bloody mess on the floor, I left the room without a backwards glance.

According to the rough diagram, Vanze's quarters were two levels up and several hundred metres to the west. I was on autopilot, not even pausing before turning blind corners or stepping out into open spaces – the hostiles I encountered were dead before they could even acknowledge me. One managed to get off a lucky shot, but

I barely felt the pain as a bullet ripped through my left arm, just below my shoulder. By the time I was a hallway from Vanze, blood had trickled down my skin like red spiderwebs, and the grip of the gun was tacky.

He was shoving more stuff into his backpack, but I was so focussed on him, I didn't even see the other hostile I ran in to. In a surprisingly good manoeuvre, which probably wouldn't have worked had I not been shot, the merc managed to force the gun from my left hand. I fired the other, but the man bowled into me and we both fell heavily to the floor. I managed to twist my head sideways in time to see Vanze disappearing down the corridor.

"No," I cried, still struggling with the sweaty ape. He'd pinned my hand to the ground, preventing me from shooting him, but with a bit of squirming I was able to reach my blade with the other. Just as he pulled back his fist to punch me in the head, I forced the knife into his neck, twisting the handle. He gasped, letting out a pained, gurgling cry, and I wasted no time in shimmying out from underneath him.

Taking off up the tunnel, I knew I wasn't that far behind Vanze, so when I rounded a corner and he was just in front of me, I knew what I had to do.

"Vanze," I shouted, firing one blast at his shoulder. He spun from the force of the shot, careening off a wall, but when he corrected himself, he had his own weapon pointed right at me. He slowly backed through a doorway into a small room and I followed. We circled each other cautiously, just like Ash and Cal had done in the cage.

The room was completely bare, but ironically the walls were covered in the beautifully ornate symbols that'd been a mystery to me my entire life. Not such a bad place to die, I thought.

"You shouldn't have killed him," I said, only just keeping my voice even.

"It's what I do," he replied, his eyes black and stolid, his expression grim. "Blain?"

"Dead." I shrugged my shoulders dispassionately, but Vanze's face darkened further. "Just like Vita," I added, twisting the knife.

Rage flicked across the man's gaunt features and he struggled to regain a sense of composure. "Then we're even," he said.

"Not even close," I hissed, tightening my finger on the trigger. I guess Vanze was just as resigned to the inevitable as I was because we both fired at exactly the same time.

The force threw me backwards against the wall, white hot pain searing though my ribcage as I fell to the floor. The hard stone was cold against my cheek, and every breath I took felt like razor-wire being dragged through my chest. I couldn't move. All I could do was concentrate on my breathing – slow, shallow, excruciating breaths.

Vanze unsteadily dragged himself to his feet. It was difficult to concentrate through the pain, but I saw how badly injured he was. He steadied himself with difficulty and took a step towards me, but his body was stubborn and unresponsive. He staggered and fell, the red stain on his shirt expanding as blood seeped from his neck wound.

I tried to move my hand towards the gun lying just out of reach, but my fingers merely twitched. I struggled to sit up, but my body refused. The pain was unbearable.

I momentarily wondered if I should be afraid of dying. I wasn't.

Vanze heaved himself closer until he was sitting right beside me. His gun-hand was clamped to his neck, blood oozing from the gapping, ragged hole with every heartbeat. He tried to get a better seal with his palm while shakily raising his gun. He pointed it unsteadily towards me, but instead of worrying about my own fate, all I cared about was that I knew his wound was fatal. I might not actually see him breathe his last, but I knew without a shadow of a doubt that he wouldn't last much longer than I was going to. I closed my eyes.

The blast reverberated loudly around the small room.

25

Vanze's head exploded in a red mist.

My first thought should've been how am I still alive, but it wasn't. It was I'm glad I got to see you die, arsehole. All three Khan siblings were dead… that was all that mattered to me.

Cal grabbed one of Vanze's boots, pulling his body out of the way so he could kneel beside me.

"I'm sorry, Shae, but this is gunna hurt real bad," he said, sliding me away from the wall so he could lay me flat on my back. I cried in pain, but it was nothing compared to the agony that followed as he pressed against my wounds, trying to staunch the blood.

After what seemed an eternity, the wave of pain dulled, my eyesight cleared, and I noticed how terrible he looked. Half his face was black and blue, one eye hidden behind swelling, and the strands of hair that had escaped his ponytail had curled from sweat.

I didn't hear Jake arrive, but I tried to focus on him when he threw himself to the floor beside me.

"Fuck! Shit!" He reached out to me. "Why aren't you healing?" he asked urgently, his wild, frightened eyes flicking from my face to the wound and then back again. "You should be healing." His voice was frantic, but in contrast, below the white-hot pain in my chest, I was totally calm. I wanted to tell him it was okay, but I couldn't get the words out.

"Colonel, get the field dressings from my bag," Cal said, but Jake didn't move. "Jake! Get the dressings," he bellowed. That time, Jake pulled his eyes away from mine and reached over to the backpack, pulling out the med-kit. He yanked out the contents and ripped open packets before passing them to Cal, who removed his hands just long enough to apply the bandages. As he pressed down, the razor-wire tore through my chest again. My brain fogged over, and my eyes closed.

"Don't you leave me, Shae. Don't you dare. That's an order." Jake's voice sounded distant, swallowed up in an abyss of swirling grey mist. I felt vigorous rubbing against my cheek and managed to force my eyes open, but everything was out of focus. "Why aren't you healing?" he repeated desperately, a pained confusion in his own eyes. "We need to get her out of here," he added to Cal.

"We can't move her, she's not stable. It'll kill her. Sir... Jake, there's nothing we can do."

"Don't say that," Jake growled, grabbing Cal by the shoulders, shaking him violently.

Cal took his hands from my chest to grab him back and the two men wrestled briefly above me. "Jake, listen to me," Cal said. "The wounds are too severe—"

"No!"

"I'm sorry. She's dying."

Jake looked hollow and broken. "Shae, you have to listen to me." He bent closer so I could focus on him. "You have to heal yourself. I'm not going to lose you, not like this."

I tried to move my hand and it cooperated briefly, but I was glad when Jake took it. I wanted to tell him... what?

That I'd given up? That I'd lost another person I loved and couldn't live with the pain? That I was sorry... for everything?

His hands warmed mine, but the rest of me was frozen to the core, and my chest felt heavy, like someone was sitting on it. I took the smallest of breaths, but it felt like my lungs were filled with liquid, and when I exhaled, the metallic taste of blood filled my mouth.

Cal pressed harder on my wounds and shockwaves of pain radiated out from my ribcage.

"What do I do?" Jake begged. "Fuck!" he yelled out of frustration, raking his fingers through his hair.

I needed him to understand.

"He's dead," I whispered. It was about all I could manage, but the unpleasant, iron-taste of blood filled my mouth again. I coughed and warm liquid trickled down my cheek.

Jake turned his head briefly towards Vanze. "Cal blew the fucker's melon off. I should hope he's dead." He forced a smile.

"No." I tried to shake my head but trembled from the resulting wave of nausea.

Jake's eyebrows knitted together. "I don't understand," he said quietly, gripping my hand as if holding on to it would somehow save me.

"Jared's dead." I barely got the words out.

"What? When?" Jake looked even more bewildered and turned to Cal, who shrugged. "Get on to Ash. I want to know what the fuck's going on."

Cal stepped away and Jake turned his attention back to me. He placed his hand gently on my forehead and stroked it softly while making hushing noises as I tried to talk.

The pressure in my chest lifted and there was a moment's respite from the pain, but then my whole body stiffened from the lightning bolt that pierced through my chest, radiating out to the ends of every limb. After my body relaxed, nothing hurt anymore.

I struggled to breathe, but at least the razor-wire had disappeared. I felt relieved and closed my eyes, letting the fatigue wash over me.

"Ash says Jared's with them and he's alive... mostly." I recognised Cal's voice, even though it was throaty and he spoke quickly.

"Did you hear that, Shae?" Jake said, rubbing my cheek again. I ignored it. "Ash has him. He's badly beaten, but he's very much alive."

I'd heard him wrong; I must have... that or Jake was trying to trick me.

"I saw him die... let me go," I gurgled through the blood, too weak to even open my eyes.

"No," Jake growled, his breath warm on my cheek. "I'm never going to let you go. Cal, get on to Ash and tell him to bring Jared here asap."

"Sir, Captain Marcos isn't in a good..." I heard the deep intake of breath. "Brother Asher needs to get him back to the *Veritas*. He needs medical—"

"What he needs is Shae," Jake interrupted. "Get them here. Now. That's an order."

"Yes, Sir."

"Open your eyes, Shae," Jake continued. "Stay with me just a few more minutes. I know you can do it, you're strong. The strongest person I've ever met."

I don't know how long I listened to Jake, but I do know his voice got more desperate with every word. I tried to squeeze his hand to show him I was alright, but I wasn't in control of my body anymore. I felt drunk, like my mind was drifting away...

"Shae!" Jake suddenly yelled, surprising me enough for my eyes to open. "Thank God! Don't scare me like that. I thought you'd... Please," he begged. "Glow, shimmer, radiate... whatever you need to do, but just fix yourself. I can't..."

I couldn't bear to see the pain etched on his face and tried to close my eyes again.

"Oh no you don't." He rubbed my cheek. "Stay with me."

There was so much I wanted to say, but I didn't have the time or energy. "The Seal," I murmured. I barely had the strength to cough up the blood from my torn lungs, but somehow I managed to point towards the backpack on the floor by Vanze's body. Jake wasn't interested though; his attention had been drawn elsewhere.

I blinked slowly, and when my eye's opened again, Ash was by my side.

"Why isn't she healing?" he asked in a moment of déjà vu. "She should be glowing. Why isn't she glowing?"

It was a good question, and the short answer was because I didn't want to. I was done.

"She thinks you're dead," I thought I heard Jake say, but that made no sense. What was he talking about? Who was he talking to? I felt him move backwards and tried to tighten my grip on his hand, but he pulled it away easily. Seconds later, someone else sat – slumped – on the ground beside me.

The man's face was so swollen he was barely recognisable. He had a raw gash down one cheek, and even though both eyes were part closed, I couldn't mistake them. He moved closer, groaned, and grabbed his side with a bloodied hand.

"You died," I whispered, struggling to stay conscious.

"It wasn't me," he said, wincing. I tried to focus on the fingers he was snapping in front of my face. "Stay with me, Shae."

"You're not real." My eyes unfocussed and it became harder to concentrate through the grey fog.

"I am. Please, it's me."

"No, it's a trick. You're dead. Vanze shot you."

"He didn't. Listen to my voice. It wasn't me Vanze shot

– he tricked you. Open your eyes, Shae. Look at me... look at my clothes." It was a weird thing to say, but somehow it got my attention. I had to concentrate hard, but after a moment, I noticed he was wearing worn, dirty overalls.

I hardly dared believe it was true, but when I looked into his swollen, bloodshot eyes, I knew. The pit of my tummy began to tingle, a tickling sensation spread like a firecracker through my veins, and my chest – what was left of it – vibrated. I don't know how, but I managed to sit up, and I grabbed Jared as tightly as I could, our bodies pressed together. The sudden blaze of iridescent, silver-blue light was so excruciatingly bright, I had to shield my eyes.

I knew the light meant I was healing, but as I gulped for air, I felt blood trickling from the side of my mouth. Was it too late? Had I left it too long?

Jared's arms tightened around me and my body automatically responded to his touch, to his heartbeat, and I began to relax. As I did, bit by bit, my breathing got stronger and my head cleared.

I closed my eyes and concentrated on the rhythmic circles he drew on my back. I couldn't say how long it was before I felt the tingling heat in my chest start to diminish, but when I opened my eyes again, the silver-blue had almost dissipated, replaced by the pale glow of the chem-lights.

"Welcome back," Jared said with a worried half-smile. His skin was soft pink, his eyes were wide and intense blue, and the cut on his cheek had disappeared. When he moved to pull me into another hug, he did so without any indication of injury. I guess I'd fixed us both at the same time – that was another first to add to a growing list.

I took a long, deep breath, trying out my newly healed lungs. A dull ache lingered at their fullest, but there was no pain. I held up a hand and touched his face with the back of my fingers, still unable to quite believe he was alive.

"When Blain took my uniform and told me what they

were going to do, I felt sick," Jared said. "I wanted to kill him."

"I did that for you," I said, surprised by the normality of my voice. A hint of a smile appeared on his lips and my chest warmed. "Who was it? Who did Vanze kill?"

"No idea. Someone they already had in their cells, I guess."

"You mind?" Ash said tapping him on the shoulder. Jared let go of my hand and Ash pulled me off the floor. I wobbled slightly, still a little shaky, but he held me close for a moment while I regained my balance. I wondered why he'd removed his tactical vest until he passed it to me. "You might want to cover up," he said quietly, pointing to my shredded top.

I smiled happily and nodded, hardly able to believe that just minutes earlier I'd been so destroyed by Jared's 'death' that I was ready to give up everything – everyone. I glanced around the room at the assembled men: Ash, Jake, Jared, Cal…

"Where's the Wolfpack? Are they okay? Do you have Phina? Is she okay?" I garbled all in one sentence.

"Relax, Babe, everyone's fine. The Wolfpack has taken the Princess back to the *Veritas*," Jake explained. "She's okay." he added, rubbing my shoulder.

"As much as I'm happy you guys are… better," Cal said, looking awestruck, "time's running out. Who's got the Seal?"

"It's in the bag." I pointed.

Cal picked up my backpack and went to retrieve the Seal from Vanze. He tucked the object safely inside the bag and slung it over his shoulder before bending down to retrieve a small object from the floor.

"Um, slight problem," he said, holding up a clear glass remote that looked uncomfortably similar to the one we'd found on Jesper. "Either this clock is broken, or we need to get the fuck out of here."

I watched numbers counting backwards: 8.03, 8.02, 8.01...

"That's our cue people. Let's hustle," said Jake.

"What about the prisoners?" I asked.

"We don't have time," Cal replied.

"But—"

"Go!" Jake shouted, physically pushing me towards the door. "You sure you're okay?" he added quietly.

"I'm fine. I'll keep up," I assured him, but when I got to the doorway, I stopped so abruptly he ran into me. "Keep going, I'll be right behind you," I said ducking around him and heading back to Vanze. I rummaged through his pockets until I found my necklace, but when I turned to take off after the others, I saw they'd all gathered at the doorway waiting for me.

"What? You didn't think we would leave without you, did you, Babe?" Jake said. Jared raised his eyes briefly.

Cal led the way. I'd told Jake I was fine, but it was a struggle to keep up with him until Jared took my hand, giving me strength. We tore through the complex, taking stairs several steps at a time, navigating through rooms and tunnels without pausing. We headed through the beautiful hall and I slowed momentarily, realising the objects around the top of the columns I'd noticed earlier, were explosives. I felt sick that all that history was about to disappear for good, but Jared tugged at my hand and I sped up again, heading towards the utility tunnels.

I let go of his hand, practically sliding down the shaft into the fissure, but the moment he landed behind me he reached for it again. We were almost out when I staggered from the first explosion.

I grabbed my rebreather on the fly, holding my breath as I threw myself out of the small opening. Hands grabbed at me, pulling me to the side, just as flames burst out behind me. Dust and debris followed as the ground shook. I covered my head and ducked against the wall while dislodged rocks fell from the canyon side. It was only my lungs objecting to a lack of oxygen that reminded me to put on the rebreather. I pulled on the mask and took a deep breath.

"Those Khan Brothers sure do keep things interesting, don't they?" Cal joked, breathing heavily.

"Yeah, well… not anymore," I replied.

We started our descent towards the plateau, but if I'd thought the path had been perilous before, it was nothing compared to walking it in the dark.

"How are we doing for time?" Jared asked, helping me over a large bolder.

"You don't want to know," Cal replied, slipping down a couple of metres on loose rubble.

"I realise the urgency, people," Jared said once Cal had secured his footing, "but I'm not going to lose anyone tonight. Watch your feet everyone and take things carefully."

It was hard work and painfully slow going, and the only saving grace was that we were heading down rather than up. I don't think my tired legs would've managed that.

The *Veritas'* ramp was down when we got to the ship, and Ty was on hand in a rebreather to help everyone in. The engines were already impatient, and the ramp was only halfway up when Conner took off in a giant cloud of rock dust. As soon as the hold was pressurised with breathable air, I ripped off my mask and took several long, deep breaths, noting that even the dull ache had gone from my lungs.

I caught Ash's eye and he gave me a happy, lop-sided grin, but the hit I got through the Link was very different. I took a step towards him to give him a reassuring hug, but the *Veritas* jolted violently, throwing me off my feet. At first, I thought Connor must've hit the canyon wall again, but after glancing at Jake, I knew it was something different.

"Weapons fire," he shouted, picking himself off the

floor and racing for the stairs.

We arrived en masse at the Flight Deck and Jake threw himself into the navigator's seat, immediately checking tactical data and terrain sensors.

I stared at the front screen, half of which displayed an image from the rear sensors. A ship was closing on us fast. "Who?" I asked.

"Must be Fletcher," Connor replied. "Rear shields are down to sixty percent… and manoeuvring through these canyons while avoiding weapons fire is a little tricky." He banked hard to port to avoid an incoming missile.

Jake accessed the *Veritas*' weapon's systems, charged the plasma cannons, and deployed a volley of concussion mines into the ravine behind us. Jared opened a com-link to the *Defender*, ordering Tel'an to bring the ship into Tartaros' orbit and dispatch Hellfires.

"Connor, can you lead Fletcher to the *Defender*?" Jared asked.

"Honestly? Not sure. Only reason we're still in one piece is because he's having trouble targeting us in the canyons. If I break cover, I might not be able to evade him, and our rear shields are… hold on." We did a hard right, but the *Veritas*' ultra-powerful xenon lights suddenly lit up a bridge of lethal rocks just in front of us. We dropped sharply to duck under the outcrop, veering left and right to avoid ledges before drifting around another tight turn to level out. "Holy crap that was close!"

"Now that's why we pay you the big bucks, Con," said Jake, white fingers still gripping the arms of his chair.

"Yeah? Remember that when you get the repair bill," Connor commented, giving an apologetic shrug of the shoulders. "Whoa!" he exclaimed as we took another blast from Fletcher. "You know you can return fire whenever you're ready, Boss."

Jake scowled at him. "The quartzide's playing hell with our sensors. I'm trying to do it manually, but I can't get weapons lock."

"Rear shields down to thirty-five percent," said Connor.

"We're going to get ripped to shreds if we stay down here," Jake replied. "Con, make a break for the *Defender*. Away from the surface, I'll be able to lock-on plasma cannons... we don't have time for this cat-and-mouse bullshit."

"You're the boss." Connor looked unconvinced. "Hold on."

We ascended quickly, breaking free from the valley before snaking through a tight mountain range. Within seconds we were in free sky, heading for orbit, but Fletcher was right behind us.

"Almost..." Jake said, working the weapons system. "Almost..." Just as we were leaving atmo, we jolted again, more fiercely than anything previously. "Shit, rear weapons are offline. Another shot like that and we'll lose aft shields as—"

The ship juddered violently, and the lights dimmed. Alarms blared, and the control panels in front of Jake and Connor flickered.

"What the hell was that?" asked Jared

"Teslax pulse," Connor replied. "Don't worry, Ty's patch seems to have worked."

"But Fletcher doesn't know that." Jake immediately disengaged weapons and took all sensors off-line. "Cut engines," he ordered Connor.

"What?"

"Cut main engines and play dead. Do it now."

The power shut down and the *Veritas* drifted.

"You're playing a dangerous game, Jake," said Jared. "I hope you know what you're doing."

"So do I," Jake replied. "Look, he's coming around. The cocky little fucker wants to be looking right at us when he finishes us off. Guess he's been working for the Khans too long. Wait for it..."

"Jake…" Jared said slowly as an alarm sounded and the computer told us we'd been targeted.

"Wait… wait… now!" Jake re-engaged sensors, locked-on, and fired a volley of plasma missiles. The starboard hull of Fletcher's craft disintegrated before the ship exploded in a ball of flames.

"Yes! Well done," I said, hugging him from behind.

"It was nothing," he replied with mock modesty. Connor coughed loudly, bringing the engines back online.

"You did good too," I said before hugging him as well. He blushed.

I left the others celebrating on the Flight Deck and headed towards the cabin to find Phina, pausing to talk to Cal who was heading in the opposite direction.

"You saved my life down there, Cal. I'm indebted," I said.

"I won't even try to understand how you do it, but I don't think I had much to do with saving you," he replied.

"Maybe not the actual healing bit, but I wouldn't have had the opportunity if you hadn't taken out Vanze, so… thank you."

"You're welcome. I kind of had my own score to settle there anyway." He smiled broadly. "Oh, I believe these are yours," he added, rummaging around in the backpack before handing over my com-pad and earpiece.

"Thanks." I started to walk away but paused. "Wait… You went into the complex, Cal. I thought you wouldn't go underground again?"

"When I realised you'd lost coms and sensors, it seemed like the right thing to do." He shrugged his shoulders and tucked a loose piece of hair behind his ear. "I thought you could use the assist."

"You're a good man, Lieutenant. I didn't know your brother, but I'm sure he would've been very proud of you."

"Thanks, that means a lot," he said before excusing himself.

I found Phina in the main cabin, where Ty was giving her a once over with a bio-scanner.

"What's the verdict?" I asked, glad to see her – even if she did look weird in dirty overalls.

"Dehydration, borderline malnutrition, but on the whole… could be worse," replied Ty, tucking the scanner back into its case before leaving us to catch up.

Jared caught me looking at my com-pad as we disembarked the *Veritas*. I showed it to him and he frowned; it was almost a full hour past our midnight deadline.

Commander Tel'an approached, flanked by a woman with short, curly, red hair.

"Captain, we've set course for Decerra, but even with all engines at maximum, we're not going to make it in time for the start of the Sector Senate Meeting," Tel'an explained.

"Not acceptable, Commander," Jared blasted, causing several ground crew to look around. "We haven't gone through all this sh…" He paused to control himself. "We haven't gone through all this pain to miss our deadline by sixty minutes. Hannigan, you're Chief of Engineering; there must be something you can do?"

She thought for a moment, her red curls jiggling as her head bobbed from side to side. "I suppose if we…" She fell silent, tapping furiously on a data-pad.

"Talk to me, Chief?" Jared pushed.

"If we shut down all internal and external non-essentials, reduce life support to minimum, re-direct power from the aft shields, and override some of the safety protocols, we might just make it… but," she added worryingly, "there's also a chance we could fry half the ship's systems – and that's best-case scenario."

"Worst case?"

"We lose reactor containment and the ship disintegrates into a billion sparkly pieces." Her face was deadpan, and I wasn't sure whether she was joking or not. "Realistically," she continued, "there's a possibility we could lose an engine or two, but barring catastrophic failure, I'll be able to take them offline before they do any major damage."

Jared rubbed his chin, weighing up the consequences. "Do it," he ordered.

"Yes, Sir." Chief Hannigan disappeared, giving hurried instructions over a com-link.

I noticed Doc trying to persuade Phina to lie on a gurney, but she pushed it away in protest.

"I'm perfectly fine," she said, her voice weaker than usual with a harsh edge I'd never heard before.

"Princess," I said. "I'm sure if King Sebastian were here, he'd insist that Doctor Anderson check you over... even if you do feel okay now," I added quickly as she opened her mouth to object. She pursed her pale red lips. "You want my honest opinion?" I asked.

"You know I've always valued your judgment, dear friend."

"Then you look like crap, Phina," I offered bluntly. She didn't say anything for a moment, and Doc held his breath at my lack of Royal protocol, but then she laughed. "Do it for me, Phina. I need to know you're really okay."

"Alright," she conceded. "I'll go to Med-Bay... but I'm not going strapped to a gurney like an invalid."

Doc was happy with the compromise and ushered her out of the hangar before she could change her mind.

"I've already updated the King on our status," Tel'an was telling Jared, Jake and Ash when I returned to them. "He's unsurprisingly thrilled Princess Josephina is unharmed and wishes us God's speed. He also reiterated the consequences of the Third Seal not being on display when the doors to the Sector Senate Meeting open."

"As if we don't already know that," Jake grumbled.

"So, what now?" I asked, stifling a yawn.

"Nothing to do but wait," replied Jared. He took a look at the beaten hull of the *Veritas*. "No offence, Jake, but I think we'll take a Warrior to the planet when we get there. Commander, make sure one is prepped and ready to go the second we arrive in orbit."

Jake grimaced as he scanned his ship. "Could be worse," he said pragmatically.

I was physically and mentally exhausted, but there was no way I'd be able to sleep; besides, I didn't want to leave Jared. Part of me feared I could still lose him and there was no way I was going to let that happen. I failed to stifle another yawn.

"You should sleep. You've had a tough few hours," Jared suggested, but I shook my head.

"Not until this thing's over," I said adamantly, daring anyone to disagree.

"Then how about a drink," he suggested. "Kill some time?"

"That's the best idea you've had this mission." Jake grinned. "I think we all deserve it. You mind?" he asked, indicating to the Wolfpack.

"Not at all," Jared replied. "But I suggest a shower and a change of clothes for everyone," he added, picking at his own dirty overalls. "I for one, want to wash the stink of the Khan's off me. Meet back here in thirty?"

Malcolm was on duty when we arrived at the Queen's Tap Officers and VIP bar. The Pack was hesitant to enter but when Jared personally ushered them in, they loosened up. It wasn't busy, and we were able to spread out, taking over one whole section. We may have ditched our dusty, bloodied clothes, but there was no hiding the disturbing array of injuries and bruises. We easily stood out from the intrigued crowd, a stark contrast against the pristine regulars.

We were all there: Jared, Jake, Ash, Cal, Kaiser, Ty and Connor. I marvelled at the fact we'd all made it through in one piece, even if it had been a rocky road at times. My healing abilities had certainly had a good workout during the mission, not to mention my newfound skills…

My new skills.

For a moment, a wave of fear rippled through me. What was happening to me? And why? But I was too tired to be scared, so instead I pushed the thoughts aside.

Without making a conscious choice, I sat on the sofa next to Jared. He wordlessly shifted position so I could shuffle up against his side and I felt the comforting heat of his body. He smelled faintly of sandalwood and musk, and I pulled up my legs as he closed his arm protectively around my shoulders.

A part of my brain tried to remind me why I'd stayed away from Jared but after what'd happened, after coming so close to losing him, that logic didn't seem to carry much weight anymore.

I surveyed the battered group, lounging on chairs and sprawling on the floor. I wanted to know what they'd been up to on Tartaros, and how they'd sustained such an impressive collection of injuries – all of which I'd fix when I was stronger. At that point, I don't think I could've healed a papercut.

A fair amount of the journey time back to Decerra was spent listening to stories of fights, ambushes, and impenetrable cell security systems. It felt familiar as the Wolfpack launched into a graphic re-enactment of one of their bloodier encounters.

Gradually, I noticed eyes closing and heads starting to nod, and even though Jared offered quarters to everyone, no one wanted to leave the bar. Eventually my own eyes began to droop, and my head lowered on to Jared's shoulder. It only seemed like a second later that I was jolted awake.

The ship juddered for a few seconds before lurching and slowing. Jared automatically looked at his com-pad for information, but his wrist was bare, and I remembered I'd left it on the desk back in the Khans' office. I moved out the way so he could stand.

He crossed the bar quickly and spoke into a com-panel on the wall opposite. I rubbed my eyes, forcing myself fully awake before checking the time. It was just shy of zero-nine-hundred and I was surprised at how long I'd been asleep.

When Jared returned, he was agitated, and his tone urgent. "One of the engines is out – burnt through a rotation coil. Hannigan's had to shut it down to prevent a containment breach and we've reduced speed to prevent the others from overheating. We're still at FTL, just, but at our current velocity, we're not going to make it to Decerra in time. The good news is we're close enough to take a Warrior from here, but whether we get there in time is another matter."

Everyone stood to leave, but Jake caught Jared's look and stood down Cal and the Pack; it didn't need all of us to go to Decerra. Strictly speaking it only needed Jared, but there was no chance in hell, Jake, Ash, and I weren't going to see the mission through to the end.

Jared paused briefly in the hangar to receive a new com-pad and earpiece from an ensign, but we were star-side before I'd even caught my breath from the sprint to the ship. Ash and Jared went to get an eta from the pilot, leaving me with Jake in the main cabin.

"Checking the time every five seconds isn't going to make us go any faster," he said.

"I know. I just don't know what else to do." I turned to pace, but his hand caught mine.

"I meant what I said the other day," he whispered. "When I told you I loved you and that I wasn't going to give you up without a fight."

"Jake, I—"

"Don't say anything," he interrupted. "Not now. We're all tired and emotional from the last couple of weeks. After what happened on Tartaros… just promise me you won't make any rash decisions."

"Rash decisions? I don't understand."

He smiled and shook his head lightly, his thumb gently caressing the underside of my wrist. "You're—" He stopped as Ash and Jared appeared. "No rash decisions, please," he added quickly before letting go of my hand.

"We've spoken to the Palace," said Ash, giving Jake a cautious glance. "They've given us priority permission to land and cleared us through Security in advance. Now all we have to do is get there."

"It's going to be very, very close," Jared added, checking his new com-pad.

We had boots on Decerra at exactly three minutes to ten-hundred. My heart was already pounding in my chest when Sergeant Mollere met us, and we wasted no time on pleasantries. Our team raced across the landing pad and breezed through the Security checkpoint without slowing.

"The Senate Committee's been told there's a slight delay because one of the stewards dropped a tray of glasses in the Assembly Hall," Mollere puffed as startled employees moved out of our way. "But the King can't stall for long."

The bells in the clock tower rang loudly as we ran through the courtyard, and my chest constricted even further.

"This way," he said a couple of minutes later, skidding around a corner before sprinting down a plain hallway where an army of stewards waited with carafes of water.

We burst through an unassuming door into the Assembly Hall, which was thankfully deserted.

"Hurry," Mollere snapped urgently. "I've just been informed that the Committee's on its way."

Jared flipped open the box and removed the Third Seal, practically throwing the case at Jake before using a shirttail to polish the hexagonal platinum disc and its embossed insignia.

"That'll have to do," he said, carefully placing the Seal in its glass showcase.

He closed the lid and stepped out of the way, just as a set of large double-doors swung inwards, held open by two King's Guards in full ceremonial uniform. I was happy the Seal was back in its rightful place but wondered how we were going to explain our presence in the hall. I followed Ash's lead and stood my ground, trying to look like I was supposed to be there.

King Sebastian looked drawn as he entered the room ahead of the other Senate members, but the moment his eyes fell on the Seal, his entire demeanour changed. The dark shadows across his face disappeared and his eyes cleared. He squared his broad shoulders and even his walk took on a new energy.

Senate members filed in after him, each with mixed expressions of intrigue and confusion at our presence. A hushed ripple of inevitable questions ran through the assembly, but Sebastian ignored them all. Instead he turned to address the group, radiating the natural command and authority I recognised from before the Khans' attack.

"Ladies and Gentlemen of the Senate," he began, strong and confident. "As you're probably aware, two weeks ago there was an incursion at the palace. The perpetrators were foiled in their attempts to steal precious Earth artefacts, but in an attempt to get away, they kidnapped my precious daughter, Princess Josephine."

A few murmurs filtered around the room, but the King dismissed them with a casual wave of his hand.

"In a combined REF and Brotherhood of the Virtuous Sun mission, the people responsible have been brought to justice, and I'm delighted to advise the Princess is safe and on her way back to the palace as we speak. I can assure you none of our precious heritage was taken, thanks to the people you see in this room today. I've invited them here today, before we begin the Summit, so that you can join me in thanking Captain Marcos, Colonel Mitchell, Brother

Asher and Shae, for their dedication and time."

Whispers were replaced by open comments of appreciation. King Sebastian moved his attention to us. "Captain, please pass on my utmost appreciation to the appropriate people."

"Of course, Your Majesty," Jared replied.

"Thank you… for everything. Don't let me keep you further."

26

As soon as the Assembly Hall door clicked shut, I let out a long, relieved, puff of air.

"Well, that was too close for comfort," said Mollere as he walked up the hallway, wiping his brow with the back of his hand. "I have to say, none of this has been good for my nerves."

"Not good for your nerves?" Ash said, raising both eyebrows.

I laughed… and so did Ash, then Jake and Jared joined in. It was relieved, exhausted, and slightly crazed laughter.

The stewards, even Mollere, stared at us like we were insane, but I didn't care because we'd avoided a Sector-wide disaster again. Against all odds. Not only had we retrieved the Third Seal and returned it to its rightful place, but we'd found the Princess alive and in relatively good shape. I couldn't have wished for a better outcome.

No, that wasn't true.

The icy chill of disappointment rippled through me and I stopped laughing.

There could've been a better conclusion. I could've got the answers I wanted, but I hadn't. All I had were more questions. I absentmindedly rubbed the pendant between my thumb and fingers in my pocket, frustrated that I'd got nothing from Vanze. And to add insult to injury, the complex on Tartaros had been utterly destroyed. It could offer no further insight.

I felt despondent, and I'm sure Ash and Jared picked up on it through the Link, because they'd stopped laughing as well. Suddenly everything seemed too much: the Seal, Phina, my failed personal mission to find out who I was, Jake and the booby-trap, thinking Jared was dead...

I couldn't breath and my eyes blurred. Beads of sweat sprung up on my forehead, and my heart thumped hard in my chest – every beat like a hammer to my ribs. I staggered, feeling light-headed, but strong arms folding around me, catching me, stopping me from falling.

Ash's deep, rhythmic voice comforted me, just like it always did. I concentrated on his words, pushing all other thoughts out of my head until my breathing evened and the shaking calmed. When my eyes focussed, I noticed the worried look on his face.

"I'm okay," I said unconvincingly. Jared opened his mouth to say something, but then his expression changed and he indicated he was receiving a call. He stepped away to talk privately.

He wasn't gone long, but by the time he returned, I'd managed to persuade Ash and Jake that they could stop worrying about me. I'm not sure whether they really had, or whether they were humouring me, but at least they'd stopped looking at me like I was about to break.

"The *Defender's* just arrived in orbit," Jared said. "Princess Josephina's on her way down to the planet with Doc Anderson – eta six minutes. She's fine; there'll be no lingering effects of her ordeal... at least no physical ones anyway."

"I'm delighted to hear that, Captain," said Sergeant Mollere. "So what now... for you I mean?"

"There are a few formalities we need to conclude before I can officially close Operation Fallen Star," Jared replied.

"Anything I can help with?"

"Actually, yes. Can you arrange priority departure authorisation for my Warrior? I'd like the team to return to the *Defender* asap."

"Of course. I'll inform Flight Control immediately. If you'll excuse me?" Mollere left us to deal with the request.

Jared reached for my hand and I took it, intertwining my fingers with his. I felt the strength of his grip and the warmth of his skin against mine, and it made me feel safe.

But more than that, his closeness made my insides tingle. He looked down at me smiling and my stomach flipped.

"Come on," he said. "Let's go home."

We were almost to the landing pad when he slowed his pace and we fell back slightly from Ash and Jake. He lent towards me and I felt his warm breath on my cheek.

"When we get back to the *Defender*, you and I are going to talk," he whispered.

"Talk?" I whispered back, looking up at him wide-eyed.

"If you remember, the last time we 'talked', you told me you could never be with me, but now..." he lifted our joined hands, "I'm hoping things have changed. At least I think they have from these bizarre feelings I keep getting through the Link – which is still really, really weird by the way."

"I know. It takes some getting used to, doesn't it? And you're right, things have changed. I guess we do have a lot to talk about," I conceded. "I just..."

"What?"

"I wish it could just be about us – you and me. Not Operation Fallen Star or our Guardian team. Not even about the REF or the Brotherhood. And certainly not about my freaky abilities."

"You know, your weird freakishness is one of the things

I love about you."

"It is?"

"Yes. That and your charming naivety."

"Doesn't sound like I've got a lot going for me," I said. "How could you possibly be interested in someone like me?"

Jared stopped abruptly, letting go of my hand, and I panicked that he'd seen the light and realised I wasn't worth all the shit that came with me. I was about to tell him that I'd understand if he backed away, but instead he raised his hands and cradled my face before brushing his lips against mine. Just the softest of touches.

"You," he said, looking deeply into my eyes, "are the most amazing person I know." He kissed me again – just the lightest touch before pulling away. "I love you." Another kiss. "All of you." And another. "And everything that comes with you." That time his kiss was passionate and hungry, and he didn't pull away.

His hands wrapped around me, pulling me closer, and in that moment, I don't think I'd ever been happier.

"Ahem."

Jared's lips parted from mine, but he didn't loosen his arms and our bodies remained pressed together. I turned my head towards the noise, catching Ash's eyes. I giggled nervously and buried my head in Jared's chest to hide my blushes.

"I guess we better go," Jared said reluctantly.

The Warrior's pilot was on the landing pad chatting animatedly to two of the ground crew when we arrived, but he headed over as soon as he saw us.

"Captain, we pushed the ship pretty hard to get here, and the post-flight diagnostics identified a micro-fracture in one of the engine's cooling systems. Ground-crew is just finishing the repair, shouldn't be more than ten minutes max."

"Acknowledged. Let me know when we're ready to

leave," Jared replied.

"Yes, Sir. I'll go and check on—"

His last words were drowned out by a short blast from the tannoy system.

"To all ground personnel: be advised that Brotherhood vessel the *Aldrin* is on final approach to the West landing pad," announced Flight Control through the speakers. "Immediate turnaround is required. Refuel and prep for lift-off as priority. Repeat: to all ground crew – the *Aldrin* is to be refuelled for immediate priority departure."

The wind picked up and I looked to the sky, wondering what could be so urgent that they couldn't stay. I watched the ship come in to land about four hundred metres further down the concrete, shielding my eyes from the leaves and debris whipped up by the reverse thrusters.

As soon as I heard the engines powering down to idle, the *Aldrin* was swamped by an army of ground-crew, all working in flawless synchronisation. A lone monk descended the steps and jogged the distance between us, but I didn't recognise who it was until he was much closer.

"Good to you, Ash. You too, Shae. It's been too long," the newcomer said, shaking Ash's hand.

"Indeed it has, Anton. Let me introduce you to Captain Marcos and Colonel Mitchell. Jared, Jake, this is Brother Anton, Captain of the *Aldrin*."

"Pleasure to meet you both. I've heard so much," Anton said, extending a hand to each of them in turn.

"What's up?" asked Ash. "Why the urgent turnaround?"

"You don't know?"

"Know what?"

Anton frowned. "I'm here to pick you both up and return you to the monastery with haste. I apologise for the confusion, I thought you'd been informed."

I couldn't read Ash's expression, and I was picking up so many feelings through the Link, it was impossible to decipher who they belonged to. Jared took a step closer to me and I didn't need the Link to tell me what that meant.

An awkward silence lingered, during which time Anton flicked his gaze around the group.

"Why the urgency though?" Ash pressed after some thought.

"No idea. I got the order because the *Aldrin* was the closest ship to Decerra. All I was told was to come here, pick you two up, and ferry you home without delay. That's it."

I reached for Jared without realising it.

"Brother Anton," Jared said as he took a firm grip of my hand. "Shae and Brother Asher have their After-Action reports to write up for the Tartaros mission. I suggest they return to the *Defender* and—"

"Captain," Anton interrupted, turning so he was square on to Jared. "I'm sure Ash and Shae can complete their reports on our way home and submit them via secure comlink. I see no reason to delay our departure." His words were polite, but his tone had hardened.

"Maybe so," Jared accepted. "But as Officer in Command of Operation Fallen Star, it's within my purview to order a full, post-operational debrief with all key assets in attendance... which I'm doing, if I hadn't already made that clear." He matched Anton's posture, but the monk wasn't easily dissuaded.

"Do I need to remind you, Captain, that Brotherhood assistance in Fallen Star was offered as a courtesy to King Sebastian? The rules of the Constantine Agreement haven't changed, and you have no authority over our representatives. You'll need to conclude your debrief without them."

"This is ridiculous," Jake waded in. "Shae and Ash were an integral part of the operation. They should be there. Surely your Primus will understand?"

"Who do you think gave me my orders, Colonel? Orders I intend to follow by—"

"Okay!" Ash's voice cut through the conflict. "Everyone needs to just calm down," he added, looking pointedly between the three men. "Maybe the Primus is unaware of the operational protocols still outstanding. Give me a few minutes to contact him and I'm sure we can straighten this all out... without straining relationships between the Brotherhood and the REF, yes?"

"Of course," Anton replied before the two of them sprinted back to the *Aldrin* to contact Noah.

"Captain," The Warrior's pilot jogged down the ramp behind us. "Repairs are completed. We can leave on your order."

"Outstanding," replied Jared. "Get her ready, we'll be leaving shortly."

"Yes, Sir." He disappeared back into the ship.

My insides knotted at the thought of leaving Jared. I hadn't had any time alone with him to tell him how much I needed him, how much I wanted him. But at the same time, I couldn't bear the thought of not seeing Jake. He was family, and I loved him, even if it wasn't the kind of love he wanted from me.

I was still agonising over things when Ash returned alone. To begin with, I thought that was a good thing, but when I saw the look on his face, I let down my mental roadblock and felt his disappointment.

"I'm sorry," he said. "Orders stand. We're to return to the monastery immediately."

Three voices merged into a cacophony of noise.

"What? No," Jared cried.

"That's crap and you know it." That was Jake.

"What if I don't want to go?" All three men turned to look at me, and the enormity of what I'd said sank in. "What if I want to go to back to the *Defender* with Jared and Jake?"

I was surprised it hadn't occurred to me before, but once I'd said it out loud, I began to panic.

I didn't want to let Jared out of my sight, but I hadn't considered the consequences. My insides instantly knotted. I loved Jared... but the Brotherhood was my family. Ash was my brother in all but blood.

How could I walk away from either?

"Oh crap," I said, constantly swallowing to fight off the nausea. I felt guilty and wondered if Ash would be disappointed or angry with me for even considering it?

I prepared myself for the worst, but it was as if he didn't know what to say. He seemed just as torn as I was.

"Come with me for a moment," Jared said, taking my elbow, but as Ash began to object, he added, "It'll be alright, I promise."

He led me towards a crate of boxes, lifting me up to sit on one. He opened his mouth but couldn't get the words out, so instead he took a couple of deep breaths.

"Just say it," I said. "Say you don't want me to come with you."

"What? No! That's not... that's not what I was going to say at all." He sounded hurt. "I want to fight for you, Shae. I want to tell you that you have to come with me. God knows I want that more than anything. The thought of you leaving again is crushing me, but you're not ready."

"I am," I replied, but deep inside, a part of me I didn't want to acknowledge, agreed with him.

"The Brotherhood has been everything to you for so long it would be wrong of me to expect or even encourage you to disobey a direct order. Just like you'd never let me disobey a direct Fleet order. Besides," he grinned, "now I know you love me, I can wait for you."

"I always loved you," I corrected. "But I thought distancing myself would ease the pain if something happened to you."

"But it didn't."

"No, it didn't." I shuddered at the memory and my eyes began to well.

"Hey, don't cry," he soothed. "At least if you're at the monastery I know Jake can't get his hands on you."

I wasn't sure if he was serious or joking until his beautiful blue eyes crinkled and a grin lit up his face. He folded me into his arms.

"Go back to the monastery with Ash. Find out what all the drama's about, and then, when you can, you come back to me. You hear? Surely the Primus can't deny you some vacation time after the last few weeks. And in the meantime, we can com-link – if you answer them this time."

"I will," I said, wiping away the last of the tears. "I promise. I do love you, Jared."

"I know," he said gently. "I love you, too. But if you don't go soon, I might have second thoughts about letting you leave. I have an urge to put you over my shoulder and forcibly abduct you as it is… but the paperwork would be a nightmare." He grinned, and I pulled him closer so our lips could touch. I didn't care who was watching.

Ash was pleased I'd decided to return to the monastery, but Jake made it clear he was unhappy, continuing to argue that I had every right to make the decision to stay if I wanted to.

"Jake, promise me you'll take care of yourself," I said. "I won't be there to mend you, or re-attach anything, if you get hurt again. You're family, I love you, and I'll see you again soon." I pulled him into a tight embrace, not wanting to let him go. "Promise me," I repeated when I eventually let him go.

"I promise," he replied reluctantly.

"And tell the Wolfpack the same. I know what you guys are like – not happy unless you're shooting guns and blowing shit up."

Jake laughed, but then he got serious. "They'll miss you. We'll all miss you, Little Wolfpup."

"You make it sound like we're never going to see each

other again. We're Guardians; the four of us are a team," I said, more to convince myself than them.

I felt Jared's pain through the Link and knew it was time to leave before one or both of us gave in. We said our final farewells, but I couldn't move until Ash put his arm around my shoulders and physically lead me away. My heart ached as I turned to wave goodbye.

The *Aldrin* arrived at Lilania a little before twenty-two hundred that evening. After the rush to get us there, I was expecting to be ushered straight into some kind of special meeting with Noah, so when Brother David met us on the landing pad, I was raring to go.

"Ah, Brother Asher, Shae. It's so nice to have you back," he said warmly, but his casual greeting and lack of urgency confused me. "Oh dear. What's happened?" he asked, looking worried.

"I could ask you the same question," Ash replied, his own concern thrumming through the Link. "We received orders to return immediately. I was expecting... actually I'm not sure what I was expecting, but certainly something that would explain the urgency."

"I'm at a loss," said David, rubbing his head. "The Primus asked me to greet you when you arrived and inform you that he'd like to see you at oh-nine-hundred tomorrow. There didn't seem to be anything out of the ordinary in his request."

"What's going on?" I asked Ash, trying to keep the irritation fluttering in my chest from seeping into my voice.

"I have no idea," he replied quietly.

I felt suspicious... and then I felt guilty for feeling suspicious. This was the Brotherhood – my family – I shouldn't doubt their motives. Yet, there was something...

"Brother Thomas thought you might be hungry after your journey," David continued, thankfully oblivious. "There's food waiting for you all in the refectory, and

Brother Francis asked me to tell you he'll be with you shortly."

I wasn't hungry, and I was close to excusing myself so I could return to my quarters and wallow in my own self-pity, but then I thought about seeing Francis. So instead, I trudged after Ash, Anton and the rest of the *Aldrin's* crew towards the refectory.

I picked lethargically at a lump of fresh bread until I was crushed by a pair of muscular arms that closed around me from behind.

"Welcome home, I've missed you," Francis mumbled into my neck before letting go. He embraced Ash then joined us at the table, tucking in to breads and cold meats as if he hadn't eaten for a week. I asked him what he knew about our orders, but he seemed as mystified as we were.

After a while, I excused myself and returned to my quarters. I contemplated trying to contact Jared, but as much as I wanted to see his face and hear his voice, I wanted his touch more than anything. I worried that seeing him would make things more difficult, especially as I was so raw about being called back for nothing. Instead, I took a quick shower and curled up in bed, wrapping my favourite hand-woven throw around me for comfort.

I was asleep before I knew it.

Just before oh-nine hundred the following morning, Ash and I arrived at the Primus's Outer Chamber as requested.

"He'll be with you shortly," David said, and I found myself resenting his cheerfulness. A good night's sleep had done nothing to help improve my mood.

Noah was sat behind his desk when we entered, but he stood immediately and came around to greet us. I hadn't noticed the other person in the room, so when Investigator Manus said, "Good morning," I was startled. What the hell was he doing there?

"Firstly," Noah began, "Supreme Primus Isaiah has asked me to pass you both his congratulations on the success of Operation Fallen Star. Not only did you manage to return the Princess safely to her family, but we have successfully cemented relationships between the REF and the Brotherhood. Well done."

"It was a team effort," said Ash. "We couldn't have done it without Captain Marcos, Colonel Mitchell, the Wolfpack, and the crew of the *Defender* – not to mention our own brethren."

"Precisely." Manus beamed. "It was a true collaboration, and one to be extremely proud of. It bodes well for all our futures."

"Forgive my bluntness, Primus," said Ash, ignoring the investigator. "But I was hoping you could explain why we had to return to the monastery so urgently."

Manus and Noah shared a brief look.

"While the Brotherhood is keen to cooperate under certain circumstances," Noah explained after a thoughtful pause, "the Supreme Primus wants to ensure the REF doesn't get too comfortable with our alliance. Once the Princess was returned to Decerra, Isaiah felt our part in Operation Fallen Star was concluded."

It was a logical explanation, and one that was no doubt true… but the cautious glances towards Manus, and the careful choice of words, suggested there was more to our recall than he was saying. And I wasn't prepared to leave it at that.

"But you just said Supreme Primus Isaiah was happy with our cemented relationship," I said. "And we may have taken care of the Khans, but what about this Outsider person they were working with? He's still a threat."

Manus looked displeased. "Isaiah is thrilled with our collaboration, but wishes for the Brotherhood to maintain a diplomatic detachment from the REF He doesn't want them to make the incorrect assumption that they can simply snap their fingers and we'll come running. The REF can deal with this Outsider character."

"Primus, I understand everything that's been said, but we still had mission protocols to complete with Captain Marcos," Ash explained. "And as Shae said, the Outsider could still cause trouble for the Sector."

"Yes, yes, you made me well aware of that yesterday, Ash." Noah pinched the bridge of his nose and looked harassed. For a moment, I felt sorry for him; it didn't seem fair that he should have to deal with all of this so close to being appointed into the role. It certainly seemed like a baptism of fire.

Manus took the momentary lapse in conversation to interject again. "Orders are made to be obeyed, Brother Asher," he said bluntly. "And Primus Noah's were to recall you. You should accept that without question."

"And here we are. As ordered," Ash replied calmly, but I felt a confusing hit of frustration and anger crackle through the Link. Noah gave him a warning look before flicking his eyes quickly towards Manus.

A quiet unease bubbled in my chest and I hated feeling that way about the Brotherhood. But ever since Finnian died, things had started to make a lot less sense.

"This is bullshit," I said out loud without realising.

"That's enough, Shae," Noah warned. "You may—"

"The Supreme Primus has reasons for all his orders," Manus interrupted, his face hard, his lips drawn into a tight, uncompromising line. "Sometimes they're not always obvious, but you have to have faith that what is done, is done for the good of the Brotherhood... and for you, Shae. Perhaps it is for the best. Isaiah is troubled that your association with the REF has put you in unnecessary danger."

"What?" I wanted to punch him, even if he was a monk.

"He also has concerns over your... um, relationships with Captain Marcos and Colonel Mitchell," he continued, ignoring the pure look of hatred I gave him. My whole body shook with anger and I felt heat rising in my cheeks.

"Now just a minute, Manus," Noah cautioned. "I think we're heading off-topic." He turned to face me. "Shae, Isaiah worries about your safety, that's true, but he's just as worried about the safety of every other monk in the Brotherhood." He sighed heavily. "You have to admit that since you and Ash have been working with the REF, you've found yourself in some challenging situations. You've used your powers extensively to heal people outside the Brotherhood."

"But that's—"

"I'm not saying you shouldn't have. I'm saying you're visible to a lot of people now, people who might want to hurt you if—" Manus coughed loudly, stopping him mid-sentence. Noah paused to decide on his next words. "Would it be such a bad thing if you dropped off the grid for a while? Let things settle down? You could take some time to fully recharge."

Put like that, it was difficult to argue with Noah's logic, but I couldn't help feeling trapped. Something I'd never felt before on Lilania.

"Perhaps you're right," I conceded. "Perhaps I do need some personal time. In fact, Captain Marcos has offered me quarters on the *Defender*—"

"I'm sorry, Shae, that won't be possible," Noah interrupted.

"But—"

"Your orders are to stay on Lilania."

"For how long?"

"For the foreseeable future."

"Primus, that's not necessary," argued Ash, but I was hardly paying attention. Why were they putting me on lockdown? Was I being punished for something?

"I think we should leave things here for the time being," Noah said. "Obviously this is an emotive topic, but I must stress the order for Shae to stay on Lilania has come directly from the Supreme Primus. I have – we all have – a duty to comply. We'll talk again tomorrow." His words were final.

"Of course, Primus," Ash replied, heading towards the door. I followed on autopilot.

"Oh, I almost forgot. I was going through Finnian's things and came across this," Noah said, retrieving a small pouch from a desk drawer. "It's for you," he added, handing it to me.

I looked at my name, written in Finnian's blocky writing.

"What is it?" I asked, my eyes brimming with unexpected tears.

"I've no idea. It was amongst his personal papers. Everything will be okay, Shae," he said, rubbing my arm. I wasn't sure whether he was talking about Finnian or my confinement to the monastery.

I didn't say a word as we walked back through the inner courtyard towards the main hall, but eventually Ash said, "I'm not going to ask if you're okay, because I know you're not, but Noah was right about one thing: dropping off the grid and resting up for a while isn't such a bad thing. I think they've just gone about it the wrong way, and that officious little ba…" He stopped himself. "And Manus doesn't exactly help matters, does he? All I ask is that you don't do anything rash. Give it a few days – let me talk to Noah again."

"Okay." It was all I could say, but he looked relieved. I stared at the pouch in my hand. "I'll catch up with you later, Ash."

"Sure. Just yell if you need me."

"You know I will." I tried to give him a reassuring smile, but I think it came out more like a grimace.

I sat on my bed, staring at the small bag for almost an hour before I opened it and tipped out the small, silver data-disc – the only thing in it. It took me another half hour to pluck up the courage to get off the bed and move to the plexi-screen on my desk.

My breath froze in my lungs as Finnian's face appeared.

He was in his office, sat at his cluttered desk with a mug of steaming Goldflower tea – just how I remembered him.

"My dearest Shae," he began. *"I suppose the traditional way to start one of these things is to say: if you're watching this, it's because I'm no longer with you. I hope mine was a truly honourable death, and that I didn't trip and fall over a cliff – or die in some other, equally embarrassing way. Oh, and I hope there was lots of singing and drinking at my funeral."*

I smiled through the tears, because that was the Finnian I knew and loved, but as I continued to watch, his grin faded and his face clouded over with a sadness I'd rarely seen.

"In all seriousness though, I'm truly sorry. Not because I've passed, but because I've left you… because I'll no longer be there to look out for you – to protect you."

He paused, looking uneasy, and I wondered what he'd meant by protect me.

"Although, after what I'm about to tell you, you may be glad I'm no longer around. And I wouldn't blame you."

I gasped, choking on my own breath. Finnian continued talking, but the words blurred as I gulped for air, unable to believe what I'd heard. In what Universe could I ever be glad he was dead? My mind scrambled as I continued to cough. Gradually I got myself under control.

"Pause," I said, my head pounding. "Rewind sixty-seconds. Play."

"…be there to look out for you – to protect you. Although, after what I'm about to tell you, you may be glad I'm no longer around. And I wouldn't blame you. The Brotherhood has been my whole life, but it's no secret I thought of you as my daughter. From the moment I held you in my arms as a baby, I've loved you. I've always considered myself one of the luckiest men in the Four Sectors – I got to follow my calling, while enjoying the riches of being a father. You make me very proud, Shae, and I don't think I told you that enough. You're the most amazing person I know, and that's not just because of your gift, but because of the wonderful, thoughtful, loving person you are."

I had to pause the recording to retrieve a tissue because I was crying so much, I couldn't see the screen anymore.

"I was in the Brotherhood long before you came along, and it's a vocation I still believe in with all my soul. My vows are as strong today as they were when I took them back on my eighteenth birthday... but there's one order that's never sat well with me."

He shook his head before looking down and picking at his nails.

"I'm torn, Shae. I took an oath a long time ago to protect a secret – one I vowed to take to the grave unless specifically ordered to divulge it. I've never received that order, but now I find myself with a dilemma: protect the secret, or protect you."

What on Lilania was he talking about? What secret?

"You need to be very careful, Shae. There are people out there who'll come for you if they find out who you are. The signs are clear: something bad is coming, and unless you're prepared, I fear for the future of all Humankind – no, I fear for all races. There are so many things I'd tell you if I could, but that would mean breaking my vows – something I still hold very dear. I hope that in time you will come to forgive me."

I realised I was holding my breath and had moved to the very edge of the seat, leaning towards the screen. I wanted to tell him I didn't blame him for not breaking his vows, I knew how important they were to him, but what could be so significant that he'd been tempted? And what signs?

"You must find out who you really are. You must find out the truth about your past to prepare for the future. You're the key, Shae. Go back to your beginning."

I was stunned. What did he mean by who I really am? And why was I the key?

"Ever since you were old enough to understand, you've asked questions about your parent's death and why the Brotherhood adopted you – and I answered all of them as best as I was... able. But I'm just one person, and... well, the memory can play tricks on you."

"Pause," I practically screamed. Had Finnian really just told me he'd been lying to me all this time, and that someone had ordered him to? "Rewind ten-seconds. Play." I listened again, my hand over my mouth.

"You used to question what the Nakomo *was doing in that region of space in the first place, and the answer was always the same: a humanitarian mission. But you never asked what humanitarian mission we were on. What were we doing out there – just when your parents needed us? Was it just coincidence?"*

"There's no such thing as coincidence," I said automatically. It was the first thing Finnian had taught me – he would've known my reaction.

"I'm in danger of saying too much, Shae. I'm truly sorry for leaving you to deal with this without me. When you don't know who else to believe in, trust Ash. He'll keep you safe. Let him see this message, but don't tell anyone else about what I've said. No-one – even though you may be tempted. Ash only," he reiterated. *"I love you."*

He lent forward to stop the recording but then paused and sat back looking conflicted again.

"One final thing… find the Harbingers. Ask them about the Helyan Codex."

The message ended.

I couldn't move. I could barely even breathe.

ABOUT THE AUTHOR

British author, S.M.Tidball, has been writing since her teens, starting with poetry before moving on to short stories. Despite the challenges of being diagnosed with dyslexia, she has continued follow her passion, and now shares her epic vision of secrets, danger, and rebellion in the Helyan Series.

Books available in the Helyan Series:

Part One: Guardians of the Four
Part Two: Fallen Star

Don't miss out:

Follow on twitter: @SarahTidball

Like on Facebook: @SMTidball

Follow on Instagram: @SMTidball

Printed in Great Britain
by Amazon